GOERING'S GOLD

Also by Richard O'Rawe

A RUCTIONS O'HARE NOVEL

GOERING'S GOLD

RICHARD O'RAWE

MELVILLE HOUSE
BROOKLYN • LONDON

GOERING'S GOLD

First published in 2022 by Melville House
Copyright Richard O'Rawe, 2022

First Melville House Printing: April 2022

Melville House Publishing
46 John Street
Brooklyn, NY 11201

and

Melville House UK
Suite 2000
16/18 Woodford Road
London E7 0HA

mhpbooks.com
@melvillehouse

ISBN: 978-1-61219-965-8
ISBN: 978-1-61219-966-5 (eBook)

Library of Congress Control Number: 2022930621

Printed in the United States of America
10 9 8 7 6 5 4 3 2 1

A catalog record for this book is available
from the Library of Congress

GOERING'S
GOLD

PROLOGUE

September 1944. Hermann Goering's private home, Carinhall,
in the Schorfheide forest outside Berlin …

HERMANN GOERING, REICHSMARSCHALL OF GREATER
Germany, pops a morphine tablet into his mouth and washes
it down with a swig of red wine. His eye catches a speck of
fluff on his white uniform. He flicks it off with his fingernail.
Yellow-blue sparks explode from the wooden logs in the gran-
ite fireplace of the *Jagdhalle*, his medieval-style reception room
and council chamber. As he sits back in his easy chair, his enormous frame flattens the cushions. He reaches for his Cuban
cigar and takes a draw, careful not to inhale. Looking into the
fire, he is reminded of the flames from the twenty-two allied
planes he had shot down during World War I. It's a time for
introspection, mostly about his life and the war, that accursed
garotte coiling around his neck, strangling his life force …

His mind flicks back to happier times, to sun-kissed memories filled with deer and pheasant shoots, and shotgun-toting diplomats binging on Beluga caviar and lobster thermidor in Schorfheide Forest in east Germany; of despots and crackpots and sexpots guzzling magnums of Dom Perignon champagne, and laughter and bonhomie and abandon in the *Jagdhalle*. Now there is only greyness, with the thudding of anti-aircraft batteries and the boom of Allied bombs exploding in obliterated streets, of firing squads, of the gallows – and of the Führer, staring at him, his hypnotic eyes apportioning blame, but never accepting it. Goering has come to the realisation that the war is lost. The Soviet armies are pushing German forces out of Poland and the Allies are almost at the Rhine. Soon they will be at the gates of Berlin – and they will be unforgiving.

He hears the anti-aircraft fire and the heavy drone of Allied night bombers. Two SS soldiers march into the hall and stand on either side of Goering. 'Herr Reichsmarschall, may we escort you to the bunker?'

Goering opens a glass door, sticks out his head, and listens. He reckons that it's a one-thousand-bomber raid on Berlin, the city of rubble. He proceeds to his underground bunker, thirty-six feet below ground and lined with eight-foot concrete walls. His wife, Emmy, and their six-year-old daughter, Edda, are already there. Edda runs to her father, who whirls her up into his arms.

When the bombing ceases, Hitler's deputy goes back to the *Jagdhalle* and once again plants himself in his front of the fire. His hand reaches for his Reichsmarschall's ceremonial baton, presented to him by Adolf Hitler in June 1941. Arm straight, he holds it out in front of him, then brings it closer and rubs the gold Luftwaffe eagle on the end cap.

An SS officer approaches, carrying some files to his breast. 'Herr Reichsmarschall ...'

'Yes?'

'Those files you asked for …'

Goering wags his baton, and the SS officer places the files on the ivory coffee table in front of Adolf Hitler's deputy leader. 'Herr Hans Winkler has arrived, Herr Reichsmarschall,' the SS officer says.

Goering lifts the top file and peruses it. The SS officer steps back and stands rigidly to attention. The fire crackles. Goering sets down the file on the coffee table, lifts a poker and rams it into a log, sending a salvo of yellow and red sparklers up the chimney. He lifts the file again, turns a page, scans its contents. Then he looks blankly at the SS officer and says, 'Send him in.'

'Very good, Herr Reichsmarschall.'

Outside the entrance to the room, Hans Winkler stands, wringing his hands. He is worried. He cannot fathom why the Reichsmarschall of Germany would want to see him. He examines his conscience again but cannot find one sin.

The SS officer escorts Winkler into the reception chamber. 'Herr Hans Winkler, Herr Reichsmarschall,' the SS officer announces before clicking his heels and leaving.

Winkler stands rigidly to attention while Goering continues reading his file. A bead of sweat trickles down Winkler's forehead. Eventually, Goering turns around and looks at him. Bald, bespectacled, nondescript: the Nazi leader's ideal image of an archaeologist. 'Sit down, Herr Winkler,' he says softly, indicating that he wants Winkler to sit across from him. 'Would you like some refreshments? Coffee? Tea, perhaps?'

'No, thank you, Herr Reichsmarschall.'

Goering lifts his glass of wine. 'A glass of wine?'

'No, thank you, sir.'

'I see you worked with Adolf Mahr in Ireland.'

'Yes, Herr Reichsmarschall. Herr Mahr was the first Keeper of Irish Antiquities and director of the National Museum of Ireland from 1934 to the start of the war, and it was my privilege to be one of his assistants.'

'I've always wanted to visit Ireland. Is it as beautiful as they say it is?'

'It is quite spectacular, Herr Reichsmarschall.'

'And the Irish ... what are they like?'

Winkler hesitates. 'They're an eccentric people, sir. Fiercely independent, wonderfully traditional; they appreciate music ... they like their Guinness and having a good time.'

'They like their Guinness ... but they don't like the British.'

'No, Herr Reichsmarschall. Historically, British imperialism has resulted in great suffering in Ireland, and the Irish have long memories.'

'And are they hostile to the Reich?'

'The Irish Republican Army are sympathetic to the Reich, Herr Reichsmarschall, but only because it suits their own ends; they strenuously oppose our system of governance every bit as much as the British.'

Goering has read about this. 'What's the maxim they hold – "England's difficulty is Ireland's opportunity"?'

'That sums it up exactly, Herr Reichsmarschall. It is my view that the general population are neither pro-German nor pro-British.'

Goering swirls the wine in his glass. 'An assistant to the Keeper of Irish Antiquities ... must have been an interesting job?'

'It was, Herr Reichsmarschall.'

'And you met the Irish prime minister, Herr de Valera?'

'Yes, Herr Reichsmarschall, I did meet the Taoiseach.'

'Taoiseach? Is that Irish for prime minister?'

'It means chieftain, or leader, Herr Reichsmarschall.'

'Like Führer?'

'Yes, Herr Reichsmarschall.'

Goering chuckles. 'Ha! Two Führers. I don't think our beloved Führer would like that.'

Winkler detects a seam of sarcasm in Goering's voice, but he remains stoic in the knowledge that to join in the Reichsmarschall's merriment could be deemed a capital offence.

'Hmm ... What type of man is this Irish Führer?'

'I found him dour, Herr Reichsmarschall.'

'Dour,' Goering repeats, smiling. Grim-faced images of Hitler and Field Marshal Keitel and Admiral Karl Dönitz flash before him. 'I know people like that. Sullen, unimaginative people: students of stupidity.' He stands up, his baton in his hand. 'How would you like to go back to Ireland on a very important mission, Herr Winkler?'

Winkler looks mystified. *Me? Going back to Ireland? What's there for me?* 'Whatever you say, Herr Reichsmarschall. It would be an honour to serve the Reich and yourself in any way I can.'

'Good. That settles it, then. We'll talk again.' Goering waves his baton. 'Goodnight, Herr Winkler.'

CHAPTER ONE

IN THE NARROW COBBLESTONED STREETS AND ALLEY-
ways of the town of Saint-Émilion, in the French prefecture of
Bordeaux, men and women dressed in crimson soutanes, ermine
surplices, and Phrygian hats hold up torches as they march in
the annual Procession of the Jurade. These leading winemakers
and prominent citizens make their way to the King's Keep in the
town, where a firework display heralds the opening of the annual
Bordeaux grape harvest.

IRA Commander Robert 'Tiny' Murdoch, all six foot six
inches of him, peeps at the procession from the side of a frosted
window in a stone-walled wine bar, but the face he has been
looking for for three years doesn't seem to be in the parade. Has
James 'Ructions' O'Hare, the man who robbed the National
Bank of Ireland in Belfast of £36.5 million and who, in the process, had engineered Tiny's kneecapping by his IRA comrades,
eluded him again?

Hughie O'Boyle, Tiny's cousin, has a red face and a blond

Tintin quiff. He peers through the other side of the window and says, 'This is something, isn't it?'

Tiny groans and rolls his eyes. It seems to him that all his life he has been surrounded by dimwits, and nothing has changed. As the procession passes by, Tiny softly says, 'He's not there.'

'Maybe your source got it wrong.'

Tiny slowly turns his head towards Hughie, lifts his empty glass, and shakes it.

Hughie walks towards the bar. Tiny looks out the window again. 'Boss,' Hughie shouts. 'Small or large?'

Tiny turns to make a 'large' sign with his hands, then turns back to the window only to feel his heartbeat break into a canter, then into a full charge: a cloaked figure in jurat costume is staring back at him from just outside the window. Tiny, mouth ajar, brings his face so close to the glass that his nose is almost touching it. The figure replicates the motion. Tiny scratches his ear. The figure scratches his ear. His eyes widen. It's ... it's him! Ructions O'Hare! The cocky little prick! Tiny's noxious thoughts stop abruptly when Ructions brings a gun muzzle to the glass, directly in front of Tiny's forehead. Stunned, Tiny staggers back and collapses onto a chair, which topples over, sending him to the floor.

Hughie rushes to lift his commander. 'Are you alright, boss?'

Tiny is quickly on his feet again. He points to the window. Hughie looks out, then turns to Tiny quizzically. Tiny looks out. Ructions is gone.

A buzzing, like a bee trapped inside a matchbox. Tiny takes his phone out of his pocket and looks at the unregistered number. He knows who's calling him.

'I could have nutted you just now,' Ructions says.

'You *should* have nutted me just now. *I* wouldn't have hesitated.'

'Go back to Ireland, Tiny. Go home before this gets out of hand.'

Tiny needs to assert himself, to take control of this conversation. 'It's already out of hand.'

'No, it isn't. All that's been hurt is your pride.'

'Haven't you forgotten something?'

'I don't think so.'

'You got me kneecapped by the IRA *and* stole our money.'

'*Me?* Pray tell, dear boy,' Ructions says in a posh voice, 'what money would that be?'

'The bank money, dear boy,' Tiny says in an equally pukka voice.

'I don't know what you're talking about, my man.'

'Shall I enlighten you?'

'I await your elucidation.'

Gone is the frivolity. Tiny's voice is backstreet Belfast. 'Yes, you. When you robbed the National Bank, you left us a lot of traceable notes while you made off with twenty million in untraceable notes. We want our fifty per cent cut of that. Ten million. There. Is that elucidation enough for you? Get it to us, and we walk away.'

Holy shit! thinks Ructions. Big Tiny's back in the 'RA!

Tiny hears Ructions's intake of breath. '"We?"'

'Yes, fucking "we."'

'And what "we" would that be?'

'The royal fucking "we." The "we" that sticks hot pokers up the asses of dickheads like you.'

Ructions, forty eight years old, blond hair, athlete's build, gets into his car but doesn't turn on the engine. 'I haven't a clue – what National Bank job are you referring to? Was a bank robbed?'

Tiny is not amused. He makes a fist and purses his lips. 'Is that the way you fucking want it?' He speaks slowly to emphasise his words. 'If you try to fuck with me, prick—'

'Tiny, son, you're one ungrateful old revolutionary! I just spared your life, and now you're calling me a prick. Is there no appreciation in this world anymore? No gratitude?' Ructions turns on the ignition and drives off.

'Ungrateful? Because of you, asshole,' Tiny says, 'I was on the front pages of every newspaper in Ireland: "Terror boss kneecapped." You must have felt good when you read that!'

'And you're blaming me for that? Man, you allowed yourself to be taped threatening the life of the chairman of the IRA Army Council. What did you expect them to do? Give you a promotion? Give you a by-ball? Tiny, the 'RA forgive nothing and remember everything. But then you found that out the hard way, didn't you?'

'Never you mind what the 'RA forgive. You just remember one thing: you're not forgiven. You'd better keep looking behind you, dear boy, 'cause I'm coming for you – and the next time you won't see me.'

'We've all got to take our medicine, Tiny, you, more than most, know that.'

'You'll be taking yours soon enough.'

'Go home, Tiny, before you're brought home in a wooden box,' Ructions says before hanging up.

Tiny sits down. Head bowed, he funnels out a stream of breath.

Hughie pulls a chair up beside him. 'Are you okay, boss? You look like you've seen a ghost.'

Tiny's head swivels, his eyes flicking open. 'I *have* just seen a ghost.'

'I don't believe in ghosts,' Hughie says. 'My da used to say—'

'Your da was full of shit. Tell the team to step down. Tell them to go back to Belfast. It's over.'

Hughie cocks his head. 'I don't get it. Why would they go back to Belfast?'

'Just do what you're told, will ya?'

'If you say so.' Hughie takes out his phone and walks into the hall.

Tiny stirs his glass of wine. How did Ructions know the IRA was in town? How long did he know? Long enough to bring a shooter to the show. Who has he bought now with his millions? Cops. Cops like fat envelopes. Tiny can feel himself getting angrier by the second. Or maybe there's an informer in the ranks? That wouldn't surprise him. What will the bold Ructions do now? He'll run, like a frightened little gazelle. Tiny has an image of a gazelle leaping across the Serengeti. He smiles as he thinks, *Gazelles get caught by lions – and eaten!*

CHAPTER TWO

IF TINY IS IN A REFLECTIVE MOOD, SO IS RUCTIONS.
How did Tiny know he was living in Saint-Émilion? How did
the IRA leader know he'd be in the Procession of the Jurade
tonight? Cops, has to be cops. The IRA must have leaky cops on
their payroll. It stands to reason that Tiny also knows the location of the farm. He congratulates himself on having evacuated
Eleanor from the farm. Someone has tipped Tiny off. Someone
who knows who he is and where he is.

He phones Serge Mercier, the Frenchman who had laundered
the twenty million pounds that Ructions had stolen from the
National Bank in Belfast four years earlier.

At seventy one years old, Serge is more like a cuddly grandfather than an international playboy who, it is rumoured, had an
affair with the Hollywood actress Brigette LeBlanc. Tonight, he
is in the library of his Lake Geneva home. It is a large, cavernous
room, crammed with thousands of books. More books are stacked
high on the floor and on three large mahogany tables. Serge likes

his library, the fusty smell of books, their sense of order, meaning and reliability. When his nephew, Alain, tried to break Serge's sentimental attachment to his books by offering to store some of the older volumes off-site for him, Serge had rounded on him, inquiring from him who he would put in storage? Aristotle? Voltaire? Dickens? 'Alain,' he informs his nephew, "when I die, the books will be yours, but until then the romantics, and the dreamers, and the poets, they're all my friends.'

Serge answers his phone. 'Cher ami,' he says to Ructions, 'how did it go?'

'I've marked his card,' Ructions says.

'Will he listen?'

'No.' As if struck with an afterthought, Ructions says: 'He was here on behalf of the IRA.'

'Is that so? I'm surprised they took him back after kneecapping him.'

'The same boyo could always turn big money for them, so I'm not surprised he's back in the fold,' Ructions says, then raises his voice. 'But he turned up here, Serge, on my patch! Someone told him I'd be walking in the procession tonight. Have you told anybody—'

'Have *I* told anyone? Is that a joke?'

'No, it's not. I trusted you with my security, and it's been breached so, no, I'm not fucking joking.'

'This is unjust,' Serge says. 'This is absurd. There are many ways you could have been compromised. It could be as simple as someone visiting the town having seen you. There could be a trail, a letter, an email, a postcard, a—'

'It could be that one of your law enforcement friends accepted a bigger envelope than mine.'

'It could be a lot of things,' Serge says, putting a glass of red wine to his lips, 'but it's not my fault.'

Ructions feels a ripple of contrition, but no more than a ripple. He sighs. 'You're right. It's not your fault.'

Serge smacks his lips in dismay. The guys in law enforcement won't like any of this. They won't want any trouble. Tiny won't take any stupid risks. Or will he? What will Ructions do? 'So, what are you plans?' Serge says.

'I'm upping sticks,' Ructions says, 'at least for a while.'

'Tonight?'

'There's no point in hanging about. I'll let you know where I'm going.'

'No, don't do that,' Serge says, a bit too anxiously for Ructions's liking.

'Why don't you want to know?'

Serge empties his glass of wine. 'Because what I don't know, I can't be accused of revealing.'

'Maybe I deserved that,' Ructions says. A silence. 'Something's worrying you.'

'It's nothing.'

'It's more than nothing. Do you want me to come to you? I could catch a flight in the morning.'

Serge thinks before speaking: 'No, but let's meet soon.' Serge looks at his diary. 'What about the nineteenth of this month? The usual place?'

'I don't know yet. I'll phone you back.'

'Fine.'

Ructions hangs up as he pulls into the laneway of the farm of his friend Jean-Claude Caron. In the darkness, his headlights light up the dark plum grapes on the vines that envelop both sides of the laneway.

After the yearlong, around-the-world cruise in the wake of the bank robbery, Ructions and his partner, Eleanor Proctor, had retired to the Bordeaux countryside, to two years of pruning, harvesting, crushing, pressing, fermenting, aging, and bottling wine. The former wife of an executive of the National Bank in Belfast, Eleanor had discovered that her husband was having an affair with his secretary and, rather than confront him directly, had secretly sworn revenge.

Against the background of her husband's infidelity, Eleanor and her friend Stacy had gone to a Bruce Springsteen concert in Dublin in 2003, where, while perusing a merchandise stall outside the RDS stadium, a young thug had snatched Eleanor's bag and run off. Luckily for the damsel in distress, a handsome knight in shining armour just happened to be nearby and gave chase to the bag-snatcher. Once out of sight, the bag-snatcher stopped running, turned around, and handed over the bag to the knight, who, in turn, handed over money to the miscreant. In that instance, Ructions had succeeded in his task of building a bridge to Eleanor, his mark, and warranting her gratitude in the process. Such was her appreciation of Ructions retrieving her handbag that Eleanor agreed to have dinner with him that night. A love affair ensued. Initially, for Ructions, romancing Eleanor had been all about creating a pathway that he hoped would lead to her helping him clean out her husband's bank. What he did not factor into the equation was the possibility that he and Eleanor might fall in love.

Ructions's plan worked to such an extent that Eleanor had supplied him with the crucial staff rotas on which were the names of the employees who would be working on the day of the robbery. Consequently, in the mouth of Christmas 2004, armed with the staff rotas, Ructions organised his gang to hold hostage the families of two members of staff, both of whom had keys to the bank's vaults. The gang members then compelled the two employees to bring out the bank's money to other gang members, who were waiting outside the bank in a large lorry. And the employees did bring out the money, all of it, emptying the bank's vaults to the tune of £36.5 million.

As ever with super-robberies, complications set in. The IRA were blamed by the governments on both sides of the Irish border for the robbery and that upset them. They felt that, as they were getting the blame, they were entitled to the spoils. Ructions had other ideas, believing that, as he had robbed the bank, the money belonged to him. He got wind that the IRA had found out where the money was being stashed in the Irish Republic and went back to scoop all the unmarked notes, leaving the IRA robbery team, led by Tiny Murdoch, the useless marked notes.

Tiny didn't like being made to look like a fool by someone whom he regarded as an upstart. And to make matters worse, having failed to sequester the bank robbery money, he had fallen foul of Paul O'Flaherty, the chairman of the IRA Army Council, the organisation's seven person ruling body and policymakers. Not only that, but Tiny had unwittingly been secretly recorded saying that O'Flaherty might have to 'go,' a euphemism for being shot dead. As a result, the IRA kneecapped him. Fair or not, he blamed all his misfortune on Ructions.

Eleanor Proctor is no derring-do adventuress. A plain-living, well-brought-up Catholic Irishwoman, she likes the stability of a regular home life, the friendship of neighbours, the solace of God and church on Sunday, and the comfort of a fat bank account. And she likes Saint-Émilion. Unlike the showery skies of Belfast, it had promised an idyllic life and temperate Burgundy has not disappointed her. She and Ructions took pride in the finished product. Their fellow winegrowers and peers in the surrounding vineyards had embraced them as their own. And then had come the phone call from Serge: the IRA and Tiny Murdoch were in France – and en route to Saint-Émilion.

Eleanor is waiting outside Jean-Claude's farmhouse, arms folded. Dressed in a black woolly sweater, beige slacks, and knee-length black boots, she pulls hungrily on a cigarette. Then she throws it away and gets into Ructions's car.

Neither speaks. Eleanor, a fresh-faced thirty-five-year-old, doesn't look at Ructions, who taps a beat on the steering wheel. 'We have to move away tonight,' he says.

'Says who?'

'El, I told you, Tiny Murdoch knows we're here.'

She holds out her palms. 'So what if the IRA know we're here?'

'So they'll try to kidnap you,' Ructions says, his voice slightly raised, 'or kill me.'

'You—' She shakes her head in disgust. 'You promised me, when we got out of Northern Ireland, that all this IRA crap would be behind us.'

'Ahh, now, that's not strictly true.'

Eleanor turns to Ructions, her fiery eyes amplifying her rage. 'Isn't it? Do you remember our conversation in the Gresham Hotel? After the robbery?'

'Every word of it.'

'Every word of it? Then you'll remember I told you I didn't want to be skulking about in hotels for the rest of my life, and you said ...' Eleanor puts an extended finger to the side of her lip and then points at Ructions. 'What was it you said?'

'I said it wouldn't happen.'

'But it did happen, didn't it? It's happening right now.'

'This will only be for a short while, love.'

Eleanor slaps Ructions's face. 'Don't you dare bullshit me! And don't dare call me "love"! This is a fucking life sentence! Until I met you, I'd never broken the law *in my life*. You, on the other hand ...' – she spears Ructions's chest with her index finger – 'robbed the fucking National Bank. And now I'm looking over *my* shoulder for the rest of *my* life. I don't even know anybody in the fucking IRA! I don't even know Tiny fucking Murdoch!'

Ructions recognises that nothing he might say will go down well, so he opts for silence. He so badly wants to start the car and drive off, just to be able focus on something other than Eleanor's fury, but his instinct tells him that wouldn't go down too well, that Eleanor would see that as a brush-off.

'This isn't working out,' she says.

Ructions's teeth are clenched tightly in case the wrong words should accidentally tumble out of his mouth.

She raises her voice. 'I said, this isn't working out.'

The voice in his head screams: For fuck's sake, give me a break, will ya? Do you think I want to move from here? Do you think I'm enjoying having an IRA posse hunting me down? But over the years, Ructions had acquired an appreciation of quotations, one from Mahatma Gandhi in particular, 'Speak only if it improves upon the silence.' He knows that nothing he would say would improve upon the silence, so he keeps his screams in his head.

Eleanor sighs. 'You've nothing to say?'

'El, please ...'

'Please what, James? Please stop badgering me?'

Ructions pushes the search button in his brain to find the right words, but the screen is blank.

'Is that what you think this is?' she says. 'I'm badgering you? I'm giving you a bit of lip? Is that it?'

'Well, aren't you?'

'Ahh, Christ.' Eleanor's head slumps back against the headrest. She reaches again for her cigarettes, but the pack is empty. Ructions lights up two and gives her one. She exhales out the window before looking straight ahead. 'What ever possessed me to think I could live like this? How naïve I was. I'm not angry with you, Ructions, I'm fucking raging with myself. I've behaved like a silly schoolgirl who had a crush on her teacher.' She turns to Ructions, whose hand is caressing his forehead. 'I don't know—'

'El—'

Eleanor turns her head towards the open car window and exhales smoke. 'I thought I could handle this life, but no, I can't, I just … I can't, I can't do it. I need roots …' She slowly shakes her head. 'And I'm never going to have them when I'm with you. The sad thing is I'm still in love with you, but I fucking hate you.'

Ructions leans over and gently kisses Eleanor on the lips. She opens her mouth to the kiss. 'We can have roots,' he says. 'We can have it all.'

She smirks.

Ructions reckons that the red mist has lifted so he starts the car and gently pulls away. 'All we've gotta do is to set up somewhere where no one will ever find us.'

Eleanor laughs, but it's a who-do-you-think-you're-kidding laugh. 'Those words were our lighthouse four years ago. Don't you remember saying them? I do. "Somewhere where no one

will find us." Saint-Émilion sounded like a place where no one
could find us. But they did. And they're here. To kill us, James?
Are they here to kill us?'

'I don't know, El.'

'And what if … just suppose we do find another place where
no one will find us, who'd be our next-door neighbours? Lord
Lucan? Jimmy Hoffa?'

Ructions sniggers. 'That's actually quite funny.'

Eleanor had been trying to be spiteful, but she can't help gig-
gling. She feels the venom being sucked out of her anger.

The car turns on to a main road. In the distance, two cars are
driving towards them. Ructions leans forward to get a better view
of the cars. Taking no chances, he turns on to a side road, pulls
into in a picnic area that overlooks the road, and switches off his
lights. A car and an articulated lorry drive past. As he puts his hand
on the gearstick to drive off, Eleanor holds his forearm and stares
into his eyes. Ructions hesitates, then talks, rapid-fire: 'El, let's not
jump off the cliff just yet. Let's get away from here. We'll think this
thing through. We have to try, haven't we? We can't just let what
we have go. You and me, kid; we don't quit. We pull together.'

Eleanor bows her head before getting out of the car. She
paces for a while and then gets back in again. 'One more chance,
James.' She holds up a finger. 'But only one.'

'We only need one.'

'I mean that, James.'

'I know you do.'

'Is it safe to go back to our farm? I've things to pack.'

'It could be risky.'

'I have stuff I'm not leaving behind – personal stuff.'

'Okay, but we have to leave in fifteen minutes,' Ructions says.

CHAPTER THREE

RUCTIONS IS FAST ASLEEP BESIDE ELEANOR WHEN THE phone rings. He lets it ring in the hope that the caller will have the good manners to hang up, but the caller seems to have limitless patience. Ructions puts on a bedside light. The name 'Henry' shows on the phone's display. Ructions lifts the phone. 'Serge, it's …' – he looks at the clock on the bedroom cabinet – 'half three in the morning.'

'I know.'

'What's wrong?'

'I'm going to die.'

'So am I, eventually.'

'But I'm gonna die before you. I'm gonna die soon.'

Ructions sits up and braces himself. 'All right. Let's have it.'

'I've prostate cancer.'

A pause. 'Is that all? I know a fella, Eamonn Caulfield, and he had prostate cancer. He went into hospital, had the operation, and was let out on the same day. No more cancer.'

'What age was Eamonn?'

'About fifty-six.'

'I'm seventy-one, and I have to wear a piss bag for the rest of my life. A fucking piss bag! "Is that all?" You can be an insensitive bastard, Ructions. I don't deserve that.' Serge pauses. 'I can't have the operation. My cancer's too far gone.'

Ructions feels his stubbled chin, 'Sorry, Serge. Have they given you … you know?'

Serge takes another drink of wine. 'Two years at the most.'

'A lot can happen in two years.'

'Yes. I can stop breathing.'

'So what are you gonna do? Drink yourself to death? Are you drinking now?'

'Of course I'm fucking drinking now!' Serge says, his voice raised. 'I'm getting … what's the word … plastered.'

'Get plastered. Get all that self-pity out of your system. But when you wake up tomorrow morning, phone me, y'hear?'

'And are you going to make the cancer go away in the morning?'

'Just fucking phone me!' Ructions says and hangs up.

The hornet flies over the ten-foot wall. Its tiny infrared beam picks up a movement in the wooded area. A squirrel breaks cover and runs to a fallen acorn. In a black van, outside the wall, a young man sits, looking into a laptop computer. *'Guten Morgen, Herr Eichhörnchen.'*

The hornet circles the pool area with its soft blue lighting. *'Wie schön,'* the young man says. The hornet is orbiting the outside of the villa now. Hovering. Buzzing. Deploying from window to window around the villa. Backwards and forwards, up and down. Spying. Scanning. *'Ich sehe dich, aber du siehst mich nicht.'* Descending towards the library. Entering through an open window. *'Danke, Herr Mercier.'*

A stirring in his booze-drenched brain instructs Serge to lift up his head, to open his eyes. He tries to ignore it, but it persists, stubbornly, and goes further, telling him that the piss bag needs emptied.

Serge Mercier's head feels like it has been superglued to his desk. The sharp stabbing pain in his lower groin is real though. *Open your eyes!*

The buzzing hornet hovers two feet above Serge's mass of long white hair. It slowly propels forward to within an inch of the Frenchman's head. As Serge's hand caresses his strained neck, the hornet flies backwards and lands on his desk in front of him. His head slowly rises. He parts his hair with his fingers, half opens his bloodshot eyes and plops his head down again. His head arises a second time, and once more he partitions his hair with his fingers.

The hornet oscillates in front of his computer screen, which is filled with data: money transactions, times, dates, people's names, and businesses. Scribbled on a sheet of paper to the left of the screen is the name RUCTIONS and a telephone number.

A packet of headache tablets throbs like the strobe lights on an ambulance beside the desk lamp. On the right side is a half-full bottle of Côtes du Rhône. Serge pushes back the chair he has passed out in. The wheels grind into glass, making a crinkling noise. Looking down, he sees broken glass and an empty wine bottle lying on its side. His tongue feels as if it has been marinated in cod liver oil and vinegar for a month, but that doesn't stop him from running it around his arid lips.

He shakes his head, rubs his eyes. 'What are you?' he mutters. 'A bee? No, you're too big to be a bee … too big, too big. What are you, little one?' Serge bends forward until his face is within an inch of the airborne hornet. A thin, red light shines from its one eye into Serge's left eye, making him blink. He moves his head to inspect it from different angles. The red light follows him. 'Am I looking at you, or are you looking at me?' As his finger moves to prod the sinister body, it takes off and floats in front of him.

Serge is perplexed. Looking around the library, he observes that, other than the desk lamp light and the little flying entity with the red light, the room is in darkness. His fingers pluck the underside of his lips.

Serge pops two of the headache tablets into his mouth and, lifting the wine bottle to his lips, takes a swig. Another painful convulsion in his groin reminds him that his catheter bag is full.

Hooligan thoughts riot in his brain. He has an image of a long-faced, hairy young man, a burning cigarette glued to the side of his lips, leaning forward, peering into a screen, at him. He wonders where Smokey-Joe might be? Outside the main gates? Inside? On the other side of the windows? Couldn't be in the house … could he? He wants to flee, to escape the little flying monitor, but he must be calm. Smokey-Joe is watching.

Grabbing his phone, Serge gets slowly to his feet. For the first time he can smell his own foul breath. As he walks towards the library door, the hornet follows him. He abruptly turns and tries to slap it with his hand, but it is too agile and evades his attack. He lifts a book from a table and throws it at the hornet. Once more it escapes his wrath but, in the time it takes to evade his fury, he manages to slam the room door on it.

He breathes hard as he leans against the library door. As if suddenly realising that his fly is undone, Serge reaches down, and locks the door with the key. Relieved, he exhales. Another agonising tremor in his groin. He runs haltingly towards the stairs. From his left, another hornet appears, flying from side to side, the thin red light dissecting his every movement. Serge is sweating profusely now, his face a bitter brew of pain and apprehension.

'Sal! Up! Up! Get up now, Sal!'

Serge tries to run up the stairs but trips and bangs his head on the floor. He staggers upright and steadies himself by holding on to the handrail. The hornet is inches in front of his eyes, bobbing back and forth, like a pendulum on speed, inspecting, examining. 'Get away!' he shouts. 'Get away from me!' He again tries to swat it with the back of his hand, but he is too slow. 'Sal!'

Sally, Serge's young English girlfriend, appears at the top of the stairs in her nightgown. 'The gun!' Serge shouts. 'Get the gun out of the drawer. Quickly!'

In the library, infrared beams penetrate the Venetian blinds, crisscrossing the room. The door that leads from the library to the pool area opens, and five individuals enter; all are wearing biker helmets and are dressed in black. Armed with Heckler & Koch MP5 submachine guns with silencers, the five adopt the tactics of a SWAT team, pointing their weapons in all directions while making, in single file, for the door into the interior of Serge Mercier's Lake Geneva mansion. The door is locked. A heavy shoulder takes out the lock.

'Ja.' One of the invaders points a finger at the cellar door on the right. Turning to two subordinates, the same terrorist says: 'Bringen sie Diener in den Keller.'

Holding on tightly to Sally's hand, Serge steers her down the concrete cellar stairs. In his other hand is the gun that Sally had fetched for him. The hornet buzzes in front of him. 'This way, Sal,' he urges. 'Hurry!' The hornet flies into his face, as if trying to stop him from reaching the bottom of the stairs. 'Fuck off!' Serge swipes at the hornet with the barrel of the gun but it easily dodges his pitiful attack. 'Fuck you,' Serge says grimly. He fires a shot at the hornet. It misses. At the bottom of the stairs, two lights hang from the concrete ceiling. Serge fires three more bullets at the hornet. One shot splinters a light bulb into dozens of tiny needlelike shards, and another lucky shot strikes the hornet. It disintegrates. Serge smiles at his success.

The door at the top of the stairs swings open, letting in a halo of light from the hall. The leader of the invaders steps onto the small landing, looks down at Serge, and points the submachine gun at him. Serge can feel trickles of sweat running down his back. Standing in the doorway, he pushes Sally into the safe room with his free hand. 'Lock the door, Sal,' Serge says quietly. 'Lock it now.'

'No,' Sally says.

'I said, lock it!'

'No.'

The door remains ajar. The terrorist leader and Serge stare at each other before the former holds up the submachine gun in a gesture of surrender. 'Monsieur Mercier,' an echoey male voice says, 'let's talk, *ja*? I have no wish to hurt you.'

'Okay,' Serge says, before quickly stepping into the safe room and pressing a button, which locks the door.

In the safe room, Sally Nixon, a pretty thirty-year-old Cambridge law graduate with long red hair, is crying bitterly. Serge leans against the door, blowing hard, his hand pressed against his chest. He looks down at Sally, who is seated. 'Don't worry,

Sal,' he says as he tries to catch his breathing, 'we're completely protected here.'

'Why are you holding your chest like that?' she asks him. 'Have you pains there?'

Serge removes his hand. 'No. I'm just ... what's the words you English use ... out of puff.'

'Are you hyperventilating, Serge?' Sally says, standing up now, staring anxiously into his face. 'Are you alright?'

'No, no. I'm good,' he says, his chest slumping as he exhales. 'It's just ... I'm okay.'

'Serge, I don't understand this. I don't understand ...' she makes a sweep with her hand, 'any of this. Why are armed ... what do I call them? Robbers? Terrorists? Why are they here, Serge? Are they here to murder us? Is this about money? Why am I locked in a safe room with armed people outside the door?'

Serge kisses Sally on the forehead. 'No one is going to murder us. Remember, Sal,' Serge makes a circling motion with his index finger, 'this is a safe room. That means these walls ... are made of reinforced concrete and steel, so no one can get in here. And this glass is one-way; we can see them, but they can't see us. We're safe. Now, I've got to phone the police, but before that I've got to go in here.' He walks into the small toilet and drains his catheter bag. A feeling of absolute relief envelopes him.

Sally deems herself entitled to answers. 'You never answered my question.'

Serge is dialling the police. 'I don't know who these people are.'

Sally reaches for a bottle of water out of the tiny fridge, but in her head, she is beginning to realise that there is another Serge, a stranger she barely knows.

The previous night's boozing, the exertion, the trauma of

the house invasion, the threat to his life, have all taken a toll on Serge's appearance. He slumps into a chair and gasps for air, swallowing chunks of it in greedy gulps.

As Sally puts the bottle of water to her mouth, she is taken aback at the deterioration in her lover and how like an old man he looks with his waxy, wrinkled skin. An image of crack cocaine addicts she had encountered at a party in Temple Court, Cambridge, flashes in front of her. They had the same skin texture as Serge.

The invader who had spoken to Serge walks down the stairs, accompanied by a colleague. He approaches the safe room, pulls up an old chair and sits down, folding his legs. 'I know you speak very good English, Monsieur Mercier. I also know your safe room is equipped with a television monitor and a microphone, so you can see and communicate with me.'

While holding the phone, Serge looks at the television, which is divided into four screens. He is speaking to a local police officer. 'I can see two invaders. They're dressed in black with biker helmets. The male speaking to me seems to be in command. Hard to say. Thirty, maybe. I can't be sure. About five foot ten, slim build. Yes. They're armed.'

The leader says: 'My name is Hermann Goering, after the Reichsmarschall.' He giggles. 'Not my real name, obviously.' A silence. 'You don't want to speak to me? That's okay.' The door at the top of the cellar opens. Hermann looks up. 'Ahh, here come the proletariat. Bring them here.'

Two more of the intruders manhandle the six-foot-five butler, Clément Beauregard, and the teenage maid, Nicoline, down the steps to the cellar floor. Both are in their pyjamas and are petrified. Beauregard's thick white hair is standing upright. Nicoline, shivering and whimpering, doesn't lift her head.

'We want the Reichsmarschall's ceremonial baton,' Hermann says. 'That's all. Give it to us, and all your problems vanish. We go away, and we don't come back. Herr Mercier, this does not have to be painful. All we want is what is ours. The Reichsmarschall's baton, *bitte*. Open the door.'

Serge and Sally look out at the terrorists. 'I don't understand,' Sally says. 'What's he talking about?'

Serge puts his finger to his lips. 'Shh.'

Hermann's tone is laced with menace. 'Open the door, I said.'

Serge leans forward, lifts a microphone and presses the push-to-talk button. 'Unfortunately, I don't know what you're talking about.'

'Ah, *Guten Morgen*, Herr Mercier, *aber bitte!*'

Serge folds his arms defiantly.

'You don't want to give us back our property? I see.' Hermann walks over to Beauregard, puts his hand around the servant's neck, and pulls him close. 'Look at this poor man, Herr Mercier. What is he? A worker. A slave. I'd bet he hasn't one hundred euro in the bank. Have you one hundred euro in the bank, old man?'

'Je ne parle pas anglais, monsieur.'

'Il ne parle pas anglaise. Quel est votre nom, vieil homme?'

'It doesn't matter what his name is,' Serge says, 'he has nothing to do with this.'

'He's got nothing to do with what, Herr Mercier?'

Beauregard clears his throat. '*Mon nom est* Clément Beauregard, *monsieur.*'

'Herr Mercier, he's got nothing to do with what?'

Serge does not answer.

The terrorist leader stands directly in front of Beauregard and strokes his cheek with his hand. 'Clément Beauregard. A fine name.'

'What does he want?' Sally says, her eyes searching Serge's face.

'Field Marshal Hermann Goering's baton.'

'And do you have it, Serge?' Sally says, her voice shrill. 'If so, fucking give it to him.'

'I haven't got it, and if we open that door, he'll kill us all.'

'You don't know that.'

'For Christ's sake, grow up, woman!'

'Don't you tell me—'

'Who do you think you're dealing with here? The Fairy Godmother? He's a Nazi, Sal, and he's going to pump us full of bullets the minute he gets his hands on that baton.'

Hermann sniffs the air and stands up. 'Do you smell anything, Herr Mercier? It's the smell of …' he pulls out a handgun from a holster at his hip, sticks the muzzle of the gun under Beauregard's chin, forcing the servant's head back, and pulls the trigger. A fountain of blood and bone explode from the top of Beauregard's head. He drops to the ground. The terrorist sniffs again. 'It's the smell of cordite. Can you smell it, Herr Mercier?'

Nicoline stumbles, as if she is going to faint, but she grabs on to a chair and remains on her feet, even though her bulging, bewildered eyes give the impression that her spirit has fled her body.

Sally's hand covers her mouth. 'Oh, Jesus!' she mutters. 'Oh, my God!'

Hermann goes over to Nicoline and lifts her head with his cupped index finger. Her mouth is open, but her eyes are closed. 'I do not want to end this girl's life, Herr Mercier,' he says, his face turning to the secure room. 'She has not done me harm. Her only crime is that she is poor, and she is your vassal. Do you

not feel any responsibility for her, Herr Mercier?' A few seconds
pass. 'She is ... what is the English word – expendable: *ja*, she is
expendable. So be it. It will be on your conscience, not mine.' He
puts the gun into Nicoline's mouth. Then his head tilts. He takes
the gun out of Nicoline's mouth and walks aside, listening to the
radio in his helmet.

'Ja. Ja.'

He turns to Nicoline and tenderly strokes her cheek with the
barrel of his gun. 'It's your lucky day, poor vassal.' Facing the
safe room, he says: 'Herr Mercier, we will be back, and we *will*
take the Reichsmarschall's baton.'

The helmeted men retreat up the cellar steps and disappear
through the corridor of light.

A large black van approaches a deserted airstrip. A man in dark
clothing opens two gates, and the van drives into the airstrip.
On the tarmac is a small Cessna Pilatus PC-12 plane, its engine
running. The van pulls up thirty yards from the plane. Six people, dressed in casual clothes and carrying hand luggage, step
out of the van and board the plane. The person who had opened
the gates also gets on board. The plane starts taxiing along the
runway.

Onboard, they relax into their seats, but one of them, a man
with blond hair and azure eyes, leans out of the open door of the
plane, points a remote control in the direction of the van, and
pushes a button. The van explodes. The plane takes off.

CHAPTER FOUR

FRENCH POLICE SUPERINTENDENT THIERRY VASSEUR is six foot eleven inches tall, and his bald head almost touches the ceiling of Serge Mercier's cellar. Beside him is his second-in-command, Inspector Pierre Robillard, lean and black-haired. A forensic team examine and photograph the cellar and the safe room.

Vasseur and Robillard look down at the body of Clément Beauregard and the pool of coagulated blood that surrounds his head and shoulders. Encased in white Tyvek crime scene suits, masks, and blue booties, the two policemen walk along a narrow corridor and peer into the safe room. A fridge, a telecommunications system, including a phone, a safe, a toilet. Nothing seems amiss. They proceed up the cellar stairs, and Vasseur stops. He looks back down the stairs, prompting a bottleneck of questions: Who is Serge Mercier? What was the rationale behind these criminals invading his home and murdering Clément Beauregard? Where did they come from? When did Mercier become a target? Why did he feel so threatened that he built himself a safe room? Mercier has secrets. The man is no innocent.

Vasseur and Robillard walk into the library. Again, crime scene officers are dusting it for fingerprints and taking photos. Vasseur goes to Serge's desk and looks at the label on the bottle of wine: *Châteauneuf Lafite-Rothschild, 1971*. Vasseur sees the sheet of paper on the desk, on which is written RUCTIONS, along with a telephone number. He turns to Robillard, perplexed: 'What is "RUCTIONS"? This is unfamiliar to me.'

'It means ... chaos or confusion. It could be someone's codename, sir.'

'Find out, will you? And I want to know who this number belongs to.'

Robillard nods.

They walk into the hall. Vasseur points to a close-circuit television camera on the ceiling cornice.

'Yes, sir. We have them on CCTV,' Robillard says.

'Where?'

'Everywhere. The house is completely fitted out with CCTV cameras.'

'Has Monsieur Mercier seen the footage?'

'No, sir.'

'Where is he now?'

'In the dining room, along with his partner, a Mademoiselle Sally Nixon.'

'And the maid?'

'She's been taken to hospital. I'm led to believe she's in deep shock.'

'Is someone with her?'

'Yes, sir.'

'I want a statement from her as soon as she recovers.'

'That may take some time, sir.'

'I don't care, Pierre. I want to know what she knows. Now, let's see what happened here before we speak to Mercier.'

Tiny Murdoch flicks up the collar of his leather jacket as he walks out of Terminal One in Dublin Airport and into the short-term parking area. A young man with a skinhead haircut standing beside a Toyota Corolla wags a finger at Tiny and gets into the driver's seat of the car. Tiny gets into the back of the vehicle.

Paul O'Flaherty, the seventy-five-year-old chairman of the IRA Army Council, is seated beside Tiny. He finishes off eating a pear and puts the core into a brown paper bag, which he sets in the door-well. 'Drive,' he says. The car takes off.

'Paul—'

'Here you are, looking like you're just back from a pleasant sojourn in the sun.'

'Paul—'

'Where's our money, Robert?' O'Flaherty says.

Mindful that O'Flaherty was the man who had presided over the IRA court-martial which had resulted in him being knee-capped, Tiny replies with subdued deference, 'He had the drop on us, Paul. He knew we were there and where we were staying. The fucker pulled a shooter on me.'

'I don't like bad language, Robert.'

Paul doesn't like bad language, Tiny thinks, yet he would order someone's execution and not lose a second's sleep. But he doesn't like bad language. 'Sorry,' Tiny says.

'This perplexes me,' Paul says. 'Does it not perplex you?'

'For sure.'

O'Flaherty opens a bottle of water, takes a drink, and twists the cap back on the bottle. The chairman has a rambling way about him, but appearances can deceive; he is far from a ditherer. Almost imperceptively, he initiates a probing interrogation of Tiny.

'How did he know you were in Saint-Émilion?'

'I don't know.'

'You didn't travel under your own name, did you?'

'Of course not.'

'Of course not, you say.' O'Flaherty frowns. 'Of course, that leaves us with only two options: either he's got someone on our side on his payroll, or someone on his payroll in the authorities identified you in transit.'

'The latter's the way I see it.'

'If you're right, and you were identified at the airport under a bum passport, why weren't you arrested?'

'I haven't a clue, Paul. Maybe they let me through immigration to see where I was going and what I was up to.'

'That's possible, in fact, probable. But that doesn't answer the big question: How did Ructions find out you were in town?'

'As you say, maybe he has on his payroll someone in authority in Saint-Émilion, a local cop, maybe.'

'Maybe this, maybe that.' O'Flaherty puts his hands inside the pockets of his overcoat and leans back and closes his eyes. 'You're not the worst, Tiny.'

'Glad to hear that from you, Paul.'

'You know, I didn't want to see a man of your calibre humiliated. You're a bullshitter and a gobshite – everybody knows that – but, as I told the Army Council, your heart's in the right place.'

Tiny, bullshitter and gobshite, draws a deep breath.

'I didn't want you kneecapped, even though you allowed yourself to be recorded saying you were considering stiffing me. But I knew you were a buffoon and didn't mean it.'

A buffoon … on top of a bullshitter and a gobshite? Why don't you just pretend I'm not here, Paul? Tiny wonders.

'Unfortunately, a majority on the Army Council didn't agree with me.'

'So, my court-martial was a foregone conclusion?'

'Come on, Tiny! How many court-martials have you sat on? How many people have walked away from them free?'

'Not many. Were you surprised that I wanted to get back into the 'RA?' Tiny asks.

'I'd have been surprised if you hadn't.'

'Oh?'

'Expulsion from that which you've held most dear all your life is always emotionally difficult,' Paul says. 'It's the power that's in it, y'see. The comradeship, the intrigue, the stature that people bestow on you … you're a Gaelic god amongst mere mortals when you're in the 'RA … you know what I mean, don't you?'

'Sure.'

'So, no, I wasn't at all surprised. *I* was dismissed once, y'know,' Paul says matter-of-factly.

'Oh?'

'Yeah. I shot a fella in the hand. You 'member Jimbo McArdle?'

'Ironfists?'

'That's him. He gave me an awful beating 'cause I stopped him from throwing wee Noel Gilmartin out of his house.'

'Why did he want wee Noel out?'

'So he could put his newly married son in the house.'

'What had that got to do with you? Noel was an alcoholic, wasn't he?'

'He was, but he was my best friend at school. Anyway, I used the 'RA's name to stop him. Then, after he beat me up, I used one of their weapons to shoot him.'

'Why shoot him in the hand?'

'I was aiming for his chest, but he was running.'

'Rightyo.'

'Anyway, I was dismissed, and I was damned lucky the 'RA didn't shoot *me*. Six months I was out of the movement; the longest six months of my life.'

'How did you get back?'

'I had a friend in the leadership at the time, Billy McKee. He spoke up for me.' O'Flaherty goes on to say that he has dedicated his life to the Republican Movement and the cause of Irish freedom. His conversation meanders until it turns into a rant against ' ... the social climbers, the counterfeit revolutionaries, the aspiring politicians, and those bloody trendy lefties ... I detest those trendy lefties more than any of the others. Every time we got up a head of steam, they undermined us with their Marxist drivel.'

'I'm with you there, Paul.'

'I'm burned out, son.'

'It's a wonder you're still at it, Paul ... at your age, like.'

At the inference he might be over-the-hill, O'Flaherty springs upright as if he had just been resuscitated with a heart defibrillator. He blinks repeatedly. 'Where were we? Yes.' He coughs. 'Some people, important people, think we should call time on this Ructions thing. Too dangerous, politically, you know? It's not the issue it once was.'

Tiny snorts, his hands flail. 'That's the ...'

'Speak your mind, man,' Paul says, 'it'll go no further: you've my word on that.'

Paul O'Flaherty's word is regarded by his friends and enemies alike as gold standard.

Tiny says: 'All right. To this day, everybody thinks the 'RA robbed the National Bank, yeah?'

Paul shrugs and nods.

'Everybody thinks this was a job for the boys, the IRA leadership's pension fund robbery. Is that to be our legacy, Paul? Is that how we're to be remembered? As a criminal gang who pulled off the robbery of the century? What would our patriotic dead think of that?'

'As a rule, I never listen to dead people's opinions,' Paul says, stroking his chin contemplatively, 'but there's merit in what you say. I don't like people thinking we pulled off that job any more than you do.' The old IRA man looks directly at Tiny. 'Tell me: short of dragging O'Hare into court and putting a gun to his head in order to force him to confess in front of a judge, how are we going to prove he pulled off this robbery?'

'We have to find his weak point. Everybody has one.'

There follows a discussion on what exactly Ructions's Achilles heel might be and, again and again, Eleanor's name keeps coming up. In the end, O'Flaherty concludes, it comes down to how much Ructions loves Eleanor because, as he points out, if he doesn't love her, his incentive to help her in a kidnap situation is greatly diminished.

Tiny, for his part, reiterates his belief that Ructions does love Eleanor and that he would be vulnerable should she be kidnapped by the IRA.

O'Flaherty remains unconcerned. 'Sometimes you have to cut your losses, Robert.' The old-timer grabs the handrail of the car door. 'I'm thinking maybe we should just let this one go. Put it down to experience.'

'We can't let him walk away, Paul!' Tiny slams the side of the car with the side of his fist. 'We've taken *his* hit, and one way or another, he *has* to take ours.'

O'Flaherty sighs. Deep down, he knows that Tiny is right. He muses: money or death? Why does it always come down to the Kray option?

'Is it the woman – the banker's wife? Is she your way in?'

Tiny pouts reflectively. 'I'm not sure.'

'Does he not care for her?'

'I'm sure he does.'

'But not enough?'

'We can't say that.'

'You sound pessimistic.'

'It's just … I can't make a judgement on how much he loves her.'

'Are you confident you can retrieve our money?'

'There are no guarantees, but I think it'd be easier to get the money than force him to own up to robbing the bank in a court of law.'

'He'd let the woman swing first, would he?'

Tiny nibbles at a rag nail on his big finger. 'I don't know.'

CHAPTER FIVE

THE KULM HOTEL, IN THE PANORAMIC SWISS TOWN OF Sankt Moritz, is 1,800 metres above sea level, and was the first hotel to ever promote winter sports. For the last two years, Eleanor and Ructions have been regular guests in the Alpine ski resort. Eleanor is the more accomplished skier.

Sitting in the multi-pillared, caramel-coloured reception, Eleanor glances out the window at the snow-covered Albula Alps, and then turns to Ructions, who is busy trying to make a phone call. Her mascaraed eyes survey his face, trying to pick up a read. His taut lips tell her he is vexed, and this is reinforced by his eyebrows, which undulate as one toxic thought preempts another.

He pushes the hang-up button on the phone, and it rings again. Once more, to his disgust, he gets an engaged tone. He immediately redials.

Eleanor lifts the morning newspaper. The headline is stark: 'Stock Markets Crash: Dow Drops 777.68 Points: Largest Point Drop in History.' Eleanor reads on before showing Ructions the headline. 'Is this something we should be worried about?' Ructions does not reply. She continues to stare at him.

'Stop it,' he says.

'Stop what?'

'Gawking at me.'

'Don't you think I should know what's wrong?'

'When I find out, you'll find out. Okay?'

Eleanor is not a lady who crumples in the face of discourtesy. 'Hey! There's no need to bite my face off.'

'Bite your face off?' Ructions looks away, looks back at Eleanor, and cynically smiles. 'To answer your question, yes – there's a very good possibility that our money is going down the plughole. We could end up skint before this day's out.'

Eleanor's head nods ever so slightly. She makes a meal out of unwrapping a mint and then doesn't eat it, setting it at the side of the saucer instead. Then, pinkie finger extended, she puts the coffee cup to her lips, but doesn't drink. She holds the cup with both hands to her chest. 'And is it my fault?'

''Course it's not your fault.'

'Then why do you expect me to take your shit?'

Ructions has long forsaken the notion that he is in Eleanor's league when it comes to giving cheek, so he hides his sassy attitude behind an iron curtain of apprehension. 'I'm sorry, El. I've a lot on my mind just now.'

'It's okay.'

'But that's just it, it's not okay.' Ructions lets out a deep, desolate sigh. 'Stock markets around the world have crashed.'

'Ah-ha?'

'And we've a lot of money tied up in them; a lot of money. And, to make it worse, Freddie isn't taking my calls.'

'Who's Freddie?'

'My investment broker.'

Eleanor glances at the newspaper. 'I see. So—'

Ructions's phone rings. He answers immediately.

'Freddie!'

'Yeah, I have.'

'It's pretty grim reading, but I've nothing to worry about, have I?'

'I see.'

'Okay.'

'Right.'

'You're supposed to be on top of this, Freddie. You should've seen this coming.'

'Now just stop right there—'

Ructions raises his voice: 'You should've—'

'Of course I fucking knew the risks, but you said—'

'I know that.'

'You assured me it was a licence to print money—'

'No, Freddie, *you* hold on. You promised me my money would be safe, but you—'

'I don't need to cool down.'

'Let's hope so.'

'I know you will.'

'I know that.'

'I'm depending on you, Freddie.'

'Bye, Freddie.'

Ructions bows his head.

Eleanor is really troubled now. She had been dangling on Ructions's every word, and now she feels like she can barely hold on. There is trepidation in her voice: 'So, are we broke?'

'Not exactly,' Ructions says, 'but it looks like we might have lost millions.'

In Serge's home office, Thierry Vasseur watches the security video of the terrorists entering the Mercier residence and invading the basement. The scene comes up where the terrorist pulls out his handgun and shoots Beauregard Clément. His eyes frequently flick to Serge. So stoic. Is it possible for someone to be so emotionless when watching such a grotesque scene? Does the spilling of innocent blood not appall this man? Seemingly not; he looks like one of those Easter Island statues, looking out indifferently as a storm approaches. The recording ends.

A junior police officer asks: 'Should I run it again, sir?'

Vasseur shakes his head and rubs his bearded chin with his fingers, as he looks at Serge downing a glass of cognac.

'Who are they, Monsieur Mercier?'

'I haven't a clue.'

'They know you.'

'Obviously.'

'It would appear that they've profiled you.'

'Yes.'

Germans … they seem to think you have Hermann Goering's baton. Do you have it?'

'No.'

Vasseur frowns. 'I find this puzzling. These terrorists put themselves in considerable danger and committed murder because they think you have Goering's baton. Why you? What would've convinced them that *you* had the baton?'

'I wish I knew, superintendent.'

Vasseur waves a finger. 'Monsieur Mercier, a very serious threat exists on your life. In fact, I don't think these people will stop until they either get caught by the police or they get what they want. Monsieur, you must be honest with me if I'm to protect you. *Oui?*'

'I am being honest, superintendent.'

'I want you to think carefully before answering my next question: Do you have Hermann Goering's baton?'

There is no hesitancy in Serge's reply. 'No, I don't.'

You're lying, Vasseur thinks.

'Can I say, superintendent?' Serge says. 'If I'd thought that by opening the door to the safe room, I could have saved Clément's life, I would have done so.'

'You made the right decision, monsieur. I think they'd have murdered you and' – he looks at his notebook – 'Mademoiselle Nixon. You made the right decision.'

'Clément worked for me for twenty-two years,' Serge says. 'He wasn't just an employee; he was a dear friend.'

Vasseur stares at Serge. 'It appears your attackers were neo-Nazis ... I say appears ... because they may have wanted us to believe that. Can you think of the significance of Goering's baton?'

'I would imagine that since it belonged to Goering, it would have considerable monetary value. I really don't know.'

Vasseur wraps himself in silence, but his eyes do not leave Serge. 'I think you know more than you're prepared to reveal, Monsieur Mercier.'

'Are you calling me a liar, superintendent?'

Vasseur pouts his lips, looks at a spot on the floor, and lets his gaze return to Serge. 'I'm not calling you anything – yet.'

CHAPTER SIX

RUCTIONS STANDS IN FRONT OF DANIELE DA VOLTERRA'S *David and Goliath* in the Louvre.

'Poor Goliath,' a voice says behind him.

Without turning around to see who had just joined him, Ructions, his hand covering his mouth, replies, 'Why poor Goliath? Because David is about to cut off his head?'

'I'd say he was rather fond of his head, wouldn't you?'

'Without a doubt.'

'But I don't think he'd have feared death.'

Ructions turns to look at Serge. 'Then why poor Goliath?'

Serge is also covering his mouth with his hand. 'Because, *mon cher*, he was just about to go down as the world's most infamous loser, a fool who was outwitted by a punk kid with a sling. I don't think a patriot like Goliath deserved that notoriety.' They walk through the room, Serge a little in front.

'Were you followed?'

'Don't you know?'

'Cops?'

'Yeah. I lost them.'

Standing in front of a bank of television screens, in the Louvre's security room, is Thierry Vasseur, Pierre Robillard, and two senior Parisian police officers. Vasseur points to Serge and Ructions on a screen. 'Close-up on these two men, please.' As the camera closes in, it is clear that, although Serge and Ructions are not looking at each other, one is speaking to the other.

'A meeting of conspirators,' Vasseur says. 'They are covering their mouths with their hands so they can't be lip-read. Innocent people don't do that.' Vasseur strokes his bald head. Almost to himself, he says softly: 'What are they plotting? What have they got to conceal?'

'I'd give a month's wages to hear what they're saying,' Robillard remarks.

'So would I, Pierre,' Vasseur says. 'Mercier is no stranger to antisurveillance measures.'

'He changed cars three times en route to Paris. We actually lost him for a while.'

Vasseur turns to a Louvre security officer. 'Can I have a glass of water, please?'

'Would you like tea or coffee, sir?'

'No, water is fine.' Vasseur's attention reverts to the screen. 'Where would he have learned such elaborate countersurveillance measures? And why?' Vasseur looks baffled. 'I had never heard of Serge Mercier until his servant was murdered.'

'He has no police record, sir.'

'Ah, but he's a crook, Pierre. A clever crook, but a crook nonetheless.'

Vasseur points to Ructions. 'We need to know who this man is and what possible connection he might have with Mercier. There's a lot going on here that we don't know about.'

'I was sorry to hear about your investments,' Serge says.

'So was I,' Ructions says.

'If you remember, I—'

'You told me not to play the markets. I know.'

'But you're not completely wiped out?'

Ructions, his hand still covering his mouth, sits on a padded bench. Serge joins him. 'I have enough to tide me over if I cut back on the champagne and caviar. It's kinda weird, isn't it?' Ructions half turns. 'One minute you've crossed the Rubicon and chased Pompey out of Rome – you are the emperor of the world – and then bang!' Ructions punches his open palm, then quickly covers his mouth again. 'You get stabbed in the back by the market. Who would be Caesar?'

'If I remember right, I gave you another analogy about the stock market? Playing the stock market is like—'

'Dabbling with a Ouija board – you never know what demons are waiting on the other side. I remember.' There is a silence between the two men. 'So, tell me, how did Tiny Murdoch know I was living in Saint-Émilion?'

'We've had this conversation already. *I* didn't tell him.'

'Was it Louis, your French police contact?'

'Don't be ridiculous. It was Louis who told us that Murdoch was in town.'

'That doesn't mean he wasn't burning the candle at both ends.'

'Louis has never betrayed me. I owe a lifetime of anonymity to him. Look elsewhere for your informer, Irishman.'

From across the room, a fat man with greasy hair and a deep dimple in his chin wearing a flowery Hawaiian shirt and white flannel trousers, is video recording a young girl with blonde hair. He makes sure that Ructions and Serge are in every shot.

Serge stands up, followed by Ructions. They walk along. 'Then who?' Ructions asks.

Serge stops and turns to Ructions, his hand still over his mouth. 'What do you want me to say?'

Ructions shrugs. They walk into the area that houses Leonardo da Vinci's *Mona Lisa*. A crowd congregates around the portrait. A Chinese couple stand up, and Serge and Ructions take their places on a wooden bench.

The fat man and the young girl walk into the room, and the male once again begins video recording.

'So,' Ructions says, 'these fucks that invaded your house – who are they?'

'In public they don't exist, but amongst their confederates, they call themselves the "Das Reich SS division."'

'Who are they though?'

'The original Das Reich was a branch of the Waffen-SS. Fierce fighters, fanatics: loyal unto death to Hitler. The Das Reich people who shot old Clément see themselves as the custodians of the sacred tradition.'

Ructions stops and swivels his head, as if exercising his neck. 'What's going on here, Serge?'

There is a dryness in Serge's voice. 'Ructions, I'm in real trouble. I'm in the telescopic sights of the Fourth Reich, who don't officially exist either.'

Rather than bombard his friend with piercing questions, Ructions quarantines his inner thoughts: The Das Reich people doesn't officially exist, the Fourth Reich doesn't officially exist, meaning Clément Beauregard was murdered by ghosts. For what? Is this some sort of bullshitters' ball? Instinctively, his fingers caress the Immaculate Conception medal which hangs around his neck. He shifts uneasily. 'That's fucking lovely, that is,' he says. 'That's fucking dandy. And here's me wallowing in self-pity because I've lost a few million on the stock market.' Ructions stands up and immediately sits down again. Through gritted teeth, he says: 'The neo-Nazis want something from you: What is it?'

'Hermann Goering's Ceremonial Field Marshal's baton.'

'That thing that sits in your cabinet in the dining room?'

Serge shakes his head. 'That thing that used to sit in the cabinet in my dining room. I decided that maybe that was not the smartest place to leave it.'

'That looks like one of your better decisions. So, where's it now?'

'In a security box in Paris.'

'Serge, you don't need this crap. Why not just give the baton to the Nazis and be done with it? It's the baton they're interested in, not you.'

'What makes you think they're not interested in me? Ructions, Nazis – even twenty-first-century ones – are litterers; they have a nasty habit of littering the streets with dead bodies. Can you be certain they don't see me as litter? I think … I think that once they have the baton, they have no excuse not to kill me.' Serge slips an envelope into Ructions's coat pocket. 'Don't put your hand into your pocket.'

'What's that?'

'It's a letter. Read it later.'

Ructions looks around him and sees the blonde woman and the man in the Hawaiian shirt with the video camera. He remembers that he had spotted them before, in the Denon wing. *Are they cops?* he asks himself. *Probably.*

'Those two,' Vasseur says, pointing to the man and woman, 'are following and videoing Mercier and his friend.'

'Should I pull them?' Robillard says.

Vasseur shakes his head. 'No. That wouldn't solve anything; they'd say they are tourists and we wouldn't be able to disprove it. But I want to know who they are and what they represent.' Vasseur asks the CCTV controller: 'Can we go back to the original two men?' The image of Ructions and Serge comes up on the screen. Vasseur smiles. 'Look.' The recorder shows Ructions concentrating on the fat man and the girl, who try to look away from him. Vasseur points to Ructions on the screen. 'This guy has spotted Hawaiian Man and Blondie. Mercier hasn't.' Vasseur points to Ructions on the screen. '*You* really interest me.' The detective takes a nasal spray out of his coat pocket, sticks it in his left nostril, and inhales. He performs the same procedure on his right nostril before pointing a finger at Ructions. 'What do you see, Pierre?'

'Well, sir, when he listens, he really listens. It's as if he's banking every word Mercier is saying. And his eyes don't blink.'

'Why's that?'

'He doesn't want to miss as much as a flutter of Mercier's eyelashes,' Robillard says. 'He's deciding if what Mercier is telling him is the truth.'

'Formidable. And Mercier?'

'I get the impression he's eager to convince the other guy that he's sincere.'

'Yes,' Vasseur says. 'Did you ever get the feeling you've stumbled onto something huge?'

'Not really,' Robillard says.

Vasseur points to Ructions. 'Look, they're breaking up. Meeting over.'

Ructions and Serge go their separate ways.

In her office at Ludwig-Maximilian University in Munich, Professor Brigitte Meyer, known to everyone as Gitte, scans her eleven students. The eyes of the professor of antiquities and German history involuntarily narrow and rest on Albert Fischer's porcelain-smooth face and full lips. The strikingly beautiful, five-foot-six inches tall professor tears her eyes away from Albert and looks vacantly at her remaining students. But those eyes return to Albert, who exudes a corseted sigh. 'Albert?'

'Yes, Frau Meyer?'

'I detect boredom. Am I boring you?'

'No, Frau Meyer.'

'Good. In our last class we examined the Nuremberg trials and their effects on postwar Germany. Of all those who were put on trial by the Allied powers at Nuremberg, the Reich Chancellor, Hermann Goering, was the most important and certainly the most charismatic. Why was that? What was so remarkable about him?'

'On his own, and arguably on Germany's terms, Herr Goering stood out as a great patriot,' Albert says.

'A great patriot? Many would contest that claim.'

'I don't see why,' Albert says defiantly. 'He was unquestiona-
bly a World War One hero.' Albert counts on his fingers: 'He was
the last commander of Manfred von Richthofen's *Jagdgeschwader
No. 1* flying squadron; he shot down twenty-two enemy planes by
the end of the war; and he was awarded the *Ordre pour le Mérite*.'

'Also known as *der Blaue Max* – "The Blue Max,"' Gitte says.
'He was certainly not a coward, that much is true. But was he a
patriot? Perhaps the question is: Was Nazism, to which Goering turned after the First World War, a patriotic ideology? And
what compelled him to go down such an extreme path?'

'We tend to think of situations in twenty-first-century terms,
Frau Meyer,' Albert says. 'But we don't know hunger; we don't
know what it's like to stick our heads in bins, looking for food
to eat; we don't know destitution. We have fixed, internationally
agreed-upon borders; we work in union with our neighbours
for our mutual benefit. That wasn't the case in post–First World
War Germany. The people were starving and impoverished. The
Treaty of Versailles had seen large tracts of our country handed
over and occupied by other states, and then, of course, there was
the noose that was war reparations. It was not a good time to be
a German, but it was a good time to fight for a new Germany.'

'So you have sympathy for the Nazis?'

'Most certainly not, but I can see why a man like Goering
would find Nazism attractive and why he would have been a
more competent leader than Adolf Hitler.'

'Why?'

'Goering didn't think Germany was ready for war in 1939. He
was proved right. He opposed the invasion of the Soviet Union.
He was proved right. He was demonstrably someone who could
see ahead, who was led not by emotion, but by logic and good

sense. So, arguably, yes, had he been given the opportunity in postwar Germany, he could have been a very good leader.'

Gitte looks to the other students. 'But he was narcissistic, hedonistic, and a megalomaniac, and, we must remember, he had never shown much enthusiasm for democracy. Hans?'

'More than anything else, Frau Meyer, it was the Reichsmarschall who signed off on the 1938 Nuremberg Laws, and it was he who wrote to Heydrich in 1941 ordering the "Final Solution" to the Jewish question. That, it seems to me, is what made him a monster and thus politically obnoxious to the Allied powers.'

'Was he naïve, then, in thinking he could have a leadership role in Germany after the war? Elica?'

'Undoubtedly,' Elica says.

'Then surely that calls into question his intellectual and political judgement?' Gitte says.

'Yes, it does, Frau Meyer. He was a clown.'

'A clown? Fritz, is that how you see him?'

'Frau Meyer,' Fritz says, 'the American psychiatrists who studied the Reichsmarschall for the Nuremberg trials said' – Fritz looks at his notes – '"He is neither stupid nor a fool in the Shakespearean sense but generally cool and calculating. He is able to grasp the fundamental issues under discussion immediately. He is certainly not a man to be underrated." Goering made mistakes, certainly, but those mistakes were often predicated on Hitler orders and obduracy.'

'So, was he the Führer's puppet?' Gitte says.

'No more so than Keitel, Jodl, or the others.'

'Doesn't that make him a clown?'

'Frau Meyer, they were all clowns.'

CHAPTER SEVEN

NOT SURPRISINGLY, RUCTIONS FINDS THE OPULENCE of the south of France irresistible. As he strolls towards the world-famous Hotel Negresco, on the Promenade des Anglais, with a biography of Hermann Goering in his hand, he hears young Belfast voices. Looking across the road, he sees a lanky young man with an infant on his shoulders, accompanied by a blonde-haired lady holding the hands of two little girls. The adults are arguing about who should have packed the towels for the beach. The accusative Belfast tones draw him back to his previous life and its petulant past ...

He cannot remember much about his parents. His mother, Isobel, had died giving birth to him, and his father, Bobbie, had been an alcoholic. After Bobbie's death, when Ructions was seven years old, he was reared by his uncle Panzer, who treated him as if he were his oldest son. On the farm, he learned from an early age how to feed the chickens, to milk the cows, to ride bareback on a horse and whisper in its ear, to clean out stables, to pick potatoes from drills in the fields, to drive a tractor, to sell illicit cigarettes and videos and vodka out the side of a van, to collect debts from shop owners who had bought Panzer's goods, to handle a gun, to rob post offices and banks, to kneecap those who crossed Panzer.

What Panzer did not teach him was to dabble in republican politics. The senior O'Hare had republican sympathies, but he made sure his support did not go further than hiding someone on the run from the authorities or providing a room for a meeting. Ructions, on the other hand, did not want to be an in-betweener; he went in, all the way, when he was twenty years old.

It was 5 May 1981, the day that IRA hunger striker Bobby Sands died. It was a day that saw Northern Ireland convulsed in gunfire and bombings, an event that guaranteed the continuation of a war that had been raging, on and off, for more than eight hundred years and which threatened to plunge the beleaguered province into civil war. Appalled that the British government had allowed Sands to die, Ructions applied to join the IRA by approaching Tiny Murdoch, a renowned IRA man.

Tiny liked the cut of the intense young man. He knew of Ructions's illegal activities on Panzer's behalf and of his reputation as an enforcer, but he figured that enforcers could handle themselves and could be useful in a fight to the death. And Ructions fought, tenaciously. He proved to be a formidable volunteer in the Ballymurphy IRA, with his organisational talents quickly being spotted by his superiors. He rapidly rose in the ranks and became Belfast Brigade Operations Officer, serving under Tiny, his mentor and commanding officer.

But, by the time of the 1994 ceasefire, most IRA operations was being thwarted by precise, up-to-the-minute British intelligence with many operatives being arrested and charged with varying offences, and others being slaughtered in British army ambushes. Ructions reluctantly concluded that the IRA had been completely penetrated by British intelligence and that the war was unwinnable. It was time to bail out.

Tiny Murdoch tried to persuade Ructions not to cut and run, but his mind was made up. The war was over ... time to move on. Ructions's departure was seen by Tiny as a personal betrayal, and he never forgave his prodigy.

Ructions's return to his old gangster ways on Panzer's behalf seemed to add insult to injury and, in 1997, it cost Panzer fifty thousand pounds to persuade the IRA to remove an execution order on his nephew after Ructions had shot an IRA volunteer in the shoulder. The volunteer had pulled a gun on Ructions, intending to kneecap him for robbing a post office van. The robbery had resulted in the post office being closed for two weeks. Tiny had opposed the removal of the subsequent execution order but had been overruled ...

Decades later and Tiny is still trying to hurt me, he thinks as he walks into the lobby of one of the most glamorous hotels in the world. Who would hold a grudge that long? When am I ever going to get him off my back? He goes over to Eleanor. 'Do you know something, girl,' he says, 'I reckon you're getting better looking in your old age.'

'I'd like to say the same about you,' Eleanor says smiling, 'but ...'

'But what?'

'But I don't want to.'

'Am I not even passable?'

Eleanor studies Ructions, her fingers caressing her chin.

'Maybe.' They laugh and then leave to walk along the fabled promenade with its blue chairs, white pergolas, and palm trees. They make their way to the beach, where they take off their sandals and stroll along the water's edge.

Eventually they find the Café Frei in Rue de France, behind the salmon-domed Hotel Negresco. On the back wall of the café are maps illustrating the dozens of coffee beans that go into the making of what the Irish pair believe to be the best coffee in the world. They sit at an outside table and a waiter approaches them. Ructions orders a noisette for himself and a café crème for Eleanor. Eleanor lifts Ructions's book and opens the first page. 'I'm surprised. You don't usually go in for history.'

'Goering was an interesting fella.'

'In what way?'

'Well, besides being second only to Hitler in the Third Reich, he had a fondness for gold bullion, old masterpieces, fine food and furnishings, the hunt, the Führer, and morphine.'

The waiter brings the coffees. 'Didn't I read somewhere the Americans found his art and money at the end of the war?'

'Not all of it. There's one and a half billion euro of old Hermann's treasure still knocking around.'

'What are you smiling for?'

Ructions sips his coffee and sets down the cup. 'Oh, I was just thinking ...'

'What?'

'How long it is since I was on a treasure hunt.'

A look of horror clouds Eleanor's face. 'It's only three years since you were on a treasure hunt. Oh, no. No way, Ructions.'

'I was only dreaming,' he lies.

CHAPTER EIGHT

DRESSED IN BLACK THIGH-HIGH LEATHER BOOTS AND A red basque, Gitte Meyer smokes a long, thin cigar at the window of Karl Keller's attic apartment in Schwabing, a bohemian district of Munich. Karl, the leader of the Fourth Reich party, is handcuffed and tied naked to a four-poster bed. Gitte looks through the streams of rain on the windowpane and observes the fat man with the dimpled chin, who had followed Ructions and Serge in the Louvre, crossing the square. He looks up. Gitte pulls away.

'You've got company, slave,' she says.

'Who?'

Gitte gives Karl a wicked, sideward glance. She walks over, reaches down, and squeezes his testicles. 'Who?' she shouts. 'Who's "who"? Are you addressing me, slave?'

'Yes, mistress,' Karl spits out through gritted teeth, 'I'm addressing you, mistress. I'm sorry, mistress. I apologise, mistress. Please forgive me.' Gitte squeezes harder. Karl's azure eyes look as if they're ready to pop out of his eye sockets. 'I'm sorry, mistress. Oh, please, mistress.'

'You'd better be sorry,' Gitte says, releasing her grip on his testicles, 'or I'll tell the world what an utter fucking wimp the great Führer really is.'

'Thank you, mistress.'

Gitte lifts a key from the dressing table and uncuffs Karl. 'Now hurry up.'

Eduard Richter stands with his back to a roaring fire in Karl Keller's large living room. 'I'll be with you in a second, Eduard,' Karl shouts from another room.

'Take your time,' Eduard shouts back, 'I'm in no rush.' He looks around. As a former antiques dealer, he knows good furniture when he sees it. He runs his hand over a Chippendale revival display unit. A maroon chesterfield leather sofa and two chairs occupy the space on either side of the fire. On the red-bricked wall, opposite the fireplace, is a full-size portrait of Jacques-Louis David's *Leonidas at Thermopylae*. Eduard examines the thirteen-by-seventeen-and-a-half-foot portrait.

'Do you like it?' a voice says.

Eduard spins around as Karl, now casually dressed in black trousers and a white, open-necked shirt, enters the room. 'It's good,' Eduard says.

'Only good?' Gitte says as she also enters the room, changed into an ankle-length blue dress with a slit up the side. 'Even though his army is facing annihilation, Leonidas is still the strong man, still in total command.'

'A bit too French, for my taste, Gitte,' Eduard says.

'Ah, that's where you're wrong, Eduard,' Gitte replies. 'Yes, the artist was French, but Leonidas' – she waves an extravagant hand – 'he belongs to the universe.'

Eduard wishes that Gitte belonged to him. He knows that Hans Weber and Dieter Schneider are in love with her too, but their love pales in comparison to his.

'And look …' Karl says, pointing to a naked man carving something on the rock. 'Do you know what he's carving?'

'No, Führer.'

'"Go tell the Spartans; you who passeth by; that here, obedient to their laws, we lie."'

'Very profound,' Eduard says.

Gitte walks to a drinks cabinet and pours herself a bourbon and ginger ale. She pours Karl a mineral water and then turns to Eduard. 'What would you like?'

'A bourbon and ginger ale, if you have it.'

Gitte glances at Eduard. Is it a coincidence that her favourite drink is also Eduard's? She doubts it. She mixes the drinks and then dangles Eduard's drink seductively in front of him. 'Bourbon,' she muses, an impish smile on her face. 'You can't be a serious lover of Bourbon unless you can recite what Mark Twain said about it.'

Eduard smiles hesitatingly. 'Let me see,' he says, his hand stroking his dimpled chin. 'Was it: "If I cannot drink Bourbon and smoke cigars in Heaven, then I shall not go"?'

'Bravo, Eduard.' Gitte gives Eduard his drink. 'To the Fourth Reich,' she says. Eduard returns the toast. Gitte studies Eduard. She can see a want in his eyes … She is assailed by a vision of Eduard and she in bed, of him on top of her, pumping, grunting, foaming at the mouth, like a rabid dog. She smiles politely and leaves the room.

Karl smiles, businesslike. 'So, Eduard ...'

Eduard lifts his briefcase and sits down alongside Karl. He had backed another candidate against Karl for the leadership of the German Nationalist Movement. He liked Karl and had admired him for his strong opinions. But for Führer? Eduard did not think so. That all changed for Eduard when Karl spoke at a closed leadership selection meeting in 2000: 'Comrades, I say to you tonight: Be ready. Be absolutely ready, because the Fourth Reich is coming,' he had shouted at the two dozen delegates who were meeting in an upstairs lounge of a backstreet bar in Munich. 'And you,' he had wagged his finger, Hitler-like, 'you shall be its leaders!' His vision had prompted uproar, much tapping of beer bottles on tables, frantic Nazi salutes, and manic cries of 'Sieg Heil!'

'Our beloved Führer, Adolf Hitler,' Karl had continued, 'spent almost fourteen years in the political wilderness before becoming chancellor and then president.' His voice was low, his head nodding rhythmically for effect. 'That was a long time. And it demonstrates the reservoirs of patience and tolerance that the Führer possessed. But, comrades, we have neither patience nor tolerance.' Another rumpus erupted. Karl's voice got louder: 'The Führer, I'm sorry to tell you, had faults.' Murmurs of discontent. Karl put up his hands appealingly, knowing that any criticism of Hitler was anathema to his audience. His voice lowered again to lend reverence to what he was about to say: 'It ill behoves me to criticise the Führer, and I know it will probably destroy my candidacy for the leadership, but I don't care, comrades. The Führer had imperfections.' More muttering. He held up his hands. 'Comrades ...' The furor did not abate. 'Comrades!' he shouted. 'Hear me out!'

Eduard had sensed then and there that there was something different about this man, something profound. He stood up and appealed to his fellow neo-Nazis to give Karl a hearing. Eventually, the audience settled down.

'The Führer,' Karl continued, 'allowed his patience and tolerance to cloud his judgement. He did not, comrades, take the opportunity, presented by the war, to fully solve the Jewish question.' There wasn't a sound as the audience inhaled every word. 'Otherwise ... otherwise, there would be no Jews in Europe today.' A rowdy round of applause. Karl's voice became louder. 'Think about it. The victors ask us to believe that, had the Führer decided to eliminate all the Jews in Europe, he could not have done so. That is ridiculous. This ...' His pointed finger wagged as if it was on the receiving end of electric shock treatment. ' ... This lie, this pernicious invention that the Führer eliminated six million Jews ... where did it come from?' he squealed. 'Where did it come from?'

'International Jewry,' someone shouted.

'Correct,' Karl said, his voice returning to normal. 'International Jewry did a deal with the Allies ... And what was that deal?' Karl looked around the assemblage for dramatic effect. His voice seemed to rise organically, as if he was mining his soul: 'They agreed to bankroll the Allied war on the understanding that the Allies would not stand in the way of the creation of the State of Israel. And they didn't.'

Such was the fervour generated by Karl's demagoguery that some of his followers were waving guns. 'And the Jewish press sold the illusion. That is why, when we come to power, we will shut down this – this unGodly Zionist press. That is why we, the Fourth Reich, shall hold the media to our breasts and never let it go. We alone, my fellow Nazis, know what is good for the German people. We alone, the chosen elite, shall light beacons that will tell our beleaguered people the time of their liberation and exaltation among the nations has come. *We* shall make Germany great again.'

There is thunderous applause and the stamping of bottles on tables. In the election that followed, Karl won over three-quarters of the votes and became leader of the Fourth Reich.

'You've something for me,' Karl says brusquely.

'Yes, Führer.' Eduard reaches into his briefcase, takes out and opens his laptop. He puts a USB stick into the laptop. Footage emerges ...

On-screen, Serge and Ructions are looking at various paintings.

'Who's that with Mercier?' Karl asks.

'He's an Irishman called James "Ructions" O'Hare.'

'An Irishman? What's an Irishman doing with an international money launderer?'

'O'Hare is a bank robber. Our sources in the police tell me that he robbed a bank in Belfast three years ago of over thirty-six million pounds.'

Karl wolf-whistles. 'Wow! Where does he live?'

'He was living in Saint-Émilion, near Bordeaux—'

'Was?'

'He doesn't live there now. It seems he has no fixed address.'

'People with no fixed addresses are homeless, and people who are homeless have problems. What's O'Hare's problem?'

'The IRA want to kill him.'

Karl nods. 'Now, that is a problem. Do we know why?'

'It seems he didn't give them their cut of the robbery money.'

'Not good business.' Karl purses his lips. 'I don't want any complications with the IRA. They are extremely capricious.'

The recording reaches the room in the Louvre that houses the *Mona Lisa*. 'Stop it there!' Karl commands. Eduard stops the recording. 'Rewind.' Eduard rewinds the footage and hits the play button. The segment plays out where Serge slips Ructions the envelope. 'Rewind.' Eduard rewinds. 'There!' Eduard freezes the recording. 'See?' Karl says, pointing to the screen where Mercier slips something into O'Hare's pocket. 'What's that?'

Eduard enlarges the image. 'It's an envelope, Führer.'

'What are we looking at? An exchange of money? If so, why?'

'Could be anything.'

'This man O'Hare interests me ... I'd like to know more about him. Have we friends in Ireland?'

'Yes,' Eduard says. 'Combat 18, also known as "18."'

'Combat 18? Remind me about them.'

Eduard tells Karl that Combat 18 were formed in 1992 and that the "18" comes from the initial letters of the Führer's two names, A for Adolf, being "1," and H for Hitler, being "8." 'They are small,' Eduard says, 'but they have stockpiles of weapons and are dedicated national socialists.'

'If we must send people to Ireland – and I hope we don't – can rely on Combat 18 to supply us with weapons?'

'I believe so.'

'Can we rely on their discretion?'

'They seem to be fairly security-conscious.'

'"Fairly security-conscious" isn't good enough, Eduard. We have to be certain about them.'

'I'll investigate them and get back to you, Führer.'

'And when you're at it, find out what weapons would be available to us.'

Wanting to please his Führer, Eduard goes on to say that the party's police contacts in Munich are friendly with members of the Northern Ireland police, and that they should have access to high-grade intelligence.

'That is good.' Karl gathers his thoughts. 'O'Hare is a bank robber,' he says. 'Logic would dictate that he was meeting Mercier about laundering money.'

'I agree, Führer.'

'But the bank robbery happened three years ago,' Karl says pensively. 'It's not inconceivable that he has waited until now to move on the money.' He opens a walnut box on the coffee-table, takes out a cigar, smells it from end to end, and lights it. Exhaling, he turns to Eduard: 'We need to know everything about Mr O'Hare. You said he was called James something?'

'James "Ructions" O'Hare, Führer.'

'Ructions ...' Karl swirls the name around his tongue. 'Ructions, Ructions ... I've never heard that name before.'

'It's a nickname.'

'What does it mean?'

'It means chaos, anarchy, uproar.'

Karl nods thoughtfully. 'I like anarchy; it's essential at times. But it's inherently uncontrollable. Is this Ructions going to be uncontrollable, I wonder?' Karl smokes his cigar. 'You say the IRA couldn't control him ... what does that tell us?' He taps the ash from his cigar into an ashtray. 'We need to find a way to talk to Mercier. This man, Anarchy—'

'Ructions, Führer.'

'*Ructions*. We need to find out who, exactly, we're dealing with, but ... Might this Ructions carry a message to Mercier for us?'

CHAPTER NINE

LARGE RAINDROPS DETONATE ON TINY MURDOCH'S car windscreen. Even though his full beam is on, Tiny has to lean forward to see the road in front of him. He looks in his rear mirror: no lights; no cars; blackness. *Take it slowly, big man. No rush.*

His car turns left down the Glen Road, off the Belfast to Bangor road. As he approaches a railway bridge, he sees the headlights of a car coming towards him. He pulls over and lets it pass before continuing towards Belfast Lough. He reaches the end of the road and steers the car into a small, undulating parking area, pointing his car out to sea. A cross-channel ferry, lit up like a tall ship, is inching down the lough.

The tempestuous wind pinballs a white plastic bag across the lot until it lands on Tiny's windscreen. The windscreen wipers sweep the bag to the bottom of the window. He looks around. Nothing. Tiny looks in his rear mirror. A beam from a flashlight. He gets out of the car and his face is immediately pepper-sprayed with horizontal, slicing rain. He gesticulates with his hand, indicating that he wants the person holding the flashlight to come to him.

'No,' shouts police officer Daniel Clarke, who seems to have walked to the meeting. Clarke, a chief superintendent in the police service of Northern Ireland, is wearing a grey duffle coat, the hood of which completely covers his head.

Tiny is wary. He reaches into his car and takes out a revolver from underneath the driver's seat, holding it by his side.

Clarke approaches. He throws back the hood of his duffle coat as a measure of recognition. 'Follow me,' he yells.

'No,' Tiny screams. 'Get into the car.'

'But—'

'Get into the fucking car. Now!' Tiny himself gets into the car, followed by Clarke. Tiny slips his gun under the seat. They drive up the Glen Road. 'Are you wired?' Tiny asks.

'No,' Clarke replies.

'You'd say that anyway.'

'How do I know you're not wired?'

'You don't. As it happens, I'm not. So what now?'

'We get out of the car.'

Tiny is aghast at the suggestion. 'And walk in the middle of the road? It's bucketing down! I don't think so.' Tiny pulls the car over to the side of the road, reaches over and opens the passenger-side door. 'Fuck off.'

'For Christ's sake, man, pull yourself together,' Clarke says.

'You wanted this meet, not me. I'm outta here.'

'Okay, okay. We talk here.'

'Look, I don't want to be talking to you any more than you want to be talking to me.'

'We should've been talking about a whole range of things a lot sooner than this, Tiny. We're on the same side now.'

'We are?'

'Aren't we? Doesn't the IRA want to pursue its goals through exclusively peaceful means?'

'Of course. We've made that abundantly clear.'

'And neither party want a return to war.'

'That goes without saying.'

'It does. My point is: that puts you and me on the same side, 'cause I want exactly what you want – peace.'

'I guess you're right.'

'I have to pat you down.'

'Be my guest.'

Clarke pats Tiny down. 'I want to have a dekko around the car.'

'Fire away.'

Clarke leans forward and looks in the glove compartment and feels under his seat. Under Tiny's seat, he feels the gun. 'You came prepared, I see.'

'And what?'

'You were taking a chance, weren't you?'

'I don't think so. You wouldn't be here unless you wanted something really bad from me. Now, I want to pat *you* down.'

Tiny pats Clarke down and finds a holster and gun tucked into his waistband. 'You came prepared yourself.'

Clarke shrugs. Tiny sits back.

'Your people were in Saint-Émilion recently,' Clarke says.

'Saint what?'

'Let's not play games, Tiny. I know the last time you took a crap.'

'I don't know what you're talking about.'

'You and some of your friends were recently in Saint-Émilion, looking for a certain gentleman.'

Tiny makes no attempt to subdue or hide a yawn, his open mouth showing a set of custard-coloured teeth.

'Old habits die hard, don't they?' Clarke says. 'I remember you yawning like that in Castlereagh interrogation centre. You—'

'Look, get to the fucking point. What's all this about?'

Clarke takes out his notebook and writes the name RUCTIONS.

'You've got my attention,' Tiny says.

'Is the car wired? Truth?'

'No.'

Clarke nods. 'I believe you. Okay. I don't know how you found out our friend was in Saint-Émilion, but you did.'

'He's not my friend, and his name is Ructions O'Hare. I told you, the car isn't wired. We can speak freely.'

'We don't care about the money, but we want this guy brought to book for the National Bank robbery. And we need your help to do that.'

'Sorry, go back a bit: You don't you want the money?'

'It'll be well buried in the financial system by now, and besides, we don't anticipate your crowd handing us millions of pounds in stolen bank notes – that is, if you find it.'

'Very perceptive.' Tiny rubs his bristled chin. 'We have problems already.'

'Oh?'

'You want him locked up.'

'That's it.'

'You're talking about *prima facie* evidence.'

'Yes.'

'I very much doubt if he'd have any of the original bank money lying about.'

'Unlikely.'

'So, basically, the only real *prima facie* evidence that's left, that would stand up in court, is a signed confession.'

'Exactly.'

'And he'd be up for that, would he?'

'He wouldn't be the first bank robber who cleared off to foreign parts, got homesick, and decided to give himself up.'

'I see where you're coming from. Dan – you don't mind me calling you Dan, do you?'

Clarke does mind. He figures that Tiny, by being deliberately disrespectful, is testing him. He buries his angst under a broad grin. 'Not in the slightest.'

'You're thinking of Buster Edwards, the Great Train Robber.'

'And his partner, Ronald Biggs.'

Tiny tries desperately not to laugh. 'What a robbery! 1963, wasn't it?'

'Yes.'

'I'd love to have had a hand in that one.'

'You'd have ended up in jail.'

Tiny shakes his head. 'Don't think so. Nope.' He holds up a finger: 'The first rule of any robbery is to make sure your runback is airtight. Yeah?' Clarke's face is expressionless. 'And the second rule is to know everything there is to know about forensic science so that you don't leave any evidence behind when you leave the runback house. The Great Train Robbers left evidence everywhere. Sloppy. And, just while we're on the subject, the cops didn't catch Buster, he was skint when he gave himself up, and Biggsy was dying.'

'The system broke them,' Clarke offers.

Tiny leans towards Clarke, 'A bit of advice, Dan: Don't underestimate Ructions O'Hare. He's more of a mastermind, like Bruce Reynolds was for the Great Train job, than a Buster or Biggsy.'

'Reynolds was caught too.'

'But he didn't give himself up. And you're missing something else, Dan.'

'What's that?'

'Ructions isn't on the run. He can come back here tomorrow, and there's fuck all you or the PSNI can do about it.'

'That's where *you* come in, my friend.'

'You want us to persuade him to come back and make a confession?'

'More or less.'

'You want us to become cops.'

'I wouldn't go that far.'

'Just as a matter of interest, Dan: How are we going to secure this confession?'

'You'll think of a way.'

'And supposing we were able to help you – what's in it for us?'

'You get to keep whatever money you recover.'

Tiny bursts out laughing. 'That's very generous of you, Dan.'

'Your sarcasm is wasted on me, Tiny.'

'Are you rattled, Dan?'

'Me? Never.'

Tiny guffaws. 'I tell you what, you weren't as funny as this when you were interrogating me for the National Bank robbery.'

'Ah, now, I had my moments.'

Tiny grabs a paper handkerchief and rubs his eyes. He stops laughing and holds up his hands apologetically. 'Dan, when we make a withdrawal from a bank, we *never* give the money back.'

'No, you don't. Okay, here's the deal: I've been authorised to say that we won't pursue the money, should you recover it ...'

'Ah-huh?'

'And we'll issue a statement saying we don't believe the IRA carried out the National Bank robbery.'

'And?'

'And that's it.'

'That wouldn't be enough.'

'It's all there is.'

'We'd need more.'

'Such as?'

'We'd need to know that, down the line, your people would help us out, if necessary.'

Clarke doesn't like the way the conversation is going. 'In what way, help you out?'

'A situation could arise where we might have to chastise individuals who threaten ours and your interests—'

'Pardon me?'

'You can't control the dissident republicans. We can. And, as you yourself said earlier, we're on the same side.'

Clarke realises that Tiny has given some thought to their meeting. 'I see. And by "chastise" do you mean murder?'

'Let's put it this way, there are a lot of dissidents who are angry that the leadership ended the war and embraced the peace process. They might attack us and force us to defend ourselves.'

'And there's me thinking the IRA had decommissioned all its guns in 2005.'

Tiny smiles.

Clarke puts his hands behind his head and links his fingers. 'I appreciate your concerns, but I haven't the authority to adjudicate on the matter. I will, however, pass on your comments.'

'Supposing we could cut the deal,' Tiny says. 'Would your offer be in writing?'

'Ah, come on, Tiny: you know better than that.'

Tiny reaches for a cigarette.

'I'm allergic to smoking,' Clarke says.

Tiny puts the cigarette in his mouth, holds the glowing car-lighter close to it, puts the car-lighter back in its well, and tosses the cigarette on the dashboard. 'An act of goodwill,' Tiny says.

'Appreciate that,' says Clarke. 'If we pull this deal off – and we're taking a huge punt—'

'As are we.'

'If we pull this off, you and I will liaise on a one-to-one basis. I'll keep you posted on our friend's movements and his activities; you keep me posted on what moves you intend to deploy to bring him to heel.'

Tiny grimaces. 'Are you sure you want to know how we'd get to him? It could be messy.'

Clarke hesitates. 'Come to think about it, I'd prefer the *fait accompli*. No details on the how and when. That sounds about right, but I'll get back to you on it.' Clarke holds out his hand.

Tiny looks down at it for a few seconds before taking it. 'I never thought I'd see the day when I'd be shaking hands with a Peeler.'

'And I never thought I'd see the day I'd be shaking hands with an IRA general headquarters staff officer. I hope you don't mind me saying it ...'

'What?'

'No, it doesn't matter.'

'It does. Speak your mind, Dan.'

'It's just ... I'm surprised old man Flaherty and the Army Council allowed you back into the organisation after having had you kneecapped. He must be going soft in his old age.' Clarke holds up his hands. 'No offence meant.'

That, coming from a peeler? Are you joking? Of course, I'm taking offence, you fucking prick. Time to put some manners on this boy. 'Y'know, I had you once ...'

Clarke frowns. 'What do you mean you, had me once?'

'You live in a cul-de-sac, number 12 Cheshire Close in Bangor. Your next-door neighbours are called Brian and Sally Andrews, and they drove a blue BMW.'

Clarke tries his best to remain calm, but gremlins are playing basketball in his stomach. This has suddenly become very personal. 'Go on.'

'You have a son called Derek, a nice-looking kid, about eight, as I recollect.'

'As you recollect? You've seen him? You've seen my son?'

Tiny wants to burst out laughing, but he controls himself. *Not so fucking cocky now, are you, big ears?* 'A man sees a lot of things.'

'What are you telling me here?'

'Oh, nothing,' Tiny says nonchalantly, 'except you live in number 12 Cheshire Close in Bangor and have an eight-year-old son called Derek.'

'You were in Bangor to kill me,' Clarke says. 'You were outside my fucking house, you cunt! You fucking IRA ratbag!'

'For fuck's sake, man, give your head a shake!'

'Fuck you! You were going to kill me.'

Tiny reaches over and opens the front seat passenger-side door. 'Get out! Go on, fuck off.'

Clarke hesitates. He knows that if he walks away from Tiny now all chance of convicting Ructions will walk away with him. He stares ahead, closes the door, and puts both hands on the dashboard.

'Look at me,' Tiny says.

Clarke continues to stare ahead.

'Are you fucking deaf? I said, look at me.'

Clarke turns his head.

'Don't you ever try to be smart with me again. Don't you fucking dare,' Tiny scowls. 'You owe me, big time.'

'How?'

'There were people in a car who were looking at you, who were gloved and suited up and who wanted to stiff you, and I ...' Tiny stabs his chest with his fingers, 'I stopped them.'

Suddenly it dawns on him that he is only having this conversation because Tiny reigned in the IRA hitmen that were outside his home from shooting him dead. *Why?* he asks himself. *How many murders has Murdoch been involved in? Ten? Twenty? He's one of the most prolific killers of the Troubles. Why didn't he murder me when he had the chance?* Clarke coughs. 'Thanks.'

'Don't thank me, thank your son.'

'My son?'

'Yeah. Derek bears a remarkable resemblance to my own son.'

Derek. Clarke is left blinking, and can only mutter, again, 'Thanks.'

Tiny nods.

Clarke feels a swelling in his chest. 'I mean that,' he says.

'I know you do.' It's not often that Tiny gets the opportunity to put a cop in his place, and this one is particularly sweet. 'Okay. Let's move on. Where's Ructions now?'

'On the Côte d'Azur with his girlfriend. In the Hotel Negresco, in Nice, to be exact. Last I heard, he was whooping it up on the 'RA's money, spending it like there was no tomorrow. I've gotta love you and leave you,' Clarke says, pulling up his hood.

Just as Clarke is about to get out of the car, Tiny says, 'Hey, pal ...'

'Yeah?'

'Pull that plastic bag off the bonnet for me, will you?'

'Sure thing.' Clarke gets out of the car. Another car speeds out of the rain and the blackness and stops abruptly. Clarke turns to Tiny and peers into the car, his hood still up. 'I really wasn't wired,' he shouts over the wind and rain.

'Neither was I.'

Clarke gets into the other car and drives off.

Tiny reaches his hand down towards the pedal into the underside of the dashboard and retrieves a small tape recorder.

Clarke, in the back of the car that picked him up, on his way to police headquarters, screws off a button from his duffle coat.

'Did you get it all?'

'Yes, sir.'

CHAPTER TEN

RUCTIONS WANTS TO FIND OUT THE STRENGTHS AND weaknesses of the Fourth Reich. He leans over his laptop computer. On-screen is Karl Keller, looking down from a brightly lit upstairs window, giving the Nazi salute to men dressed in brown shirts, with swastika armbands, at a night-time rally. A caption describes Karl as the leader of the Deutsche Nationalistische Partei. The more that Ructions reads about the Fourth Reich, the more obnoxious he finds it. He wants to believe that people like Keller don't really exist in postwar Germany, but the evidence tells him otherwise. Hitler never exterminated six million Jews? Where did they disappear to?

Reading on, Ructions discovers one German politician describing Karl Keller as 'the most dangerous Fascist in Europe.' A government minister calls him an 'astute demagogue and the person most likely to unite the far-right in Germany.' A political opponent states that big business has secretly funded the Fourth Reich to the tune of tens of millions of euro. Further investigation reveals that Karl is the grandson of former SS paratrooper Captain Adelbert Keller, winner of the Iron Cross, first-class, for his valour during the German invasion of Crete in 1941. From what Ructions can tell, Adelbert is not an active member of the party, but a voice in Ructions's head sounds a note of caution. *Iron Cross, first-class, Adelbert*, the voice echoes. *Who are you really, old man? Are you still a Nazi? Why wouldn't you be?*

Ructions consistently views photographs of Karl in the company of a woman named Gitte Meyer, one of which catches his attention. They are at a dinner dance, and a group photo has been taken at their table. An elderly man with a thick mane of white hair is sitting to one side of Karl, while Gitte sits to the other. You must be Adelbert.

Meanwhile, in *his* study, Karl looks at a police mugshot of Ructions on his computer. In the photograph the roots of a beard are clearly shown, and Ructions's long blond hair is dishevelled, with two ringlets dropping down on each side of his face. Karl reads the police assessment of Ructions: 'James O'Hare, aka "Ructions," is an extremely dangerous criminal, who is believed to be the brains behind at least eleven bank robberies, including the 2004 National Bank robbery, during which over £36 million was stolen in a tiger kidnapping.' Karl looks up tiger kidnapping: 'A tiger kidnapping involves two separate crimes. The first crime usually entails the abduction of any person that someone highly values. Instead of demanding money, the captors demand that a second crime be committed on their behalf. The second crime could be anything from robbery or murder to planting a bomb.' *This Irishman is not to be underestimated*, Karl tells himself.

In her apartment, Gitte is looking at the computer. She reads that Ructions was born into a criminal family, which was led by his uncle, Johnny O'Hare, aka 'Panzer.' According to the police file sent to her by Karl, Ructions had been in the IRA during the 1980s and into the early 1990s. The same file said that he had been the senior operations officer in the IRA's Belfast Brigade and had been responsible for organising a large number of robberies, as well as numerous shootings and bomb attacks on members of the security forces. He left the IRA in 1994, the year that the IRA called a complete ceasefire and took its first faltering steps along the pathway to peace. Since then, Ructions has used his considerable organisational talents in pursuit of personal gain and had emerged as the de facto leader of his uncle Panzer's criminal gang.

Reading on, Gitte finds out that a woman called Eleanor Proctor, the wife of a leading National Bank official, had been groomed by Ructions into helping him pull off the robbery. The file also said that, while initially appearing to be the leading witness for the prosecution in the court case against Ructions, Eleanor had been, in fact, a Trojan horse, whose job description – as dictated by Ructions – was to become the virus that would crash the case. After she did so, the two lovers had left Northern Ireland to start a new life abroad – presumably with the proceeds of the bank robbery. 'And you orchestrated all this?' Gitte says giddily, clapping her hands. 'Ructions O'Hare, I simply have to meet you.'

Thierry Vasseur looks into a webcam. A grainy image of Daniel Clarke comes into view. 'Hello, Dan,' Vasseur says.

'Hi, Thierry.'

'As I said in my email, I'm looking for information on James "Ructions" O'Hare in connection with a murder.'

'Did O'Hare murder someone in France?'

'No, but he is a person of interest to us.'

Clarke hesitates. 'May I ask why?'

Vasseur sniffs. 'The person who was murdered was an employee of a Serge Mercier. Does that name mean anything to you?' Clarke shakes his head. 'It appears the employee was murdered by neo-Nazis because Mercier would not hand over Hermann Goering's baton to them.'

Clarke cannot hide his amazement. 'Hermann Goering? Neo-Nazis? What on earth has Ructions got himself messed up in now?'

'I don't think O'Hare *was* involved with the neo-Nazis. I'm not even sure Mercier was involved with them. But they might be now.'

In the far reaches of his mind, Clarke is trying to make sense out of something that appears senseless. *Who is Mercier?* he thinks. *Why haven't we heard of him before? And what's his relationship to Ructions?*

'We checked Mercier's phone,' Vasseur says, 'and the last person he called before the neo-Nazis hit his home was O'Hare. In fact, there have been numerous calls between the two over a considerable period.'

'May I ask what a considerable period constitutes, Thierry?'

'As far as we can tell, it goes back years.'

Incubating inside Clarke's head is the suspicion that, somehow, Serge was connected with the National Bank robbery. 'That's interesting,' he says.

'Also, the two met recently.'

'*After* the neo-Nazi raid?'

'Yes.'

'And did Mercier meet anyone else after the raid?'

'No. Only O'Hare.'

'Ructions doesn't do chitchat—'

'Chitchat?' Vasseur asks.

'Camaraderie, small-talk. He doesn't waste time on people

who are of no use to him, which means that this Mercier fellow is important to him. Can I ask … where did they meet?'

'In the Louvre. And Mercier employed elaborate countersurveillance measures to prevent us finding out about the meeting. We almost lost him.'

'Those are not the actions of an innocent man. You know, Thierry, the more I'm hearing about this Mercier, the more I suspect he and Ructions are partners in crime.'

'You think Mercier was involved in the National Bank robbery?'

Clarke looks away, then looks back. 'Maybe. It'd be useful to have a historical record of Mercier's banking arrangements, although I'm not sure they would reveal too much.'

'I've already done that. Mercier's accounts show a man of modest means.'

'They would, wouldn't they?' Clarke says. 'What happened in the Louvre?'

'Their meeting was surreptitious. They deliberately kept their hands over their mouths in case they were being lip-read. Watched everything and everybody.'

'Ructions always does that in public.'

'Does he?' Vasseur says. He thinks, *Should I tell him the neo-Nazis were following them? No.* 'We have them on CCTV. I'll send a copy over to you.'

'Much obliged, Thierry. I'm surprised you were able monitor Ructions.'

'It was Mercier we were monitoring. He led us to O'Hare.'

'Where's O'Hare now?'

'We lost him.'

Of course, you did.

'Have you any idea where he might be?' Vasseur asks.

'Sorry, Thierry. You may as well ask me for the combination to the Vatican's vaults.'

'Who is O'Hare? I've read his file and his role in the National Bank robbery, but tell me about him, Dan.'

Clarke shifts in his seat, as if he is warming up to his favourite subject. 'He's ex-IRA leadership. Smart. Different.'

'What way different?'

'As a rule, he doesn't mix socially with other criminals. He doesn't loose-talk. He's not a big drinker. And he can think ahead, Thierry. That's what makes him unique from every other criminal I've ever come across.'

Vasseur speaks slowly, as if he knows what Clarke is going to say next. 'So why do you think they met in the Louvre?' He sighs. 'Dan, I'm worried about this.'

'I wouldn't be too exercised till I found out what's going down.'

'A French citizen has been murdered by Nazis, Dan. I'm already exercised.'

The alarm bells were already sounding in Clarke's head. 'I think Mercier must have the original baton—'

'So do I.'

'And obviously so do the neo-Nazis.'

'Plus, Mercier witnessed the murder of his servant, which makes him a potential future witness in any prosecution. It also means that his staying alive leaves things untidy for those neo-Nazis.'

'It's possible Mercier will drop off the radar, become an invisible.'

'He doesn't need O'Hare's help to do that.'

Clarke smiles and slowly shakes his head. 'No. He doesn't. He needs him for something else.'

CHAPTER ELEVEN

ELEANOR COMES ONTO THE BALCONY IN HER DRESSING gown, holding a glass of white wine. 'Who's he?' she asks as she peers over Ructions's shoulder at the computer screen, on which Karl Keller is debating with other leading German politicians on a television programme. Even though Ructions does not speak German, he can see from Keller's demeanour that he is dominating the discussion.

'His name is Karl Keller.'

'Weird eyes, hasn't he? Why are you interested in him?'

'He's a neo-Nazi, the head of what is euphemistically known as the Fourth Reich.'

'Are these the people you were telling me about? The ones that raided Serge's home?'

'Yeah.'

'He doesn't look like a terrorist.'

'Terrorists try not to look like terrorists, El.'

'I suppose so.' Eleanor sips her wine. 'I don't understand ...

didn't I read somewhere that it's illegal for a Nazi party to exist in Germany?'

'Yeah, but they use different stratagems to outflank the rules. These guys, for example' – Ructions nods to the screen – 'they call themselves the Fourth Reich but never in public and never in writing.'

Ructions hands Eleanor the letter that Serge had slipped into his pocket in the Louvre. Eleanor tries to read it, but she is not fluent in French. 'I can understand an odd bit of it, but that's all,' she says, passing the letter back to Ructions. 'What does it say?'

'Before I translate, do you remember Hermann Goering's baton?'

'The one in the cabinet, in Serge's dining room?'

'The one that *used* to be in Serge's dining room, yes.'

'That baton was the reason why Serge's home was raided.'

'And they murdered Serge's servant for some fat Nazi's baton? Is it valuable?'

Ructions massages his chin. 'Valuable enough for Serge to put it in a bank safety box.'

Eleanor looks out over the balcony. 'What's it worth?'

'Maybe a million euro, maybe two, given that it was Goering's. It's studded with gold eagles and platinum crosses and was presented to him by Hitler.'

'How did these Nazis know Serge had the baton?'

'I haven't a clue.'

'Serge must know.'

'He doesn't.'

Eleanor turns abruptly and leans in over the computer. 'Can I cut in?'

Ructions nods.

'Let's see where we are,' she says, typing in HERMANN GOERING'S CEREMONIAL BATON. A picture of the baton appears on-screen. 'Says here that Goering surrendered the baton to the Americans on 9 May 1945 ... and it's on display in the West Point Museum, New York. How can Serge have the original baton if it's in New York?'

Ructions starts typing and a different image of a 'Goering's baton' is displayed. He points to a sentence in the middle of a paragraph: ' ... but it was widely known in the upper echelons of the Nazi regime that Goering had exact replicas made of both his Luftwaffe and ceremonial batons, right down to the precious stones and metals, in case of mishap.'

'How do you know then that Serge has the original baton if Goering made exact copies?'

'The neo-Nazis think his is the real one, otherwise why come to France to retrieve it and kill old Beau in the process?'

'They could be wrong.'

'Could be. They could just as easily be right.'

'You really like Serge, don't you?'

'He's an eccentric, El. Always has been, but he's honourable. And another thing: he's one of only two people who have never let me down.'

'Who's the other one?'

'You.'

Eleanor pulls up a seat beside Ructions, leans over and puts her head on his shoulder. 'So, what's all this got to do with you, or, should I say, us?'

Ructions puts his arms around her shoulder and says, 'Serge has offered to go fifty-fifty with me on the baton.'

Eleanor is stupefied. She stands up and leans her hands on the railings of the balcony. That old sinking feeling is back again. Belfast in the rare old times is back. Skulduggery is back. Danger is back. She can smell the fickleness in the Mediterranean breeze, the flopping wings of dragonflies in her stomach, the invidious thought that it is all going to happen again. She turns on him. 'What does that mean? Are we talking about the sale of the baton? Would that bring you into conflict with the neo-Nazis too? Tell him you want nothing to do with it.'

Ructions turns his face away.

'What? You can't look at me?'

Ructions turns back to her, but his lips are welded together.

'Why on earth would you want to take on this grief? You're already got Tiny Murdoch and the IRA combing Europe, looking to kill you, and now they could very well be joined by a bunch of fanatical fucking neo-Nazis. Fucking brilliant! Well done, you.' In a show of faux praise, Eleanor claps her hands. 'Surely you're not going to stop with the IRA and the neo-Nazis? What about the Jihadis? Those guys – now *they* are serious McMurphys … they make the IRA and neo-Nazis look like altar boys with their trousers 'round their ankles.'

She just flops on a chair. 'Do you realise that if the IRA and the neo-Nazis end up looking for you, they'll end up looking for me too?'

'Sweetheart, no one will ever hurt you. Not while I'm alive. It won't come to that.'

Eleanor doesn't know whether to laugh or cry. It isn't as if she is unfamiliar with Ructions's swashbuckler attitude – she has experienced it firsthand before he robbed the National Bank in

Belfast. She puts the palms of her hands to his cheeks. 'Ructions, you don't need the fucking money. What's a million more?'

'Ahh, but there's a lot more than a million in this.'

'Okay. Two million.'

'Let's round it off at, say, between a half a billion and a billion euro.'

'What?'

'If this *is* the authentic Goering baton, it could be worth a billion euro, of which I would humbly receive fifty per cent. I like the idea of fifty per cent of a billion euro. I guess you could say I'm a fifty-per-cent man.' Ructions holds up the letter, which Eleanor had completely forgotten at this point. 'That's what this is all about. According to Serge's letter, Goering realised the war was lost and so transported tons of gold to neutral countries for the expected rainy day. The writer says the Reichsmarschall's baton is the key to part of the yet-to-be-recovered fortune, which, again, according to the writer, is estimated at between a half a billion and a billion euro.'

Eleanor reaches for her drink but stops. 'Whaaat?'

'I don't know – yet.'

Eleanor looks at the letter. 'Who sent this?'

'It's unsigned.'

'An unsigned letter? An invisible key ... that says it all, doesn't it? It's not worth the paper it's written on.'

'Not so, El. I've thought long and hard about this, and all the pieces fit.'

'Fit what?'

'The conclusion that Serge has the real Hermann Goering ceremonial baton and that it's a signpost to a billion-dollar payday.'

It seems to Eleanor that Ructions *wants* the pieces to fit, but he sees her disbelief, and continues.

He holds up one finger: 'One: the neo-Nazis are convinced Serge possesses the real baton. In fact, they're so convinced, they mounted an armed raid on his home. Not only that, but they murdered old Clément in an attempt to force Serge to hand over the baton to them, and they were prepared to murder Nicoline, the maid, only they ran out of time.'

He holds up a second finger. 'Two: Serge is adamant that the baton he has in the safety deposit box is authentic. And ... '

He holds up a third finger. 'Three: there's this.' Once more Ructions waves the letter. 'Whoever wrote this letter clearly knows about the raid and, crucially, also believes that Serge has Goering's baton. And the author has to be close to the leadership of the Fourth Reich to have this information because there's been no mention of the Reichsmarschall's baton in the media.'

Eleanor looks at him disdainfully. 'Why didn't they just try to buy it from Serge? He's a businessman. If the money had been right, he'd have sold it.'

'I don't know why. Could be they didn't have the money. Could be they didn't want a paper trail linking them to the baton. I simply don't know.'

'I hate it when you do this.'

'What?'

'Break scenarios down into calculations and numbers. It's so condescending, so fucking superior.'

'Sorry. It's the way my mind works.'

'I know the way your mind works. All you just laid out lends weight to what the author of the letter has written about Goering's gold. Is that how you see it?'

'Enormous weight.'

The chess game is still in session, and Eleanor is not yet ready to knock over the king. 'Okay, let's assume that the contents of the letter are true: What's in it for the author?'

'Could be he was overlooked for promotion. Or he'd a falling-out with someone in the neo-Nazi hierarchy. Or he found a seam of decency. El, I'm no expert in the mindset of Nazis.'

Eleanor wonders aloud why the author wouldn't go to the police if he or she really wants to hurt these people.

'Maybe he or she doesn't like the police. Maybe that would have been self-incriminating. Could be—'

'This is all speculation and "what ifs," isn't it?' Eleanor says. 'What if Serge has had a row with the Nazis over another deal and they were sending him a message?'

Ructions is beginning to run out of patience. 'They *were* sending him a message. If they don't get the baton, they'll be back.'

'Supposing – I shouldn't have used that word—'

'Supposing—'

'I'm totally against you taking on this—'

'I know.'

'What would you call this thing you want to do? Hardly a robbery.'

'A project. Let's call it a project.'

'Okay. Supposing you take on this project, what would you have to do to get to Goering's treasure?'

'I don't know.'

Eleanor starts to leave the balcony but stops at the doorway and, without looking back, says: 'It's not about the money, is it?'

'It is.'

'No, it isn't! You need the adrenaline hit. You told me that the National Bank robbery was the big one – and at the time you probably meant it.' Eleanor turns around and strokes Ructions's face. He bends his cheek to her caressing hand. Sounding forlorn, she says: 'But for you, lover, there'll always be a bigger one. You're like an ancient mariner who can't resist sailing his boat towards the edge of the world.'

Ructions knows that there is a modicum of truth in what Eleanor says. He chooses silence.

'I won't be involved in this,' Eleanor finally says.

'You don't have to be.'

'Don't lie to me, Ructions! I won't have it. If you want to chase up Goering's gold, then go for it, but don't fucking lie to me. And don't treat me like a Barbie doll. I can't just walk away from this ... wish the hell I could. Nah, Ructions, I'm like Helen of Troy. No escape. No redemption. Your enemies will always be at the gates, and they'll always see me as a way to get to you.'

'El—'

Eleanor turns and walks back into the room.

Ructions feels a knotting in his stomach. He sets the laptop on the glass table, follows her into the room and takes her two hands. 'El, will you marry me?'

Astonished, Eleanor's mouth fell open. *What is it they say? From enmity comes salvation? Or is it bliss?* She can't remember. 'You ... you want me to marry you now?' she says, her voice barely above a whisper. 'When I've just told you I've had enough?'

'Yes. Yes, I do. Please, will you marry me, El?'

Eleanor shakes her head.

'I'll let this Goering thing go, El. I'll tell Serge I don't want to be a part of it.'

Eleanor lifts a hairbrush and pats her hand with it. 'Don't you see? There'll be another' – she makes quotation marks with her fingers – '"project." You are what you are, Ructions. You can't change.'

'I can. I swear I can.'

Eleanor shakes her head slowly. 'You are what you are.'

Ructions puts his arms around her and kisses her. 'I love you, El. I don't know what else to—'

Eleanor puts a finger to Ructions's lips. 'I know you love me. The sad part is: I love you too.' Eleanor feels a riptide of tears on its way. 'I've got to get out of this room.' Without looking at Ructions, she pushes away from him and leaves the hotel room.

Once outside the door, she stands with her back to the corridor wall, yields to a withering sigh, and cries.

Ructions steps out onto the balcony, makes fists, and stretches his arms. He feels the wrenching in his stomach and, in his head, he hears a familiar echo telling him that it can't end like this, that he won't let it, that he'll make it work … it can't end like this. I won't let it. I'll make it work out. There's a screamer in his head who won't be ignored. *Listen, you selfish bastard, the decent thing to do is to let her go, give her a chance to have a life. Do it, man! She wants out; don't make it hard for her. She doesn't deserve that.*

As days go, Ructions considers this one has been otherworldly. Life had taken a bite out of him. *Who goes from planning the biggest job of his life to proposing marriage?* he asked himself. He lights a cigarette. The Nice-to-Corsica ferry is already clear of the harbour. Out to sea, the lights on at least twenty yachts flicker, like glowworms in an overhanging cave. Ructions can make out tiny figures of people dancing on the deck of the nearest yacht. Behind the yacht, a full moon lights up a hitherto secret pathway to the shore. Below the balcony, on the Promenade des Anglais, a young Franco-Algerian woman is arguing with a young man. She rips a ring from her finger, throws it at him, and storms off. The man stands, rooted to the spot, looking after her, wondering if he should follow her. He turns and walks in the opposite direction.

Ructions wants to shout: Hey! Fella! You! Turn back. For Christ's sake, turn back!

The man walks on.

CHAPTER TWELVE

THE TAXI MIGHT AS WELL BE A HEARSE. ELEANOR SITS, nun-like, her hands clasped on her lap, staring out the car window. Ructions, beside her, continually counts the joints in his fingers with the tip of his thumb as the taxi approaches the airport. He wants to say something, but he doesn't have any words at hand. *Have a good trip home* hardly seems appropriate.

His phone rings. 'Hello?'

'*Guten Tag*, Herr Ructions,' a male voice says.

Eleanor looks at Ructions quizzically, her eyes darting around his face. He shrugs. 'Who's this?'

'A friend you have yet to meet,' Karl Keller says in his heavy Bavarian accent.

'Listen, fella—'

'*Stop*. Don't burn bridges, Herr Ructions. You know better.'

The engine in Ructions's mind is now fully cranked up. 'Were you the man in charge in the raid on Serge's home, Herr Keller? Was it you who killed Clément Beauregard?'

'I don't know what you're talking about.'

'What do you want?'

Keller and Gitte are power-walking along Leopoldstrasse in the Schwabing district of Munich. Keller decides to be direct. 'I believe you are on your way to the airport. I hope you're not leaving us.'

Ructions spins around and looks out the back window. Eleanor takes her lead from him and also turns. 'How do you know that?'

'It doesn't matter.'

'Oh, but it does. It does, mister. Unless you tell me who you are and what your beef is, I'm hanging up right now.'

'My beef? I don't understand. What is beef?'

'What do you want?' Ructions says forcefully.

Eleanor's apprehensive stare interrogates Ructions, but he shakes his head.

Keller and Gitte reach the gateway to the Schwabing district: the Siegestor, a victory arch crowned by a quadriga drawn by four lions, commissioned by King Ludwig I and completed in 1852. 'I believe you have access to something I want, Herr Ructions; something I'm prepared to pay a lot of money for. You like money, don't you?'

'I've yet to meet anyone who doesn't.'

'An honest answer.'

The taxi pulls up outside the airport terminal. 'We need to talk,' Keller says.

'Says you.' Ructions hangs up.

'Keller?' Eleanor asks, wringing her hands. 'What did he want?'

'To talk.'

'And?'

'And I hung up on him.'

'Why?'

'Because he'll phone back and I'll control the conversation, not him.'

'Is he gonna make you an offer for the baton?'

Ructions vacillates before answering. 'I think so.'

'Will you take it?'

'The baton's not mine to accept or reject an offer on.'

'But you'll relay any offer to Serge?'

'Of course.'

'Why did you look behind you when you were taking the call?'

'He knew we were on our way to the airport.'

'Christ Almighty! They've followed us here?'

'Not us; *me*.'

As Eleanor's eyes involuntarily scan the immediate area, Ructions puts on his flat hat, gets out of the taxi, and steps up on the sidewalk, studying the traffic passing along the drop-off area. *Someone is watching me right now*, he thinks, *probably taking photos*. He doesn't want Eleanor to see him spooked. He goes around to the car's boot, where the taxi driver has already taken out Eleanor's cases. Ructions pays the fare. As they are about to walk into the terminal, Eleanor stops abruptly. 'I need a smoke.' They light up.

'So, the game begins,' Eleanor says, taking a deep drag. 'I'm sorry I can't help you, Ructions.'

'El, it's me who should be apologising.'

A porter approaches and offers to take Eleanor's luggage. She declines the offer. More taxis pull up. Neither can help scrutinising the occupants.

'I need to know the truth,' Eleanor says. 'Did you mean it when you asked me to marry you?'

Ructions's doleful eyes hold Eleanor's. He wants to find the right words but he's not sure they exist. 'With all my heart. Marry me, El, please.'

'El,' Eleanor says, smiling. 'In all the years I was married to Frank, he never called me El.'

'I don't want you to go.'

Eleanor smiles. 'Dammit, Ructions, you can be a real heart-breaker when you want to be.'

Ructions extinguishes his cigarette and grabs Eleanor by her elbows. 'Nobody's heart needs to be broken. I love you, El. I want us to spend the rest of our lives together.'

Eleanor looks into Ructions's eyes. 'I believe you, but this is the way it has to be. You can see that, can't you?'

'No, I can't,' Ructions says defiantly. 'I can sort this, if you give me a chance.'

Eleanor resolutely shakes her head. 'But that's my point: you can't. These are Nazi fanatics, Ructions, and they now believe you have access to this baton, so, even if you wanted out, I'm not sure they'll let you go that easily. I mean … ' Eleanor rubs his arm. 'They will *kill* you for that baton.'

'They'll try.'

'There you have it,' Eleanor says, jabbing her cigarette in his direction. 'All that's left is for fate to decide whether or not they succeed in killing you.' Eleanor can feel a run of tears coming. She drops her head. 'I'm sorry, Ructions.'

Ructions also feels a dryness in his throat and decides to lift the mood by cupping a finger under Eleanor's chin. Making a decent fist of impersonating Humphrey Bogart, he says, 'Here's looking at you, kid. We'll always have Paris.'

Eleanor looks at Ructions as if he has suddenly grown horns. 'Pardon?' she says timidly.

Ructions grins. 'I said: "We'll always have Paris."'

Eleanor shrugs and shakes her head.

'Humphrey Bogart?' Ructions says. 'Ingrid Bergman? *Casablanca*?'

Eleanor doesn't know whether to laugh or cry. She gives him a look that says *Are you for real?* and laughs. 'We're splitting up, and you give me Humphrey Bogart? Lover, you're a nutter.' She eventually curtails her merriment and says: 'I didn't think I'd be laughing today.'

'Does this mean you're not leaving me?' Ructions says, his eyes whizzing around Eleanor's face, looking for a sign that she has changed her mind.

Eleanor puts her hand behind his head, draws him close, and kisses him lightly on the lips, before whispering in his ear, 'It's over, love.'

'What if I make all this shit disappear?'

'How many times do we have to go through this, Ructions? You haven't made it disappear in the three years since the robbery. Have you forgotten already? It's not that long ago that the IRA were in Saint-Émilion, trying to kidnap me, or kill you, whichever took their fancy.'

'I know, but—'

Eleanor turns away and stamps on her cigarette. She turns back and once more and kisses Ructions on the lips, her eyes open this time. 'I'll go on in,' she says softly.

Ructions puts up a hand to stop her. 'There's one more thing before you go,' he says. 'If things get rough—'

'What do you mean by rough?'

'It's just … if you're picked up by any of these characters – the cops, or the IRA, or these neo-Nazis—'

'You … you think I'm going to be picked up by the cops or the IRA?'

'No, I don't, but if you do—'

Eleanor's voice is barely audible. 'You think I'm gonna be a target—'

'I don't think that!'

She shakes her head in disbelief. Words that should tumble out are stuck to her tongue.

Ructions puts up his two hands, attempting to appeal to her reason. But Eleanor does not think like him – to her, his warning to be careful almost amounts to a premonition. *Oh, Christ Almighty*, she thinks, *how did I ever get mixed up with this—*

'You do what you have to do to survive,' he says, 'and if that means shopping me to them, you go right ahead.'

'But—'

'No buts, El. You survive, y'hear me? That's all that matters. And don't worry about me—'

'But I *do* worry about you.'

'I make a habit of having multiple strategies in place to cover every possible eventuality. I will survive; you can depend on it.' He points a finger at her for emphasis. 'But you fucking survive too. You do it.'

Eleanor, overwhelmed, just stares at him numbly.

He reaches to grab the handle of her case, but the movement reanimates her, and she beats him to it. 'Goodbye, Ructions,' she says, grabbing it and turning to walk into the terminal. But before stepping inside she spins around slowly. 'One thing I will say about you … you were never dull.' And then she's gone.

CHAPTER THIRTEEN

KELLER AND GITTE ARE SITTING IN THE HOTEL LEOP-
old in Munich. He holds up his mobile phone and shakes it,
clearly trying to make up his mind if he should make a call.

'Phone him,' Gitte says.

Keller punches in the number.

Ructions, who is in the back of a taxi, looks at his ringing
phone: *International* has come up on display. 'What kept you?'

Keller taps a beat on the arm of the seat. 'After you hung up
on me, I was trying to decide if I wanted to be courteous to you
or not. And I've decided to give you a chance.'

'What makes you think I want to give *you* a chance?'

Keller laughs. 'Ructions – may I call you Ructions?'

'You can call me Otto von Bismarck, if you want.'

'I think you and I can do business.'

'May I call you Karl?'

'You can call me Michael Collins, if you want.'

'I'll settle for Karl.'

Keller decides to inject some gravitas. 'It seems to me you have no idea who or what you are dealing with.'

'If that's an attempt to bully or intimidate me, I can tell you now: I don't give a Kaiser's fuck who you are.'

'There's no need to be vulgar, Ructions.'

'Get used to it.'

'I thought it appropriate and timely to—'

'I'll tell you what I think is appropriate and timely, shall I?'

'Please do.'

'I knew Clément Beauregard.'

Keller is confounded. 'That's twice you've said that name. Who is this Clément Beauregard?'

'Clément Beauregard was an innocent old man who worked for a friend of mine. Some Nazi thug put a gun under his chin and blew the top of his head away.'

'I'm sorry to hear that, but what's this got to do with me?'

'I thought you might've known that Nazi thug.'

'Why would you have thought that?'

'I have my reasons.'

'You accuse me of being in league with murderers, but you offer no proof. Is it a habit of the Irish to be so discourteous?'

'We Irish are known throughout the world for our courtesy.'

'Then why are you being so belligerent to me?'

'You're mistaking directness for belligerence.'

'Do my politics offend you?'

'I don't do politics.'

'What do you do?'

'Money.'

'Then we have something in common. We need to talk, don't you think?'

'First things first. I presume I'm being observed?'

'Yes.'

'Call your hounds off or I'll disappear, and you'll never hear from me again.'

Keller is impressed. He thinks, a power play. And you leave me little choice other than to give in to you. 'Consider it done. Now, where shall we meet?'

'I'll have to think about the where and when. Give me a contact number, and I'll get back to you.'

'I hope you won't keep me waiting too long.'

'I'll let you know soon.'

After the call, Keller gazes straight ahead.

'Well?' Gitte asks.

'He says he'll get back to me.'

'*He'll* get back to *you*? You're the leader of the Fourth Reich, and you let some bank robber dictate terms to you?'

'It wasn't that easy. He knows he has what I want, and that gives him the power.'

The waiter comes and leaves them two mineral waters. Gitte takes a sip. When she lowers her glass, she observes: 'Poor you. Mugged by a common criminal.'

The two officers in the police car at the entrance to Serge Mercier's estate are bored to distraction. André yawns. He looks at his crossword again. Two down: Strong son of Jupiter. He knows the answer, but downloading 'Hercules' from a brain that wants nothing other than to shut down is no mean task. His partner, Roseli, is busy on her Blackberry.

The electric gates to the entrance of the estate slowly open.

Initially, neither André nor Roseli see the emergence of a Land Rover, followed by a black C-Class Mercedes-Benz C300, and a second Land Rover. Then André radios in that a convoy of vehicles have come out of the Mercier estate. They are instructed to follow the convoy.

Five minutes later, a Peugeot SUV, in which only the woman driver is visible, emerges from the estate. 'Are we being followed?' Serge asks, his head down in the back seat.

'No,' Sally Nixon says.

Serge sits up. 'Pull in, Sal. I'll take over from here.'

In the sky above, a drone follows the Peugeot. In police headquarters, Thierry Vasseur looks at a screen. He points to Serge as he's getting into the driver's seat, then turns to Inspector Pierre Robillard. 'Why doesn't Monsieur Mercier want us to find out where he's going? I want maximum surveillance, Pierre.'

Serge's car travels up a small country road. 'Where's he going?' Vasseur asks.

'He's taking countersurveillance precautions,' Robillard says.

Vasseur looks at a map on the wall. 'Where does this road take him?' He follows the road with his pen. 'I guess he could conceivably turn here,' he points to a junction on the map, 'and cut back here, and here, on to the Paris road. That's where we can pick him up.' Vasseur moves back to the screen and says, 'Be careful with Monsieur Mercier, Pierre.'

The disc jockey in the Café del Mar on Ibiza's Sunset Strip gives Patricia Kelly the thumbs-up as he plays a raved-up version of Samuel Barber's *Adagio for Strings*. 'Be careful with Ructions, Billy,' she tells her husband as she sips a sex-on-the-beach cocktail. 'Sooner or later, his luck is bound to run out.'

Billy's luck hasn't run out. In fact, as Ructions's close friend and colleague in the Northern Bank heist, his fortunes have flourished.

The pint-sized, former weight-lifting champion sips some water. 'What are you blathering on about, woman?' he asks her.

Patricia is too apprehensive to rise to her husband's impoliteness. 'He's tried to phone you twice already tonight. He needs you, but you don't need him.'

Billy sighs. ''Tricia, let's just watch the sun go down, eh?'

A yacht swivels slowly on a dead-calm Mediterranean. Swirling lights – red, indigo, and yellow – illuminate the deck of the yacht, on which three women in bikinis and two men in shorts are holding drinks and dancing. A sagging, orange sun melts into a velvet sea.

Thoughts tumbleweed across the prairie of Billy's mind: Twice he's phoned. He must have something on. Must be something big if he's coming out of retirement after the bank job. *I want this. Bring it on, Ructions.*

The sky is deeply dark now and a cheer erupts from the young revellers who are drinking carry-outs on the small rocky bay below the café.

Billy's phone rings. He takes it out of his pocket and looks at the name on the screen: RUCTIONS. He gets up, walks towards the back of the café, and takes the call.

Patricia tries to get a read from his face when he comes back to the table. 'Was that him?'

Billy nods as he sits down. He looks meditative, as if he is oblivious of what, or who, is around him.

Patricia waits and waits. She opens her makeup bag, making sure that the flap is resting against her handbag. Peering into the mirror on the makeup bag, she puts on some lipstick. Then she inspects her skinny face, pulling her sun-burned cheeks in opposite directions. 'I don't like these laughter lines.' She moves her face from side to side to get a better look at herself. 'They don't suit me. What do you think? Do they age me?' Billy stares ahead. 'I think I'll get collagen injections to fill them.' She puts the makeup bag back in her handbag then raises her breasts with her hands. 'I may as well get a boob job too, while I'm at it.' Patricia is waiting for Billy to reenter the earth's atmosphere. His eyes flutter. Patricia says, 'You haven't heard from Ructions since the bank job. What does he want?'

'He wants to talk.'

'Is he in trouble?'

'Nope.'

'But he wants to talk business to you.'

'Yes.'

'Business,' she says contemptuously. 'Is that the business of robbing banks?'

'He never said.'

'But you're gonna drop everything – including me – to find out what he has got planned for you?'

'I don't know if he's got anything planned.'

'Billy Kelly, you can be so smart and so stupid. Why haven't you heard from him in three years?'

'He's been keeping his head down.'

'My arse! He's been living the life of Riley, that's what he's been doing. And now he wants to *use* you again.'

'In case it's escaped your notice, Patsy, *we've* been living the life of fucking Riley! We've been to Florida twice and gone on two cruises. Not only that, but we're a million quid richer *because* he used me!'

'He's in trouble, and he needs you to bail him out.'

'He's not in trouble.'

'How do you know?'

Billy stabs his temple. "Cause he's a thinker. He sees trouble coming, and he avoids it. That's why he never gets caught.'

'He's been lucky, that's all.'

By now, Billy's patience is wearing thin. 'Look, love, Ructions is my best friend, and he has never done us any harm.'

'Yeah, he gave you the guts of a million pounds out of the National Bank robbery, but he walked away with almost thirty-four million. He cut you up, but you can't see it.'

'No, he didn't.'

Billy realises that he needs to divert Patricia away from the subject of Ructions. He waves his hands and, looking about him, indicates how much he is enjoying the heady ambience. 'C'mon, 'Tricia, let's boogie,' he says.

'Boogie? In front of all these people?' She laughs. 'I've a better idea. Let's go back to the apartment. You can entertain me there, lover-boy,' she says seductively.

Patricia thinks Billy is smiling at the prospect of imminent sex, but he has other things on his mind; he can smell dosh. It's time to go to work, time to go to Ructions.

CHAPTER FOURTEEN

'WE'RE BEING FOLLOWED,' SERGE SAYS INTO HIS phone. 'Cops. They picked me up when I came back onto la Périphérique. He looks in his rearview mirror. The Parisienne traffic is flowing freely. He leans forward and looks up to the sky to see if he can spot a helicopter. 'Can't see one, but they could be using drones.' He listens to the person on the other end of the line. 'Got that. Be with you soon.' He hangs up. 'I'm going to drop you off in a few minutes,' he says to Sally. 'Just get a taxi back home. And don't talk to anyone.' The car stops at a traffic light.

Sally takes a cigarette out of its packet. Her hand is shaking so violently that the cigarette falls into the foot-well. She picks it up and nervously holds it to her lips. Serge removes the car-lighter from its receptacle and holds it to her cigarette. Sally barely exhales before taking another draw. 'Will *I* be followed?' she asks.

'I don't know. Possibly.'

'By the police?'

'Possibly.'

'Not those neo-Nazis?'

'No.'

'Why are the police following you?'

'I thought that would be obvious … to protect me.'

'Don't you want their protection?'

'No.'

'Neo-Nazis want to kill you, and you don't want the police to protect you?'

A blue van appears alongside them at the next traffic light. Ructions, wearing a thick false moustache, heavily rimmed black glasses, grey overalls, and a flat cap, looks over at Serge. The light changes, and Ructions takes off, followed by Serge. 'I saw the look on that man's face,' Sally says. 'He knew you. Who is he?'

'A friend.'

Sally feels as if someone has lit a fuse in her head. 'What the fuck's going on here, Serge? Stop the car.'

'Sal, don't do this.'

'Stop the car, I said. I'm getting out.'

'And then what?'

'Then I'm going home.'

'Back to the villa?'

'Yeah, to get my stuff. Then I'm going back to England, back to sanity. Now stop the car.'

'Sal, this is not the right time—'

'Stop the fucking car!'

Serge pulls over. The police tail drives past.

'Sal, don't be hasty now. We can—'

Sally gets out of the car. She leans in the window. 'Goodbye, Serge.' She walks away and, with a sigh, Serge drives off.

Thirty minutes later, Serge pulls into a multistoried car park. Halfway up one of the two single-vehicle lanes to the second storey, he turns the car so that it is blocking both lanes. He gets out, taking the keys with him. Walking briskly, not looking behind, he continues towards the second floor and gets into the open, side door of the blue van that Ructions has been driving and lies flat on a wooden bench. Horns hoot loudly, as traffic backs up at Serge's abandoned car. Ructions drives away, leaving the car park by a secondary exit.

Driving through Paris, Ructions keeps looking in his rearview mirror. 'We've lost them,' Ructions says, 'but you stay back there for the time being. Where did you say your bank was?'

Serge clicks his fingers, as if that will help his memory. 'It's the Europe Arab Bank.'

'Where's that?'

'The Champs Élysées.'

'Don't be making this any easier, whatever you do.'

Eventually, Ructions pulls up outside the bank. Serge, now wearing a camel button-down overcoat and a trilby, gets out of the van and goes into the bank. Ructions pulls into the nearby Marriott Hotel and parks. After fifteen minutes he gets a phone call from Serge saying that he is leaving the bank. Ructions picks him up.

Serge sits beside Ructions in the front of the van. 'Did you get it?' Ructions asks.

'Yes,' Serge says, patting a leather pouch.

'Good man.'

Ructions drives down the Rue de Belleville between the 20th arrondissement and the 19th and stops. He looks in the rear mirror for the last time, takes off the flat cap, and pulls away the false moustache. Strapping a small holdall across his shoulders, he gets out of the car, followed by Serge. They walk a short distance. People are sitting outside a bistro called the Vieux Belleville. 'I know this place,' Serge says. 'I was here last year, as it happens.'

'Oh?'

'I was meeting Adelle—'

'Not another lover?'

'No,' Serge says, a hint of irritation in his voice. 'Her name is Adelle Cordier. She's a young artist I'm helping. Fabulous talent. She'll be extremely collectible in a few years. You should buy some of her paintings now. They'll be a good investment.' Ructions smiles. He hopes to be investing in gold bullion soon. 'Anyway,' Serge continues, pointing to the Vieux Belleville, 'there's a little lady who plays the accordion in there, and if you didn't know any better, you'd swear she was Edith Piaf.'

'That's a hell of a compliment.'

'Piaf was born around here. On the Rue de Belleville. In a doorway, as I recollect reading.' Serge sniffs the air. 'Garlic,' he says.

'And steaks,' Ructions says.

'With sautéed onions.'

'Are you hungry?'

'Famished,' Serge replies, rubbing his stomach. 'Cop chases always leave me starving.'

'Jaysus! You're right back to your old self, Sergey! Whatever happened to that miserable old shit who was crying down the phone to me about dying of prostate cancer?'

'That miserable old shit is still going through six incontinence pads a day, but he's been given a new lease of life.'

'Good to hear,' Ructions says. 'I've booked us into the Ritz, under false names, of course. Have you got your André Dennel passport with you?'

'Yes.'

'We'll check in and examine the baton. Then we'll head out for a bite to eat.'

'Fine,' Serge says.

'Did I tell you I've bought three replica Goering batons online?' Ructions says.

Serge stares open-mouthed at Ructions. 'No. Why? And why three?'

'It's simple enough: walking around with one baton might cause suspicion, but three? Wrapped up like Brighton rocks? They look like souvenir purchases.'

'Good thinking. Did you get anywhere with the Nazi leader? What's his name again?'

They approach a white Toyota Corolla in the car park of a pub. Ructions clicks the car open and they get in. Ructions starts the car and drives off.

'Karl Keller. I've spoken to him.'

'And?'

'I think this thing has the potential to get pretty messy.'

'How messy?'

'Well, if Goering's gold exists, and if the estimates are right, then there's perhaps hundreds of millions of euro in gold bullion in the pot and I think the neo-Nazis will want to kill everybody who has any knowledge of that gold – and that includes you – especially you, in fact. So, my friend, you have decisions to make. To be blunt: I can bring you along with me, but I'll be carrying you, and you might be too heavy.'

'Ructions O'Hare, you won't be carrying me because I'm not going anywhere with you!'

'I didn't mean any disrespect, buddy.'

'I know you didn't. You said I had "decisions" to make?'

'Yeah. The other thing is ... I can tell you everything as it develops, but if the wrong people get to you, they'll make you tell *them* everything.'

'So, you think it best I'm not kept in the loop?'

'No, I'm not saying that, but, for security reasons, you don't need to know the everyday stuff. Now,' Ructions says, 'that doesn't mean you're not important.'

Serge grins. 'Are you buttering me up, young man?'

'No fucking way! You have contacts in authority who will be useful to us ... '

'Okay ... '

'You're also very resourceful ... you have access to various modes of travel and the means to make items of value disappear into the system. So, no, you're not getting out of this that easily.'

'It's nice to be appreciated. Can I think about it, Ructions?'

'Look, Serge, it's your call. Whatever road you choose, I'm okay with it.'

The traffic light changes, and Ructions drives off. Almost as if his innermost thoughts are spilling out, he mutters, 'This could end up a bloodbath.'

Eventually, Serge finds his voice. 'Poor Clément.' He looks ahead, his eyes misty. 'I loved that man. He was a gentle giant, Ructions.'

'I know, I know.'

Serge squints as if he's unable to see the road ahead and then, submissively, he surrenders his face to the solace of his open hands. 'Can I tell you something, Ructions? I prefer agreement to disagreement.'

'Who doesn't?'

Serge looks like he's having difficulty finding the right words. 'No, what I'm saying is this: we should try to find a ... ' – he clicks his fingers – 'what's the English phrase? Common denominator. *Oui*. We should try to find a common denominator with the neo-Nazis, a way where we all come out of this wealthier and alive.'

'To be frank, Serge, I don't think that's possible. Even if we were to give them the baton, I reckon they'd still come after us.'

'I'm sorry I ever bought the bloody baton. I should drop it in the ocean.'

'It wouldn't make any difference now. The Nazis are convinced you have it, and they wouldn't believe you've destroyed it – even if you had a video of yourself throwing it into the deepest ocean. They'd think you were trying to stitch them up.'

Ructions pulls in. 'I need to get cigarettes.' He gets out of the car and goes into a shop.

Serge's mind spins: Ructions thinks this could end up a blood-bath. *Not for me. I don't want to be a part of this.*

Ructions returns. They drive along in silence. 'Goering paid off an American GI called Wolfe Paterson with the baton,' Serge says. 'Did I tell you that?'

'Yeah.'

There are things that are better left unsaid ... *Yeah, you did*, Ructions thinks. At those dinner parties, where you fetched the

baton out of the display cabinet and fêted us with the proposition
that we could be a Reichsmarschall for a few minutes.

Serge continues as if Ructions had not answered in the affirmative: 'Paterson smuggled in the cyanide capsule that killed him.
Then Goering's wife, Emmy, passed the baton on to Paterson. I
remember, I was so excited at acquiring it. God, that was some
day. What I also remember, but I ignored, was the irritating little
voice in my head that was telling me: "This is trouble".'

Looking in his rearview mirror, Ructions can see a police car,
but he decides not to tell Serge they have company. 'How were
you to know the trouble it would bring?'

'I knew the baton's provenance. I knew its historical value.'

Ructions says, 'For the record: Keller wants to meet me.'

The siren on the police car goes off. Startled, Serge's heart
jumps. His head spins around. 'Are they pulling us over?'

Ructions glances in his side mirror. The police car overtakes
the Toyota and drives on past them. 'That was close,' Serge says.
Then, 'You haven't said yes to meeting Keller, have you?'

'Tacitly. I'm still working out the logistics in my mind.'

'It has to be on your terms. And it has to be in a safe location
– somewhere that takes him out of his comfort zone.'

'That goes without saying.'

Serge looks pensive. 'I'm not sure such a safe location exists.
Does it?'

Ructions nods vigorously. 'Oh, yeah. Definitely. It definitely
exists.'

CHAPTER FIFTEEN

DANIEL CLARKE HAS SOME EXPERIENCE IN AVOIDING the attention of nosy people. During the thirty years of war and mayhem in Northern Ireland and beyond, he had handled many informers and had arranged meetings in the most innocuous places. While residents in remote villages like Moneymore, Gilford, and Ballywalter slept in their warm beds, Clarke was in their pub and community centre car parks, debriefing some of the most important informants in the IRA and the loyalist paramilitary organisations. Tonight, though, it's not an informer he is meeting, but Tiny Murdoch.

In the County Down village of Dundrum, the IRA chief sits behind the wheel of his Land Rover on the main street, his head stuck in a newspaper. His passenger-side door opens and Clarke get into the car, two ice-cream cones in his hands. He hands a cone to Tiny.

'It's vanilla,' Tiny says, looking at the cone in his hand.

'You don't like vanilla?'

'I asked you for honeycomb.'

'Sorry about that,' Clarke says. 'I'll remember next time.'

The Murlough Bay Nature Reserve is a six-thousand-year-old sand dune system, owned and managed by the National Trust. Dusk is descending as the two former adversaries, now wary allies, pull up into the car park and get out. Clarke's phone rings. He looks at Tiny, who shakes his head, takes his own phone out of his pocket, and leaves it on the seat of the car. Clarke follows Tiny's example.

The men walk along a boardwalk and onto Murlough Beach. The tide is in, and with it, an ear-biting squall that sounds like an aeroplane about to take off. To their right, the Mountains of Mourne snuggle into the sea. A young couple walk along holding hands. A man with a mane of curly white hair and flushed cheeks walks by with his fox terrier. He bids the cop and the former revolutionary good evening. Only Clarke returns the greeting.

Tiny lifts a stone that has been polished smooth by a billion waves and tries skimming it. Three skims before sinking. Could do better.

'I love the smell of the sea,' Clarke says as he bends down, picks up some seaweed and holds it to his nose.

'My people were originally from this area,' Tiny says. 'I used to holiday down here when I was a kid.'

'Is that so? I was born and reared in Newcastle myself.'

'It's a small world. Are you a … ' Tiny's bushy eyebrows arch.

'No, I'm a Catholic, but all my mates were Prods.'

'You're not a true-blue then?'

'Definitely not. Can I ask you, why did you get involved with the IRA?'

Tiny takes a deep breath. 'Didn't have a choice, really. Whole Catholic streets were being burnt down, people shot dead in their homes, firstly by loyalists and then by the British army.' Tiny shrugs. 'And you? Why did you become a Peeler?'

'I'd like to say I had a noble calling, but I'm afraid that wasn't the case. Joining the police was a career opportunity.'

They walk along the stony beach, both unsure if they want to take this conversation any further. The sky is turning the colour of soot. 'I still have aunts who live about here,' Tiny says. He puts his hands in the back pockets of his jeans and kicks the sand. 'So, what's on your mind, comrade?'

Clarke chuckles. *Comrade*, he thinks, *that'll be the day*. He takes a photograph from inside his coat and hands it to Tiny, who stops, takes out his lighter, holds the flame up to the photo, and studies a printout of Eleanor Proctor coming through Belfast International Airport. 'When was this taken?' Tiny asks.

'Five days ago.'

'And her boyfriend?'

'He wasn't with her.'

Tiny turns and stares at Clarke. 'What do you make of it?'

'I'm not sure.' Clarke reaches out and turns over the photo. An address is written at the top of the page. Tiny reads it and nods. Clarke takes back the photograph and puts it in his coat pocket. 'I don't want her hurt.'

'Neither do I,' Tiny says.

They walk up the beach. 'By the way,' Clarke says, 'does the name Serge Mercier mean anything to you?'

'Why?'

Thirty years of experience kick in. No instant denial – *Tiny knows him*. 'His name has come up in relation to Ructions.'

'In what way?'

'First of all: Who is he?'

'In what way has his name come up?'

'It seems Mercier and Ructions have got themselves into pretty serious trouble with some neo-Nazis. A man has been murdered.'

Tiny stops. 'By Ructions?'

'No. By the neo-Nazis.'

'Fuck me! Ructions and neo-Nazis? What's that all about?' Clarke looks at Tiny, then out to the darkened sea. 'C'mon, Dan, out with it. If we're to trust each other, we've got to be open.'

'Then answer my question: Who's Mercier?'

Sometimes willpower and self-preservation aren't enough … Tiny realises there's no other way for it but to come clean: 'He's an international money launderer and fence. Big into high-end art and jewellery. No Micky Mouse stuff with this guy. Has to be big dough in it for him or he doesn't get out of bed. He laundered the National Bank money for Ructions.'

'Now I get it.'

'Your turn.'

Dispensing information to someone he still instinctively regards as a terrorist does not come easily to Clarke and, even with Tiny's revelation about Serge out in the open, he wrestles with his dilemma. He ignores his instinct to hold his tongue. 'It's about Hermann Goering's Reichsmarschall's baton.'

Tiny is lost. 'What?'

'Hermann Goering's baton.'

'What the fuck?'

'You asked me a question,' Clarke says. 'I gave you a truthful answer.'

Where is sanity when you need it? Tiny thinks. *Neo-Nazis? Ructions? Give me a break.* 'Okay, okay … what has Hermann Goering's baton got to do with Ructions?'

'I don't know, but neo-Nazi paramilitaries raided Mercier's mansion looking for the baton and murdered one of his servants because he wouldn't hand it over to them.'

Tiny tries to unravel his mangled thoughts, eventually coming up with the primal question: 'How much is the baton worth?'

'I haven't a clue.'

'Millions?'

'I genuinely don't know.'

As they walk on, Tiny's cynicism is unclamped. 'Ructions has millions in his back pocket. Even if the baton was worth, say, a million – for the sake of argument – would that be enough to entice him to cross swords with a gang of murdering neo-Nazis? I don't think so. What do you think, Dan?'

'I don't know Ructions as well as you.'

'For him to involve himself in Mercier's shit with neo-Nazis paramilitaries, he'd be expecting a huge payday.' Tiny looks quizzically at Clarke. 'There's got to be big dough here. Big. I can smell it.'

Clarke cradles the thought that he should tell Tiny he's letting his imagination run away with him. 'This is a French investigation, Tiny. I really don't know any more than I've told you.'

'Find out where the money is, will ya?'

'I'll try.'

Tiny lifts a fallen twig and beats it against his leg. 'I expect to be kept informed about this baton business.'

You expect? Clarke thinks. Best not to douse expectations then. 'Okay.'

'I mean it, Dan.'

'And I mean it when I say I don't want the person in the photo hurt,' Clarke says.

'But you do want her kidnapped and used as bait to bring in the boyfriend?'

'I didn't say that.'

'Sometimes you don't need to say anything.'

CHAPTER SIXTEEN

RUCTIONS REACHES DOWN TO TOUCH THE REICHSMAR-
schall's baton on the dresser, his fingers curling around its ivory
stem. So bitingly cold. He opens and closes his free hand. 'Is it
freezing in here, or is it me?'

'It's actually roasting,' Serge says.

Ructions holds up the baton and stares at it. 'Adolf Hitler
touched this,' he says sombrely, then shivers. 'I didn't expect this.'

'What?'

'To react to it like this,' Ructions says. 'Not me. This is ... I don't
know ... this is unholy.' He looks at the engraving on the baton.

'It's not every day you get to hold history in your hand,'
Serge says.

'How do you rate Goering? Seems like a Falstaffian character to me.'

'Au contraire,' Serge says, 'he was far from Falstaffian. Goering might have looked like the jolly clown, but he was highly
intelligent, much more so than Hitler. And he was complicit in

the extermination of millions of Jews in the death camps.' Serge raises a finger, 'Not once, *not once* did he raise an objection. He was a monster with a smile.'

'I've never heard that before ... What else do we know about him?'

'He loved praise and titles.' Serge puts his hand into his suitcase and takes out some printed papers. 'These are archive prints from the *Hamburger Anzeiger* newspaper of the twentieth of July 1940, the day after Hitler had promoted him to Reichsmarschall of Greater Germany.'

Ructions reaches for his glass of whiskey. 'Should be interesting.'

'And here's what Hitler said of Goering,' Serge says, reading from a page: '"As leader of the German Luftwaffe, he, in the course of this war, had helped lay the foundations for victory. His merits are unique! I proclaim him Reichsmarschall of the Grand German Reich and award him the Bid Cross of the Iron Cross."'

'He was the Führer's blue-eyed boy then?' Ructions says.

'Very much so. And, as ever in life and in death, it's all about timing ... Operation Barbarossa, for example – the invasion of Russia, had been launched a month earlier, on the twenty-second of June, and the German armies were annihilating the Soviet armies and advancing on all fronts. To the German people, Hitler seemed like Jesus and Odin rolled into one. His dream of *Lebensraum* was coming to fruition.'

'*Lebensraum?* What's that?'

'Living space. It was a Hitler credo that advocated the expansion of Germanic people into the east.'

'I see,' Ructions says, but he doesn't see. Ructions waves the baton in the air. 'It's not as heavy as I thought it would be.'

'It weighs about five pounds.'

Ructions turns the baton over in his hands. 'It would have been an expensive piece in its day.'

'Made by J. Godet and Sohn of Berlin,' Serge says. 'The leading jewellers in Germany at the time.'

'Jeweller to the Führer. Things must have been good for the Godets.'

Serge takes a small notebook out of his pocket and reads: 'It's made of ivory. The shaft is decorated with twenty gold-plated Wehrmacht eagles and twenty platinum iron and Balkan crosses. The end caps are made of gold and are decorated with six hundred and forty diamonds.'

'Six hundred and forty diamonds?' Ructions exclaims.

'And see here and here?' Serge points to the ends of the baton. 'At this end of the end cap is the Luftwaffe iron cross and at the other end is a swastika in platinum, mounted in diamonds.'

'And here and here?'

'Those are the inscription rings. They have Goering's name and promotion date.'

'And what does this inscription say?'

'"The Führer to the Reichsmarschall of Greater Germany".'

Ructions holds the baton in both hands. 'It is a beautiful work of art.' He puts his hand around an end cap. 'Do the caps screw off?'

'I don't know. It never occurred to me that they might.'

'Let's see.'

'Be careful,' Serge urges.

Ructions tries to unscrew the end cap with the swastika on it, but nothing happens. 'Hold that end,' Ructions says to Serge. 'This thing probably hasn't been opened since 1945, so it's liable to have seized up.'

'For Christ's sake, Ructions, be careful you don't damage it.'

'I won't.' Ructions lifts a small hand towel, wraps it around the end cap to give him a better grip, and tries to loosen it. Nothing shifts. 'Let's try the other end.' Breathing heavily, Ructions tries to turn the end cap.

'They don't screw off,' Serge insists.

Ructions turns the baton around in his hand. 'This is a key,' he says. He repeats the inscription that Serge had translated, '"The Führer to the Reichsmarschall of Greater Germany ... The Führer to the Reichsmarschall of Greater Germany" ... We're missing something and it's staring us in the face.' He brings the baton closer and picks at a Balkan cross. 'Do you think there's a message below these crosses?'

'If there is,' Serge says, 'it's, "Don't be so fucking lazy, Irländer."'

'This Irländer is hammered. I've got to freshen up.'

Ructions goes into the bathroom and throws cold water around his face. He dries his face slowly with a hand towel, all the while looking at himself in the mirror. He rubs his chin, contemplates a shave, but decides to wait until the morning.

Returning bare-chested to the bedroom, he reexamines the baton. He sets it down on the bed and starts pacing the room, his head bowed in thought. The television has been switched on in his mind, and he can see Goering in his white uniform, his shoulders heaving, and his fat, rippled face distorted with laughter. He is pointing his baton at Ructions, and saying, 'Don't be so fucking lazy, Irländer.' Sighing, Ructions stops pacing. 'This enigma isn't going to be as easy to crack as I thought.'

'You thought Goering was going to leave a treasure map on the baton?' Serge says.

'I don't know what I was thinking. For now, I don't trust

hotel safes, so I'm keeping the baton close to me from now on. Are you okay with that?'

'Sure.'

Ructions puts the baton into its leather pouch and takes a large roll of clear tape out of his holdall. Then he begins strapping the pouch to the right side of his chest. 'Would you notice the pouch?'

Serge inspects Ructions. 'Not if you keep your coat on.'

As Ructions puts his hand on the front door handle, his phone rings. He looks at the display on his phone. It's Keller. He shows his phone to Serge, then takes the call. Serge listens in.

'Did I not tell you I'd get back to you?' Ructions says.

Keller ignores Ructions's question. 'Are you with Herr Mercier?'

'I'm going to hang up.'

'You are with Herr Mercier. Hello, Herr Mercier.'

Ructions hangs up.

Serge has a strange look on his face. There is puzzlement but also a hint of recognition.

Ructions's phone rings again. He lets it ring. 'Answer it, please,' Serge says. 'I want to hear what he has to say.'

Ructions, with Serge listening in, takes the call. 'This is beginning to get boring. What do you fucking want?'

'I want to congratulate Herr Mercier on so skillfully shaking off the police surveillance today. Strictly between us, the Préfet de Police is most annoyed.'

'And you'd know that, would you?'

'As it happens, I have friends in—'

'You're beginning to sound like a jilted lover, pal,' Ructions says. 'What do you want?'

'He's listening in, isn't he? Well done, Herr Mercier.'

'He's not here.'

'Oh, I think he is. I can always tell when someone is lying,' Keller says.

Inexplicably, Ructions believes him. 'For the last time: What do you want?'

'What's mine.'

'What you think is yours isn't yours.'

'I guess by now you've had a good look at it.'

'I'm hanging up.'

'I'll pay one million euro for the baton.'

Serge looks at Ructions, unsure how he will react. He doesn't have long to wait. 'Not interested,' Ructions replies.

'You can turn down one million euro without even considering it?' Keller says incredulously. 'Who would do that?'

'Someone who doesn't like Nazis.'

'A lot of people don't like Nazis,' Keller says, 'but that doesn't mean they don't do business with them. No, that's not the reason. I've read your police file and you make a virtue out of not allowing politics to influence business decisions. Is revenge driving your illogicality? You really do think I was involved in the murder of Monsieur Mercier's servant, don't you?'

Ructions decides against answering Keller's question.

'When you reason things out, Herr Ructions, you and Herr Mercier will realise that you need me; that it's better to have me as a friend than an enemy.'

'I don't need anybody,' Ructions says, 'and I don't buckle under threats from whackos. I'll phone you if and when I'm ready to talk. Don't phone back.'

Ructions hangs up and looks at Serge. 'What do you think?'

Serge sits down on the edge of the bed, looking thunderstruck. His hand quivers as he reaches for a cigarette, puts it to his lips, but doesn't light it. Something has spooked Serge.

'What is it?' Ructions asks.

Serge mutters, 'He called me Herr Mercier.'

'Well, Serge, he is German, after all.'

'I hear that voice every night.' Serge says quietly. 'It'll never leave me.' He looks at Ructions, as if seeing him in the room for the first time. 'That's the voice of the man who murdered Clément Beauregard in my home.'

CHAPTER SEVENTEEN

ELEANOR PROCTOR DECIDED TO STAY IN THE OLD INN in Crawfordsburn because it was a quiet, out-of-the-way hotel. Established in 1614, the hotel was sandwiched between the middle-class, north County Down towns of Holywood and Bangor.

Room 105 smells of lemon zest and eucalyptus. A fresh morning breeze gently buffets the beige curtains through the open window. Eleanor sits in front of a large mirror, applying makeup. Satisfied that she has not overindulged, she leans over and blows out the Yankee candle.

Her phone rings. It's Ructions. She lets it ring until he hangs up. That was his fourth attempt; there would be a fifth and a sixth, she knew. Had she taken the call, Eleanor is convinced that Ructions would have pleaded with her to come back to him, telling her he would sell Hermann Goering's baton to the neo-Nazis in exchange for their lives. Life would return to normal. She can almost hear herself rebuffing him, telling him that normal to him is only having one gang of murderers on his tail instead of two.

Ructions sits at a breakfast table in the Bar Vendôme brasserie in the Ritz in Paris, staring at his phone before him. He reaches for his tea. Serge comes over with a plate of ham, cheese, croissants, and bread. He looks at Ructions's face and realises that, once again, Eleanor didn't take his call. Serge cuts a croissant in half. 'So what now?' he asks, applying soft cheese to the bun.

'That's a good question,' Ructions replies. 'Do you think there might be writing on the baton?' He leans forward and wriggles two fingers. 'Minute writing, so small it's not visible to the naked eye?'

Serge puts down the knife and croissant and scratches the back of his neck. 'It's possible, I suppose.' He winces. 'Seems a bit of a long shot though.'

'Long shots are all we have.'

A tall bald, figure with a jutting jaw approaches and pulls up a chair. Ructions doesn't like it. He knows a cop when he sees one. His eyes don't leave Thierry Vasseur, who is equally transfixed with Ructions. 'And you are?' Ructions asks.

Serge does the honours. 'Superintendent Thierry Vasseur, meet—'

'James "Ructions" O'Hare.' Vasseur puts out his hand, which Ructions takes, noting to himself that Vasseur has a firm hand-shake. 'I've read a lot about you, Monsieur O'Hare,' Vasseur says, 'or should I say, Mr Charles Dillon. Who is Charles, by the way?'

'Charlie Dillon was a bricklayer. Died four years ago. A decent man.'

Vasseur nods. 'And you decided to become Mr Dillon?'

'Only when I don't want to be Ructions O'Hare.'

'I can have you put in prison for possession of a false passport.

Or I can have you deported back to Ireland.' Vasseur takes out the two false passports that Ructions and Serge had deposited at the reception desk when they booked in and thoughtfully pats his hand with them. 'And you, Monsieur Mercier, using a false passport in your own country. Who is André Dennel?'

'He used to work for me.'

'I see.' He looks at Serge. 'What do you think, Monsieur Mercier? Should I put Ructions and you in prison?'

'That's a matter for you, superintendent. I'm sure you'll do whatever you think best.'

'Part of me wants to put you on a flight back to Belfast, Mr O'Hare. How would you like that?'

'I wouldn't like it.'

'I thought not.' Vasseur sets the false passports on the table, puts his hands in his pockets, and leans back in his chair. 'You're a remarkable man. How you pulled off that bank job in Belfast … how you managed to … ' – Vasseur pulls an agonised face and rotates his hand – 'screw the police and the IRA at the same time. That was quite an accomplishment.'

'I didn't screw anybody.'

'Of course you didn't. Where was I? Yes. I *should* put you on a flight back to Ireland.' Vasseur looks for a flicker of dread in Ructions's eyes but can't find it. 'I'm a Jew, you know – not a particularly devout one – but a Jew, nevertheless. My great-grandfather, who was also called Thierry, his wife, and my grandfather's brother, Jacob, were gassed to death in Auschwitz. My grandfather escaped the roundup only because he was sleeping over with a Christian friend when the Nazis came. He was hidden in a convent for the duration of the war by Catholic nuns.' Vasseur lifts a slice of ham with his fingers from Ructions's plate and pops it into his mouth, chewing on it slowly. 'Neo-Nazis murdered a man in my district. I don't like that. I loathe neo-Nazis. You can understand that, can't you, Ructions?'

'Perfectly.'

'The question I ask myself is: Why?' Vasseur turns to Serge. 'Why did the neo-Nazis murder Clément Beauregard?'

'I told you, superintendent, they wanted Hermann Goering's baton.'

'But you say you hadn't got Hermann Goering's baton.'

'Tell that to the Nazis,' Serge says.

Vasseur leans in. 'Have you the baton?'

'*Non.*'

'I expected you to say that.' Vasseur has a way of cocking his head, as if it will make the bearer of his gaze uncomfortable. It usually works, but not on Serge. He knows that Vasseur has no evidence to connect him to any crime. 'I don't mind saying that I've lost sleep over this business,' Vasseur says. He lifts a spare fork, spikes a slice of cheese and puts it in his mouth. He looks ahead. 'I keep asking myself: Why?' He turns his head back to Serge. 'Why, Monsieur Mercier?'

Serge sets down his knife and fork. 'I keep telling you, I don't know.'

Vasseur tries a different tack. 'If the Goering baton were to come up on the open market, how much would you expect to get for it?'

'Nothing. I don't own it.'

Vasseur smiles sardonically. 'A good answer. So how much could one expect ... in your estimate as an antiques dealer?'

Serge picks his tenses carefully. 'I believe it would fetch at least one million euro at auction.'

'Yes, on the open market, but would that sum be worth the risk of sending assassins into another country to steal it and to murder someone?' Vasseur looks directly in Serge's eyes. 'Here's one of the things that has been troubling me. Once the neo-Nazis invaded your property and murdered Clément Beauregard, they forfeited the right to display the baton in public, or to sell it, and any person who did display it in public, or tried to sell it, would automatically become a suspect in a murder investigation.'

Serge touches his lips with a napkin. 'Superintendent Vasseur,' he says, 'I don't think they ever intended to put it on the market,' Serge says. 'I don't think this is about money. It's about symbology.'

'Oh, I agree, absolutely. But the symbology theory is limited too, because if a leader appeared at a rally or a political meeting brandishing that baton, he or she would be immediately arrested on suspicion of murdering Clément Beauregard.' Vasseur turns to Ructions. '*You* can see my problem, can't you, Ructions?'

'Definitely.'

'Would you be able to offer an alternative motive?'

'I'm afraid not, superintendent.'

'That disappoints me.' A faint smile spreads on Vasseur's face. He knows Ructions is lying. *Should I arrest Ructions on a charge of possessing a false passport?* he wonders. He decides, instead to see where Monsieur Ructions leads him. 'Thank you, gentlemen,' he says, standing up to leave. Hovering above Ructions, he hands him the false passport. 'I believe this is yours, Monsieur Dillon.' Then he gives Serge back his false passport.

Vasseur walks away, then stops, as if he just remembered something. He turns back towards the table and tilts his head pensively. 'Have either of you been speaking to Karl Keller?'

Serge says, 'The name isn't familiar to me.'

'Do you know Karl Keller, Monsieur Dillon?'

Ructions shakes his head.

'May I ask, superintendent,' Serge says, 'who he is?'

Vasseur shifts his gaze to Ructions. 'Perhaps Monsieur Dillon could answer that question. He strikes me as a man who makes a virtue out of knowing his enemies.'

Ructions remains expressionless.

'The time may come when you need me,' Vasseur says as he fishes a calling card out of his wallet and gives it to Ructions. 'If it does, you can get me at this number, day or night. *Bon journée, messieurs.*' Vasseur walks away.

Gazing intently at Ructions, Serge says, 'How did he find us?'

'He didn't find *us* ...' Ructions points a finger at Serge. 'He found you, and through you, me.' Ructions puts his finger to his lips.

'What was he hoping to achieve by coming at us like that?'

Ructions runs his finger under the part of the table where Vasseur had been sitting. When he brings his hand back up, there is a small, battery-like object in it. Ructions smiles and puts the listening device back under the table. 'The gentleman was just introducing himself. Let's go.'

Serge walks towards the elevator, but Ructions puts his hand in front of him and whispers in Serge's ear. 'No.'

Serge nods.

They make their way to Bar Hemingway, where a barman is polishing a glass behind the counter. Another barman is taking photos of an elderly American couple standing beside a bust of Ernest Hemingway and a typewriter, presumably Hemingway's. Serge and Ructions perch themselves on green leather barstools. 'I've seen Hemingway's typewriter before,' Serge says. 'What was the bar called?' His thoughts ricochet between exotic locations around the world until, finally, he settles on a crusty Cuban watering hole. A five-piece band was playing beside the door ... a wafer-thin man with a waxed, handlebar moustache played bass, a young trumpet-player, so good he reminded Serge of Dizzy Gillespie, and a bulky lady with a husky voice sang 'Guantanamera.' 'It was the El Floridita, in old Havana.'

Staring ahead at the bar, Ructions muttered, 'Hemingway had lots of typewriters.'

A barman approaches and Ructions orders a mineral. Serge asks for coffee. 'How does Vasseur know about Karl Keller?' Serge asks.

'He doesn't. He was looking for a reaction from us. Keller's in the frame; why wouldn't he be? He's the leading neo-Nazi in Germany.'

Serge looks relieved as he stares at Ructions. 'You said I had a decision to make.'

Ructions nods.

'Well, I'm leaving it all to you.' As if reprieved from execution in the electric chair, Serge sits back and fold his arms. 'I don't see any other way.'

'Are you sure?'

Serge puts a reassuring hand on Ructions's shoulder and smiles: 'The good ship *Hispaniola* will have to sail without me. Go find the crock of gold at the end of the rainbow, Irishman, and the best of luck to you.'

'You trust me that much?'

'More than that.'

'I believe you do.'

The barman returns with the mineral and tea, and both men sip their drinks.

Ructions finds himself getting emotional. 'I won't let you down,' he says.

'I know that.'

A gentle silence. Then, Ructions comes to.

'The minute you walk out the door,' he says, 'the cops will be following you.'

'Comes with the territory. You'll be careful.'

'Sure,' Ructions says, smiling. But behind the façade of the obligatory smile lurks something else: relief.

'You're setting your face against some very dangerous people.'

'I seem to have made a virtue out of doing that,' Ructions says. They stand up and hug. Ructions walks Serge to the lobby. Once more they shake hands before Serge, head erect, strolls briskly out of the hotel.

Ructions's eyes follow the Frenchman. He thinks, *Is this the last time I'll ever see you, Serge?*

CHAPTER EIGHTEEN

RUCTIONS HAS LITTLE TIME TO PONDER SERGE'S departure – he must depart himself and, in doing so, find a way of evading the police.

But then he notices a bank of reporters shuffling backwards through the reception area towards the exit, a tall woman in a white fur coat before them. Sparks fly in Ructions's brain.

Rumours have been circulating that Marcy Courtney, the Oscar-winning Hollywood actress, had been dropped from her latest movie because of her worsening crack cocaine habit. Her appearance does nothing to dispel the rumours. Even though she is wearing a white fur coat, there is no hiding her lifeless blonde hair and pallid, emaciated cheeks. And her eyes? If she were to croak, you'd think she was a frog. But it isn't only that. Dark eye shadow, heavy eyeliner, pale foundation, and ruby-red lipstick add to the general impression that she looks like a washed-out zombie in a B movie.

The reporters' questions are savage: 'Have you been dropped

from *Sin*, Marcy?' 'Are you a crackhead, Marcy?' 'Has Tom left you?' 'When's the last time you saw your two kids, Marcy?'

Security men and women in red ties and navy blazers try to shield her, but they are barely holding off the press. Ructions puts on his flat hat, takes out his phone, holds it in front of him, and joins the press throng.

Marcy is escorted out of the hotel, where hordes of paparazzi are gathered, pushing and jostling, taking snaps of the superstar. She puts up her hand to shield her face, which makes matters worse. Uniformed police push back against the paparazzi and the fans. A brawl breaks out as a security man elbows a member of the paparazzi and knocks him down. Ructions stays close to Marcy.

Vasseur and Robillard are standing across the road from the hotel. Vasseur is speaking into his phone: 'Tell him I'm busy right now.' As Vasseur puts the radio back into its mount, he looks over at the melee in front of the hotel. 'Is that man punching that security guy? He is!' Vasseur peers forward as he tries to get a better look at the ruckus.

In the pushing and shoving beside the limousine, Marcy is knocked over. Ructions bends down and pulls her up with one hand. With his arm around Marcy's waist, the bank robber and the superstar dip low, out of sight.

Vasseur's head swivels back to Robillard. 'Was that ... C'mon, Pierre! It's O'Hare!' The two police officers rush across the road.

Ructions is in Marcy Courtney's limousine. *'Conduire la voiture!'* he shouts. *'Vite! Conduire!'* The vehicle starts pulling away from the hotel.

Vasseur comes to the left rear-passenger window and tries to open the door. Ructions puts his face to the window and looks out at the superintendent. He can't help but smile. Vasseur runs alongside the limousine, his eyes welded to Ructions's. Ructions wiggles a few fingers as the limousine gathers speed. Vasseur stops running.

In the limousine, Marcy looks at Ructions. 'Who the fuck are you?'

'I'm the man who saved you from being trampled on back there.'

Marcy has an uncertain look on her face. 'I asked you a question: Who the fuck are you?'

'I'm Ructions O'Hare.' He offers his hand to Marcy, but she doesn't take it. Instead, she puts the end of her index finger into her mouth. 'I'm wondering … are you a cop? Truth, now.'

'No.'

'What are you, then?'

'Truth?'

Marcy nods.

'I'm a bank robber.'

Marcy claps her hands in glee. 'I knew it! I fucking knew it! A bank robber. I love bank robbers! What banks did you rob?'

'The cops think I robbed the National Bank in Belfast.'

'You're Irish?' Ructions nods. 'I fucking love the Irish. What's that black beer you guys drink?'

'Guinness.'

Marcy points a finger at Ructions. 'I fucking love Guinness! How much did you get? Did you clean out the fucking bank? Did you get away with millions?'

'As it happens, the cops are alleging that I *did* clean the bank out—'

'How much? How much?'

'They're saying I got away with over thirty-six million pounds.'

Marcy leaps up on the seat. 'Awesome!' She looks Ructions up and down. 'There's a real-life Danny Ocean in my car! What did you say your name was?'

'Ructions O'Hare.'

Marcy shakes Ructions's hand. 'Ructions? As in ... bedlam?'

Ructions nods.

Marcy once more claps her hands. 'Ructions ... Fucking brilliant! I love it.'

'You do?'

'Sure.' Marcy holds up two fists. 'Bank robbers ... balls of steel. I don't suppose you've any gear on you?'

'Sorry, I don't do drugs.'

Marcy puts her hand on Ructions's crotch. 'What do you do?'

'Bad timing, Marcy.'

Marcy glances out the side window. A paparazzi on the back of a moped is snapping photos. She looks out the back window, where at least another ten mopeds, with paparazzi in the pillion seats, are following the limousine. Behind them are the screaming sirens and flashing lights of police cars. 'Fucking paparazzi,' she says, pulling her legs up into her chest and leaning her chin on her knees.

Ructions looks out the car window. An anthill of people are mingling, muttering, getting directions, looking in shop windows, sitting at cafés, philosophising, comforting, popping questions, arguing, people-watching, being seen. The limousine approaches the Galeries Lafayette department store on the Avenue de l'Opéra. 'Driver! *Arrête la voiture!*' Ructions kisses Marcy full on the lips, pulls his flat cap down over his face, jumps out when the limousine stops, and disappears into the crowd.

Eleanor Proctor congratulates herself on having disappeared into the County Down countryside. No one knows she is here, not even Ructions. Sitting in the restaurant at the Old Inn, she dabs her lips with a white linen napkin. She had been famished, not haven eaten since breakfast, but that's not unusual. And she has always detested eating alone. Even when she was married to Frank, she had habitually waited until he came home from work before eating the evening meal, even if he was working late.

The Old Inn is busy. Eleanor watches as Danny Rice, the colourful hotelier, flits from table to table, making sure everyone knows they're his VIPs.

'Was your meal satisfactory, ma'am?' the tall maître d' with the black moustache asks Eleanor.

'Yes. It was excellent,' she replies.

'Ma'am, that gentleman' – the maître d' nods to a middle-aged man in a black pinstriped suit – 'has asked if he may buy you a drink.'

Eleanor looks in the man's direction. He has combed-back white hair and is clean-shaven. Eleanor reckons he looks a bit like Charlie Watts, the drummer for the Rolling Stones. He smiles at her and graciously nods. He seems charming, elegant even. Why not? 'Tell him I'd like a brandy and ginger ale, please.'

The maître d' goes over to the man and then walks to the bar. The man hesitates for a minute, as if making up his mind what to do next. He leaves his table and approaches Eleanor. 'Hello,' he says in a foreign accent.

'Hello.'

'May I?' he says, his hand beckoning to the seat across from her.

Eleanor returns the gesture. The man sits down. She notices that he is wearing highly polished, black Oxford shoes. 'Forgive me for being cavalier—'

'Don't worry about it.'

'My name is Fabian Hoffman.'

'And I'm Eleanor Proctor.'

They shake hands.

'If I may say so, Eleanor – may I call you Eleanor?'

Eleanor nods.

'It seems strange to me that a woman of your beauty should be eating alone … ' Fabian raises his hands. 'I am sorry; that was tactless, yes?'

She thinks it was corny. 'Fabian Hoffman – is that a German name?'

'Yes. I live in Munich. Have you ever been to Munich, Eleanor?'

Suddenly, the walls of the room begin to bleed. Someone has turned up the volume in the busy restaurant to a pitch where it is hurting her ears. All Eleanor can see is Hoffman's face. His lips may be smiling, but his deep blue eyes are cold, measuring, taunting. Eleanor feels a pulse of revulsion and panic. He's German, she thinks, and he lives in the same city as that neo-Nazi … oh, what's his name? Karl something. Keller. Karl Keller.

'Are you okay, Eleanor?' Hoffman says. 'You look as if you've seen a ghost.'

'I'm fine,' Eleanor lies. Her stomach feels as if it's in a cement mixer. She has an irresistible urge to wretch. She grabs her napkin, holds it to her mouth, and hurries to the ladies' room, where she enters a cubicle and throws up. She sinks to her knees, her head above the toilet bowl. Her eyes and nose are running. A cold sweat has broken out on her forehead. A second wave hits her. And a third. She wipes her mouth with the napkin.

The toilet door opens. Her head turns instantly. Loud footsteps, not high heels, seem to be coming towards her. The footsteps stop outside her cubicle. Two light knocks on the door. 'Eleanor,' Hoffman says tenderly, his forehead almost touching the door, 'Are you all right?'

The voice in her head tells her not to answer him, but she wants to plead with him, to declare her innocence, to assure him that she knows nothing about Hermann Goering's baton. *Ructions, where are you? Where the fuck are you?*

'Eleanor, are you all right?' Hoffman asks again. 'Can I get you anything?'

'No,' she says feebly.

'You're sure?'

'Yes, thank you.'

Hoffman smiles indulgently. 'I have to go now. You know, it was such a pleasure meeting you. I do hope we meet again.' He turns to walk away, then stops, as if he has had an afterthought. 'Oh, ahh, would you be so kind as to give my best regards to Ructions?'

Eleanor dry-heaves into the napkin. Her eyes distend and become vacant.

'Auf Wiedersehen.' Hoffman calls out as he walks away. Then he stops. The scorpion's venomous tail is raised. It is time to deliver the venom. 'I forgot to say … ' There is a click, like shoes clacking together. 'Heil Hitler!' Eleanor hears the door to the bar open and close.

CHAPTER NINETEEN

ELEANOR HAS NOT LEFT THE TOILET CUBICLE. 'AND then he followed me into the toilet. And I knew it was him. And I vomited,' Eleanor says into the phone. 'And he tapped the door and asked me if I was all right. And he said, "Give my best regards to Ructions."'

Ructions thinks: *Keep her calm.* 'What else?'

'And then he walked away and clicked his heels and shouted, "Heil Hitler." *Heil fucking Hitler!* And then—'

'Slow down, love. It's okay.'

But nothing Ructions could say to Eleanor is going to be well received. 'Are you insane? It's fucking *not* okay. The Nazis followed me to County Down. *They followed me into the toilet.* For all I know he could be standing outside this stall listening to me right now!' she shouts. 'Are you listening to me now, you Nazi cunt? Help! Someone help me!'

'El!'

'Help!'

'El!'

'What?' she snaps.

'Listen to me—'

'Listen to *you?*' Eleanor puts her head to the floor and looks below the partition to see if any shiny Oxford shoes are lurking, waiting for her to appear. 'It's been listening to you that's got me looking under toilet doors for Nazis. It's been listening to you—'

The door to the ladies' room opens and someone comes in.

An Irish female voice says, 'Did someone call for help?'

Making no sound, Eleanor gently slides the bolt on the cubicle door across and peeks out. A waitress is standing in the middle of the floor.

Eleanor opens the door and looks behind the waitress.

'Are you okay, ma'am?' the waitress asks.

Stumbling from one word to another, Eleanor warily asks if the waitress had seen a man entering or leaving the toilet. When the waitress confirms that she has not seen anyone, Eleanor expels a sigh of relief.

Ructions is now shouting down the phone to get Eleanor's attention. Hitting the terminate button, she puts the phone in her handbag, goes over to the sink, and splashes water on her face. She pulls a cloth towel down from a dispenser and pats her face dry. Looking in the mirror, she recoils in horror at what is looking back at her. She wants to put on makeup, but that would be time-consuming and, more than anything, she wants to get out of the toilet and be surrounded by people who aren't threatening her life.

Her phone rings as she leaves the toilet. She takes Ructions's call. 'El,' he says quickly, 'don't hang up. Hear me out.'

'What is it?' she says pugnaciously.

'Love,' he says in a sweet, velvet voice, 'here's what I want you—'

'I don't care what you want!'

'El, listen to me.'

'I'm going somewhere where none of you maniacs can find me.'

'Listen,' Ructions pleads, 'I'm going to send someone down from Belfast to you. You know Billy Kelly, don't you?'

'No.'

'He'll know you. He'll look after you.'

'What does that mean? What, in the name of Jesus, does that fucking mean?'

'It means he'll keep you safe.'

'I'll keep myself safe.' She hangs up again.

She walks over to the reception and asks the receptionist if she can book a taxi to pick her up in fifteen minutes, explaining that she needs to pack her cases and check out. Eleanor then goes to her room and quickly packs. When she returns to the hotel lobby, she pays her bill, and the receptionist tells her that there is a taxi outside. Eleanor walks outside and speaks to the taxi driver. 'Can you drive me to the Newtownards Road in Belfast, please?'

'Sure, miss,' a red-faced driver with a blond Tintin quiff says. IRA man Hughie O'Boyle adjusts his mirror so that he can see Eleanor as she settles into the back of the taxi. 'Are you alright, miss?'

'Yes.'

The taxi pulls away from the hotel.

CHAPTER TWENTY

AFTER THIERRY VASSEUR CONFRONTED RUCTIONS IN
the Ritz, everything changed. The police chief may as well have
written Ructions a note saying, 'You're at the top of my watch
list.' And Ructions reads notes. Which had made it imperative to
him that he needed to get out of the French capital.

He is in the lounge of the Hôtel La Résidence du Vieux Port
in Marseilles. A waiter brings him a cognac. A pianist plays
Johann Pachelbel's Canon in D Major. The calming music does
nothing to slow down Ructions's racing mind ... How far does
the neo-Nazis' reach extend? They not only knew that El was
in Northern Ireland, but they knew exactly where to find her.
How would they know that? Cops. Has to be cops. No one else
would have that information. He pops some nuts in his mouth
and chews slowly as thoughts and questions crisscross his mind.
*What are you trying to tell me, Karl? That you can kill Eleanor
any time the notion takes you? But you can't, 'cause if you do, I've
no reason to deal with you. And I'll fuckin' come after you, boyo;*

I'll fucking catch you when you're least expecting it. So, you have powerful friends in the intelligence services ... never doubted it for a second. Oh, I get it, yeah, you're telling me you can bring me down any time you want? Don't think so, fuckhead, or you'd have done so already.

Ructions leans his arm back in the hollow of the chaise longue sofa and slowly looks around. What does a twenty-first-century Nazi look like?

He feels very alone. True, even when Eleanor was with him, he sometimes felt alone, but not like this. As if it was time for a well-earned thinking break, Ructions drains his cognac, but the questions show no signs of retiring for the night. One keeps coming back: *Where are you, Karl?*

Karl is with Gitte in a box in the Gasteig Philharmonic Hall in Munich for a performance of Rossini's *The Barber of Seville*. Also with them is Karl's grandfather, Adelbert Keller. Despite being ninety years old, Adelbert still works out in his home gym every morning. He smiles at Gitte and puts his hand affectionately on hers.

In the foyer at the intermission, Adelbert speaks to a police chief, Manfred Dortzer, while Karl and Gitte sip cocktails and make small talk with the mayor of Munich and his entourage. Karl turns on his phone. Nothing from Ructions. He is surprised. He would have expected Ructions to have contacted by him by now, to have threatened him with death and ruination. But nothing. That is disturbing. Debilitating thoughts speak to him in a familiar voice ... Ructions must know that his woman has been visited by now. Doesn't he care about her?

He walks outside the concert hall and lights a cigarette. His phone rings. 'Hello?' he says.

'It's me. You wanted to meet?'

'Yes.'

'The Shelbourne Hotel, Dublin, twelve o'clock midday, Saturday fortnight.'

Keller grimaces and grips the phone tightly. *This bloody Irishman is infuriating*, he thinks. 'But that's over two weeks away! And Dublin? Out of the question. It doesn't work for me. I won't be there.'

'That's up to you.' Ructions hangs up.

Karl stamps on his cigarette and returns to the lobby, making himself comfortable on a dark-blue sofa, propping a brown cushion behind his back. Gitte joins him.

'You look distracted,' she says. 'Is everything alright?'

'I've just heard from Ructions O'Hare.'

'Oh?'

'He wants to meet me in Dublin.'

'Dublin?' Gitte blows out her pursed lips. 'You're not going, are you?'

'I don't see that I've much choice.' Karl throws back his head and looks at the ceiling. 'Go on in. I'll be with you in a minute. I need to think.'

Gitte goes back into the auditorium.

This is not the turn of events Karl had expected. He had expected fire and brimstone down the phone. But that was too predictable, and the more he confronts him, the more Karl is beginning to realise that this Ructions O'Hare doesn't do predictability. He likes keeping his adversaries off-balance. Had he behaved as a normal person would, Karl would have let Ructions purge himself of his anger, certainly, he would not have retaliated in the face of multiple insults. He would have reminded the Irishman that he could have, but didn't, hurt Eleanor. Surely that counts for something? Apparently not. Ructions didn't even mention Eleanor's brush with Fabian. And then – the cheek of him – he commands that the Führer attend a meeting at a time and place of his choosing? That's not right. That's not how the game is played.

'The second half is about to begin. Are you coming in, Karl?' his grandfather asks. Karl's head spins around. He smiles and stands up. 'You have much on your mind,' Adelbert says as they walk towards their box. 'Can I help?'

'No, grandfather.'

'Can I give you advice?'

'Of course.'

The nonagenarian's voice is remarkably strong, 'Be careful in whom you confide.'

Karl looks at him nervously. His grandfather doesn't normally say much, and when he does it is usually profound. Something is eating at him. 'I am careful,' Karl says.

Adelbert oscillates a finger and brings his mouth close to Karl's ear: 'Not careful enough. Manfred has just told me that you've a police mole in your ranks. Very highly positioned. He doesn't know the mole's identity, but he emphasised that this person is close to you.'

'A mole?' Karl murmurs. 'Close to me?' A shock wave makes him shudder. He pulls back dramatically to look into his grandfather's face. 'Who would do this?'

'Don't be demonstrative,' Adelbert says. 'People always note anger.'

A strained smile crosses his face. 'Sorry, grandfather.'

'Come over here,' Adelbert says. They walk to the side. 'This person is a police officer. He has been undercover, inside the organisation for years, and he is now in a position of trust. You have to consider that he has recruited others.'

'Others?'

'Traitors,' Adelbert says. 'There could be any number of people who wish you and the organisation harm.' Adelbert greets a friend who passes by. 'Someone – perhaps more than one – may have become disillusioned with the cause. A comrade mightn't like you personally, might want your job. A rat may be angry because you've ignored him or her when doling out positions or money. Take your pick,' the old man says. 'Traitors invariably have a dozen reasons to justify their treachery. Leadership is a lonely post, Karl. You have no friends. Get that into your head. Some people, not all, whom you think are friends, will be out to harm you. I've seen it before.'

The former SS captain beams at another person who nods respectfully to him. 'Oh, and when you discover who the parasite is, be very careful not to cause him or her any injury. They will have security force backup and a traceable history of his or her dealings with the organisation, and with *you* in particular. What I'm saying is: the last thing you need right now is the full weight of the state coming down on you. Now, smile. Compose yourself. We've an opera to enjoy.'

They reenter the box, but Karl's interest in the opera has taken flight. Now his mind is plagued with the faces of his leadership team. As he surveys the gallery of Nazi illuminati, he thinks … none of these people can be trusted. Who then can I trust? Only those who were on the Mercier raid with me. None of them gave away the operation or else the French police would have arrested or killed us.

Once again, Karl sieves through the faces of his remaining top brass. It could be any of them.

CHAPTER TWENTY-ONE

PROFESSOR DERMOT MCCRACKEN IS IN A DITCH IN County Tyrone with an archaeologist trowel in his hand. He grimaces and rubs his rheumatic knee. Comes with the job. Too many digs. Too much time stuck in mucky trenches on barren landscapes. He looks up at a combustible sky. The light is fading. The first brush of rain spits in his face. 'We'd better wrap it up for today,' he says to his students. 'Come on, everyone, hurry it up. It's gonna lash down in a minute.'

The professor of archaeology at Queen's University, Belfast, climbs out of the ditch. He removes his large brown Stetson to reveal – despite the white ponytail that stretches down to the small of his back – a shining bald head. He runs his fingers through the underside of his grey goatee. Two hooped earrings decorate his right ear, and another on his left. A student brings him a coin, which he examines. The face of Queen Elizabeth I, alongside the Tudor rose, appears on one side. On the other side is a quartered coat of arms on which the three lions occupy the second and third quarters and the fleurs-de-lis the first and fourth. 'Very good, Bronagh,' he remarks. 'Where was it?' Bronagh brings him to where she was digging. 'Where there's one, there's more,' McCracken says, looking first into the ditch, and then up at the sky. He is mortared with hailstones. They scurry to a tent where he holds the coin in the palm of his hand and asks Bronagh what it is.

'It looks to me like an Elizabethan hammered silver sixpence, Dermot.'

'Excellent. And tell me ... when did hand-hammered coin-making end in England?'

'1662.'

Dermot nods approvingly. Then he rubs his lower lip. He thinks, that's two tanners and three groats found on this site. Is there a money pit here? Could be. Could be some sort of medieval bank. 'Hmm ... I'm wondering ... is it part of a collection?' The noise in the tent is deafening now as the hailstones clatter down. 'It's always the way of it, isn't it?'

'Pardon?' Bronagh shouts.

'The minute something exciting happens, nature closes us down.'

Dermot's phone rings. 'Hello?'

'Dermy, it's Ructions.'

'Who?'

'Ructions O'Hare.'

Dermot is vexed ... Ructions O'Hare? It must be seven years, no, make that eight. Has to be something hooky. *For Christ's sake, don't piss him off.* 'It's bucketing down here,' he yells, 'I can't hear you.'

'It's me ... ' Ructions screeches.

'I got that. What about ya, man?' Dermot calls cheerily. 'Ructions, phone me back in a minute, will ya? I need to find somewhere quieter.' Dermot hangs up.

Just as quickly as they had started, the hailstones stop and are replaced by soft rain. Holding the sixpence, Dermot says: 'Bronagh, please get this bagged and labelled with a context number, will you? And make sure you record it in the context sheet.'

Dermot walks out of the tent. His phone rings. 'Ructions! I haven't heard from you since—'

'Since I helped you out with that other little matter,' Ructions reminds him.

Eight years earlier, Dermot, a leading gay-rights activist in Belfast, had been returning home from a night out when he was beaten up for the third time by a gang of youths from a nearby estate. On that occasion, he ended up being rushed to hospital with a fractured skull and broken cheekbone after being hit repeatedly with a baseball bat. When the police visited him the next day and asked him to name the culprits, Dermot replied that he didn't know them. (He did.) Could he pick them out of a lineup? He didn't think so. (He could.) Was the attack related to his public persona as a gay-rights activist? The youths had been shouting anti-gay obscenities at him while they battered him.

His ordeal made headlines in the local newspapers: GAY ACTIVIST BEATEN WITH BASEBALL BAT. City councillors and politicians had visited him and expressed their determination to arrest the hooligans who had carried out this dastardly act ...

Words. Dermot had heard them before. He reckoned he'd hear them again because, if he knew anything, it was that there was another beating waiting for him whenever he was released from hospital, unless ...

Dermot was mortified when Ructions O'Hare sauntered into his hospital ward at eight o'clock in the morning. Now, years later, standing outside the tent, Dermot smiles. He can still see Ructions that morning. He was wearing a black open-neck shirt, cream trousers, and a white, fedora straw hat. Ructions's finger was in the loop of his jacket, which he carried over his shoulder. Dermot thought he looked gorgeous. He had always fancied Ructions, but pride and the inevitable rejection would not allow him to reveal his true feelings for his friend. The two had been best mates at school, so much so that Ructions had been the first person to whom Dermot had revealed his homosexuality. And Ructions had kept the secret. But school was over and close school friendships tend to corrode with separation and time. Dermot had gone on to Queen's University, where he was eventually offered a professorship in archaeology, while Ructions majored in bank robbery for the IRA and thievery at the 'Panzer' O'Hare's University, Belfast.

Bringing Ructions's muscle into play did not come easily to Dermot. But needs must and, above everything else, Dermot needed to survive. The only way he could see that happening was to persuade his former schoolmate to back him up.

Any anxiety he had was blown away when Ructions unleashed his wide smile, tilted his hat, spun around, and humorously sang the Rod Stewart song, *'Some guys have all the luck.'* Dermot had laughed and then immediately grimaced, his hand reaching for his cheekbone. His luck was about to change.

'I'll sort it' had been Ructions's last words before leaving the ward. Dermot never heard from the youths again. He hadn't heard from Ructions either.

'Dermy … Dermy!'

The academic shakes his head. 'Yes. Ructions. Ahh ... how's it going, man?'

'Okay. How have you been doing?'

'Fine. Yeah, struggling on, digging.'

'Listen, I have to make this short. Are you still working at Queen's?'

'Still on the old merry-go-round for my sins.'

'You fucking love that merry-go-round.'

'I've a wonky back, rheumatic knees and fingers, my bones are brittle ... How could I not love it?'

'Have you time to hear about my afflictions? There's my broken heart—'

'You have a heart?'

'Bought it in Rome,' Ructions says, 'but it's past its sell-by date; can't bring it back.' The laughing fades. 'Look, I'm coming over to Belfast soon, and I need to talk to you.'

'What about?'

'I can't tell you over the phone, but I think it's something you'd be interested in.'

'I'd rather not—'

Ructions's soothing tone abruptly changes. 'Not what? Help me? You'd rather not help me? Is that what you're saying, Dermy?'

Dermot wobbles immediately ... don't even think of telling Ructions O'Hare you can't help him! 'I didn't say that, Ructions,' he says.

'It sounded very like it to me. Look, I need your professional eye, nothing else. I'm not asking you to do anything illegal.'

Dermot breathes a sigh of relief. 'I'm at your service, mate.'

CHAPTER TWENTY-TWO

THE MUNICH HEADQUARTERS OF THE GERMAN NATION-
alist Party does not match the organisation's grandiose political ambitions. In fact, were it not for a plaque advertising the
organisation's name above the front door of the nondescript,
red-bricked building, no one would know the neo-Nazis occupied the building.

In the directors' room, the executive committee of the Fourth
Reich stands around the refreshments table. The eleven men are
all formally dressed in suits and ties. Looking down on them from
a photograph on the wall – as if reminding them that duty to the
Fatherland is absolute – is Adolf Hitler, his piercing eyes watching every corner of the room. On another wall is a swastika. A
long china cabinet stands below the swastika, within which is an
SS dagger, some ceremonial swords, a collection of decommissioned handguns, and an assortment of regimental insignia. In
another corner is a mannequin dressed as an SS soldier, complete
with uniform, helmet, and Schmeisser submachine gun.

The directors chat, drink tea and coffee, and nibble biscuits. The door opens and Karl Keller, dressed in a Waffen-SS uniform, complete with black hat bearing the scull of bones below the Nazi eagle, cross belt and belt, black trousers, and high boots, walks into the room. Behind him is his secretary, Gitte. The men turn and come to attention. All raise their arms: 'Seig Heil!' Keller returns the salute. He sits at the top of the long table as each of the directors takes their seat.

Keller does not say anything for a full minute, each director awaiting the reason he had called this unscheduled meeting. Finally, he takes out his phone and dials a number: 'Come in, please.'

The five men who had accompanied Keller on the raid of Serge Mercier's house enter the room are all dressed in Waffen-SS uniforms. The directors look askance as if they are being threatened.

'What's this, Führer?' Dieter Neumann asks. 'The Night of the Long Knives revisited?'

'Something like that,' Keller says. The five men stand menacingly around the table. 'Gentlemen, I'm afraid I'm going to have to ask you to put your hands on the table and keep them there where we can all see them.'

'How dare you treat us like this!' Jochen Schulze says.

Keller bangs the table with his fist. 'There is a traitor at this table!'

'A traitor?' Neumann says. 'Here? Hell no, Führer. You're mistaken. I know every man here. I'd vouch for every last one of them.'

'There is a traitor at this table,' Keller repeats. 'Don't ask me how I know it, but I do.'

Jochen Schulze stands up. 'I'm not letting you or anyone else accuse me of being a traitor.' Schulze tries to leave but is pushed back into his seat by an SS man.

Keller goes to the China cabinet and removes the Cherusker, the copy of the ancient sword used by Arminius, when his Germanic armies defeated three roman legions at the battle of Teutoburger in 9 AD. He waves the sword in front of him.

'Jochen, no one is accusing anyone of being a traitor – yet. What I have done is to have this room swept for bugs earlier on and we found three. Still, I'm not sure we found them all, so if you don't mind, I'd like you all to come with me to the basement.'

'The basement?' Schulze exclaims. 'We're going to have an executive meeting in the basement?'

'I need you all to put up your hands where I can see them, if you please.'

'I'm protesting in the strongest possible terms.'

'Protest noted,' Karl says.

'I hope you know what you're doing, Führer,' Neumann says. 'Once again, I want it noted in the minutes of this meeting that I strongly protest at the way my fellow directors and I have been treated this evening.'

'So noted, once again,' Karl says. He sets the Cherusker down on the table and twines his fingers together before him on the tabletop. Taking his time, he looks every one of the directors in the eye. Finally, he says: 'What I propose to do now is to take a gamble.'

'What sort of gamble?' Neumann asks.

'I'm gambling that someone's phone is activated, and our conversation is being listened to by intelligence agents. Or else, someone is wearing a wire.' The directors are completely silent. 'If I'm wrong, I'll leave the room in order to give you time to determine whether or not you still wish me to lead the party. I will abide by any decision you might make, of course.'

'Just how far are you prepared to go with this … this farce?' Schulze says.

'As far as I have to, Jochen. Are you the traitor?'

'I most certainly am not.'

'Perhaps you'd prove it by handing over your mobile telephone.'

'How dare you call me a traitor! You're insane!' Schulze snarls. 'I'm not handing over anything to you.'

'Well, I'm no traitor,' Neumann says. 'Here's my phone.' An SS guard takes Neumann's phone and opens its audio files. After a thorough examination, the SS guard looks at Keller and shakes his head.

'You're not going along with this, are you, Dieter?' Schulze says.

Neumann stands up and starts opening his shirt. 'There,' he says. 'No wire.'

One by one, the directors stand up, hand over their mobile phones, and open their shirts. Only Schulze is left. 'I'm not doing it,' he says, grabbing his phone and turning it off at the same time.

Two SS guards grab him by the arms and tear open his shirt. Taped to Schulze's chest is a small microphone.

Keller comes around the table. He lowers his face to the microphone. 'We wish your spy no harm. We want no trouble.

We're a peaceful political party, but we will be bringing this matter up at the highest level of government. Get out, Dieter, or whatever your real name is,' he says. 'Go on. Out.'

Schulze looks disdainfully at the people around the table, one after another, leaving no doubt that he despises them. Head erect, he walks out of the room.

Neumann stands up, turns to Karl, and gives the Nazi salute. The other directors join him. Neumann then leads the executive in a stirring rendition of 'Deutschland über Alles.'

CHAPTER TWENTY-THREE

RUCTIONS ADJUSTS HIS CLERICAL COLLAR AND LOOKS straight ahead as he approaches customs at Dublin airport. He hands over his passport. The customs officer looks at it, then at Ructions, then his computer. He gives Ructions back his passport and motions for Ructions to proceed. As he begins to pass through the NOTHING TO DECLARE aisle, another customs official stops him to inspect his luggage. The suitcase is put through the X-ray machine. At the other end, Ructions is asked to open it. Very visible on top of his clothes are three batons, wrapped together in stripy souvenir paper. The customs official points to the bag.

'Can you tell me what is in here, Father Fitzsimmons?'

'Sure. They're replica military batons. German generals used to carry them about. A status thing, you know.'

'Can you open the paper for me, please?'

Ructions unwraps the batons. The customs officer looks

closely at them. 'They're well decorated, aren't they, Father?' he says, without looking up. 'And these diamonds look real.'

Ructions laughs with gusto. 'I wish! They do look good though, don't they? Coloured glass. Machine-made in Germany. Look. There's the receipt, 99.99 euro a baton. That's not bad when you think about it.'

The customs officer holds a baton in his hand. 'Strange-looking things.' The customs officer waves the baton in his hand. 'I don't get it. What's their purpose? Who'd want these, like?'

'They have no purpose, other than to fill a general's hand and ego. Sorry, I didn't catch your name?'

'Philly McDavitt, Father.'

'Well, Philly, history teachers, academics, love this sort of stuff. I'm giving one to Professor Conchúr Richardson; he teaches modern European history at Trinity. And Father Seán Barry, he's getting one. Seán teaches philosophy at University College Cork. And then there's one for the Reverend Roy Salters.' Ructions whispers in the Philly's ear, 'He's a Protestant preacher from Belfast.' He puts up a neutral hand. 'Not that I've anything against Protestants. Roy's the salt of the earth.' Ructions looks ahead, as if he is recollecting a distant memory. 'I can hear him now: "The wages of sin is death." First time I met him he tried to convert me. It was outside a bank in the centre of Belfast, if I remember right. That's where he preached. Can you believe that? Outside a bank. Roy reckons he's saved hundreds of souls from eternal damnation. Personally, I think it's difficult to calculate how many souls a clergyman can save in his lifetime, and I'm not all that sure souls saved by Protestant ministers count. Now, take me, for instance. I couldn't say how many souls I've saved, but—'

Fearing he is about to be on the receiving end of a soul-saving sermon, Philly jumps in. 'Each to his own, Father, that's what I say. Sorry for bothering you. We have to do our job, y'know?'

'That's not a problem, Philly. It's been a pleasure talking to you.'

Ructions is having a smoke outside the airport terminal when his phone rings. He doesn't recognise the number, so he hesitates before pressing the answer button. 'Hello?'

'Ructions, dear boy.'

If Ructions didn't recognise the number, he certainly recognises the voice. 'Dear Tiny, the biggest thief in Ireland.'

'Oh, no,' Tiny Murdoch says. 'That honour belongs to you.'

Ructions detects a gloating edge to the IRA man's voice. He can feel the muscles contract in his stomach. 'Out with it.'

'I've got her.'

Ructions instantly knows that Tiny is speaking about Eleanor. He walks away from the airport in case an announcement should come over the tannoy that would indicate his location. 'Excellent,' Ructions says. 'Now, she likes sugar in her cornflakes, and she doesn't take milk in her tea. Oh, and by the way, she's a nooner.'

Tiny can't resist it. 'What's a nooner?'

'She doesn't get out of bed until noon.'

'Amm, amm, amm … ' Tiny sputters. 'Don't you be a cute whore with me, O'Hare. I'm the man here.'

'Congratulations. You know, my friend, that's music to my ears. She needs a strong man about her.'

'It's not like that.'

'Hey, it's none of my business. Good luck to the both of you.

I hope you have beautiful kids. Call one of them after their uncle Ructions, won't ya?'

'I said,' Tiny repeats, his voice bordering on the hysterical, 'it's not like that.'

'Whatever. Look, I'm up to my neck in stuff. I've gotta shoot the crow.'

Tiny cannot disguise the panic rise in his voice. 'Now hold on, fella. This isn't a social call. I've got her and you know—'

Tiny hears the line go dead.

He runs his hands through his hair. I hate this man! How is it that every time I talk to this shithead, I come away feeling I've just been kicked in the balls? He immediately phones again.

Ructions lets the phone ring out.

Tiny phones again.

Ructions waits until the tenth ring before answering. 'Do you ever take a hint, man? Do ya? Eh? Do you ever—'

'What are you fucking playing at?' Tiny says.

'Actually, I'm about to play a game of beach volleyball on this beautiful beach in beautiful Saint Tropez,' Ructions says before shouting, 'I'll be over in a minute, Monique.'

'Listen, you,' Tiny says angrily, 'you're starting to annoy me.' Ructions puts his hand in his mouth to stop himself from laughing. 'Do you hear me?' Tiny shouts.

Ructions composes himself. 'Look, fella, I'm very busy here.' He calls out, 'I'm coming now!'

'Will you pay attention?' Tiny shouts.

'Okay, okay! Hurry up, will ya? I've people waiting.'

'If you want to see your lips again, you be in Belfast for twelve o'clock tomorrow.'

'Not poss, dear boy. Nipping over to Venice for lunch with a

film producer tomorrow. They want to make a film of my life …
can you believe that? And anyway, she's not *my* lips.'

'Not poss? You mean, not possible, don't you?'

'Yeah, yeah, not poss.'

'What the fuck has happened to you, boyo?'

'This is boring me; I've gotta go.'

'You go, and you won't see Eleanor again.'

'Good.'

'You want her dead?'

'Oh, no. I want her to have a long and happy life – with you.
She's *your* lips.'

'I didn't say that!'

'Yes, you did. She's a handful and she's your problem now. I
couldn't get rid of her quick enough. Fair play to you for taking
her on.'

'She's not my fucking problem!' Tiny screams.

'Well, she's not mine!'

'You be here tomorrow at noon or—'

'Are you a nooner too?'

'Fucking be here!' Tiny screams.

'Nope. Can't do tomorrow at noon. I just told you, I've—'

'Gotta be in Venice.'

'You're a good listener. Look, Tiny, you'll just have to do
whatever you have to do without me. Sorry.'

Now bordering on desperation, Tiny sputters, then says,
'Well, when can you do?'

'I'm in Saint Tropez now; I'm meeting Tyrell, that's the film
producer, in Venice tomorrow, and I'm tying in with Florence
in Monte Carlo on … the earliest I could get there would be …
let's see … would be … Thursday … no, make that Friday –
but no promises.'

'Friday at noon. Be here. I'll phone you at noon to tell you where we can meet.' Tiny hangs up quickly.

Ructions looks at his phone. He walks over to a seat and plops himself down. Reaching into his pocket, he takes out a packet of chewing gum, folds a stick in half, and pops it into his mouth. It strikes him that Tiny isn't much good at handling phone calls, even when he has lumped the cards.

His thoughts turned to Panzer. What was it his uncle had taught him? Expect the unexpected, keep calm, and adjust accordingly. Sounds straightforward when you say it quickly. He thinks, Tiny has Eleanor. No, get it right: the IRA has Eleanor. How do you adjust accordingly? Fury trumps clear thinking. He thinks of their last phone call, when he'd tried to advise her, and she'd hung up on him. He is momentarily enraged. But when he runs out of expletives, he realises that feeding the negativity won't help.

It's time to bring in the cavalry.

Ructions phones Billy Kelly, and, without being explicit, tells him he hasn't yet sorted out his travel arrangements, but he'll be staying in Belfast and Dublin for the next two weeks.

Billy understands this to mean he is being told to organise transport, and to secure safe houses in Belfast and Dublin. He arranges to meet Ructions in a coffee shop in Lisburn in three hours.

Then Ructions proceeds to the car hire kiosk and rents a Ford Mondeo in the name of Father Seamus Fitzsimmons. As he drives out of the airport, he thinks of Eleanor and sees her face convulsed in terror. He doesn't think they'll harm her. It's not in their interest. When they get their dough, they'll let her go. He hopes.

Eleanor is sitting on a chair in a dimly lit room; the windows are covered by heavy curtains. Two women are behind her. One is a brute of a woman in her midforties with fat, calloused hands, a quick temper, and a foul tongue. The other seems to be embarrassed by the crudeness and viciousness of her comrade. When, earlier, Eleanor had stood up and said that she'd had enough and was going to leave the room, the bigger woman had violently shoved her into the corner and punched the back of her head and back continuously. Eleanor had been rendered unconscious, only to be revived by the second woman, who bathed her face with a wet flannel and led her back to her chair.

A man had come in and dressed down the guard who had beaten Eleanor, then ordered her out of the room. He then apologised to Eleanor for the violent behaviour of his comrade. *He sounded sincere*, Eleanor thought, before she told herself that good liars always sound sincere.

Tiny hadn't wanted to frighten Eleanor: she was frightened enough. He had expressly ordered that she should not be ill-treated, yet Big Grainne had slapped her about, and was now in trouble for disobeying orders. But meanwhile, Tiny had questioned Eleanor. Did she want to tell him how she had co-operated with Ructions to rob the National Bank? Where had she been with Ructions since the robbery? What had Ructions done with the money? What had life been like in Saint-Émilion? He said that he had been there and that it was a beautiful part of the world …

In that instant, Eleanor knew that she was being questioned by no less a person than Tiny Murdoch himself. He had guessed she would know his identity once he said he had been to Saint-Émilion. He had wanted her to know. 'Do you know who

I am?' he had eventually asked her. She resisted the temptation to say yes. Where was Ructions when she had left him to come to Northern Ireland? Had their relationship broken down completely? Had she been fed? It was on the tip of her tongue to say no, when Ructions's words echoed in her head: *'Interrogators will ask you if you want to shower. Or if you want water. They'll ask you if you'd like something to eat. They'll do whatever it takes to get you to speak. They'll say your father has had a heart attack or your mother's crying outside the door. Don't, whatever you do, get into conversation with them. Don't even nod your head.'*

And so Eleanor said nothing.

'I'm away to speak to Ructions,' Tiny eventually said. 'Is there anything you'd like me to say to him?'

Eleanor could think of many things she would have liked to say to Ructions O'Hare, but those words weren't for Tiny Murdoch's ears.

CHAPTER TWENTY-FOUR

SUPERINTENDENT THIERRY VASSEUR STANDS LOOKING at a bank of television monitors on which ten senior police officers from across Europe are looking back at him. Standing to the side of Vasseur and out of view is Inspector Pierre Robillard. Vasseur has a remote control for his presentation in one hand and a wand indicator in the other.

Vasseur starts his address by thanking everyone for answering his call. 'By now, you will have received the brief I sent you. As you will be aware, my inquiries concern several people, one of whom is this man … ' Serge's face comes up on the screen. 'His name is Serge Mercier. He's an international money launderer and a dealer in stolen art and jewellery.

'Mercier's luxury home on Lake Geneva was recently raided by people whom we believe to be neo-Nazis from Munich. They were looking for a ceremonial Nazi field marshal's baton that once belong to Hermann Goering, but they didn't find it.'

'I take it that you haven't found it yet?' asks Chief Supervisor

Daniel Clarke of the Northern Irish police.

'No,' Vasseur says. 'But we're fairly certain Mercier has it. Probably in a safety deposit box in a bank.'

Superintendent Stephen Matlock of the British police asks about the value of the baton and why, exactly, the neo-Nazis were prepared to kill for it.

Vasseur replies that it could be worth up to one million pounds before saying that he does not think that value is the motivating factor in this case.

Perplexed that one million pounds seems of so little consequence, Matlock asks if the baton is the Holy Grail of Nazism.

'The value of relics is always in the eye of the beholder,' Vasseur says.

'How do we know they were neo-Nazis?' Clarke asks.

'They were neo-Nazis,' Vasseur says. 'The Fourth Reich, to be totally accurate. Ludwig?'

German Police Senior Counsellor Ludwig Huber clears his throat and tells his fellow officers that German intelligence sources have indicated that it was the Das Reich Division, the military wing of the German Nationalist Party, who carried out the Mercier raid, but that they don't know for sure who murdered Clément Beauregard.

Matlock persists. 'But, again, to what purpose, Ludwig?'

Huber buries his head in papers.

'Go on, Ludwig, tell them,' Vasseur says.

Huber takes a deep breath: 'I can confirm that the leadership of the German Nationalist Party, also known as the Fourth Reich is convinced the baton will give them access to Hermann Goering's gold.'

Everyone's ears prick up at the mention of gold.

'Hermann Goering's gold?' Clarke says. He flips a hand. 'I'm lost. What's that?'

Huber relates how, in the autumn of 1944, when it began to be clear Germany was not going to win the war, Hermann Goering had begun to hide his hoard of looted gold bullion in neutral countries; an intelligence agent inside the leadership of the Fourth Reich had confirmed the organisation was actively pursuing that gold. Thence, the raid on Mercier's home.

There is a buzz. Vasseur realises that he needs to retake control of the meeting. 'Ludwig's agent's account is, unfortunately, hearsay, except for the raid on Mercier's home,' he clarifies, and goes on to show a photograph of a dead Clément Beauregard and then one of Karl Keller, whom he describes as the chief suspect in Beauregard's murder and the leader of the Fourth Reich.

'What's his background?' Clarke asks.

Vasseur looks to his notes. 'Keller's Nazi credentials are impeccable. His grandfather – still alive – is a former SS paratrooper, Captain Adelbert Keller. The captain was a friend and confidante of the notorious Nazi SS Lieutenant Colonel Otto Skorzeny.'

'Skorzeny?' Matlock says. 'That's a very familiar name. Wasn't he the guy who ordered SS divers to blow up the bridge in Remagen?'

'Yes,' Vasseur says.

'He also led the raid on the Campo Imperatore Hotel in the Gran Sasso massif, which freed Mussolini in 1943,' Italian police superintendent Christiana Esposito says. 'My grandfather was a porter in the hotel.'

'Nazism is in his blood, then,' Clarke says.

Vasseur wants things to keep moving. He clicks the remote

control, and a photo of Ructions and Serge in the Louvre comes up on the screen. 'This man here,' Vasseur points with the wand, 'uses multiple aliases, but his real name is James "Ructions" O'Hare. He's a bank robber by profession and is suspected of having robbed the National Bank in Belfast of thirty-six million pounds in December 2004. O'Hare is a close friend of Mercier's, who probably laundered the money from the bank robbery.'

Irish police chief Manus O'Toole visibly straightens. 'What's O'Hare got to do with Goering's baton?'

'We're not sure if he has anything to do with it,' Vasseur says. 'What we do know is that he was the last person Mercier spoke to before the raid and the first one after it. We had a tail on him, but he shook it off.'

'If I may come in here, Thierry … ' Clarke says.

'Please do, Dan.'

'I know Ructions O'Hare well – that's what he's called, by the way: Ructions. He and I have crossed swords before. If he thinks there's a scintilla of truth in this rumour about Goering's gold, he'll stake a claim on it.'

'I notice no international arrest warrant has been issued for Ructions,' O'Toole says.

'He's not a wanted man,' Vasseur says, 'but he is in hiding.'

'Why? Who from?'

'From us, from the IRA, from anyone who wishes to harm him. He likes anonymity.' Vasseur comes to the crux of the matter, saying that there are several important uncertainties in the ongoing inquiry. 'We believe the neo-Nazis will continue to pursue the baton and that they've already killed to get it. We also believe the baton is in Mercier's and O'Hare's possession. Our view is, the potential exists for further violence and murder.

'Messieurs,' he says, 'should violence occur as a result of this collision of circumstances, it may well be multi-jurisdictional and substantial. My feeling is that O'Hare will be central to everything. I have to know where he is, and I need your collective assistance to help me find him.'

CHAPTER TWENTY-FIVE

A STORM HAS SPITEFULLY CROSSED THE ATLANTIC AND made landfall on Ireland's west coast. Not that you'd have known it if you were in Teach Jack's Pub in the County Donegal village of Derrybeg. Outside the pub, a drunken wind angrily lashes a sober land. Inside, musicians, armed with tin whistles, banjos, guitars, concertinas, violins, and bodhráns, belt out a reel, 'The Belfast Hornpipe.' An appreciative crowd have pulled their seats around the musicians. A Swedish tourist with an enormous red beard and clapping hands asks a local what time the bar closes and is told 'about January.'

Comfortably planted in a quiet corner of the bar is Paul O'Flaherty, his daughter, Deirdre, and her husband, Roddy. The chairman of the IRA Army Council is tired. More out of manners than anything else, the teetotaller lifts his glass and brings the straw to his lips, but he doesn't drink the orange mineral.

Deirdre looks lovingly at her father. She embraces the thought that his head looks as if it is too heavy for his body as it nestles comfortably on his chest. As if contradicting his daughter's observation, Paul's head springs upright. He makes his way to the toilets. The popular republican leader is a well-recognised and a much-admired figure in Derrybeg and people like to speak to him, to shake his hand, to let him know they respect him. He responds politely. But a drunk, his eyelids almost touching, grabs O'Flaherty roughly by the arm and garbles something about how he and the IRA had 'sold out.'

O'Flaherty is embarrassed, and when he tries to break free, the man grips his arm tighter. A black-haired man with a pale face, prominent cheekbones, and no upper lip, appears out of nowhere, prises open the drunk's fingers, and ushers him towards the exit. O'Flaherty nods his appreciation.

The toilet door opens, and a man enters. Paul is at a urinal, and the man picks the urinal beside him. Both men look at the wall in front of them.

'Hello, Paul,' Ructions says.

'Hello.' O'Flaherty glances at the man. He is vaguely familiar. 'Have we met before?'

'Not that I can remember.'

O'Flaherty does a double-take. 'Who are you?'

'James O'Hare.'

'James "Ructions" O'Hare? Panzer's nephew?'

'Yes.'

'I've got you now.' O'Flaherty pulls up the zip of his trousers. 'Are you here to kill me, young O'Hare?'

'Why would I want to do that?'

'You might have your reasons.'

'I might, but I'm not here to harm you or anyone else.'

'So, if you're not here to kill me, you're here to talk to me.'

'Yes.'

'There are rules, O'Hare, procedures. You've been knocking around long enough to know that.'

'I tried, Paul, but your secretary wouldn't give me your phone number or email address, and I didn't want to leave my calling card – just in case someone other than yourself got it.'

'Secretary?' O'Flaherty smirks. 'I heard you were a smart-ass.'

'I'm just circumspect, that's all.'

'I'm circumspect myself. What you want is to talk business, and I never talk business when I'm having a piss.' O'Flaherty goes to the basin to wash his hands.

'I'm afraid I'm going to have to ask to break that particular rule.'

O'Flaherty studies Ructions. 'And what if I say no?'

'Then I walk out of this toilet, and you never see me again, nor the substantial donation I'd like to make to the cause.'

'The IRA isn't the Salvation Army. It's not a charitable institution.'

'But it does accept charitable donations,' Ructions says.

O'Flaherty knows when he is being baited. 'Have you ever heard of Ralph Waldo Emerson, O'Hare?'

'Nope.'

'He was a nineteenth-century American essayist and poet. Amongst other things, he said: "Money often costs too much." I've had to use that quote many times over the years to inform people that they'd be making a mistake if they thought I could be bought. I can't. Not only that, but I've a suspicion your money will cost.'

'Doesn't all money?'

'As I recollect, you've had ample opportunities in the last three years to make a substantial donation to the cause, and you didn't take any of them. Something has made you change your mind. I wonder what it might be? A woman, perhaps?'

The black-haired man who had rescued O'Flaherty at the bar from the drunk comes into the toilet and stares at Ructions. He takes a gun out of a holster beneath his coat and holds it to his side.

The toilet door opens again and, upon entering, Billy Kelly stands immediately behind the IRA man. He sticks a gun at the nape of the man's neck. 'I'll take that piece, if you don't mind,' Billy says.

'No, Billy,' Ructions says. 'It's alright.'

O'Flaherty waves his hand. 'It's all good here, Seán,' he says. 'I'm just having a friendly yarn with this gentleman.'

'You're sure, Paul?'

'Yes.'

The man gives Ructions an icy stare and pushes past Billy, who follows him out.

'You've been nothing but a pain in the butt to us,' O'Flaherty says. 'Do you know that?'

Ructions dons a face of celestial innocence. 'If it's any consolation,' he says, 'the cops think I'm a pain in the butt too.'

'There y'are then. We can't all be wrong. All right, I can't talk to you now, but let's get our heads together tomorrow? In the bar, here, five o'clock?'

'No messing about, Paul?'

'No.'

'Five it is, then.'

If Thierry Vasseur hadn't pursued his vocation to be a policeman like his father before him, he would have opted for a career as a musician. He's practising his bass guitar in his garage, accompanying Nina Simone in her song *Feeling Good*. He always gets high on this song. It purges negativity and breathes meaning and vitality into his life.

Vasseur's wife, Emily, appears in the doorway that leads from the house. Her presence bleeds his happiness because she's wiggling the phone in her hand.

Vasseur likes the odd moan. Occasionally, not often, he likes the thought of being a victim. He mutters, 'Can't a man get an hour's peace? Just an hour? Is that too much to ask?'

Emily holds out the phone.

He goes over to his recorder and turns off the music. 'Who is it?' he asks gruffly, taking off the bass guitar and pulling out the lead.

Emily looks around the garage. 'Look at the state of this place.'

'I'll clean it up later.'

'You'd better because I'm not doing it. I'm fed up—'

Vasseur takes the phone from her hand and sits down. 'Vasseur.'

'Thierry, it's Manus O'Toole.'

'Hi, Manus. Good to hear from you.'

'I just thought you'd like to know that your friend Ructions O'Hare is in Ireland at the minute.'

A look of consternation crosses Vasseur's face. 'Ireland? What's he doing there?'

'Beats me. We put an alert for him at all airports and channels crossings and, lo and behold, we got a hit.'

'Oh?'

'Yeah. He came through Dublin airport yesterday, disguised as a Father Seamus Fitzsimmons.'

'A priest?'

'And get this, Thierry: he had *three* field marshals' batons in his suitcase.'

'Three?'

'Yip. He said they were souvenirs.'

'Is there a video of him at the airport?'

'I'll get it over to you.'

'Thanks, Manus. Have you any idea where he went after that?'

'He hired a car and drove to Lisburn, a small town outside Belfast. The PSNI believe he met up with an old friend of his, a Billy Kelly. Kelly's a former IRA man turned criminal.'

'And then what?'

'That's it. He and Kelly disappeared. What do you make of it, Thierry?'

'I don't know,' Vasseur says. 'Ireland? I thought he was persona non grata there. Aren't the IRA looking to kill him?'

'They are.'

'Then why go into the lion's den?'

'Your guess is as good as mine.'

'Whatever the reason was, it must have been very important to him.' Vasseur wants to mine as much information from Manus as possible, but his thoughts are tripping over one another. 'When he came through the airport, was he alone?'

'Yes.'

Vasseur says, 'His girlfriend, Eleanor Proctor, she went to Ireland last week, didn't she?'

'Yip.'

'I wonder ... yes, it makes sense. He's going back because *she's* there.'

'It's possible.'

'But he's hardly going to make a new life for himself in Ireland ... not with the IRA on the warpath.'

'Seems highly unlikely.'

Vasseur rubs his cheek with the phone. 'Where's Eleanor now?'

'I don't know. She flew into Dublin International and got a bus to Belfast.'

'Could Ructions have done a deal with the IRA?' Vasseur asks. 'Is it possible he paid his taxes in exchange for being allowed to live peacefully in Ireland?'

'It's possible.'

'Would they be up for doing that deal, Manus?'

Manus offers that the IRA likes money, and plenty of it, especially now that they have a voracious money-eating political project to shepherd. 'Would they be up for doing a multimillion-pound deal with Ructions? You can bet the Palace of Versailles on it,' he says.

'Could he be collecting money he'd hidden from the robbery until the heat died down?'

'Maybe, but why send Eleanor here before him?'

'Good question. My hunch is he's come back because of Eleanor, not because of the bank money. Okay,' Vasseur says, 'let's assume he hasn't done a deal with the IRA. Let's assume he's come back to Ireland to bring Eleanor home.'

'Therein might lie the crux of the problem, Thierry. He doesn't *actually* have a home, not in the conventional sense, anyway. For all intents and purposes, he – and she – are homeless; they live out of suitcases, constantly looking over their shoulders for fear of being murdered by the IRA. That's hardly a recipe for a healthy relationship.'

'It's not. I've met him, and he didn't strike me as the type who would let a woman dictate his actions.'

'Love makes unreasonable demands on us all.'

'And you don't know where Eleanor is?'

'I don't,' Manus says. 'She headed straight to Northern Ireland after her arrival.'

'Would Dan Clarke know where she is?'

'I'd be surprised if he didn't.'

'I'm wondering why Ructions brought *three* Goering batons to Ireland.'

'That I can answer,' Manus says. 'Because three is less suspicious than one. He told the immigration officer they were reproductions, presents to two academic friends from the Republic, and a Protestant cleric from Belfast called Roy Salters, whom O'Hare said had tried to save his soul outside a bank in Belfast. Dan Clarke thought that was funny.'

'Why?'

'Because he interviewed a Reverend Roy Salters, who told him that he had attempted to save the soul of a man who was loitering outside the National Bank on the night it was robbed, but he couldn't identify Ructions.'

Vasseur gives no sign that he appreciates Ructions's sense of humour. 'We have to presume that the real baton was amongst the three, *n'est ce pas*? Otherwise, what's the point in bringing them in at all? But why would he bring the real baton to Ireland? Why not leave it in the relative safety of Paris, or wherever Mercier had it stashed? Could it be that he thinks the gold is in Ireland?' Vasseur ventures. 'It was a neutral country during the war, after all.'

'It's possible.'

'Ructions's trip to Ireland opens things up a bit.'

'In what way?'

'For a start, it tells us that Ructions, as I suspected, is the playmaker here. It also tells us that Mercier isn't selling Goering's baton to the neo-Nazis – that sale could more easily have been concluded in mainland Europe.'

'I don't mind telling you, Thierry, this whole thing is getting weirder by the minute.'

'It is weird, isn't it? Amm ... I appreciate your help and advice, Manus.'

'You're welcome. And be assured: he won't escape our attention for long. Ireland's a small country, and we've a good record for finding fugitives.'

'He's not a fugitive.'

'I know that.'

'I'd like to talk to O'Hare, Manus. Just a talk, mind; I don't want him arrested, *oui*?'

'I hear you, Thierry.'

CHAPTER TWENTY-SIX

CHIEF SUPERINTENDENT DANIEL CLARKE LOOKS OVER the rail of the Rainbow Bridge at the Ess na Larach waterfall in Glenariff Forest Park, County Antrim. A foggy dew surrounds the one-hundred-foot, double-drop waterfall as it incisively slits a narrow gorge out of the hard basalt rock.

Tiny Murdoch holds on to the wooden rail as he descends the side of the gorge. He reaches the Rainbow Bridge. Clarke turns towards him. 'Magic, isn't it?'

Tiny stops and, mouth open, gazes at the waterfall. 'I've lived a few dozen miles down the road from this all my life, and I didn't know it existed,' his voice barely audible over the crashing water. 'Christ Almighty, it's magnificent!' he turns to Clarke. 'It's worth fighting for.'

'But is it worth dying for?'

Tiny shrugs. They walk along the trail. 'How are things, Dan?'

'Okay. And you?'

'Paying the bills; shooting some pool when I get the chance.'

'That's good.'

They stroll along in silence. A cautionary voice tells Clarke to let Tiny speak first. Tiny gets the message. 'Sooo, here we are,' Tiny says. Clarke smiles. 'What've you got for me, Dan?'

'We need to talk about a couple of things,' Clarke says.

Tiny doesn't like Clarke's tone. It sounds jittery. 'Like what?'

'Eleanor Proctor, for one.'

'What about her?'

'Have you got her?'

Tiny makes no reply.

A silence can sometimes be as good as an admission. 'I see,' Clarke says. 'I want the IRA to release her.'

Tiny feels undervalued. 'Do you now? And what makes you think the IRA have her?'

'Your silence when I asked the question.'

Something tells Tiny to marshal his words carefully. 'If the IRA did have her – and I'm not in the IRA, so I can't say if they have got her or not – my information is that you, personally, Chief Superintendent Daniel Clarke, along with your PSNI colleagues, told the IRA where she was. Do you deny that?'

'I'm not fucking taping you, Tiny. It's gone too far for that.'

Tiny nods. 'Fair enough.'

'So?'

'So what?'

'So are you going to release her?'

'You can't just come to us now and say, "Oh, by the way, lads, I've changed my mind." Big boys' rules, Dan.'

'The big boys *are* changing the rules.'

Tiny grabs Clarke by the elbow to stop him from walking on. 'Something's spooked you. What is it?'

Clarke turns towards Tiny so that the IRA man will not miss the gravitas in his words. 'This thing's getting out of control.'

'How's that? I told you we weren't going to hurt the woman. What more do you want?'

Clarke looks around to make sure no one is watching or listening. 'You've had her for four days now.'

'And?'

'And the longer a person is held by paramilitaries, the greater the possibility exists that person will end up dead.'

'That won't happen.'

'Tiny, I'm gonna spell this out so there's no misunderstanding. Very important people are getting nervous. Interpol have been asking if we've surveillance on Proctor, and I can't give them a positive answer because I don't know where she is. This is embarrassing, Tiny. We want her released – now.'

Tiny senses panic in Clarke. 'I don't have the authority to make that decision, Dan.'

Clarke softly pumps Tiny's chest with the index finger of his clenched fist. 'Then get it – and get it quickly – before this thing becomes public property.'

They walk on, each immersed in his own thoughts. 'By the way,' Clarke says, 'there's an international manhunt underway for your pal Ructions.'

'He's not *my* pal. And, if you must know, he's in France.'

'Who told you that?'

'He did.'

Clarke purses his lips and shakes his head. 'No. He's in Ireland.'

Furrows appear on Tiny's forehead. 'The bastard' is as much

as he can muster at the spur of the moment. Tiny finally finds his voice: 'He's here to free his girlfriend. I need to have her moved.'

'You need to have her released.'

'I told you, Dan,' Tiny says, his irritation evident, 'that's not my decision, and, if I'm honest with you, I don't think the Army Council will agree to it.'

Clarke brings his hands together as though he were praying. *It's time to play the emotional card.* 'Look, Tiny, I took a chance with you because, despite our political differences, I believed you to be a man of honour.'

'I am a man of honour.'

'I hope that's true because I'm out on a limb here. I could go to prison if this thing unravels.'

'You're not flying solo, are you, Dan?'

Clarke looks distinctively uneasy. 'No, I'm not. But I'm the front man, and that makes me vulnerable.'

'So, let me get this right: this contact isn't officially sanctioned?'

'What do *you* think?' Clarke says, his voice laced with sarcasm.

'I'll tell you what I think, you *are* flying solo.'

'Not so.'

Tiny is savouring Clarke's discomfiture. 'You haven't answered my original question: What has spooked you?'

Clarke tries to hide the shakiness in his voice. 'Has O'Hare contacted you about Proctor?'

'I've contacted him.'

'What was his attitude?'

'He didn't seem to give a fuck about her.'

'He gives a fuck, all right. He's here to find a way of wresting her away from you—'

'No chance.'

'That's what the National Bank people thought before he emptied their vaults.' Clarke puts his hand on the rail and looks at the clear, rippling waters of the Glenariff river. 'If he prises her away from you—'

'He won't.'

'If he prises her away from you, she might go to the police and accuse the IRA of kidnapping her. In that case, she'll be given police protection, a new identity in another part of the world – the lot.'

'But she can't bring you down,' Tiny says. 'She doesn't know about us talking.'

Clarke is far from convinced. 'How many people do know?' he asks.

'A few guys around me and the Army Council.'

'That's a lot of people.'

'Trustworthy people.'

'For fuck's sake, Tiny, do you boys ever learn? You all thought "Stakeknife" – your top enforcer – was trustworthy, and I was debriefing him every *fucking* weekend,' Clarke says. 'No one is trustworthy, fucking no one. There's another thing. If it comes out that the IRA kidnapped Proctor, the peace process will be put in danger, and this thing *will* turn into a major inquiry. Have you a cigarette?'

'I thought you were allergic to smoking?'

'Just give me a fag, will you?'

Tiny gives Clarke a cigarette, and he lights it immediately and inhales deeply. *There's something else eating away at Dan,* Tiny thinks. 'What are you worried about?' he presses. 'The

'RA will deny everything and, without successful prosecutions, who's to prove differently?'

'That won't stop a major inquiry.'

'A major inquiry ... From the minute we came here, I've been asking myself: "Why is Dan so spooked," and do you know what?' Tiny puts a cupped hand to his ear, 'I'm hearing an answer, and it's saying there's hard evidence floating about you and I plotting to bring down Ructions. Is that the way of it, Dan?'

'No,' Clarke says, his voice quavering.

'That doesn't sound very convincing.'

Clarke turns his face away. 'There's a recording of our first meeting.'

'I knew it! I fucking knew it! Where is it and who has it?'

'It's safe,' Clarke says in a less than reassuring tone. 'Don't worry.'

'But I am worried, Dan; I'm very fucking worried. You said you approached me because I was a man of honour. You gave me your word you weren't recording our conversations and now ... ' Tiny looks at Clarke as though he has grown a carrot-like nose. 'What else are you hiding?'

Clarke pulls on the cigarette as if it's lifesaving oxygen. 'Nothing.'

Clarke strolls on. Tiny comes alongside him. 'Listen, Dan, you're up to your nostrils in quicksand.'

Clarke pulls back as if distancing himself from an imminent attack. 'Is that a threat?'

'No, it's a statement of fact. One call from an anonymous source and you can kiss your career goodbye.'

'We get anonymous calls all the time and we ignore ninety-nine-point-nine per cent of them. You've no evidence we have ever met, Tiny.'

'Amm ... I wouldn't be so sure about that.'

'What does that mean?'

'Amm ... *I* might also have a tape recording, a very incriminating tape recording.'

Dan looks like he is ready to cry. 'Ahh, come off it, Tiny! You gave me your word on behalf of the organisation.'

'You fucking hypocrite!' Tiny snarls. 'It's fine for you to secretly record me, but I can't record *you*? Get a grip, Dan. I've recorded every word we've ever exchanged. I can break you like' – Tiny snaps his fingers – 'that. You know, you could well end up in the nick if it comes out you've been in cahoots with the IRA Army Council.'

'Tiny, if I end up in the nick, you'll be in the cell next to me.'

Tiny raises a finger. 'That may be so, but you're forgetting one thing ...'

'And what's that?'

'What happens between us isn't really my shout. I answer to a higher power—'

'The Army Council.'

'Exactly. And they think strategically. Would they lose any sleep if poor old Tiny Murdoch ended up doing a wee bit of bird for the cause? Nope. They'd think they'd done me a good turn, given me an opportunity to show how much I loved Ireland. You know them, Dan, and you know I'm right.' Having delivered the haymaker, Tiny changes tack. 'But look, I don't think it's in their interests to bury you or me.'

'I hope not.'

'So we're in this together. For my part, I'll do everything in my power to get the woman released.'

'Tiny, you know we're on the clock.'

'I know, I know. I can't promise a result, but leave it with me. Okay?'

Clarke nods. He stares hesitantly at Tiny, opens his mouth as if to speak, and immediately shuts it again.

The IRA intelligence officer's eyes narrow suspiciously as he wags his fingers at Clarke, urging him to open up. 'You've something else on your mind.'

Clarke theatrically shakes his head, intimating to Tiny that he is making an important decision. 'Aha,' Tiny says, smiling. The two men stare at each other. 'What about this?' Tiny says. 'Why don't you pretend you're in the confessional, Dan, and I'll pretend I'm a priest. Now, you told me you were a Catholic.'

'I am.'

Tiny makes the sign of the cross over Clarke's head. 'Come on, my son ... Bless me, Father, for I have sinned.'

Clarke remains silent.

A thin smile appears on Tiny's face, or is it a despotic smirk? Clarke cannot tell. 'So, you don't want to play confessionals?' Tiny says.

Clarke nods affirmatively.

'Let's see ... Ructions,' Tiny says. 'It's something important to do with Ructions. Am I getting warmer?'

Clarke beams extravagantly.

'What's the dear boy been up to now? Hmm?' Aiming a finger at Clarke, Tiny declares: 'It's about the international manhunt you said was underway for Ructions.'

Clarke slowly claps.

Tiny vainly allows himself a full-blown smile. 'That's it. This has got to do with Hermann Goering's baton, hasn't it? Ructions has it, hasn't he? I know he has it!'

You remembered that? Clarke thinks. *Well, why wouldn't you? Time to play my ace card.* 'Yes. He brought three field marshals' batons into Ireland a few days ago, and one of them is Goering's baton.'

'But to what end did he bring them in?' Tiny asks, wiggling his fingers. 'Come on, Dan, out with it.'

'It appears the baton is the means to uncovering Goering's hidden gold bullion.'

Tiny's eyes are now zeroed-in on Clarke. 'Gold bullion? How much gold bullion are we talking about?'

'Estimates vary from a half to a billion euro.'

'Ha! I knew there was something brewing! I fucking knew it!' Tiny tries to calm down but a billion euro is echoing like a land-slide in his ears. 'How solid is this, Dan? Is it all speculation?'

'It was, but now the French police think there's every chance Goering transferred gold to Ireland before the war ended.'

'Yo ho ho and a bottle of rum! A treasure hunt, Danny Boy? I fucking love treasure hunts! All I need now is a parrot and a three-cornered hat.'

CHAPTER TWENTY-SEVEN

PAUL O'FLAHERTY SITS ON A CHAIR IN A SMALL ROOM at the back of Teach Jack's Pub. He's not a man who rushes into situations. 'I've heard a lot about you, Ructions.'

'None of it good, I hope.'

'Very little of it.'

'I've heard a lot about you from my uncle Panzer. All of it good.'

'I liked Panzer. He passed too soon.'

'We all pass too soon, don't you think?'

'Not necessarily,' O'Flaherty says, leaning forward into Ructions's face. 'Some people pass too late. Do you know anybody who has lived too long?'

'I know people who take shortcuts. I also know people who want to take what isn't theirs.'

O'Flaherty laughs. 'That's some answer – coming from Ireland's greatest bank robber.'

Ructions does not embrace the IRA leader's sense of humour.

'I work for every penny I get, Paul. I stick my neck out. What I don't do is expect others to hand me a cut of their wages.' Ructions raises his eyebrows. 'There's a little touch of bad manners there, don't you think?'

'Bad manners and good business have never been strangers. You've been around, Ructions. You understand how big corporations work. They maximise profits. There's no sentimentality. The little guy takes the hit. That's the way of it.'

'Sometimes the little guy comes good.'

O'Flaherty waves a finger. 'Ah, but you came back to Ireland to talk to *me*.'

O'Flaherty is quite pleased with himself. Ructions wants to do a deal. Has he finally had enough? The old republican gets off his seat and looks out the window. Two men are standing on the corner opposite. He beckons Ructions with a finger, and when he comes alongside him, he nods to the window. 'This place is surrounded by IRA volunteers.'

'That sounds suspiciously like a threat, Paul.'

'I prefer to call it insurance.'

'Against what?'

'Against you.'

'What do you expect me to do exactly?'

'I don't know what I expect you to do. That's the reason why IRA volunteers are all around this building.'

'I don't like being threatened.'

'Who does? But sometimes it's necessary.'

Ructions opens the window, leans out, and waves to the two men on the corner. They wave back. 'They seem nice enough fellas.'

O'Flaherty pulls Ructions back in and closes the window.

'Come on, let's sit by the fire.' The two men move to sit beside the smouldering turf fire. 'You sought me out,' O'Flaherty says. 'What do you want?'

'That you bring your influence to bear on a particular situation.'

'And what situation would that be?'

'Tiny Murdoch is holding my former partner, Eleanor Proctor. I want her released.'

'Eleanor who?'

Ructions looks stern. 'Are we gonna start playing games now, Paul?'

'Isn't that what we've been doing since we got our heads together in the toilet last night?'

'I want her released.'

'So you said.'

There is a pause as each man evaluates the other.

'Are you going to make this difficult, Paul?'

O'Flaherty's head tilts slowly to the right, as if he is seeing Ructions for the first time. 'Have you any idea what's running through my head right now?'

Ructions shakes his head.

'I'm trying to convince myself not to have you arrested and shot dead.'

'You're joking.'

'No, I'm not.'

'What makes you think you control this situation, Paul?'

'Don't I? Aren't you forgetting the volunteers outside?'

'Aren't you forgetting you're sitting here talking to me?'

'Are you threatening *me* now?'

Ructions flicks open his coat to reveal a revolver in a holster.

'Paul,' Ructions says, 'I've got this, and it wouldn't bother me in the slightest if John Wayne, the Seventh Cavalry, and Crazy Horse were all outside the door. I've got *you*, and you, sir, are the definite article.'

Paul cranks his head to the side. 'You *are* threatening me.'

Ructions looks the picture of innocence while holding up his palms to the heavens. 'No, I'm counter-threatening you. There's a difference. One precedes and provokes the other.'

O'Flaherty looks at his shoes for a few seconds. 'Supposing I know—'

'Stop right there. Let's cut out all the supposing, Paul. There's only you and me here.'

'Okay. If I were to use my influence to get Eleanor Proctor released, what's in it for the IRA?'

'There's more to it than that. I'd need a guarantee from you that I'll no longer be on an IRA hit list, and that I can come and go in Ireland as I please without fear of the IRA killing me.'

'Aha. You want two things?'

'No, they're the same thing.'

'I don't agree. You want Ms Proctor released, *and* you want immunity from execution from the IRA. That's two demands.' Paul strokes his chin. 'I repeat: What's in it for the IRA?'

'A million pounds. In the morning. Transferred into any account you want. No questions asked.'

'That won't do.'

'It'll have to do. There's no more. I've been taken out big time by the stock market crash.'

'You're not listening. It won't do. The numbers don't stack up. I couldn't sell it to my board.'

Even before he had engineered this meeting, Ructions had a strong feeling that it would be difficult to sell a one-million-pound pay-off to the Army Council. 'That's all I have. If that doesn't work, we've no deal.'

'We've no deal,' O'Flaherty says immediately.

'Don't you need to discuss my offer with the members of your board?'

'Nope.'

'A million pounds is a lot of money.'

'It's not enough. Come up with something better.'

'There is nothing better. That's my final offer, Paul. Take it or leave it.'

'It's not the figure I had in mind.'

'For what it's worth, it's a million more than what I had in mind,' Ructions says, standing up. 'You're in danger of overplaying your hand, Paul. Can I tell you something? Eleanor and I have broken up. That was why she came back to Ireland. I told her it was a stupid idea – I even told her she was liable to end up a guest of the IRA!'

O'Flaherty smirks.

Ructions whispers in O'Flaherty's ear: 'All that said, Eleanor's important to me, Paul, and if something nasty happens to her, I'll take it very bad.'

'There you go, threatening the IRA again, threatening me!' O'Flaherty grins. 'Son, there's something about you that I like: you've balls, and I've always respected people who stand up for themselves in the face of overwhelming odds. But you're walking on very thin ice. Now slow up before you say something that I can't ignore.'

'If I don't hear within forty-eight hours that you want to

accept my offer, it's off the table.' Ructions swishes his hand. 'No extensions.' He stands up and buttons his coat, indicating that the meeting is over.

'Don't be rushing off yet,' O'Flaherty says, smiling. 'Sit down again.'

Ructions pauses, looks at him quizzically, then sits down.

O'Flaherty says, 'I'm hearing whispers, y'know?'

'What about?'

'About Hermann Goering's baton.'

'What about it?'

'You tell me.'

'I don't know what you're talking about.'

'You disappoint me, Ructions.'

'Do I?'

O'Flaherty goes over to a table, lifts a kettle, and walks to the sink behind the bar. He fills the kettle with water, puts it on the boiling ring, and comes back to Ructions. 'Tea or coffee?'

'I'm not fussy. Whatever's handy.'

O'Flaherty makes Ructions a coffee. 'Milk? Sugar?' Ructions nods. O'Flaherty takes over a bottle of milk and a sugar bowl. Ructions helps himself. O'Flaherty sits down again. 'I hear you're not a big drinker.'

'I can take it or leave it,' Ructions says.

'Wise man. I never took to the sup myself. Now to business.'

O'Flaherty settles himself, tells Ructions to appreciate that the IRA has extensive contacts with individuals in all levels of society and all religious denominations. Ructions nods on cue. The elder tells the younger that people who you would never expect to be talking to the IRA seek their assistance. He recounts how, during the war with the British, lots of unionists secretly came to the IRA and urged them to bomb their failing businesses so they could claim the insurance. 'We were happy to oblige,' O'Flaherty says, 'providing we got our cut of the insurance.' Paul waves his hands. 'Everybody came out smelling of roses. Now, here's what *you've* gotta understand, Ructions: We *always* get our cut. *Always.* Everybody pays. The other thing is … because we have such extensive contacts, we know about this Hermann Goering baton business. We know the baton is a doorway to Goering's gold.'

'Goering's gold? What's that about?'

'You tell me.'

'I don't know what you're talking about.'

'We know about the neo-Nazis killing Serge Mercier's servant in France for the baton.'

'What baton? Who's Serge Mercier?'

O'Flaherty studies Ructions's face. Both men smile. O'Flaherty drinks his tea and says: 'You and I, if we're to reach an agreement, we have to be totally honest with each other. I want you to reflect on that.'

'I'm not sure total honesty exists in our world,' Ructions says. 'Does it?'

'Do you want to know what I really think?' O'Flaherty says. Ructions nods. 'I think you'd *better* be totally honest with me 'cause I'm your only pathway to a normal life.'

Ructions bows his head, holds up his hands, and smirks. 'And I'm your only pathway to …'

O'Flaherty smiles broadly. 'Pathway to what, young O'Hare?'

Ructions lifts his head. 'To a golden future.'

CHAPTER TWENTY-EIGHT

ADELBERT KELLER IS RICH, ALTHOUGH NO ONE CAN ascertain the source of his wealth. His home, on the shore of the Chiemsee, an hour's drive outside Munich, has a twenty-five-metre swimming pool, a bar, a sauna, a jacuzzi, a spa room, a gymnasium, a billiards room, eight bedrooms, and four reception rooms. In his boathouse is a seven-berth Cayman 75 HT powerboat and three Jet Skis. The latest in a long string of females who have shared his life is thirty-year-old Candice, a former lap dancer from Dresden.

As a child and then as a student, Karl Keller had spent idyllic summers in his paternal grandfather's home. He found him a kind man, reassuring, always on hand to help or to dispense advice when needed.

Karl needs his advice now.

They walk out the patio doors of a second-floor reception room onto the overhanging balcony. Directly in their line of sight is the Chiemsee and the island of Frauenchiem, which covers thirty-eight acres. Those acres include a Benedictine nunnery, which has been there since 782, and a cenotaph to Nazi leader Generaloberst Alfred Jodl, who signed the German Instrument of Surrender on 7 May 1945. They sit down in wicker chairs at a glass coffee table, and Karl lights a cigar.

Adelbert is not his usual tranquil self. He hadn't had the slightest idea that Jochen Schulze was the mole, and the surprise was total. He liked the man. They had played golf and poker together. Schulze had stayed in the house, sailed on the power-boat, and got drop-dead drunk on Adolf Hitler's birthday. The man had cherished hearing about the old times, when the SS ruled the world.

Karl doesn't know where to start. He lifts his glass of red wine and sips sheepishly.

'What did he know?' Adelbert asks as he also sips red wine.

'Are you sure you want an answer to that question?'

'Of course I want an answer. How can I help you if I don't know what's going on?'

'He knew we carried out the Mercier raid.'

Adelbert has regained his composure. 'But he wasn't there?'

'No.'

'Then whatever he has heard is hearsay and useless in a court of law. Have you ever admitted being there to anyone?'

'No.'

'Not even to close friends?'

'No one.'

'Does Gitte know you were there?'

Karl hesitates.

'She does,' Adelbert says. 'Your hesitancy confirms it.' The older man stands up, looks out over the lake, and asks, 'Does Schulze know how important the Reichsmarschall's baton is?'

'He knows it's the key to the gold.'

'Then the authorities also know it's the key to the gold. That's not good.'

Adelbert walks along the balcony. 'Where's the baton now?'

'An Irishman has it.'

'An Irishman?'

'Yes. A bank robber called O'Hare.'

'And where is he?'

'Somewhere in France.'

'Where in France?'

'I don't know.'

'So you don't have control of the baton or the Irishman?'

'No. But he doesn't know the baton's true value.'

Adelbert gazes out to Frauencheim island. 'That's something.' The elder Nazi swirls the red wine in his glass but doesn't drink it. 'You haven't acquitted yourself very well, have you, Karl?'

Shaken, Karl draws on his cigar. 'It's been challenging.'

Adelbert sits down again. 'This Irishman ... you're in contact with him?'

'Yes. I'm supposed to be meeting him in Dublin next Saturday.'

Adelbert shifts uneasily in his seat. 'Who arranged that?'

'He did.'

Adelbert takes his time before asking: 'Is he IRA?'

'No. The IRA want to kill him.'

Adelbert groans. 'Dublin,' he says, as much to himself as to Karl. 'He'll have absolute control there. I don't like it.'

'I've no choice, Grandfather.'

'There are always choices.'

'Such as?'

'You can do the unpalatable; you can turn your back on this.'

'I can't.'

Adelbert asserts his authority. 'That's for me to decide, not you.'

'I know, Grandfather, but were we to have possession of the baton, it would open up a treasure trove with which we can finance an enormous political programme and win power, and … and because the baton rightfully belongs to us national socialists.'

'You're so headstrong,' Adelbert says, smiling. 'You remind me of someone I once knew.'

'I remind you of yourself!'

Adelbert nods. 'A long time ago, when Otto Skorzeny and I were Invincibles. Ireland …' Adelbert says reflectively. 'Did I tell you Otto lived in Ireland?'

'Yes.'

Adelbert takes a deep breath and proceeds as if Karl hadn't answered him in the affirmative. 'He moved there in 1957.'

'How was he received?'

'Oh, the Irish loved him. He was feted in Dublin by that politician … you know him … he was the Irish prime minister a few years ago.'

Karl shakes his head.

'Haughey. Charles Haughey.'

'Yes, I've heard of him.'

Adelbert recounts how Skorzeny had bought Martinstown House, a 160-acre farm in County Kildare, and how he had visited Skorzeny there. There is a glint in his eye as he recalls those halcyon days, when he, along with Skorzeny, scoured the countryside, in vain, looking for Goering's gold. 'Even after he left Ireland,' Adelbert says, 'Otto never wavered in his conviction that the gold was in County Kildare.'

'But why County Kildare?'

'Because Hans Winkler … you've heard of Hans Winkler?'

'You've mention that name before, but I can't remember in what context.'

Adelbert tells Karl that Winkler had been an assistant curator to a man called Adolf Mahr, who was the first director of the national museum of Ireland and, being so familiar with the country, it was to Winkler that the Reichsmarschall had turned when he needed to hide his gold in Ireland.

'And he hid it in County Kildare?'

'According to the diary that Winkler left.'

'He left a diary? You didn't tell me that.'

'Well, he did.'

'And Uncle Otto read it?'

'Yes.'

'Then why didn't he find the gold?'

'Winkler was careful not to go into specifics, other than those tonnes of gold were hidden in County Kildare.'

'He probably wanted to come back and retrieve the gold for himself after the war.'

'I'd say that was a distinct possibility.'

'But why put it in a diary at all?' Karl asks.

'Perhaps because Winkler was a petty bureaucrat and would have liked everything numbered and in its rightful place. And he certainly would never have expected his diary to be read by the authorities – and definitely not by the likes of Otto.'

'Where's the diary now?'

'Who knows? Otto probably had it put in his coffin with him.'

Karl laughs. As if in an afterthought, Adelbert says, 'I want to come back to the Mercier raid.'

'Okay.'

'I'm not going to ask you if you murdered that servant fellow, Clément Beauregard, but can you think of a reason why he was murdered?'

'To make a point.'

'Which was?'

'That nothing or no one would stand in the way of the person who killed him.'

'In that case, I think it was a point well made.' Adelbert looks at Karl as if seeing him for the first time. *Behind that angelic face*, he thinks, *is a true national socialist.* "Interpol is no doubt trying to build a case against you for murdering Clément, but you shouldn't worry. They haven't enough evidence to arrest you.'

'I'm not worried about being arrested.'

'Well you should be. You're the leader of the party; you should be above accusations of murder. Have you any idea how such accusations, were you arrested, would play out in the press? This is Germany, man, it's against the law to propagate national socialism, or to have a military wing.'

'The press can go to hell as far as I'm concerned.'

Adelbert sighs. 'Karl,' he says, 'you might not like what I'm going to say, but I think it's time you got out of politics.'

Karl is stunned. His grandfather had surreptitiously been a founding member of the German National Party and had spoon-fed his grandson wanton dreams of Nazi world domination. 'You surprise me. Why do you say that?'

Adelbert stands up and stretches his arms, as if expunging a lifetime of failure. 'I say it because you are naïve.'

'I've never heard anything so ridiculous in my life,' Karl says, his face crimson. 'How dare you—'

Adelbert is not the type of man who allows upstarts to usurp his authority, *'Halt den Mund!'* he shouts.

Karl shuts up.

Before Adelbert can continue, Candice comes onto the bal-cony and sits beside him. He crosses his arms and gives her a solemn look. 'Darling,' he says, 'could you excuse us, please? This is a private conversation.'

Candice does not move immediately. 'A private conversa-tion,' she says impudently. 'Not for my ears, then.'

'It's politics,' Adelbert says. 'Not your thing.'

'Not my thing,' she repeats. Candice throws back her head indignantly, and, with arms folded, she leaves the balcony.

Adelbert has a dilemma. He had always known that his nephew was capable of poor judgement, but he had hoped he would grow to be a prudent leader. Alas, he detected no sign that a transformation was in the offing. Now, he believes, it is time to apply the poultice, to draw the pus out of the wound.

'I'm sorry,' Adelbert says. 'I was hasty in my opinion of you. I apologise.'

'That's okay,' Karl says. 'In truth, things might have been done better, but I'm not ready to forsake the Fourth Reich yet.'

'Okay.'

'As long as the Irishman does not discover the secret of the baton, I'm very much in play. Now, tell me more about the Reichsmarschall's gold, Grandfather.'

'You know the story.'

'Tell me it again. Please.'

'I met the Reichsmarschall in 1944, as you know. The greatest day of my life. The man *was* power; you could feel it radiate from him. I was with Otto at the time. The Reichsmarschall was particularly fond of Otto. He confided in him. And Otto confided in me.'

'What did he tell you, Grandfather?'

Adelbert sits back, his eyes half-closed. 'You want me to bring you back to 1944?'

Karl nods and leans forward ...

CHAPTER TWENTY-NINE

16 December 1944, off the coast of Ireland near Dublin ...

A MOONLESS SKY AND A FLAT SEA. A PERFECT OPPOR-
tunity for low-lying German submarines to make good time
on the surface. Sailing at seventeen knots, U-boat U-772 cuts
through the waves, as it approaches southeastern Ireland. In
the conning tower, the submarine's commander, Kapitänleutnant Ewald Rademacher, and three other crew members
scan the horizon through their binoculars. The baby-faced
Rademacher lifts a steaming cup of tea. It's the twenty-sev-
en-year-old captain's third time going to sea in U-772 since
August, and he has yet to sink a single Allied ship. Not that
sinking Allied ships is his priority on this trip. In fact, and
much to Rademacher's chagrin, on all three trips he had been
ordered to avoid contact with Allied ships until he delivered
his cargo. This trip is somewhat enigmatic though because,

unlike the others, Rademacher, the forty-eight crew members, and the six SS guards who mount an armed 'round-the-clock guard on the cargo, do not know the nature of the freight they are transporting, although some have speculated that it is weaponry for the IRA.

When the submarine is three nautical miles outside of Dublin harbour, Rademacher asks his second-in-command how long it will be before they reach the delivery point and is told it will be five minutes. The captain will be glad when this part of the mission is completed; he does not like having armed SS men on board his vessel; they make his crew uncomfortable.

On a fishing boat outside Dublin harbour, Hans Winkler stands in the captain's cabin as the vessel approaches the rendezvous site. It's freezing, and he's nervous. He slaps his hands around his body to keep warm. The captain, a trawler skipper before he joined the Kriegsmarine, peers out the window.

Weeks earlier, Winkler had been summoned back to Carinhall, outside Berlin, to be told by the Reichsmarschall that he was not to tamper with the cargo, that even opening one of the crates would be viewed as treasonable and would result in his being shot by firing squad. To ensure absolute security, the Reichsmarschall said that six English-speaking SS men from the Fallschirm-Panzer-Division 1 Hermann Goering would be accompanying him on the mission. Winkler had looked into Goering's eyes while the latter was spelling out the consequences of his orders being disobeyed and had been gripped with a fear he had never experienced before: his life meant nothing to this man. He assured Goering that his discretion was guaranteed. In return, Goering had promised Winkler an iron cross when this business was over. Winkler was also informed that he would be picked up by submarine in the days following the arrival of the cargo and brought back to Germany.

Like the submariners, Winkler had surmised that the IRA would be collecting the cargo from the land location in which the cargo would be hidden. He did not like the IRA. His ordered archaeological mind found their incompetence disorientating.

The U-772 comes into Winkler's view, and he hears it cut engines. Winkler flashes a Morse code message and sees the signal, in turn, that the message has been received.

Below deck on the U-772, a human chain is formed, and the submariners pass dozens of heavy wooden crates of cargo along the chain to the bridge, and then up to the conning tower.

Several sailors climb onto the fishing boat as the cargo is transferred.

The transfer is completed in just over an hour, and Winkler shakes hands with the submarine's second-in-command. The ropes that hold the fishing boat to the submarine are cast off.

The six SS men who had guarded the cargo on its trip from Trondheim, Norway, stay on the fishing boat, which turns back towards Ringsend in Dublin harbour.

Rademacher is happy that all the cargo had been discharged. Now all he has to do is to wait out at sea for two nights and then return to pick up Winkler and the SS men . . .

'What happened to Winkler and the six SS men?' Karl asks.

'Rademacher picked them up according to the plan and brought them back to Germany.'

Karl holds out his hands questioningly. 'And?'

'And, after debriefing them, the Reichsmarschall sent them to the Russian front, where they all perished.'

'I guess it's safe to say that Winkler didn't get his iron cross, then?' Karl asks.

'I guess it's safe to say he didn't even get a wooden cross.'

'And Kapitänleutnant Rademacher and his crew?' Karl asks. 'Did Otto speak to him?'

'He never got a chance to interrogate Rademacher. U-772 was sunk by a British frigate a few weeks later, off the coast of County Cork.'

'So everybody on board perished?'

'Yes.'

'And by the end of the war, only the Reichsmarschall knew the location of the gold?'

'Yes,' Adelbert says.

'But Uncle Otto had Winkler's diary and he spent the rest of his life searching for the gold?'

'More or less. At the start, Otto he believed the American government had the gold. Then Emmy Goering told him that, no, that wasn't true, that the Reichsmarschall had spirited it out of Germany before the war ended.'

'She didn't know where?'

'No, but she did know that the baton was an important clue to its location.'

'And Uncle Otto went looking for the baton?'

'Yes. Emmy said she gave it to an American GI called Wolfe Paterson.'

'Was he the guard who smuggled the cyanide capsule in to the Reichsmarschall?'

'The very same.'

'And what did Uncle Otto do?'

'He hunted for Paterson.'

'In America? He got past American immigration?'

'It wasn't that difficult in those days. He was smuggled across the Canadian border by sympathisers. Don't forget: Skorzeny was a war hero. He was held in the highest esteem.'

'He found Paterson?'

'Yes.'

'And?'

'They had words. And Paterson, after some robust persuasion, told Skorzeny that he had sold the baton to an art dealer for twenty thousand dollars, but he couldn't find the receipt for the sale and couldn't remember the art dealer's name.'

'What happened to Paterson?'

'He had an accident.'

'Oh?'

'Yeah. He was drunk and drove his car over a cliff.'

Karl smirks.

Adelbert smiles. 'Now I must rest.'

'And I must return to Munich.'

After seeing his nephew drive off, Adelbert goes back into his mansion. He approaches a mirror that is hanging on a wall and swings it at one end, revealing a safe, which he opens. He takes out a diary and turns to the first page. Written in large letters is:

PROPERTY OF HANS WINKLER

73A ADOLF HITLER PLATZ

BERLIN

CHAPTER THIRTY

ELEANOR SLIDES HER TONGUE AROUND CRACKED LIPS.
Her eyes are puffy with deep shadows. She runs her free hand
through her long, knotted hair. Lying on a mattress on a floor in
a darkened room and handcuffed to a radiator, she is a long way
from the confident young woman who, just over a week earlier,
had left Ructions to make a new life for herself. The small of her
back is sore. She turns over on her side and brings up her legs
into a foetal position. Ructions's voice has been chattering away
in her brain for some time, telling her to dry her tears, to not
let them see her like this. She also remembers his words at the
airport: 'You survive. That's all that matters. And don't worry
about me. I make a habit of having multiple strategies in place to
cover every possible eventuality. I will survive; you can depend
on that. But you fucking survive too. You do it.'

Eleanor is picking at the wallpaper when two women with
scarfs around their faces enter the room. 'Time for a shower.'

Eleanor's eyes flick from one of her gaolers to the other. 'I want to talk to Tiny Murdoch,' she says in a strong voice.

'Who's Tiny Murdoch?'

'Look, no more games, please. Tell Mr Murdoch I want to talk to him.'

'Shower,' one of the guards says.

'Are you going to tell Murdoch I want to speak to him?'

'We don't know any Tiny Murdoch. Now, shower. Hurry up!'

Eleanor enters the shower room. She slowly removes her clothes and steps into the shower cubicle. She lets the shower wash over her. There is a toothbrush and toothpaste on the windowsill, and she considers brushing her teeth while in the shower, but rather than put someone else's tooth brush into her mouth, she instead squeezes some toothpaste onto her finger and runs it around her teeth.

Eleanor walks back out on to the landing. The two women are in front of her. Still drying her hair with a towel, she says, 'I don't know which of you were responsible for allowing me to shower, so I'll thank you both.'

'Eleanor, isn't it?' one of the guards says.

'Yes.'

'Well, Eleanor, we don't like this any more than you do,' the second guard says.

'Can I have a cigarette, please? I've been going crazy for a smoke.'

'Ach, give her a fag, for God's sake,' the second guard says. 'Sure, what does it matter?'

The first guard hesitates, then shrugs. 'Okay.' She puts her hand in her coat pocket, takes out a packet of cigarettes and a lighter, and holds out a cigarette to Eleanor. 'Here.' Eleanor reaches for the cigarette, lights it, and takes a deep draw. She smiles. 'Thanks.'

An hour later, Eleanor is back in the room, once more hand-cuffed to the radiator when she hears thumping heavy footsteps on the stairs. A large man appears, wearing blue jeans, a brown sweater, and a grey balaclava. 'What's going on here?'

'She's having a smoke,' the second guard says.

'Mr Murdoch?' Eleanor says.

'What did you just say?' the large man asks.

'I need to talk to Tiny Murdoch.'

Tiny whispers in a corner with the two guards and takes the cigarettes and lighter. As soon as the guards leave the room, he pulls up a foldaway chair in front of Eleanor and sits with his chest to the back of the chair. Eleanor and Tiny weigh up each other. The IRA leader is the first to break. 'I'm not enjoying this.'

'Funny that. Neither am I.'

Tiny hands Eleanor the packet of cigarettes and the lighter. She lights up and nods her appreciation.

'Why did you ever hook up with Ructions?' Tiny asks.

Eleanor blows smoke rings.

'Did you never twig that he was interested only in using you to pull off the bank job?'

Eleanor points her cigarette at Tiny. 'You sound like a police officer I once knew.'

'That wouldn't be Chief Superintendent Dan Clarke, would it?'

Eleanor is surprised. 'You know Mr Clarke?'

Tiny smirks. 'I know Danny-boy all right. He and I go way back ... the cunt. But never mind him.' Tiny stands up and goes to the mattress beside Eleanor. 'You must really love Ructions.'

'What makes you think that?'

'Why else would you protect him like this?'

Eleanor's head turns towards Tiny, settling on his eyes through the slitted balaclava. 'You know, Tiny, I've been asking myself the same question. You are Tiny Murdoch, aren't you?'

Tiny resists the impulse to remove his balaclava. 'Supposing I am Tiny Murdoch ... what would you say to me?'

'What I have to offer is for Tiny Murdoch's ears only.'

Tiny repeats the question: 'What would you say to Mr Murdoch?'

Eleanor puts her lips next to Tiny's ear: 'I'd say: "What do I have to do to be released from this dump?"'

Tiny whispers in Eleanor's ear, 'Simple: you'd have to tell all.'

'Okay, I want to do that.'

'And what's your offer?'

'That's for Mr Murdoch to find out.'

Eleanor reckons he's hooked; she knows that if she chisels away at his curiosity, it will eventually get the better of him.

'And if Mr Murdoch doesn't want to talk to you? What then?'

Eleanor turns to the wall and picks at the wallpaper with her fingernail. 'Well, he loses out, doesn't he?'

'He loses out on what?'

'That's for him to find out.'

Tiny pulls off his balaclava and runs his hand through his ruffled hair. 'Satisfied?' he says grumpily.

'Hello, Tiny.'

'Hello, Eleanor. Now, what would I lose out on?'

This moment is not to be rushed. 'Amm ... what would you lose out on? Nothing much. Just an opportunity to get your hands on a billion euro worth of gold bullion.'

———

Billy Kelly's stomach is rumbling. He drives off the M1 motorway at Belfast's Broadway roundabout. 'I feel awful weak, Ructions. I swear to God, you've no idea how weak I feel.' Ructions, sitting low in the back of the car, opens a paper and looks at it. 'We haven't eaten a bite since eight o'clock this morning,' Billy moans. 'I'd give a hundred nicker for a fish supper,' he says, looking at the car's clock. 'Aldo's will still be open. Have you ever had one of Aldo's fish suppers, Ructions? His fish are two feet long. And it's only up the street. Up that way.' Billy points a finger towards the Donegall Road.

'Just drop me to Elmwood Avenue and you can eat as many fish suppers as you like.'

As Billy drives towards the Queen's University area, Ructions folds his paper, takes out his phone, and dials a number. 'Hello? Dermy? It's Ructions. Have you had a look at that thing I gave you yet?'

'Yes.'

'I'll be with you in a couple of minutes, okay?'

'Sure.'

Billy pulls up to the Centre for Archaeology, Paleoecology, and Geography on leafy Elmwood Avenue. It's a still night. 'I'll phone you when I'm ready,' Ructions says to Billy, who drives off.

Ructions follows the signs to the archaeology department and is met at the door by Dermot. They shake hands. Dermot smiles, but it's the smile of a man who feels like he wants a good scratch; like a man who is being eaten alive by fleas. Dermot leads Ructions into the reception area. A plastic caveman in a yellow hard hat stands facing the entrance. They go along a corridor and enter a lift to the first floor. Dermot shows Ructions into a large, well-lit rectangular room. Three wooden benches take up

most of the space in the room. Two microscopes sit on a bench
attached to the far wall. An X-ray light box hangs from the wall.
They approach a table on which sit a large magnifying lamp, four
notebooks, an assortment of pens, a plastic tub containing gravel
and sediment, and the original Hermann Goering baton.

'Would you like a cup of tea?' Dermot asks.

'No, Dermy, let's get on with this.'

Dermot lifts the baton. 'I've x-rayed the baton,' he says, 'and
I've got to say, it's a magnificent piece.'

'In what way magnificent?'

'For one thing, I'm fairly sure the six hundred and forty jewels are real.'

Ructions remains stern. 'I can't see Hitler presenting Hermann Goering with six hundred fake jewels, can you?'

'No, no, you're right.'

'What else?'

'The cap ends are made of gold, but they're not twenty-four
carat, which is good for us.'

'Why?'

Dermot explains that twenty-four carat is pure gold, and that
pure gold is soft. The less carats there are in a piece, he says,
the less gold is in it, and the more durable it is. The cap ends on
Goering's baton are yellow, whereas pure gold is reddish-yellow.
He estimates that the end caps are eighteen-carat gold and that
the Balkan crosses are platinum. The broad smile on Dermot's
face conveys that he has something exciting to tell Ructions.
'And – and this is *not* the crucial bit – there are threads around
which the cap ends are fastened.'

Ructions feels as if his stomach is a nursery for baby eels. The
last time he felt like this was when he had taken an Aston Villa

grip bag, containing one million pounds, from a bank employee during the robbery of the National Bank. He tries to look cool, but his laughing eyes betray a giddy heart. 'So the cap ends screw off?' he says casually.

'Most definitely. They may be a bit tight, but you'd expect that after what … sixty-odd years?'

'You said this is not the crucial bit? What *is* the crucial bit?'

Dermot takes Ructions over to the light box and clips up an X-ray. 'This is the stem of the baton,' Dermot says, pointing to the X-ray. 'Do you see this?'

Ructions looks closely, but he doesn't see anything that excites him.

Dermot points again.

Ructions's eyes are almost touching the X-ray light box. 'I don't see anything.'

Dermot's finger outlines a faint shadow on the screen. 'Whatever this material is, it's not part of the original structure of the baton.'

'What does that mean?'

'It means that, whatever it is, someone put it there *after* the baton was crafted.'

'So what is it?'

Dermot raises a finger. 'A good question. My guess is that it's a thin layer of paper or some type of cloth-like material.'

'Can we open it?'

'I'm fairly certain that we can. But my problem is this: if we put it in a clamp and try to force it open, we might damage the gold on the end caps.' Dermot is expecting Ructions to display alarm at the prospect of damaging the gold, but Ructions's face is stoic. 'My advice is to take it to a jeweller. They'd know more about this than me.'

'Do you know any jeweller we can bring this to? Someone who'll keep his mouth shut?'

'No.'

'And neither do I. Besides, I need it opened now.'

'Okay, but I'm doing this under protest. If the gold is damaged in any way, no blame comes back to me. Fair enough?'

'Fair enough.'

Dermot lifts the baton and sprays some coconut oil on the joint where the end cap meets the stem. He tries to turn the end cap with his hands. Nothing happens. Putting the baton in the jaws of a bench clamp, he tightens the handle …

The final resting place of Father Cormac Ignatius O'Flaherty, better known as Iggy to his younger brother, Paul, is Milltown Cemetery. Paul is on his knees, in front of a large Celtic cross. The septuagenarian thumbs his prayer beads. A black car slowly pulls up on the asphalt road, alongside at the grave. Paul glances at the car and returns to his litanies.

Tiny Murdoch is in the driver's seat of the black car. His eyes do not leave O'Flaherty, whose lips seem to be moving at a rate of knots. Wearing blue jeans and a black open-necked shirt, Tiny reaches for his cigarette packet and then remembers that Paul O'Flaherty doesn't like smoking. Tapping the steering wheel, he glances out the side window.

Two lookouts – a heavy bald man with ginger hair, and a blonde-haired young woman – are routinely inspecting nearby graves. Peering out of the passenger-side window, Tiny can see another lookout viewing graves in the adjacent lane.

O'Flaherty blesses himself with the crucifix of his prayer

beads and kisses the cross before solemnly putting them into a small leather case. He stands up, walks over to a brown bin, and drops into it the white plastic bag on which he had been kneeling. Then he tries to rub some life into his seized knees.

Tiny gets out of his car and comes over to see who had been the benefactor of O'Flaherty's supplications. 'Morning, Paul.'

'Maidin mhaith, Tiny.'

'Father Cormac Ignatius O'Flaherty. Your brother?'

'Yes.'

'I didn't know you'd a brother a priest.'

'I was very nearly one myself.'

'You're joking?'

'I am not. I was a seminarian 'til I was twenty-one.'

'I didn't know that.'

'Well, there y'are now.'

'Does it bother you, being in the IRA? Ordering people to kill other people?'

'If it did, I wouldn't do it.'

'It's just … y'know, you being so holy, and all that.'

'You think I'm holy? I just hope that the Big Guy thinks I'm as holy as you do.'

They stroll through the cemetery, each with his hands behind his back. In the lanes on either side of them, the lookouts walk parallel to them. An elderly, white-haired lady in a red scarf and a pair of navy slacks is on her knees at the foot of the grave of John Henry Fallon, the Belfast IRA leader from the 1919–1921 Irish War of Independence. Wearing yellow rubber gloves and holding a trowel, she smiles and nods to O'Flaherty, who cordially returns the smile.

'I'm going to retire soon,' O'Flaherty says.

'Old republicans never retire,' Tiny says lightly. 'They simply—'

'Slip out. Tiny, I've a leg in the other world already. Look around you; all my old comrades are already there.'

'I'm not.'

'No, you're not.' *But then you're not one of my old comrades*, he thinks. 'Your friend Ructions—'

'He's not my friend.'

O'Flaherty smiles and, head bowed, glances across at Tiny. 'No, I guess not. Anyway, he has offered us a million quid for Eleanor Proctor's release and for his personal immunity.'

'And?'

'And, everything considered, the Army Council thinks we should take it and release her.'

'That's seventeen million away from where we started.'

'I can count.'

'That's a big drop.'

'I know.'

'Too big.'

'Do you know what your problem is, Tiny? You're smart, but you don't always reason things out properly. That's why you never made it to the Army Council. Your entire thought process is rooted in the today, rarely in the tomorrow.'

'Ah, come on, Paul!'

Paul shakes his head, waits, then says, 'Supposing we reject O'Hare's offer.'

'Ah-huh?'

'And supposing he walks away and leaves Proctor to her fate – which I think he's more than capable of doing?'

'Yeah?'

'What do we do then? Shoot her? Bury her in a bog? What would we get out of that, other than pain? Sooner or later, word would get out that it was us who executed her; it always does. Or do we simply release her and hope she won't tell the media it was the 'RA that kidnapped her? Either way, it's goodbye to the peace process, and, right now, that's the only strategy the Army Council is interested in.'

'I'm not advocating killing her. Far from it.'

O'Flaherty walks up the side of a grave, squats, and sets a fallen flowerpot upright.

He looks at Tiny. 'I knew this fella. Charlie Diamond. A butcher from McDonnell Street. He used to own a house in Cushendall. I stayed there a few times when I was on the run.'

Paul stares at a photo of Charlie on the headstone. Without looking around, he says: 'What *exactly* are you advocating?'

'There's been a development.'

'Oh, yeah?'

'Yeah. I've had a long talk with Proctor about this Hermann Goering baton business.'

'And she spoke freely?'

'She did.'

'No duress?'

'None. She wanted to do a deal.'

'What sort of deal?'

'She'd tell me everything she knew about Ructions in return for her freedom.'

'Did you agree to the deal?'

'I did.'

O'Flaherty stands up and joins Tiny. 'Then you have to honour it. What did she say?'

'She told me that Ructions is taking the matter of Goering's treasure extremely seriously. So much so, he rejected a demand from her to stay away from it – on pain of her leaving him.'

'That's the thing with thieves: they never know when enough is enough. And she came back to Ireland to …'

'To get away from him. To start a new life.'

'Does he have the baton?'

'Our friend, Clarke—'

'The Peeler?'

'Yes. He told me Ructions brought three field marshal's batons into Ireland with him and that one of them belonged to a certain fat Nazi.'

O'Flaherty stops, turns towards Tiny, and tilts his head thoughtfully. 'What are we looking at here? What does Master Ructions see that we don't?'

Never one to minimize an estimate, Tiny replies: 'One billion euro in gold bullion.'

O'Flaherty shakes his head as if that would awaken him from a crazy dream. 'That's a lot of bullion. And it's in Ireland?'

'Put it like this, Paul: the French police think it's here; Ructions clearly thinks it's here; and it wouldn't surprise me if the neo-Nazis think it's here—'

'And who are *we* to contradict them?'

'Exactly! Why else would Ructions bring the baton here?'

'But why Ireland?'

'Think about this from Goering's perspective, Paul. The war's going belly-up—'

'Yes?'

'And he knows the Allies are going to be beating down doors all over Germany looking for him when it's lost … . Logic would dictate he'd have a better chance of surviving if he'd a nice little poke outside the Reich to fall back on when the shit hit the fan.'

'Perfect logic. He'd be a fool not to try and insure his future.'

'But where to put it?' Melodramatically, Tiny stops, rubs his chin, and looks up to the sky. 'In a country occupied by your enemies?'

'Which would've been virtually all of Europe.'

'Or in a little neutral country that has historical issues with one of your primary foes?'

'The Irish Free State—'

'Was neutral during the war—'

'It was a lot more than that, Tiny. It was a sleepy valley. While the rest of Europe was convulsed in total war and genocide, you could've gone from Cork to Dundalk and back a dozen times and not run across a garda.'

The two men walk in silence, each turning over thoughts about their next move. O'Flaherty speaks first. 'Did you promise Eleanor Proctor that you were going to release her?'

'I did.'

'Well, you are. But not just yet. She's a high-value bargaining chip. We need to nurture her, make her comfortable. Tell her you're just waiting on confirmation from the A/C, but that you've been assured her release is only a formality. I'm gonna meet Ructions and see if I can do a deal with him over the million pounds, *plus* the Goering gold.'

'I don't think he'll go for it.'

O'Flaherty puts his hand in his pocket, takes out a bag of mints, and offers one to Tiny. 'Depends how much he loves Eleanor Proctor, doesn't it?'

CHAPTER THIRTY-ONE

DERMOT MCCRACKEN LICKS HIS LIPS.

'Are you all right, Dermy?' Ructions asks.

'Yes, yes. It's … we've just opened Hermann Goering's ceremonial baton! I mean, we're the first people in history to look inside it and unlock its secrets. Don't you find that awesome?'

'I suppose so.'

'Ructions, I want to thank you for this. Never in my wildest dreams did I think I'd ever be central to something as enormous as this.'

Dermot's excitement is starting to bug Ructions. 'Before we go any further, Dermy, I have to tell you, I'd be very annoyed with you if I lifted a morning paper and saw my face all over it and an article about what's happening here. This has to remain our secret. Forever. Okay?'

'Sure, sure, sure. You can depend on me.'

'That's why I came to you.'

'"This above all; to thy own self be true,"' Dermot says.

'Now, let's see what Herr Goering didn't want the world to discover. Hold it up.'

Ructions removes the baton from the bench clamp.

'I want you to hold it steady,' Dermot says.

'Okay.'

Dermot gently inserts forceps into the aperture.

Ructions looks on. 'Can you see anything?'

Dermot probes the baton with the forceps. 'It's some sort of cloth. Pliable, not brittle. That's good, that's very good.' Delicately picking at the material, Dermot says, 'Here we go.' Gently, he pulls, and the top of the material emerges. 'The material *is* cloth,' Dermot says. 'Looks like a hankie of some sort.' He gingerly pulls it out of the baton's stem and cautiously sets it on the table. Dermot brings his eyes to within a millimetre of the cloth and gently rubs it between his fingers. 'This is cotton.'

'Is that good?'

'Cotton is very durable. Goering picked an excellent material.'

Dermot tentatively unrolls the cloth until it is full-length on the table. It is at least a foot square. He sets a book on one end to stop it from curling up. Both men draw close to the material. Ructions pulls back and looks at Dermot. 'It's a bloody painting!'

Dermot's eyes survey a summer countryside scene of green fields, hedges and distant buildings, including an outsized obelisk. 'And not a very good one. Hold on ... there's a name in the corner ... it's not very clear ...' Dermot draws the magnifying lamp over the painting. 'L ... O ... T ... H ... A ... I ... R. Lothair.'

'Who's Lothair?' Ructions asks.

'Could be anybody.'

'Where is this setting?'

Dermot sighs, 'Could be anywhere. Lots of small towns have some memorials like this. Look.' Dermot brings his face closer to the magnifying glass. 'There are some yellow age-marks around its circumference.'

Ructions feels cheated. 'Are we talking Germany?'

'Most likely. The North German Plain ... that area, I'd guess. A lot of flat country, just like this. Fertile. Ructions, what's so important about this painting?'

'I'm not sure myself. I suspected there might be something interesting inside the baton, but I'm none the wiser now.'

Staring at the painting, Dermot says: 'You know, there's something vaguely familiar about this scene. I can't put my finger on it, but it is familiar.'

Ructions is lost in thought on something else. 'Dermy, I need a backup in case something happens to this, a replica painted on the same material that looks as unique as the original. Do you know anybody capable of that?'

Dermot smirks. 'A forgery, eh?'

Ructions smiles. 'If anything happens to the original, and we don't have a backup, we're fucked.'

Dermot, pauses, then thumps his chest with his open hand. 'Moi.'

'You?'

'My first love was art. I'd done my degree in art before I even though of becoming an archaeologist.' Dermot dismissively waves the back of his hand at the painting. 'And look at it. It's so ... amateurish. A primary schoolboy could copy this.'

Ructions stares at Dermot as if he is making an important decision. 'How long would it take you to paint a copy?'

'A couple of hours. But first, I'd have to buy the cotton and paints.'

'Go to it, then.' Ructions puts out his hand and Dermot takes it. 'You're a star, Dermy. I knew you wouldn't let me down.'

'No problem.'

Ructions nods, puts the baton in its case, and turns to leave with it.

'There's a man who might know where this is.'

Ructions turns back. 'Who?'

'Professor Robby Dunbar. Robby runs our geography department. If anyone can tell us where this is, it'll be him. Robby has an encyclopaedic mind when it comes to geography.'

Ructions looks at the floor as he weighs up his options. He turns to Dermot. 'We need to find out where this is, so show it to him. What have we to lose?'

'What if he asks me what this is all about?'

'You came across the painting when cleaning out your attic and you were wondering where it was painted.'

'Right.'

Chief Superintendent Manus O'Toole sits at his desk watching the nine o'clock television news, but his mind is elsewhere. On his computer is a police mugshot of James 'Ructions' O'Hare. Manus opens a drawer, lifts a hip flask containing whiskey, opens the cap, takes a little swig, closes the cap, and puts the hip flask back in the drawer. Manus allows himself one swig of whiskey per shift, enough to enjoy and to look forward to but not enough to interfere with his duties. He's secretly beginning to like Ruc-

tions O'Hare. He finds something appealing about an Irishman
– a Northerner too – running rings around Europe's top police
officers, the IRA, and a phalanx of German neo-Nazis. He sighs.
It hasn't been a great day.

The garda commissioner had been sympathetic at their after-
noon meeting. Manus had expressed the view that he didn't like
diverting resources from catching criminals to hunting down
people against whom no discernible charge could be levelled.
The commissioner nodded approvingly. And even if this Ructions O'Hare were to find a crock of Nazi gold, Manus had suggested, he would only be guilty of an offence if he didn't declare
the find to the state. Then Manus posed a question: How could
the state even prove that O'Hare had discovered the gold if he
chose – as he undoubtedly would – to conceal its discovery?

The commissioner said that it wasn't just a simple matter of
O'Hare finding Goering's gold bullion. Other people – and he
named the IRA and the Fourth Reich – were also seeking it, and
they saw O'Hare as the person most likely to find it. The threat
of major violence was real. O'Hare was central to that violence.
Not only that, but the Minister for Justice was insisting that maximum priority be given to the case. European politics demanded
no less.

Manus lifts a page and holds it in front of him. The Garda
Special Branch had reported that Ructions met with the IRA
Army Council head, Paul O'Flaherty, in Donegal.

His intercom buzzes. 'Yes, Oisín?'

'Superintendent Vasseur and Inspector Robillard are here, sir.'

'Show them in.'

The door opens, and the huge bulk of Vasseur fills the doorway. A smiling Manus comes from behind his desk and shakes

Vasseur's hand. He feels the bones in his own hand contract in Vasseur's shovel-like mitt. 'Good to see you again, Thierry.'

'And you, Manus.'

'Hello, Pierre.'

'Hello, Manus,' Robillard says.

'Please, take a seat. Tea? Coffee?'

'Coffee would be good,' Vasseur says.

'I'll have tea, please,' Robillard says.

The refreshments are ordered.

'You've met the commissioner, then?'

'Just now,' Vasseur says. 'He was most co-operative.'

Vasseur shifts uneasily in his seat. 'Manus, it's been a long day.'

'Tell me about it, Thierry.'

'Would you mind if I come straight to the point?'

'By all means, Thierry.'

'Can you bring me up to date with this man O'Hare's activities in Ireland?'

'Sure. The latest we have on him comes from one of our IRA informers, who confirmed that O'Hare met the head of the IRA Army Council, Paul O'Flaherty, in Donegal two nights ago.'

Vasseur's fingers are joined as if in prayer. 'Do we know why they were meeting?'

'It was a private meeting, just O'Hare and O'Flaherty. We have nothing regarding to the content of their conversation.'

'Why do *you* think they were meeting?'

Manus strikes a circumspect pose, his head tilted, finger tapping his upper lip. 'Let's look at the facts: the IRA have been hunting Ructions ever since he didn't pay his tax for the National Bank robbery.'

'They followed him to France recently,' Vasseur says, 'presumably to either force him to pay them the money they think he owes them or to murder him.'

'Could have been either, or both,' Manus says. 'My guess is he wants to settle with them, get them off his back.'

An officer brings in the refreshments and the men help themselves.

'That's interesting,' Vasseur says as he bites into a Jaffa Cake. 'Do the IRA know about Goering's gold, do you think?'

'I don't see how they would, Thierry. Why would Ructions tell them?'

'But he's still in Ireland?' Robillard asks.

'As far as I know.'

'And Eleanor Proctor … is she still in Ireland?'

'According to Dan Clarke, she hasn't been seen since she left a hotel in County Down' – Manus looks at his diary – 'eight days ago. But Dan doesn't appear to be too worried about that. He thinks she's lying low to avoid coming to the attention of the IRA.'

'Nobody's heard or set eyes on her in eight days? And you don't think that's strange? She's just vanished into thin air?' His words shred the bonhomie that had existed up to that point.

'As I say, Dan's okay with it.' Unnerved by the gobsmacked Frenchmen and feeling that he must respond to the underlying accusation of negligence, Manus says, 'There's no evidence that she came into the Republic. My brief is to find O'Hare and report back to you. Nothing else.'

Vasseur turns to Robillard. 'Make sure we put another call in to Daniel Clarke. I want to know what efforts have been made to locate Ms Proctor since our last phone call to him. I want to know if she is being regarded as a missing person and, if not, why?' Turning to Manus, Vasseur says: 'Is it possible the IRA have arrested her, and O'Hare is trying to buy her freedom?'

'In Irish we call "what if" the "impossible if."'

'I'm finding this inexplicable. Ms Proctor is the partner of O'Hare. She's been missing for eight days, Manus! Where I come from, that would be seen as suspicious.'

'I'm the wrong man to get angry with on this one, Thierry. Whatever has happened to Ms Proctor hasn't happened in the Republic.'

'I appreciate that. Let's assume, just for argument's sake, that O'Hare *is* trying to buy Ms Proctor's freedom. In that case, the IRA would be in strong position, don't you think?'

'Undoubtedly. But where are you going with this, Thierry?'

'I'm not sure. But I'm asking: Would he pay off the IRA to secure Ms Proctor's release? He might.'

'I actually think he mightn't,' Manus says. 'He's a tough man.'

Vasseur sticks his hands in his pockets and rocks backward on the two rear legs of his chair. 'You know, Manus, I've a hunch the IRA *have* kidnapped Ms Proctor.'

'I wouldn't be rushing to support that hunch without some evidence to back it up. Thierry, I think you need to speak to Dan Clarke about this; he'll fill you in better than I can.'

'I understand perfectly. What I don't understand,' Vasseur says, 'is why Dan is so blasé about Ms Proctor.'

CHAPTER THIRTY-TWO

CHIEF SUPERINTENDENT DANIEL CLARKE IS SITTING IN the front of an SUV in the long-term car park at Belfast International Airport with Tiny Murdoch precisely *because* he is far from blasé about the fate of Eleanor Proctor.

'I got a call last night,' Clarke says.

Tiny twirls a fifty-pence piece between his fingers.

'My call was from a French police superintendent with Interpol, a Superintendent Thierry Vasseur. That's the second time I've heard from him within the last week. He seems convinced that the IRA has kidnapped Eleanor Proctor. Nine days she's been missing! Not a fucking trace of her. Her former husband hasn't seen her, her sister hasn't seen her, her friends haven't seen her: she's just vanished. The chief constable asked if I thought the IRA had "disappeared" her, for Christ's sake!'

Tiny grabs the fifty-pence piece in the palm of his hand, tilts back his head and pouts. He has learned from years of experience that when an accusation is pending, as it surely is, it's better to listen rather than offer something incriminating.

'Have you nothing to say?' Clarke says.

'What do you want me to say?'

Clarke is so distraught that he feels like taking out his gun and putting it to Tiny's temple to get an answer. He puts his hand on his holster.

'You're gonna shoot me, Dan? Go right ahead. Blow my brains out.' Tiny leans towards Clarke and says in a low voice, 'But how will you explain the video?'

'What video?'

'The fucking video that's recording us right now, you wanker! Wave to the camera. Go on, wave!'

Clarke looks all around, but he can't see anybody with a video. Tiny shakes his head. 'You're an amateur ... a fucking greenhorn. Why did I ever get involved with you?'

Clarke takes his hand away from the holster. 'I'm in deep shit, and it's your fault.'

'My fault? How did you work that one out?'

'You kidnapped Eleanor Proctor.'

'You set her up! I wouldn't have got near her if you hadn't told us where she was staying.'

'Nine fucking days, Tiny! I told you to let her go, didn't I?'

I'd better pull back and calm him down, Tiny thinks, or I'll need a defibrillator to revive him. 'Chill, Dan, chill. I've it sorted.'

'What way sorted?'

'As a favour to you, I've recommended that she be released.'

'When can I expect that?'

'Soon.'

'Could she be released in the Republic, do you think?'

'You don't want her released in the north?'

'If she wasn't being held in my jurisdiction, she wasn't my problem.'

'I'll see what I can do.'

Clarke runs his hand through his hair. 'I don't think we should meet again.'

'If that's the way you want it.'

'I don't think it's worth it.'

Tiny extends his hand, and Clarke shakes it.

'And Ructions?' Tiny says.

'He's not worth me putting my career in jeopardy. Besides, he'll eventually slip up. Criminals always do.'

'I wouldn't bet on it,' Tiny says.

A phone rings. Ructions has dozed off on the sofa in the safe house in affluent south Belfast. He sits upright. 'Yeah?'

'It's me. Dermot. Robby knew where it was right away.'

'He did?'

'I should've known myself … I was on a dig just up the road from—'

'Stop! Don't say anything over the phone.'

'Righto.'

'I'll meet you outside where we met the last time. Chop chop?'

'When?'

'Half an hour.'

'Fine.'

Ructions showers and shaves, then he walks into the room

where Billy Kelly is sleeping. It's stuffy, so he opens a window wide. Billy ducks his head under his pillow. 'Close that fuckin' windy!' he snarls. Ructions keeps the window open. 'What do you want?' Billy says, bringing his head out from under the blankets.

'I've got to shoot on.'

Billy's hair is standing to attention, and he looks confused. 'What time is it?'

'Half eleven.'

Billy shakes his head. 'Shoot on where?'

'To a meeting.'

'I'll come with you.'

'No, you stay here. I'm meeting a guy, and once we've finished, I'm coming back. I've a couple of important meetings in Dublin tomorrow, and I need you to stay handy.'

A bluebottle buzzes around Billy's head, and he tries unsuccessfully to swat it. Ructions walks towards the door before turning. 'Did you get Ambrose?'

'He's coming over at one o'clock.'

Ructions still does not leave the room. 'I'm curious ... what did he do with the one million he got from the National Bank robbery?'

'The fat fucker hid it under the bed.'

'He didn't!'

'How the fuck do I know what he did with it? He didn't go on a diet, that's for sure.'

At five minutes past twelve, Ructions drives along Elmwood Avenue. He spots Dermot standing outside the entrance to the

Queen's University Students' Union. He double-parks and beckons the professor to come to the car. Dermot gets in. He looks
at Ructions as if he has just discovered King Solomon's mines.
'Robby got it. Just like that.' He clicks his fingers. 'Didn't as
much as give it a second look.'

Ructions conceals his enthusiasm. 'Are you peckish, Dermy?'

Dermot is confused. Peckish? What's that got to do with
it? 'No.'

'Well, I am. Let's get something to eat.'

'But don't you want to know where the painting was painted?'

'Right now, I want a Big Mac meal with tea.'

'But Ructions—'

'Let's get our lunch first.'

Sitting in the car park at McDonald's, Dermot hardly touches
his food. Ructions devours his and then gets stuck into Dermot's.
'Sometimes, when you're running about, you forget how hungry
you are,' he says, wiping his mouth with a serviette. 'You were
saying?'

'What?'

'About the painting.'

'Oh, yes. It's Conolly's Folly.'

'It's what?'

'The oversized obelisk at the centre of the painting.'

Ructions reaches for his shoulder bag and, opening it, takes
out the original picture that had been hidden inside Hermann
Goering's baton. He lays it out on the dashboard and looks at it.

Dermot points a finger at a small vertical, tapering structure.
'That's Conolly's Obelisk, or Conolly's Folly, as it's more com-
monly known.'

'I've never heard of it. Who's Conolly?'

Dermot takes a notebook out of his coat pocket, looks at it and explains that they are talking about Katherine Conolly, who was born in 1662 and died in 1752. He reads that she was the wife of William Conolly, MP, who lived from 1662 to 1729. Dermot continues, 'Old Willy was a Williamite land-grabber—'

'Good for him.'

Dermot gives Ructions a dirty look, '—and former Speaker of the House of Commons. It was he who built Castletown House in County Kildare in 1722. It's Ireland biggest privately owned residence.'

'Okay, spare me the history lesson, Dermy. Where are you going with this?'

'Sorry, but history plays an important part. From the early 1740s there was a famine in Ireland. People were dying of hunger. Katherine was a philanthropist—'

'A decent spud, then.'

'Oh, she was, she was; no doubt about that. Anyway, rather than just give handouts to the poor, which the gentry frowned upon, she gave them employment, and the employment she gave them was building this obelisk. It served no purpose, and the locals returned her generosity by calling it Conolly's Folly.'

'People are so ungrateful.'

'The point is: your picture is of Conolly's Folly.'

Ructions frowns. 'Where exactly is this?'

'County Kildare. Celbridge, just outside Dublin. Arthur Guinness country. I was on a dig there about ten years ago.'

Ructions grabs Dermot by the cheeks. 'Professor Dermy McCracken, you're not eighteen-carat gold, you're twenty-four carat. I'm gonna look after you. I am, I swear to God I am. I always look after my friends.'

'Thanks, Ructions.'

Ructions stares at Dermot and rubs his earlobe. 'I wonder …
would you be able to come down to Conolly's Folly with me? If
you can't, it's okay, I can—'

'Would I?' Dermot says. 'Ha! Here's what we have: Hermann
Goering's ceremonial baton, a secret compartment in that baton,
a previously undiscovered World War Two painting of Conolly's Folly apparently commissioned by Goering and painted by
someone called Lothair, and on top of all that …' Dermot leans
forward. ' … on top of that, Ructions O'Hare as the main man.
There's a plot, isn't there?'

'There's always a plot,' Ructions says, grinning.

Dermot slaps his thigh. 'I knew it. This is intrigue; by Jesus,
this is intrigue on an epic scale. I don't know what you're up to,
Ructions, but, please, please, can I come on board?'

CHAPTER THIRTY-THREE

MIDMORNING. A FAIR-HAIRED MAN HOLDING TWO whippets on leads passes by. An old man smiles and nods at Ructions, who returns the gesture. A young couple holding hands and licking ice cream cones pass by. In his head, Ructions can hear himself pleading for the ice cream, but his voice is younger, unbroken with age.

There must be close to one hundred people on the pier, if there's ten, he thinks. Why the hell did I agree to meet Paul O'Flaherty here?

'Here' is the bandstand on Dun Laoghaire's east pier, County Dublin. Hexagonal in shape, the bandstand's ornamental dome looks like a golden canopy, designed to shield an Arab sheik from the rays of a pitiless sun. Ructions doesn't like hanging about, and, were it anyone other than O'Flaherty, he would already have been gone. His eyes linger on the lighthouse at the bottom of the pier before turning to the 820-berth marina. He chides himself for not having bought a yacht. All millionaires have yachts. He promises himself that he'll buy one when this business is over.

The departing Holyhead ferry passes through the entrance to the harbour. The glassy surface of the water looks as if it has been chloroformed into conformity.

Paul O'Flaherty walks up the east pier with a limp, a relic of a gun battle with the British army in the republican Ballymurphy area in 1972. He is wearing grey trousers and a blue woolly crewneck jumper with leather arm patches. Ructions has the impression that O'Flaherty looks more like a retired university lecturer or driving instructor than a violent revolutionary leader. Beside him is the IRA man, Seán, who had followed him into the toilets in County Donegal. O'Flaherty walks up the steps of the bandstand. 'How's it goin' there, Ructions?'

Ructions notices that the IRA leader's bodyguard has held back to allow the two men privacy. 'Fine, Paul. Yourself?'

Paul nods. 'I'm good.' Both men look at each other for a second, time enough for each to look for something that would give them an indication of the other's disposition. O'Flaherty breathes deeply, his chest rising rhythmically. 'This sea air just lifts my spirits. You know, son, a man could do worse than live out his days in Dun Laoghaire.'

'Touché,' Ructions says.

O'Flaherty raises a censorious finger. 'No, no. You misunderstand. I wasn't referring to you, or your offer. I was talking about me. I like Dun Laoghaire. I'd like to retire here.'

'Sorry if I took you up wrong, Paul.'

'That's no problem. Look at these people …' Paul waves a hand and looks around the pier. 'Not a care in the world. Y'know, I can't remember a time when I hadn't a care in the world.'

'Come to think of it, I can't either.'

O'Flaherty puts his hand over his mouth and Ructions automatically follows suit. 'I'm curious, Ructions. If you'd to do it all again, what would you like to change?'

Ructions doesn't have to think. 'Are you talking about the robbery?'

'No, life. If you'd one chance to change the way life has treated you, what would you change?'

'I'd like to have met my mother.'

'She died young?'

'Giving birth to me.' Ructions feels a wave of emotion engulfing him. He needs to move the conversation. 'And you, Paul: if you'd to do it all again, what would you like to change?'

'I'd have liked a family of my own.'

'You never married?'

'Naw. It nearly happened in 1968, but I just … anyway, it didn't happen.' Now it's O'Flaherty's turn to feel the need to redirect the conversation. 'Let's walk.'

They leave the bandstand and stroll slowly down towards the lighthouse. O'Flaherty puts his hands in his pockets. 'I've spoken to the council about your offer, and they've decided, on my recommendation, to accept it for the release of the woman.'

'I appreciate your help in this matter, Paul.'

'I've gotta tell you, it wasn't easy. There was opposition. Some thought you were getting off too light.'

'As I say, I'm grateful.'

'How long would it take you to transfer the money?'

'I took the liberty of contacting my bank in order to facilitate a smooth transfer, so it's only a phone call away.'

'Good.' O'Flaherty takes a sheet of paper out of the back

pocket of his trousers and hands it to Ructions. 'That's our bank account. Make the call now.'

Ructions is suspicious. 'How long will it take you to bring Eleanor here?'

'She's a phone call away.'

'I need to see her.'

'I thought you would.' They stop. O'Flaherty looks behind at his bodyguard and nods. The bodyguard speaks into his mobile phone.

Within seconds, Tiny Murdoch slowly walks onto the pier with Eleanor by his side. Even from a distance, Ructions can see that she looks frail. 'That's that,' O'Flaherty says. 'Make the money transfer.'

Ructions walks aside and makes a phone call to his bank, transferring one million pounds to the IRA account. He ends the call and says to O'Flaherty. 'It's done.'

O'Flaherty nods to his bodyguard, who has a phone to his ear. Ructions opens his phone, removes the SIM card, snaps it in two, and flings the pieces into the sea, along with the phone.

'I see you don't take many chances,' O'Flaherty says.

'I make it my business to minimise risk.'

O'Flaherty wags his fingers, indicating that he wants Eleanor brought to him. 'Now, to your second demand.'

'There is no second demand, Paul.'

'My board disagrees and so do I. No matter what way you look at it, there are two entirely separate demands.' O'Flaherty holds up one finger: 'One, you want the woman released, and two' – he holds up a second finger – 'you want us to ignore your transgressions and let you live in Ireland.'

'I haven't transgressed against the IRA.'

'Look, Ructions, if the council decides you've transgressed

against them, then that's it. They don't care what *you* think. They make a decision about you and then move on to the next item on the agenda.'

'I've no more money to give you.'

'I put that scenario to my board, and they didn't believe you.'

'Too bad—'

'Hold on. There may be other payment options that might help resolve the second demand problem.'

'Okay, Paul, shoot.'

'You know, son, you and the IRA don't have to be at loggerheads all the time. We can be friends. Don't you want to be our friend?'

'Sure.'

'Ah, here's your lovely lady.'

Tiny and Eleanor draw near. Tiny grins as he regally waves his hand, permitting Eleanor to go to Ructions. Eleanor walks slowly towards Ructions, who opens his arms to her. She submits to Ructions's embrace. They kiss briefly. Ructions's eyes lock on to Tiny's as he whispers in Eleanor's ear that she should say nothing. They pull apart with Ructions keeping his hand around her waist.

Tiny is exhilarated. 'Good to see you're still alive and kicking, bullet-dodger.'

Ructions makes no reply.

'I told you I'd get you, didn't I? Big shot, you thought you were bigger than the 'RA. You thought you could—'

Ructions looks to O'Flaherty. 'Am I supposed to be this wanker's friend?'

O'Flaherty comes in posthaste. 'That'll do, Tiny. I'll take it from here.'

Tiny points to Ructions, then walks up the pier.

O'Flaherty puts an arm around Ructions's shoulder. 'Can I borrow him for a minute, Eleanor?'

She nods.

'I won't be long.' They walk out of Eleanor's earshot. 'So, my friend, back to our treasure hunt.'

Ructions stops and looks at O'Flaherty as if he has suddenly sprouted a third eye. 'What treasure hunt?'

O'Flaherty smirks. 'I'm talking about Hermann Goering's treasure – tonnes and tonnes of gold bullion. You have Goering's ceremonial baton and everyone – the cops, the neo-Nazis, Serge Mercier, and now my board – think that it's the abracadabra to the treasure.'

'I don't—'

'For Christ's sake, stop, Ructions! Eleanor has told us all about it.' Ructions looks behind at Eleanor. 'Don't blame her. Blame yourself. You let her come back to Ireland without my board's permission.'

Without your board's permission? Ructions wants to say, fuck you and your board, but he remains blank, unreadable.

'You're red-hot,' O'Flaherty says. 'Do you know that?'

'I heard something along those lines,' Ructions says.

'Every cop in Europe is looking for you. How do we know that? Because we've friends in the cops, and they've confirmed everything that Eleanor has told us. In fact, they've a lot more to say about Goering's gold than she has. So much, in fact, that my board has no doubts you have the ability and the means to find it.'

'Your board's faith in me is touching.'

O'Flaherty laughs. 'That's witty.' The humour instantly evaporates from his face. 'My board likes the idea of having gold reserves. So, they want the gold, or, failing that, another four million pounds in order to complete the deal.'

Ructions did not expect this. 'You're missing something, Paul.'

'What would that be?'

'At this moment, I don't have either the money, or the gold.'

'But you know where it is?'

Ructions remains stoic. 'No, I don't.'

O'Flaherty grips Ructions's bicep. 'Look, son, I'm trying to help you here. I'm your friend.'

You're the type of friend who tells the condemned that you're doing them a favour by offering them a bullet in the head rather than a knife in the back, Ructions thinks. But what he says is, 'If you really want to help me, you'll buy me time.'

'What for?'

'So that I can find the bloody gold and give some of it over to your bloody board.'

O'Flaherty bows his head and caresses his chin. 'I really should retire,' he mutters to himself. He spins around. 'I don't want to be unreasonable ...' Ructions feels like laughing at O'Flaherty's ability to understate his hand. 'You've one week,' the IRA supremo says. 'We meet at the same time in a week. I'll let you know the location.'

'Thanks.'

'If you don't show up, you're back on our hit list.'

'Have I ever been off it?'

'You're off it for a—'

'Put your fucking hands up! Now!'

As if spring-loaded, both men's heads swivel to their right where they see that the young couple who had been eating ice cream just moments earlier are in the two-handed firing position, their hand-guns pointing at them. 'Get your hands up!' the man shouts.

'Get those fucking hands up now!' the woman screams. 'Get on the fucking ground, O'Hare! On the ground, O'Flaherty! Keep your hands up!'

Ructions and O'Flaherty get down on their knees.

'Lie down flat! Arms straight out in front of you! Do it now!'

The two lie down and put out their arms. Ructions looks sideways at O'Flaherty, who seems unperturbed with the turn of events.

A bald, middle-aged man in blue, spotted shorts is standing behind the young police officers, unconnected with the evolving drama, but has the presence of mind to whip out his smartphone and take a video recording of events.

From the bottom of the pier comes the blare of sirens as police vehicles carrying members of the Garda Emergency Response Unit race up the pier. The elite officers, their faces covered with ski masks, jump out of their vehicles and take up covering positions around Ructions and O'Flaherty.

Male police officers handcuff both men behind their backs before searching them and removing their wallets and O'Flaherty's cell phone.

Petrified, Eleanor stands to the side, her fingers covering her mouth. Suddenly she faints, the back of her head hitting the ground.

With the two principal conspirators now in custody, the young female garda rushes to Eleanor and puts her arm under her, raising her head off the concrete pier.

Three members of the Garda Emergency Response Unit, their faces also covered with ski masks, stand directly in front of Tiny Murdoch, with rifles pointed at his face. An officer bellows: 'Down! Right now! Down!' Tiny sighs and nods. He's been here before. He gets down on the ground and is quickly handcuffed.

O'Flaherty's bodyguard had had time to throw his mobile phone into the sea before also being confronted by armed police and forced to lie on the ground.

The four suspects are formally arrested.

In the car park of the nearby Royal Marine Hotel, IRA volunteer Hughie O'Boyle is listening to music when the side window of his car is tapped by a police officer carrying a handgun. Hughie is taken out of the car, searched, and arrested.

Manus O'Toole gets out of a police Land Rover and approaches Eleanor, who is semiconscious and is now being attended to by a retired doctor and his wife, who happened to be strolling by. The doctor tells Manus that Eleanor is suffering from concussion.

An ambulance with flashing strobe lights makes its way along the pier. A police officer directs the driver to stop beside Eleanor. Medics surround her and she is stretchered into the back of the ambulance. She is accompanied by the female garda. The ambulance is driven away, its siren cutting the air.

Ructions and O'Flaherty have been lifted to their feet by the Garda Emergency Response Unit members. Manus, a smirk on his face, stands less than a foot from Ructions's face. He then moves on to O'Flaherty before returning to Ructions.

'James "Ructions" O'Hare. At last. I'd shake your hand, but you seem a bit tied up at the minute.' Manus titters at his joke and turns to O'Flaherty. 'Well, well, well, if it isn't the chairman of the IRA Army Council himself. I don't want to shake your hand, O'Flaherty. Too much blood on it.' Manus steps back. He turns to a subordinate. 'I've waited a long time for this. Take them away.'

CHAPTER THIRTY-FOUR

NO ONE IS WAITING TO MEET KARL KELLER AND GITTE when they come into the exit lounge of Dublin airport. Not that Keller had expected anyone. Gitte and he had passed through immigration without incident, but if that was intended to make him feel unworthy of the authorities' attention, it hadn't worked. He knew that they would be watching him; he mightn't see them, but they'd see him.

Keller had booked a double room for Gitte and himself in the Shelbourne Hotel on St Stephen's Green. Even as he enters the lobby, he feels eyes on him. But whose eyes? No Secret Sam is peeking out from behind a newspaper, no one is pretending to chat with the concierge while discreetly following his every move. Is the concierge a policeman?

Ructions is in a local police station. He stands upright, holding a small blackboard with his name on it as he faces a police camera. After his photograph is taken, he is told to turn sideward, where a side-profile shot is taken.

A garda sergeant, approaching retirement, brings him into a room where a rookie cop takes his fingerprints and a DNA sample from a mouth swab. 'Do you know who this is, Oscar?' the sergeant asks.

Oscar looks at the arrest sheet. 'James O'Hare.'

'You've never heard of him?'

The rookie shrugs.

The sergeant tuts. 'Kids. They know nothing.' After handing Ructions some sheets of soapy tissue with which to clean his hands, the sergeant says, 'It's a pleasure to meet you, Ructions.' Ructions nods. The sergeant whispers in his ear, 'And the best of luck to you, son. Spend the money wisely.'

Ructions paces, four steps up, a swivel, four steps down. The cell's outer observation flap periodically opens as individual officers come to see the notorious bank robber.

The cell door opens and two plainclothes officers lead Ructions to an interview room.

In the command/control room, Manus O'Toole sprawls out on a hard plastic seat as he looks into a television screen which shows Ructions sitting across from the officers.

'Mr O'Hare, you don't mind me calling you Ructions, do you?' asks a tall officer with a thick black moustache. Ructions shows no reaction. 'You are being held on suspicion of aiding and abetting in the kidnapping of Ms Eleanor Proctor. Have you anything you'd like to say at this stage?'

'No comment.'

'Do you know Ms Proctor?'

'No comment.'

'Do you know Paul O'Flaherty?'

'No comment.'

'You were arrested alongside Mr O'Flaherty on Dun Laoghaire pier today.'

'No comment.'

'I'm going to show you footage of you and O'Flaherty meeting today.' The officer presses a button and images of Ructions standing next to O'Flaherty come up on a television screen mounted on the wall. 'Okay, you were both covering your mouths with your hands, but you were clearly communicating. How do you know Paul O'Flaherty?'

'No comment.'

The sequence is run on to show Ructions destroying his SIM card and phone. 'Why did you destroy your SIM card and phone?'

'No comment.'

'Was it because you didn't want the police to have access to your phone records?'

'No comment.'

After the interview, when Ructions is put back in his cell, Manus O'Toole speaks to officers who had been tasked with recording the conversation between Ructions and O'Flaherty on the pier. 'Is that it?' Manus says. 'I could hardly make out one coherent word. If it sounded like mumbo jumbo to me, it'll sound like mumbo jumbo to a jury.'

Garda Joel O'Neill tries to mitigate. 'They were covering their mouths, sir, and that tends to distort words.'

'Did you get anything?'

'Well, we did, but it's disjointed. O'Flaherty's voice is naturally weak, so it's difficult to pick him up and, unfortunately, he dominated the conversation. O'Hare speaks only when he absolutely has to and, even then, his sentences rarely exceed five words.'

'What's new?' Manus says.

'It's fragmented, but O'Flaherty says …' O'Neill hits the play button. '"—*they want the gold*"' …'and then there is a break before …' '"… *or another four million.*"'

Manus shows no emotion … the IRA are signed on. They believe the gold is in Ireland. He wishes he could get a nip from his hip flask now. He needs it.

An officer comes into the control room and whispers into Manus's ear. He leaves the room.

At St Michael's Hospital in Dun Laoghaire, Eleanor Proctor is in a private ward and sitting on the side of her bed, a bandage wrapped around her head, a cup of tea in her hand. Sitting at the door to the ward is the female garda. The matron is admonishing Eleanor: 'You should be resting, Ms Proctor. You shouldn't be sitting up.'

'I'm much better, sister,' Eleanor says. 'Truly, I am.'

Manus talks quietly to the female garda, who informs him that Eleanor wants to sign herself out of hospital. He nods, taps on the ward door, and walks into the room.

'Can I help you?' the matron asks.

'I'm Chief Superintendent Manus O'Toole, sister, and I'd like a word with Ms Proctor, if that's possible.'

'Ms Proctor has had a nasty fall, chief superintendent. I don't think she's—'

'It's okay, sister. I'll speak to the officer.'

The matron is not pleased at being undermined, and the look on her face makes this clear. 'A few minutes, chief superintendent. And when you're at it, would you kindly impress upon her that she's in no fit state to go home.'

'I will.'

The matron leaves the room.

Manus offers Eleanor his hand, which she takes. 'How are you doing, Ms Proctor? Are they treating you well?'

'I'm okay, thanks.'

'That was a bad fall you had today.'

'So I'm told. I don't remember much about it.'

Manus pulls over a chair and sits beside Eleanor. He detects rebellion in her face; better not to rush in. 'Is there anyone I can contact to let them know you're in hospital? Any relatives, for example?'

'No.'

'Perhaps you'd like me to—'

'Where's Ructions?'

Straight to the point. 'He's under arrest.'

'What for?'

'He's being held on suspicion of aiding and abetting in a kidnapping.'

Eleanor frowns. 'Who was kidnapped?'

'Why, you were.'

'Was I? First I heard of it.'

Manus is taken aback with Eleanor's reluctance to admit being kidnapped. 'But this meeting on the pier was a payoff. Ructions was paying off the IRA for your freedom. That's—'

'Hold on. I don't get this. If he was paying off the IRA to secure my freedom, how could he have been aiding and abetting in my kidnapping? One contradicts the other.'

Manus makes a mental note not to underestimate Eleanor. 'At this stage, all those involved in your kidnapping are being held pending further inquiries.'

'I'm sorry ... what's your first name?'

'It's Manus.'

'Well, Manus, I don't know anything about that. I certainly wasn't kidnapped.'

'Ms Proctor, your kidnapping is not a matter of guesswork. We *know* you were kidnapped. There's no disputing that fact.'

'I think *I'd* know if I was kidnapped, don't you?'

'You were picked up outside the Old Inn Hotel in Crawfordsburn, County Antrim, and brought to a house in the Riverdale area of Andersonstown in Belfast. And we also know that Tiny Murdoch was behind your abduction.'

'Tiny Murdoch? Who's he?'

Manus finds it difficult to hide his frustration. He stares into Eleanor's eyes. 'I see.'

'Do you?'

There is a pause. 'Ms Proctor, I can't compel you to report the heinous crime that has been committed against you, but it's your civic duty to do so, and, I may add, it's the right thing to do.'

'Am I under arrest?'

Manus shakes his head. 'No.'

'Then I'm leaving this hospital and going about my lawful business, if you don't mind.'

'Ms Proctor, can I call you Eleanor?'

'No, you can't.'

Manus shrugs. 'I don't understand. The IRA have treated you abominably. Why are you protecting them? Is it Ructions? Is it he you're protecting *from* the IRA?'

'Look, officer, I appreciate you've a job to do, but if I'm not under arrest, I'm signing myself out of here.'

'Ms Proctor, you've been badly traumatised. I don't think, even if you don't want to co-operate with the police, that you should be signing out. Give yourself a few days to rest. Listen to the medical staff; they know best.'

'I'm signing out.'

'You probably feel intimidated. That's it, isn't it? Well, don't let the IRA intimidate you. You know, we've never lost anyone who went into our protection programme. We can keep you one hundred per cent safe; give you a new life.'

'Officer, if you don't mind … I need to put on my clothes.'

Resigned to the fact that Eleanor was not going to press charges against anyone, Manus stands up. 'Sure. Can I ask you where you will be going after you leave hospital? It's not safe for you on the streets.'

'I won't be on the streets. I'm going straight to Devon to visit my cousin.'

'That's a wise decision. I can give you a police escort to the airport, if you like.'

'I don't need one.'

'I think you do. Take the escort. It won't hurt you.'

Eleanor stares into Manus's face. 'If you insist.'

Manus holds out his hand again, and they shake. 'Well, good luck. I hope Ructions knows how lucky he is to have you standing by him.'

'He knows.'

Manus takes out his wallet and hands Eleanor his card. 'In case you change your mind about pressing charges.' Eleanor takes the card. 'Oh, by the way, I'll be releasing Ructions …' Manus looks at his watch, 'within the next thirty minutes. Do you want me to tell him anything?'

Eleanor has tears in her eyes. 'Tell him I love him.'

Manus nods. 'I'll do that.' He turns to leave, walks a few yards and turns back, 'Can I tell you something?'

'I can't stop you.'

'You're too good for him.'

Ructions is lying on his bed in his cell. The door opens, and Manus enters. He pulls up a chair and sits down. 'Chief Superintendent Manus O'Toole.' Manus puts out his hand, but Ructions does not take it. Manus's eyebrows rise and fall. 'I'm curious … how did you do it?' Ructions makes no reply. 'Pulling off a job like the National Bank must've taken a lot of planning.'

Ructions turns around to face the wall.

'I've just been speaking to Eleanor.'

Once again Ructions shows no reaction.

'Don't you want to know how she's doing?' Manus waits in vain for a response. 'She's okay. She has signed herself out of hospital.'

Ructions looks over his shoulder before turning towards Manus.

'She's leaving Ireland, Ructions.'

The bank robber can no longer restrain himself. 'Where's she going?'

'I'm not at liberty to tell you, but she's bailing out – and who could blame her? You dropped her right in the brown stuff, didn't you?' Manus folds his arms and crosses his legs. 'Tell me, did you ever once stop to think "This'll hurt Eleanor"? I don't think you did. Truth be told, Ructions, I think the only person you've ever thought of in your whole life is yourself. That lady is impressive.' Manus purses his lips and nods. 'She really is. No amount of persuasion was going to make her say she'd been kidnapped in case your sordid dealings with the IRA ended up with you doing time. And her only crime? Falling in love with a low-life prick. Oh, by the way, she told me to tell you she loves you. How about that?'

Ructions blinks and swallows hard.

'It's a pity really,' Manus continues. 'I'd have liked to see her give evidence against O'Flaherty and Murdoch – that would have been some feather in my cap. Now it looks like I'm going to have to release them and their flunkies.'

Manus stands up, walks to the window, and lights up a cigarette. He offers one to Ructions, who sits up and takes it. Manus gives Ructions a light before sitting down again and pointing his cigarette at Ructions. 'So, we have you on camera making a phone call and then destroying your SIM card and phone. In the meanwhile, Tiny Murdoch is bringing Eleanor up the pier to you. You paid off the IRA for Eleanor's release, didn't you?'

'No comment.'

'How much did you pay them?'

'No comment.'

'What I don't understand is why you're prepared to give them another four million since you've already paid them off for Eleanor's release. What's the extra four million for, Ructions?'

'No comment.'

'What can they give you that you already haven't got?'

'No comment.'

Manus leans towards Ructions and whispers into his ear, 'Freedom.' He pulls back. 'You want to be free to live in Ireland without the threat of being murdered by the IRA hanging over your head. That's it, isn't it?'

'No comment.'

'That's it. Can't be anything else. Personally, I wouldn't give them the kiss of life, but then that's me.'

Manus looks at his tie and picks off a tiny speck of food with his fingernail. He brings his gaze back to Ructions. 'This Hermann Goering's gold business, how real is it?'

'No comment.'

Manus stands up and turns towards the door, but he doesn't leave. Instead, one hand holds on to the side of the chair. He turns to Ructions again. 'There are people in positions of power in the land who are watching events very carefully, who are taking the Goering's gold matter extremely seriously.'

Ructions thinks, Where's he going with this?

Manus sits down again and bring his face so close to Ructions that he can smell the garlic sausages that he had eaten for breakfast. 'This is unofficial, and I'll deny we've ever had this conversation if it becomes public knowledge.' Manus looks for an indication from Ructions that what he is about to say will be treated in confidence. A slight nod of Ructions's head. 'I've been authorised to offer you a deal.'

Ructions's curiosity gets the better of him. 'What sort of deal would that be?'

'The people in positions of power—'

'The government.'

'The people in positions of power are prepared to allow you to get clean away with twenty per cent of any gold discovered, providing you make them aware where the other eighty per cent is.'

Ructions laughs aloud. 'Their generosity is only exceeded by their humility,' he says.

'Hear me out, there's more. If you accept the offer, they will ensure that the Irish police release a statement saying that they believe all the gold has been recovered. That means you won't be prosecuted for removing the twenty per cent of the gold from Ireland – unless you're caught red-handed with it – and I very much doubt if that will happen.'

'There *is* no Goering's gold.'

Manus puts out his hand again, and this time Ructions takes it. The police officer sniggers. 'Who'd have thought that fat Hermann would've hidden his gold in the Emerald Isle, eh? Of all places. I mean … how fucking clever was that?' Manus playfully pretends to punch Ructions on the shoulder. 'Where is it, Ructions? You can tell me. Where's the gold?'

Ructions hunches his shoulders and holds up the palms of his hands.

'Fuck the government's offer,' Manus exclaims. 'If I were you, I wouldn't take it either. Here's a better offer. Why don't you and me find it and do a bunk?' The police officer laughs heartily. 'You and me … men of the world … gods of the seven universes … we can do that, can't we?'

Ructions smiles, 'I'm not a god, Manus, and there is no gold.'

'Sure there isn't. Well, good luck, tough guy,' Manus says as he walks to the cell door. But just before closing the door, Manus pops his head in again. 'Oh, I forgot to say, there are about thirty reporters at the front of the station waiting for you. Never mind O'Flaherty; you're the man in the big picture.' Manus points a finger at Ructions. 'Loved that bank job. Touch of class. Anyway, don't worry. You'll be released shortly.'

'I appreciate that.'

No sooner has Manus walked out than Vasseur walks in. 'I'm sorry to see you in a prison cell, Ructions.'

'I'm sorry to be here. The last time we met, it was in more salubrious surroundings.'

'The Ritz in Paris.'

'Thierry, isn't it?'

'You've a good memory, but then you'd need it in your line of work.' Vasseur sits down. 'I didn't want you picked up, but my Irish counterparts got excited at the prospect of such an illustrious gathering. Come on, let's get you out of here.' The two leave the cell.

In a room behind the reception area, an officer brings Ructions a brown paper bag that contains his personal belongings. 'Follow me, please,' Vasseur says. Vasseur and Robillard lead Ructions through to a car park at the rear of the station and to a Peugeot SUV. 'Get in the back and lie down,' Vasseur says. Robillard drives the car out of the station, past the swarm of reporters and photographers.

Manus O'Toole comes out of Dun Laoghaire garda station and confronts the press. Cameras roll, questions abound. 'Why is Ructions O'Hare in police custody?' 'Is O'Hare going to be charged?' 'Has O'Hare rejoined the IRA?' 'Why is Paul O'Flaherty in custody?'

Manus puts up his hands. 'Please, please. Okay. Mr O'Hare has been released without charge.'

'Why was he arrested?'

'He was arrested on suspicion of involvement in an alleged kidnapping.'

'Who was kidnapped?'

'That is the subject of ongoing inquiries.'

'Were police alleging that Mr O'Hare had carried out a kidnapping?'

'No.'

'Was Mr O'Hare in custody in relation to the National Bank robbery in Belfast?'

'No.'

'You haven't answered the question, Chief Superintendent. Why was Ructions O'Hare arrested?'

'He was helping An Garda Síochána with inquiries.'

'Has Paul O'Flaherty been released?'

'Mr O'Flaherty will be released shortly.'

'Is—'

'That's it,' Manus says, turning to walk back into the station.

Paschal O'Rourke, a reporter from the state television service RTÉ shouts, 'Chief Superintendent, was Ructions O'Hare questioned about Hermann Goering's gold shipment to Ireland in 1944?'

On hearing that question, Manus stops and spins around, surprise writ large on his face.

O'Rourke presses home his advantage. 'Is O'Hare back in Ireland because he knows the whereabouts of tonnes of Nazi gold?'

Manus turns and reenters the station and, in not answering O'Rourke's questions, seems to confirm everything.

Vasseur, Robillard, and Ructions are sitting in a coffee shop on the outskirts of Dun Laoghaire. Sitting across from them is a plainclothes female police officer. Ructions gets up and walks over to ask her if she would like a tea or coffee. She declines his offer.

Vasseur is talking on the phone when Ructions returns. 'I see. Thank you.' The French police officer stirs his coffee, his eyes fixed on Ructions. 'That was Manus O'Toole.'

'Oh?'

'Bad news. He was asked at a press conference if you were questioned about Goering's gold.'

'Are you fucking serious? Tell me this is a joke, Thierry.'

'Unfortunately, it isn't.'

'How did they find that out?' Robillard asks.

'Who knows?' Vasseur replies. 'It could have come from multiple sources. Every police force in Europe has access to this inquiry and Ructions's involvement in it … although my money would be on a local police officer.'

Ructions's chest rises. Exhaling slowly, he puts his head in his hands and without looking at the officers says, 'I'd be very surprised if this doesn't turn into an international news story.'

'Nazi gold, Hermann Goering, the IRA, a twenty-first century Jesse James … what did you expect, Ructions?' Vasseur says. 'It was always going to be an A-movie. How could it be anything else?'

'I imagine your face will be on the front page of every news-paper in Europe tomorrow morning,' Robillard says.

'Thanks, Pierre. That's cheered me up.'

With a gesture towards the female police officer, Vasseur says, 'They're going to stick to you like glue, but then you know that.'

'They're gonna try.'

'I can't imagine the pressure you must be under. The police, the IRA, the neo-Nazis, and now the world's press. It can't be easy for you at the minute.'

Ructions taps the palm of his hand with a teaspoon. 'You exclude yourself.'

'Believe it or not, I've no interest in locking you up. You robbed a bank in Ireland. So what? I hate banks. They rob people every day.'

'I'm wondering ... what am I doing here? Should I be speaking to you?'

'It's entirely up to yourself,' Robillard says, 'but it might be in your interest.'

Ructions can sense that Vasseur is concerned. 'What's on your mind, Thierry?'

Vasseur sips his coffee. 'A very dangerous man came through Dublin airport today.' Vasseur looks at Ructions's face, but that face gives nothing away.

'What's that got to do with me?'

'The man I'm talking about is Karl Keller, the leader of the German National Party. Keller is the chief suspect in the murder of Clément Beauregard.'

'You've asked me about him before.'

'That's right. I believe he has come to Ireland to meet you.'

'You can believe whatever you like.'

'Ructions, hear him out,' Robillard says.

Ructions looks at his watch. 'You've two minutes.' Ructions catches the plainclothes police officer's eye but gone is the friendliness he had shown earlier.

'I think he's here to meet you. I think he wants to do a deal with you over Goering's baton. You do have it, don't you?'

Ructions does not blink.

'Anyway,' Vasseur says, 'I want Keller and his gang for the murder of Clément Beauregard. I don't care about the gold, fuck that, but I care a lot about bringing these Nazi bastards to justice for the murder of a French citizen on French soil.'

'And if I did know this Keller fella – how could I help you?'

'You could wear a wire when you're meeting him; you could get him to admit that he murdered Beauregard.'

Ructions rubs his lower lip with his thumb. 'Supposing I *was* going to meet him, and supposing I *was* to wear a wire, what on earth makes you think he'd confess to me about the murder?'

'I'm not sure if he will or not, but how do you say … *ça vaut la peine d'un coup ne pensez-vous pas?*'

'No, it's not worth a shot. And anyway, we're only supposing.'

Vasseur locks on to Ructions's eyes and wags a finger. 'You want this bastard. I can see it.'

'Pardon?'

'I think you want Keller as bad as me for the murder of Clément Beauregard.'

'Look, Thierry, I don't know what you see, and I can't help you.'

'A pity. Help can be a two-way street.'

'What do you mean by that?'

'Strings can be pulled. Certain indiscretions can be over-looked if it's in the national interest. Ructions, we French are a generous people.'

With the Irish government's munificent offer to overlook certain indiscretions fresh in his mind, Ructions remarks, 'Everybody wants to be my friend, but their friendship comes with a price.'

'Sorry?' Vasseur says. 'I don't understand.'

'You want Keller; the Irish government want to let me walk away with twenty per cent of the gold providing they cop the other eighty per cent. Everybody wants to be my friend.'

Vasseur holds out his hands as if gripping a large parcel, 'The question is: who's friendship is more important to you?'

Ructions stands up. As he walks away, he turns around. Thierry …'

'Yes?'

'I liked Clément.

'Can I rely on your help, then?'

'If I can help you, I will – for Clément.'

CHAPTER THIRTY-FIVE

AS SOON AS HE ENTERS LOBBY OF THE ROYAL MARINE Hotel in Dun Laoghaire, Ructions goes to the hotel's public phone and rings Billy. 'Have you made the arrangements?'

'Yip.'

'And no hiccups?'

'None. Everything's sweet.'

'Don't say it over the phone, but you know what time to come in?'

'Of course. Look, relax, will you? I've got your back.'

Ructions hangs up. Afterwards, he phones Eleanor, who is about to board a flight to Devon.

She looks at her phone but doesn't recognise the number. 'Hello?'

'El, it's me.'

'Leave me alone!' Eleanor hangs up. Her phone rings again, and this time she doesn't answer it.

Ructions sighs and runs a hand through his hair. *It's going from bad to worse.* His eye catches a young man and his female companion, who are sitting across from him, making no secret of the fact that they are watching him.

He strides into the lounge and takes a seat at a window. Across from him, an old lady sits alone, supping tomato soup in front of a blazing fire. She has kind eyes and candyfloss hair that is up a bun. She smiles at Ructions, who warmly returns the sentiment.

A waiter comes along and provides Ructions with a menu. He orders lunch and a bottle of red wine. He speaks to the waiter and nods towards the two police officers, who have followed him into the lounge.

Detective Garda Deborah MacGowan is on the phone to Manus O'Toole, who is still in the Dun Laoghaire Division Headquarters. 'Of the two phone calls he made,' she tells her superior, 'the first number is registered to a Mister Carlos Marks—'

'Karl Marx,' Manus says. 'He phoned Karl Marx. For fuck's sake.'

'And the other was to a Ms Proctor. That call lasted just seconds.'

'Eleanor's hung up on him. Good for her. What's he doing now, MacGowan?'

'He's just ordered lunch, sir.'

'Lunch?'

'Yes, sir. Hold on … it looks like he's sending a waiter over to us …'

'That gentleman,' the waiter says, nodding to Ructions, 'would like to buy you lunch and perhaps a bottle of wine.'

'What's that? MacGowan,' Manus says.

'He has offered to buy us lunch and a bottle of wine, sir.'

'Well, order the most expensive item on the menu – but no wine.'

'Yes, sir.'

MacGowan looks at the waiter. 'Can we see the menu?' She waves to Ructions, who returns the gesture.

Manus hangs up the speaker phone and looks at Detective Inspector Seán de Brún, whom he'd been meeting with when the call came in. 'What's he up to, Seán?'

'Sounds like he's chilling out, sir.'

'No.' Manus points to a large photograph of Ructions on the wall. 'He's waiting for something or somebody. Have we all the roads into and out of Dun Laoghaire covered?'

'Yes, sir. We have cars at every strategic point.'

Manus is still uneasy. 'We're missing something. I'm sure of it.'

Ructions has finished his lunch and has read all the papers. He looks out the window.

A grey-haired, bespectacled man and a young, fresh-faced female with a large movie camera under her arm come into the lounge and sit down on one of the sofas. Paschal O'Rourke spots Ructions and whispers to his camerawoman, instructing her to make sure she catches every nuance of his forthcoming encounter with Ructions. O'Rourke approaches Ructions's table.

'Mr O'Hare, may I sit down?'

'It's not my hotel. You can sit wherever you want.'

The journalist holds out his hand and they shake. 'Paschal O'Rourke, RTÉ.'

'Ructions O'Hare. Innocent until proven guilty.'

O'Rourke smiles. 'Can we talk?'

'What about?'

'About your arrest. About Hermann Goering's gold.'

'That was a very clumsy approach, Paschal, for an old-hand like you. Why didn't you try to butter me up? Offer me a drink? Make small talk?'

'You don't strike me as a small-talker.'

'Good read. I'm not. So, why don't you ask questions, and I'll see if I want to answer them.'

Paschal stares at Ructions. 'Okay. Would you like to tell RTÉ's viewers what you're doing back in Ireland?'

'I'm Irish, Paschal, in case it slipped your mind, and, as it happens, I've been touring the country.'

'Was a sojourn in a police station part of your itinerary?'

'I rarely visit police stations unless I've been robbed.' He looks at his watch. 'Look, I'm pressed for time.'

O'Rourke thinks that a congenial rapport has been established, and besides, Ructions has put him on the clock. 'Ructions, would you like to tell our viewers where Hermann Goering's gold is?'

Before Ructions can answer, two dozen journalists appear at the entrance to the lounge and dash to his table.

Cameras click as hundreds of photographs of Ructions are taken. He sits, arms crossed, his face as immobile as that of a leopard stalking a Thomson's gazelle. 'Ructions, where's Goering's gold?' 'Ructions, where's the National Bank money?' 'Ructions, who was kidnapped?' 'Did you pay the IRA ransom?' The questions fly like confetti at a wedding.

Ructions's phone rings, and he takes the call, holding one hand over his mouth and the other over the phone transmitter. He ends the call, stands up, puts on his coat, and sits down again.

The photographers, reporters, and television media capture every movement.

The sound of rotor blades slice the air outside. Ructions looks out the window, stands up, and walks to the public phone box in the lobby.

'A helicopter is landing in front of the hotel, sir,' MacGowan says into her phone.

'What's he doing?' Manus says.

'He's making a phone call in the lobby, sir.'

Suddenly Ructions drops the phone and sprints out to the helicopter. The two officers and the press corps pursue him.

'He's in the helicopter, sir!' MacGowan shouts into her phone as she runs to catch Ructions.

'Well, fucking – pull him out of it!'

By the time the police officers reach the helicopter, it's six feet off the ground. Ructions wriggles his fingers at MacGowan, her colleague and the press as it rises, then turns towards Dublin.

O'Rourke turns to his camerawoman. 'Did you get that?' The camerawoman gives the thumbs up. 'Brilliant!'

'A helicopter?' Manus says. 'Why didn't I see it? Any markings, MacGowan?'

'It says Dublin Helicopters on the side, sir.'

'Tom, contact Dublin Helicopters. They'll have communications with the chopper. I want to know where it is at all times. Ructions won't be in it long. I want to know where and when it sets down. Got that?'

'Yes, sir.'

'What direction is it heading in, MacGowan?'

'Toward Dublin, sir.'

'Of course. That's where he'll be meeting Keller. Seán,

scramble our Dublin chopper. I'll brief them when they're in the air and we've a better idea of what he's up to. Jed, make sure our cars stay with him.'

'That'll be difficult, sir.'

'I know, but tell them to keep their feet to the pedals. We can't lose this guy again.'

In the helicopter, Ructions is sitting in the back seat looking out over the twisting coastline. Billy Kelly hands the pilot a wad of money in exchange for the aviator's headphones and his mobile telephone. He then orders the pilot to fly to Elm Park Golf Club in Donnybrook. The trip takes approximately five minutes.

A four-ball is putting out on the eighteenth hole when the helicopter comes in to land on the fairway. The buffeting winds from the downdraught forces the four golfers to scurry to the safety of nearby trees. The aircraft touches down, and Ructions and Billy alight, Billy still holding the driver's headset in his hand. They then run to the clubhouse car park where they get into a Vauxhall car, in which Ambrose is in the driver's seat. Ambrose Peoples, a chunky eighteen stone rock 'n' roller with an early Elvis hairstyle puts his hand out to Ructions. They shake. 'How's it goin' there, big man?' Ructions says.

'Taking in the sights, Ructions. Smiling at troubles.'

Ructions grins. 'Let's shift.' Taking the back roads, they make their way to the outskirts of Dublin, where they abandon the Vauxhall and get into a black Skoda.

In Dun Laoghaire Divisional Headquarters, Chief Superintendent Manus O'Toole is fuming. 'He's gone. Fuck!'

That night, in a flat in south Dublin, Ructions, Billy, and Ambrose are enjoying an Indian takeaway and watching television from the comfort of their easy chairs. Ructions isn't particularly hungry, so he picks at his food.

A jingle introduces the nine o'clock RTÉ news on the television. The headlines show the dramatic events that had been recorded on the phone of the bald, middle-aged man on Dun Laoghaire pier earlier in the day. The footage shows O'Flaherty and Ructions being confronted by the two, armed police officers, being forced to lie at gunpoint on the ground, with the armed members of the garda ERU taking up covering positions. It goes on to show O'Flaherty and Ructions being handcuffed.

News reporter Paschal O'Rourke stands on the spot where the arrests had taken place and speaks into a camera: 'These were the shocking scenes on the east pier of Dun Laoghaire harbour this morning when gardaí arrested five men in connection with the suspected kidnapping of a thirty-six-year-old woman from Northern Ireland.'

Footage of the arrest plays out as O'Rourke explains who was arrested, highlighting that 'Mr O'Hare was charged and acquitted in 2005 of the robbery of £36.5 million from the National Bank in Belfast.' He concludes that 'Gardaí would not confirm if Mr O'Hare was meeting Mr O'Flaherty to pay an IRA ransom for the release of a close female friend,' and notes that 'all five men were subsequently released after being interviewed by gardaí.'

Then, however, he changes tack: 'In a separate development, reliable sources have told RTÉ that gardaí believe Mr O'Hare is at the centre of a hunt for Nazi gold that was allegedly sent to and secreted in Ireland during the Second World War by Nazi leader Hermann Goering, Adolf Hitler's second-in-command. Tellingly, gardaí have not denied the reports.'

The footage runs on to show the press conference that morning where O'Rourke had put his questions to Manus O'Toole, 'Chief Superintendent, was Ructions O'Hare questioned about Hermann Goering's gold shipment to Ireland in 1944? Is O'Hare back in Ireland because he knows the whereabouts of tonnes of Nazi gold?' The video captures the look of surprise on Manus's face and his immediate retreat into Dun Laoghaire station.

Then the scene shifts to the hotel restaurant, with the video of O'Rourke trying to question Ructions himself about Goering's gold, only to be overrun by other reporters without getting an answer, and then of Ructions sprinting to the helicopter just ahead of the scrum.

The report ends with a shot of the helicopter rising above the crowd and O'Rourke's voiceover explaining that the chopper had landed in Elm Park Golf Club in Donnybrook, and 'Mr O'Hare was long gone by the time gardaí arrived at the golf club.'

Ructions slowly sets down his plate on the coffee table, goes to the venetian blinds, flicks up a slat with his index finger, and looks out. The street is quiet. No one is about. He is troubled: *This isn't right; the whole world knows my business.* He returns to his seat and stares blankly at the television.

Ambrose gazes at Ructions. He chews his food slowly and swallows, before saying, 'What are you gonna do, boss? Every peeler in the state will be carrying your photograph.'

'Fat lot of good it'll do them. The Ructions O'Hare they're looking for won't exist.'

'Shouldn't you call this whole thing off?' Ambrose says. 'Don't you think it's getting too hot?'

Ructions lifts his fork and waves it at Ambrose. 'Do you want out, Ambrose?'

'No, boss.'

'Then why ask me if *I* want out?'

'I just thought—'

'Don't think. Leave that to me.'

The next morning, Ructions is up and showered and having a smoke at the window. He likes an early morning cigarette, that few minutes before the centre of the earth erupts beneath his feet.

More than all the tumult surrounding Hermann Goering's gold and its prominence in the previous day's media, he is finding it hard to come to terms with Eleanor's departure from his life. Her phone has not been taking incoming calls. He reckons that she has changed her number. This time her break with him seems permanent. He tells himself that it's the right thing for her to do, but …

There's a knock at the door. He peers through the spyhole, then lets Billy in. Carrying some newspapers under his arm, Billy looks directly at him. 'How's your stomach?'

'Fine.' But even as he replies, Ructions can feel a flutter in his gut. *Why would Billy ask that question?*

'Have you looked at the news on the TV yet or read the morning papers?'

'I try to avoid bad news.'

'Sorry, buddy, but you're on every station. Look …' Billy turns on the television. Ructions's face is taking up half the screen on the BBC morning news. Anchor Pamela Hurst comments, ' … and now we go to our Irish correspondent, John Tucker, who is reporting from Dublin …'

John Tucker is standing outside garda headquarters in Dublin. 'Reporters from as far away as the United States, New Zealand, and Japan are flocking to the Republic of Ireland to cover a story of Nazi gold and Irish intrigue, a story that revolves around these two men …' A photo of Ructions appears alongside that of a stern Hermann Goering, wearing a wide-brimmed hat with feathers in it. 'The man on the left is James "Ructions" O'Hare, who was acquitted in 2005 of robbing the National Bank in Belfast of £36.5 million, and beside him is Hermann Goering, second only to Adolf Hitler in Nazi Germany. Strange bedfellows, you may say, but at the centre of this story is the sensational claim that, before the Second World War ended, Goering hid tonnes of gold in Ireland so that he could resurrect the fortunes of the Nazis after the war. The BBC has learned that O'Hare, who was described during his trial as a "criminal mastermind," has a treasure map and that he has the support of the IRA – in particular, this man.' A photo of O'Flaherty appears on screen. 'Republican leader, Paul O'Flaherty. Authorities are …'

Ructions flicks to another channel only to see footage of himself being arrested in Dun Laoghaire. He turns off the television.

Billy opens the paper and hands it to Ructions.

On the front page there is a huge police photo of Ructions, and above it is the headline: 'RUCTIONS CHASES GOERING'S GOLD.' He quickly runs his eye down the article. 'Jesus Aloysius Christ!'

Karl Keller is shaving when there is a knock on his door. He opens it. A uniformed bellhop is holding up a silver service food tray with one hand, and on it is a stainless-steel dinner plate cover.

'Room service.'

'But I didn't order room service.'

The bellhop looks at the room number and then at the receipt. 'Says here, Room 302, sir.'

Keller warily peeks under the dinner plate cover. 'I see. Bring it in, please.'

The bellhop walks in and leaves the tray on the table. 'Is there anything else I can get you, sir?'

'No, thank you.' Keller tips the bellhop, who leaves the room.

Keller removes the plate cover to find a mobile phone. After lifting it, he puts it down again and goes to the bathroom to finish his shave. As he is finishing, the phone rings. He grabs a towel, dries himself, and walks to the phone. 'Hello?'

'Hello,' Ructions says.

'Who's this?'

'The person you've come to Ireland to meet. No names.'

'Okay.'

'Do not use your own phone again,' Ructions says. 'It's tapped. Use this one. It isn't. You're under surveillance, but we can deal with that. I'll give you instructions. Follow them to the letter.'

'Fine.'

'I want you and Gitte to go to Grafton Street at eleven o'clock this morning. Shop for new clothes. As you buy them, wear them. Discard your old clothes, they'll be bugged. Have you got that?'

'Yes.'

'Afterwards, get tea or coffee in Bruxelles pub in Harry Street. I'll phone you later with instructions.'

'Can I——?'

The phone is already dead.

The fifth most expensive shopping street in the world is Grafton Street. It is vibrant, packed with tourists, artists, Dubliners, florists, entertainers, coffee shops, eateries, and assorted retail outlets. Outside Weir and Sons Jewellers, a teenager with a husky voice sings 'Cry Me a River' into a stand-up microphone. Keller and Gitte applaud at the end of the song. They walk back up the street. A Charlie Chaplin lookalike stands rigid, unblinkingly staring ahead, one leg across the other, his hands holding a cane in front of him. A couple of dozen yards up from Charlie Chaplin, a teenage string quartet plays Bach's 'Air on the G String.'

At the entrance to Harry Street, two flower stalls occupy most of the pavement, offering a wide selection of roses, lilies, tulips, and various bouquets. Keller looks intently at the flowers and settles for a bouquet, which he gives to Gitte, who smiles and inhales the fragrance of the flowers.

Keller walks over to a statue of the Thin Lizzy lead singer, Phil Lynott, and gets Gitte to take his photo with his arm around the musician. The two take a table outside Bruxelles pub and look at the menu. Keller's phone rings.

'No food,' Ructions says.

'But I'm famished!' Keller says. 'I missed breakfast in the hotel this morning.'

'You haven't time for food. Now, to your right is the Westbury Hotel. Go into the shopping mall. Slowly, as if you're browsing.'

'I've got that,' Keller says, looking about to see where Ructions is observing him.

Ructions, his phone to his ear, is at a window on the first-floor lounge of the Westbury. He watches as Keller and Gitte stroll over into the shopping mall.

'Right, through the mall, quickly now. Take the exit to the left. The left, not the right. You'll see red roadworks at the entrance.'

'Yes. I see them.'

'Go out onto the street. There'll be two motorcyclists there with helmets resting on the pillion seats. They're my guys. Jump on the bikes and put on the helmets. Hurry!'

Keller and Gitte scurry around the roadworks, past a refuge skip, and over to the motorcyclists. Putting on the helmets, they mount the bikes and are driven away.

Two plainclothes police officers run out onto Clarendon Street and watch the motorcycles as they speed away up the one-way street. One officer uses his wrist radio to report back to headquarters.

The bikers enter the side entrance of a block of period, single-storied cottages in the Arbour Hill area and pull up at a backyard with a blue door.

Keller and Gitte get off the bikes. Keeping on his helmet, Ambrose gets off his bike, puts a key in the back door and invites Keller and Gitte to follow him through the yard. He leads them on into a kitchen in the back of the house. Billy, also still helmeted, joins them. 'The boss will be here in a couple of minutes.'

Keller nods.

Billy produces a handgun. 'I need to search you.'

Shocked, Keller exclaims: 'What is this?'

'Safety first. Now put your hands up, please.' Keller puts up his hands. Ambrose gives Keller a pat-down.

'Ma'am, can you take off your coat, please?' Billy says.

Gitte obliges, but drops her coat on the floor. Billy picks it up, searches it and sets it down on a chair. He indicates with his gun that he wants Gitte to raise her hands. 'I'm sorry for this, ma'am.'

Ambrose quickly searches Gitte, who stands glum-faced throughout the process. She puts her coat back on when the search is over.

After five minutes, Ructions, sporting a ginger beard and thick glasses, enters the room through the back door. He smiles and says, 'Sorry I'm late,' putting out his hand to Keller. 'I'm Ructions.'

Keller does not take Ructions's hand. Ructions smiles but the smile fades almost immediately.

'So, you are Herr Ructions?' Keller says sternly. 'Then I must protest in the strongest possible terms at the way we have been manhandled. I was searched, and this man' – Keller nods to Ambrose – 'put his hands on my partner. Is that the way you treat guests in Ireland?'

'Where do you think you are, Karl?' Ructions says defiantly. 'In a five-star hotel? Precautions must be taken; security is paramount. I'd have thought you of all people would appreciate that.'

Keller is taken aback at Ructions's frankness. He reckons that it would have cost Ructions nothing to offer a token apology, but he has deliberately refused to do so. 'I suppose you have a point,' Keller says, holding out his hand. 'Please forgive my earlier reticence in shaking your hand. I was angry.'

'We all get angry, Karl.'

'It's a pleasure to finally meet you, Herr Ructions.'

Ructions takes Keller's hand. 'And you.'

'And this is Professor Gitte Meyer. She's an expert in German history and antiquities, especially memorabilia from the war.'

Ructions shakes Gitte's hand. He smiles, recognising her from his photographic research of Keller. 'Pleased to meet you, Gitte. May I say, you're even more beautiful in real life than you are on the computer.'

Gitte beams and takes Ructions's hand. 'And may I say, it's a pleasure to finally meet you, Herr Ructions.'

'And Karl,' Ructions says, 'I apologise for being so abrupt with you on the phone.'

In a spirit of freshly hatched détente, Keller waves his hand and shakes his head. 'No apology needed. I like directness.'

'Okay,' Ructions says, 'shall we be direct?'

'That would be most appropriate.'

Billy taps Ambrose. 'We'll let these guys talk.'

The two men vacate the room.

'We'd like to see the Reichsmarschall's baton, Herr Ructions, if that is possible.'

'Sure,' Ructions says. 'That, after all, is what we're here for.' He opens a cupboard, takes out the leather pouch, unzips it, removes the baton, and holds it upright in front of Keller, whose eyes are riveted to it.

'May I?' Keller asks timidly.

Ructions hands over the baton to Keller, who holds it, his grip at the top of the stem, as if it was an extension of his arm. Then he examines the platinum swastika, studded with diamonds. He studies the writing on the baton and says: *'Der Führer zu dem*

Reichsmarschall des Grossdeutschlands.' He repeats the inscription before turning to Gitte and handing her the baton.

Gitte goes to her handbag and takes out a small set of hand-held scales, a jeweller's eyepiece, and a magnifying glass. Firstly, she weighs the baton. Then she holds the eyepiece to her right eye and examines the diamonds and the platinum swastika. She clasps the magnifying glass in front of the inscription and holds it on certain letters. She goes closer, inspecting the letters, before reviewing the diamonds.

Keller looks apprehensive. Ructions, hands in pockets and quietly whistling 'The Lonesome Boatman,' looks confident. Gitte nods to Keller.

He must not show how excited he really is at this moment. He thinks: *How cruel is the suppression of delight. This Ructions O'Hare ... look at him! A dolt. An Irish peasant.* 'Okay,' Keller says. 'Gitte is satisfied that this is the ceremonial baton of Reichsmarschall Hermann Goering.'

Ructions puts out his hand and, taking the baton back from Keller, holds it tight to his chest. Paul O'Flaherty's words invade his mind: 'Everybody pays.' Is it not Karl's turn to pay – through the nose? Ructions stands straight and looks Keller square-on. 'Do you want to buy Hermann Goering's baton?'

'I might.'

'Might you now?' Ructions smirks as he puts the baton back in the leather pouch. This demonstrable act of closure is a tactic that Ructions has used on numerous occasions, especially when he knows that he holds all the ace cards.

Keller is stricken with panic. The colour drains from his face, unmasking a man in the throes of distraction. He puts his hand on Ructions's forearm. 'Herr Ructions, please—'

'It's over, Karl. I've another punter to see this evening who is exceptionally keen to buy the baton.'

'Punter?'

'Buyer. Purchaser.'

'No, Herr Ructions. You seem to think that I do not want to buy the Reichsmarschall's baton. This is not so.'

Ructions looks pensive. 'Are you saying you *do* want to buy it?'

'I do, I do.'

'Ahh, right. There's been a misunderstanding.' Ructions holds up his hands. 'I apologise. I misinterpreted your intentions.'

Keller isn't sure what's going on. Ructions's flippancy has unnerved him. He had mentally prepared a negotiating plan: He was going to be standoffish, disinterested; he was going to pretend that he was scarcely listening to Ructions's selling pitch; he was going to beat Ructions down on the price. Ructions's selling pitch? There was none. The minute Keller had raised a doubt, Ructions pulled down the curtain. No show. No baton. No sale.

'For how much can I buy the baton?' Keller asks.

'Before we get to that, you must realise that I don't deal. Karl, I'm going to be honest with you: I wouldn't know how to.' Despite being from a family of renowned dealers, Ructions looks positively naïve.

'I'm not that good at it myself,' Keller admits.

'I'm gonna give you a price. You can either take it or leave it.' Ructions has an air of *c'est la vie* about him. 'There will be no negotiation. If you don't want to pay, that's fine. That's no problem. Really. Maybe we'll do another deal someday.'

Keller nods enthusiastically.

'If you want to buy Hermann Goering's ceremonial baton, it going to cost you four million euro.'

Keller gulps. Gitte has a smirk on her face.

Ructions moves in for the kill. 'Do you have access to that amount of money?'

'Yes,' Keller says quickly.

'Karl, you must be truthful with me. If you don't have the money, say so. It's not the end of the world. At that price, I can still sell the baton to someone else.'

'I can get the money. My party has powerful backers.'

'When can we complete the deal?'

'It will take me a few days to put the money in place.'

'That's understandable. Three days from today. Does that work for you?'

'I expect to have the finances in place by then. Yes.'

'So, we have a deal, Karl?'

'I will need a bill of sale from Serge Mercier.'

'That can be done. Now, do we have a deal?'

'Yes. We have a deal.' The neo-Nazi and the Irishman shake hands. 'Can I hold it again?' Keller says.

Ructions smiles and hands the leather pouch over to Keller.

CHAPTER THIRTY-SIX

SERGE MERCIER, A PILOT SINCE HE WAS TWENTY-ONE,
brings his plane in to land at Lausanne Airport. His touchdown
is faultless. The plane comes to a halt close to the hangar. Serge
unfastens his seatbelt and walks into the hanger. A mechanic
approaches to say that there is a call for him on the public phone.
Serge unzips his green flight suit as he approaches the phone.

'Hello?'

'Calling the Red Baron. Calling the Red Baron!'

'The Red Baron was German, cher ami,' Serge says quietly.

'But a very honourable German,' Ructions replies.

'Oh, there are many honourable Germans. How are you?'

'Good,' Ructions says.

'What's happening?'

'I can't say over the phone, but things are shaping up.'

'I've heard that.'

Ructions is pacing across from Conolly's Folly in County Kildare. Staggered by Serge's reply, he stops. 'You've heard that?'

'Yes,' Serge says. Ructions awaits Serge's elaboration. 'And I know who you sold the merchandise to.'

'You do? How so?'

'Do you remember the letter I gave you in the Louvre?'

'I remember it well.'

'Well, that letter-writer has sent me a second letter.'

'Good for him, or her.' Ructions drinks from his tin of coke. 'Anything I should be worried about?'

'I'm afraid there might be. The person who has bought the merchandise—'

'He hasn't bought it yet. We haven't sealed the deal.'

'I know,' Serge says. 'He's trawling for the money.'

'Will he get it?'

'The letter-writer seems pretty confident that he will, but that's not what's worrying me.'

Ructions runs his hands through his hair. 'What is?'

'He has mobilised the individuals who visited my home.'

Ructions's fingers tap a Riverdance around the joints in his left hand.

'Of course. Let me guess … they're coming my way?'

'Yes.'

'Aha.'

'Will that be a problem?'

'I don't know. It could be. Depends.'

'Can I help?' Serge asks.

'Actually, yes.' Ructions's mind turns to Serge's nephew, Antoine, the fishing boat captain who had ferried Ructions and the proceeds of the National Bank robbery out of Ireland. 'I might need Antoine and yourself to drop anchor with me soon. Would that be possible?'

'We'd be delighted, absolutely delighted.'

'Great. I also need you to send me a bill of sale for the item as soon as possible. The vendor is insisting on it.'

'I can do that. Four million euro, isn't it?'

'Yes.'

'Where do I send it?'

'I'll contact you later with the address. Tell me: Are those people still parked outside your house?'

'They've lost interest. Today, for example, there was nobody at the gates.'

'I hope your private security is still in place?'

'Mais oui!'

'Good. I'm gonna leave it at that. I'll phone you later.'

'Do.'

'Bonne chance.'

'De même.'

His face still hidden behind a beard and thick glasses, Ructions closes his phone and walks to the front of his car. Dermot McCracken gets out of the passenger seat and comes around to stand beside him. Both men stare off at Conolly's Folly. 'So that's it,' says Ructions. 'It looks more like a giant's knuckle-duster than an obelisk.'

He looks at the information leaflet he'd picked up earlier. 'It's 137.8 feet high and decorated with stone eagles and pineapples.' He points to the two outer arches, which are topped with stone pineapples and the upper inner arches, which are adorned with stone eagles. 'Says here the workers were each paid a ha'penny a day for their work. Not a lot.'

'That ha'penny kept families alive,' Dermot says. 'Remember: Katherine Conolly built this thing just to keep people alive.'

Ructions proceeds through the open gate to the central arch and stops, looking up at the keystone. A young couple nod hello as they walk past him. He returns the greeting. Walking through the two inner arches, he strokes the brickwork.

He observes that the grass has been cut. Getting down on his hunkers, he gazes off at the road that leads up to Castletown House, almost three miles away. He goes back to the car and takes out a folder, opens it, removes the painting, and retreats to a gate post. Dermot joins him. Both study the painting and look at the obelisk. 'What do you see, Dermy?'

'Nothing I haven't seen before. This is about Hermann Goering's gold, isn't it? Don't deny it. Your face is on every television station. You have fans, you know. On a radio show I listened to, plenty of listeners phoned in to wish you the best of luck.'

'Fans? I've fans?'

'Oh, yeah. Wanna see some of them?' Dermot takes out his smart phone and turns it on. 'I recorded this … thought you might like to see it sometime …'

A video shows a reporter in Dublin's O'Connell Street interviewing passersby. A young man with green-tipped hair and wearing makeup is interviewed: 'Excuse me. Have you heard about Goering's gold?'

'Dat's dat Ructions O'Hare fella, isn't it? De man dat robbed the Bank of Belfast? Oh, he's a ride!'

Ructions laughs.

The video cuts to three twentysomething women at the Daniel O'Connell monument, one of whom says: 'Ructions O'Hare? He's lovely! And loaded too!'

Her friend chirps in, 'Yeah, loaded with Nazi gold!'

Another man in a three-piece suit is interviewed and says: 'What are you asking me about dat thievin' thug fer? He should be locked up.'

Dermot pockets his phone. He stares at Ructions before putting his hand in his pocket and nervously rattling some coins. 'It's all true, isn't it? All of it. Oh, fuck!'

Ructions looks at Dermot, and it's as if some malevolent spirit has suddenly stuck a hump onto his back. 'Dermy! I've never heard you curse before!'

'Fuck, fuck, fuck!'

'What's wrong with you, man?'

'You don't see what's wrong? Ructions, people go bananas for the noble metal,' he says, his lower lip twitching. 'They kill like bastards to get it and the whole country thinks you know where it is.'

Ructions wants to guffaw, but he keeps a straight face.

'And ...' Dermot says, pointing an inquiring finger at Ructions, 'and is it *your* gold?'

'It's finders keepers, as far as I can see.'

'Oh, no, no, no, no, no. There's no such thing as finders keepers. Under the National Monuments Act 1987, all archaeological finds must be reported to the state within thirty days. And not only that, you must have a government permit to look for artefacts in the first place. I presume you don't have such a permit?'

'You presume right.'

'So, if you find this treasure and don't report it, you're breaking the law, and, if I help you, so am I.'

'Me? Breaking the law? Perish the thought!'

Dermot sticks his hands in the back pockets of his jeans,

turns away, then turns back. He is struggling to find the humour in the situation. 'Tonnes of Nazi gold … finders keepers. Can it get any worse?'

'You could be dead.'

'That's a *real* comfort.' Dermot takes out his handkerchief and wipes his forehead. 'Look, I'm sweating.'

'I don't know why.'

''Course you don't. This is all in a day's work to you.'

Ructions has had enough fun with Dermot. He has to be sure that the archaeologist is still committed to helping him. 'Dermy, if you want to walk away from this now, go ahead. I'll understand.'

Dermot vacillates and then says: 'I've never broken the law; never had as much as a police caution.' He stares at Ructions. 'You didn't tell me I'd be breaking the law when you brought me down here.'

'No, I didn't, but then, it never crossed my mind that *I* was breaking it.'

'Neither did you tell me I'd be chasing Hermann Goering's gold.'

'But you knew. The whole fucking country thinks I know where the gold is. You said so yourself.'

Dermot is being pulled in different directions. Breaking the law is anathema to him, but the lure of finding Goering's gold is overwhelming. He asks himself: How could any archaeologist walk away from the prospect of finding such historical treasure? Would humanity forgive him? Of course, it would. Historians would put him on a par with Howard Carter, only Goering's gold would be more valuable than King Tutankhamun's. Would the Irish judiciary be as forgiving as the historians, though? That question is not so easily answered. He paces up and down, then turns to Ructions: 'I guess this is every archaeologist's dream.'

'I wouldn't know.'

'But I *do* know, and I say: Thanks, mate, I'm in. Right up to the hilt. Wow! This is exciting, isn't it?'

Ructions sighs with relief. 'Thank fuck for that, Dermy. I was beginning to think there for a second that you'd lost your balls. I'll sort you out with a right few quid when this is over – even if we don't find the gold.' Dermot nods. 'Now,' Ructions says, 'I'm going to ask you a question.'

'Go ahead.'

'Okay. Why on earth would Goering hide his gold here when there are infinitely more accessible places to stash it?'

Dermot looks off at the monument and scratches his chin. 'Ructions, I tend to avoid absolutes, but I see no logic in concealing tonnes of gold at a venue that the public visits almost every day. How could you be sure nobody saw you burying it in the first place? And how do you retrieve it? No, this would be the last place I'd hide it.'

'I have to agree. But look ...' Ructions points to the painting. 'The obelisk isn't to scale. Is that deliberate, or was the artist on the poteen while he was painting it?'

'Who knows? What if we visit Castletown House? Maybe it'll throw up a clue.'

'You mean where the Conollys lived? Sure, let's check it out.'

Malcolm Mills has the look of a hard man. Known as Big M to his comrades in Combat 18, the six-foot-three, bald terrorist comes out of his farmhouse with Fabian Hoffman, the Nazi who had intimidated Eleanor in the toilets of the Old Inn Hotel. Hoffman looks around. Not bad: a visitor's cottage, three barns, two tractors, a telescopic forklift, and about thirty cows in an adjoining field. A collie dog runs alongside its master. Big M points to the dog and clicks his fingers. The dog immediately sits, panting, its tongue dangling like that of a thirsty camel.

Hoffman feels decidedly uncomfortable around Big M. Men of few words do not appeal to him, and this guy hasn't really strung a sentence together since he came to the farm.

Big M brings Hoffman into the back of the middle barn, where a car is covered by a white tarpaulin. He pulls up the tarpaulin at the back of the car to reveal a red 1983 Ford Cortina. He opens the boot. Inside is a stash of rifles, submachine guns, and handguns. Hoffman takes out a Sterling submachine gun and looks at it. He strips it down and runs his eye along the inside of the barrel. He reassembles it and places it back in the boot, then removes an SA80 rifle. The weapon is in immaculate condition. Hoffman does not need to examine every gun. These weapons have clearly been treated with tender, loving care. He nods to Big M, who closes the boot. The two men shake hands, consummating the deal.

Another Nazi, Gunther Klein, twenty-seven, slightly overweight, comes through Dublin airport. He presents his passport at customs.

'Reason for coming to Ireland, Mr Klein?'

'I'm here on business.'

'What is your business, sir?'

'I'm a sales manager for Mercedes-Benz.'

The customs officer looks at his computer and hands Klein back his passport. 'Thank you, sir.'

Klein, the last of the five members of Das Reich SS Division who had invaded Serge Mercier's home and murdered Clément Beauregard, has arrived in Ireland.

Ructions's and Dermot's visit to Castletown House has revealed nothing. While the house was a magnificent example of how the Conolly family and the aristocracy lived in the eighteenth century, it didn't make them any the wiser about where the gold might be.

Standing at the bottom of the stairs leading up to the house after their tour, Ructions and Dermot take stock. Once again, they study the painting. 'I'm beginning to think this is a load of old cobblers,' Ructions says. 'Is this Hermann having the last laugh from the grave?'

Dermot smacks his lips. 'I don't know. There's something in this painting that we're missing, but I can't put my finger on it.'

Ructions summarises: 'Okay. Let's stop for a second and look where we're at. The Conolly obelisk isn't to scale; it's bigger than it should be. We don't know why.'

'I can't argue with that,' Dermot says. 'We've gone through the Castletown House tour and estates. Nothing. So what now?'

Ructions points to a spot on the painting. 'I think that's Maynooth Catholic Seminary. Do we visit it?'

'Why would Goering have hidden his gold there?' Dermot says. 'He'd need access, wouldn't he? And that would be a problem if it was in Maynooth. And if Goering did bring in the Catholics, the gold is probably in the Vatican bank by now. Either way, Ructions, I don't think it's in Maynooth.'

Ructions looks at the painting. 'So, where to now?'

'I don't know.' Dermot raises a consoling hand. 'I can't really help you. I think … I think I should go back to Belfast.'

'Dermy, I'd like you to stay handy.'

'I've lectures next week, Ructions. I need to get home.'

'And I've people to meet in Dublin in two days. Can you give me two days? Is that possible? I reckon, one way or another, this thing will be over in two days, and I'd like you around, you know, for your expertise.'

Dermot dry whistles. 'Two days, Ructions, but I can't stretch it any longer.'

Ructions puts his hand on Dermot's shoulder. 'Thanks, mate. Let's get some lunch. I could eat a horse.'

CHAPTER THIRTY-SEVEN

IN THE OPEN-AIR, BACK LOUNGE OF THE DUCK PUB IN
Celbridge, Ructions nods automatically as Dermot extols the
virtues of discovering a piece of pottery or jewellery that hadn't
been touched by human hands for centuries. Suddenly, tiredness
has tiptoed up on the intrepid gold-digger: Ructions just wants
to close his eyes, even for a minute, but he is trapped between his
sense of decorum and Dermot's enthusiasm for his profession.

'Take this place for example,' Dermot says. 'Arthur Guinness
was born on the site of this pub. Did you know that?'

'No.'

'Well, he was, and I guarantee you, if I were to get permission to conduct a dig here, I'd find all sorts of artefacts, maybe
even a few trinkets belonging to old Arthur himself.'

'I wouldn't doubt it.'

'He used barges to transport his beer around Ireland, y'know.
The canals of Ireland were the country's commercial arteries.
The Grand Canal's just a mile away.'

Billy and Ambrose enter and sit themselves down at a wooden bench beside them. Ructions introduces Dermot to the two men. Ambrose lifts a menu. 'Have you guys ordered yet?' he asks. 'I could murder a pint of the black stuff.'

'So, how's it going?' Billy asks Ructions.

Ructions sighs. 'It isn't.'

'I bought those two covered-in lorries and the digging gear you asked for.'

Ructions's nod is perfunctory. 'Have the lorries got tailgates?'

'Yeah.'

Billy leans towards Ructions as Ambrose and Dermot chit-chat. 'Are you all right? You look like you've been on the booze for a month.'

'I fucking wish.'

'What's up?'

'Nothing.'

'What is it? In the name of Jesus, man, I'm your mate: let me help.'

'I wish it was that easy, Bill.'

'Look, Ructions, if this thing bottoms up, you don't have to pay me.'

Touched by his friend's decency, Ructions puts a hand on Billy's shoulder. 'You'll be paid. Everybody will be paid.'

'Fuck the money! If there's no money in it for you, there's no money in it for me.'

Ructions speaks softly: 'Bill, everybody will be paid.'

'But what are you gonna do if you can't find the gold?'

'Pay you guys off and go back to my life, I guess.'

Billy has a sceptical look on his face. 'I doubt that.'

'Right now, Wilhelm, I'd give all the gold in Fort Knox just to get a few hours in my scratcher.'

A waiter brings Ructions's and Dermot's food. Ambrose and Billy put in their orders.

As people at the surrounding tables chatter, Ructions remains silent, barely touching his meal. He excuses himself, sits at another table, takes out the painting from his shoulder bag and lays it out on the table before him. He bends towards it, drawing so close that the image begins to blur. He slowly pulls back. Taking deep breaths, he closes his eyes and tried to discern what he's missing by imagining who painted this – a character he's dubbed Leonardo – and why ... Ructions opens his eyes.

The painting still looks like it always did. Rain splatters the ground outside the lean-to, and there's a stinging wind.

'Ructions,' Billy calls over, 'we're heading indoors.'

Ructions looks up. Ambrose is putting a pint of Guinness to his fat lips. Behind Ambrose, on a beige-coloured door, is a painting of a toucan, the tropical bird that was once the symbol of Guinness beer. The bird has an enormous yellow beak on which is balanced a pint of Guinness. Next to the toucan is a portrait of Arthur Guinness and a caption saying that he had been born on this site on 24 September 1725.

Ructions scratches the back of his head, looks at the toucan and then at Arthur's portrait. He studies the painting. 'You go on,' he says, 'I'll be with you in a minute. Dermy, do me a favour, will ya? Leave me your magnifying glass and laptop.'

'Sure,' Dermot says, reaching into his bag. His curiosity pricked, Dermot stares at Ructions's face. It has changed. The fatigued pallor has been replaced with a certain effervescence. Dermot has an image of rockets firing in all directions inside Ructions's head. Kaiser Ructions is clearly excited.

Dermot's voice drops a decibel: 'Anything I should know

about?' Ructions shakes his head. 'Let me know when you're ready to talk,' Dermot says.

Ructions waits until his friends have gone inside before taking the magnifying glass and bringing it to focus on the painting. He concentrates on the upper inner arches of Conolly's Folly, the areas that are adorned with the stone eagles. *The eagles look peculiar*, he thinks. Their beaks are abnormally long. And they're yellow. Ructions pulls back and looks about him. 'These eagles aren't eagles at all,' he mutters. 'They're bloody toucans.' He brings the magnifying glass closer and then pulls back. Now, it seems, the stars have aligned. Toucans, just like those on the Guinness advertisement!

Ructions walks out into the mizzling rain and turns his face to the weeping sky. Hard rain pings his soft cheeks. A headache nips at his temples and he reminds himself that he must take a couple of Tylenol. He returns to the lean-to and opens Dermot's laptop. He types in 'Famous people from Celbridge, County Kildare,' and the first face to appear on Google Images is that of Arthur Guinness. He takes out a jotter and begins scribbling ...

Ructions closes the laptop and folds up the painting, putting it into the shoulder bag. He marches into the bar and pulls up a chair.

The guys are sitting around the table. Billy dangles a forkful of prawns in front of his mouth, but his eyes are firmly fixed on Ructions. He knows the signs. He's been here before. The boss-man was working something out in the lean-to: He was sparking. He's still sparking. Billy puts down the fork. Ructions has everyone's attention.

'Lads, I've gotta go check something out. I'll be a couple of hours. Here's your laptop, Dermy.'

'Thanks.'

'Where are you goin'?' Billy asks. 'Do you need me to come with you?'

'No. I'll phone you. Don't be going too far, boys. Things might happen very quickly.'

At police headquarters in Belfast, Chief Superintendent Dan Clarke is nervous. He has been sent for by Neville Jones, an assistant chief constable. Jones and Clarke had graduated from the police academy together, but Jones's rise in the ranks had outpaced Clarke's.

Clarke knocks on Jones's door and enters. The two men shake hands. Jones invites Clarke to take a seat.

Clarke gulps even before Jones speaks.

'I want to play you a tape,' Jones says. He hits a button on his phone. Two voices can be heard: Clarke's and Tiny Murdoch's ...

Clarke: 'I don't know how you found out our friend was in Saint-Émilion, but you did ... The money doesn't matter to us – we don't care about the money – but we want this guy brought to book for the National Bank robbery. And we need your help to do that.'

Jones stops the tape. 'Need I go on?'

'No. Can I ask: Where did you get this?'

'From PSNI Intelligence.'

'C3? They found out about this? How did—?'

'Did you imagine they'd miss a senior officer having a clandestine meeting with a member of the IRA's GHQ staff? Come on, Dan.'

'Neville, I didn't want things to come to this.'

'I know you didn't, but they did.'

'For your information, I wasn't the only senior officer involved.'

'I don't hear anybody else's name mentioned on the tape.'

'That doesn't mean they're not on tape.'

'What are you saying, Dan?' Jones says. 'That there are other tapes in circulation that I'm not aware of?'

'I don't know how many tapes you are aware of.'

'Who else is involved in this?'

'I'll have to take the Fifth on that one, Neville – for now.'

'For now? In other words, should it be expedient at a future date, you will reveal who was conspiring with you in this matter?'

'May I be blunt?'

'Please.'

Clarke leans forward. 'It may well be in my interest at some time in the future to reveal everything.'

'In your interest?'

'Yes. If, for example, I were to be in the witness box, I expect I'd be asked who my accomplices were, how this project came about, who said what to whom … you know the line of questioning. What would be my options then, Neville? Lie under oath, or refuse to answer and face a further charge of contempt-of-court?'

Jones stands up and goes to a map on the wall. He speaks with his back to Clarke. 'Seems to me you've given this quite a bit of thought.'

'I have.'

'Have you taken legal advice?'

'No. I was hoping I wouldn't have to.'

Jones turns around. 'Are you blackmailing the force, Dan?'

'Certainly not, sir! I'm merely responding to your questions.'

'This isn't just a disciplinary matter; you could go to prison for aiding and abetting terrorists.'

'I—'

'Best we say no more for now, Dan.' Jones comes back to the table. 'No matter what happens, your career is over. You know that, don't you?'

There is a long pause before Clarke says, 'Yes.'

CHAPTER THIRTY-EIGHT

RUCTIONS, WEARING A BLACK WATERPROOF PONCHO, stands in front of Conolly's Folly. The rain has stopped, but it has left the walls of the monument stained and darkened. Ructions looks through binoculars at the toucans on the upper parts of the obelisk.

He takes out the painting, lays it out on top of his rucksack, and studies it. His false beard is caught in the breeze as his head flicks between the painting and the eagles. He turns and looks behind him. He asks himself, where did Leonardo set up his easel? Somewhere up there. He takes out the binoculars and inspects the horizon. Eventually his attention is drawn to a round tower on a height. He zooms in on it.

A ginger-haired female schoolteacher with a rowdy class walks past him. The kids run to the obelisk. Ructions lowers his binoculars and approaches the schoolteacher. 'Hello, I wonder if you could help me?'

'I'll try,' the schoolteacher says. 'Ciara Dillon, stop pulling Saoirse's hair! Seán Mícheál, stop that!'

'It's …' Ructions points in the direction of the tower. 'It's that round tower up there. I'm wondering what it is?'

'That's the round tower of Oughterard Cemetery.'

'Oughterard Cemetery?'

'Yes. Where Arthur Guinness is buried.'

'Arthur Guinness.' Ructions smiles broadly. He takes the schoolteacher's hand and kisses it. 'Ma'am, may I ask you your name?'

The schoolteacher smiles. 'It's Deirdre … Deirdre Mulligan.'

'Well, Deirdre Mulligan, you're a five-star lady.'

Deirdre smiles broadly. 'Thank you.' She hesitates. 'And you are?'

'Miss! Miss!' a pupil shouts, 'Rory O'Connor is eating my lunch!'

'I'm obliged, Deirdre,' says Ructions as he walks away.

Tiny Murdoch, eating a sausage roll, enters the living room of a safe house in the border town of Dundalk. He peeks out the front window. No one is about. He does not turn on the lights but sits beside a turf fire.

The room door opens, and Paul O'Flaherty walks in. He takes a seat across from Tiny and stares out the window.

'Are you all right, Paul?'

O'Flaherty doesn't answer immediately. Then he says, 'How the hell could I be all right, eh? We've a high-level informer in our ranks.'

'I know. The gardaí knew everything about the Proctor exchange. They were waiting for us, for Christ's sake.'

'Waiting for us!' O'Flaherty exclaims, 'we're lucky we're not in prison on a kidnapping charge!'

'I don't think they'd enough evidence to charge us.'

O'Flaherty casts his eyes to the heavens. 'Spare me, Lord. Tiny, you walked Eleanor Proctor along Dun Laoghaire pier after she'd been held by us for eight days! I was standing beside O'Hare! They have me on tape telling him it's Goering's gold or four million euro! Do you not think that would've counted?'

'But they couldn't have placed us at the kidnapping.'

'By being caught, red-handed, with her at the exchange, the prosecution would say we were the *principal* kidnappers! A little garda birdie told me the only reason we're not charged is that she refused to press charges.

'I want a full GHQ inquiry into this. I want you to draw up a list of everyone who knew about the Dun Laoghaire exchange, and I want every one of them questioned. I include myself in that. And I want the inquiry linked with the Saint-Émilion fiasco. Someone, probably the same person, gave that away too.'

'We've no evidence to support a connection to Saint-Émilion.'

'The Garda Special Branch knew about the Proctor exchange via our high-ranking informer, so it stands to reason that he, or she, would've tipped off them off about your trip to Saint-Émilion also.'

'That's assuming that the informer knew about it.'

'O'Hare certainly knew about it, didn't he? Who told him? The informer? I doubt that. My guess is he had bought some French police. The question is: Who told them? Answer? Our informer told his Special Branch handlers in Ireland that your team was going to Saint-Émilion and they passed that intelligence on to the French police.'

'I can't see it being any of the Saint-Émilion team … they didn't know where they were going until we got there.'

'There's nothing stopping someone making a phone call at the last minute.'

'True.'

'How many of that Saint-Émilion team knew about the Proctor exchange?'

'Only me and Hughie O'Boyle.'

'Where's Hughie now?'

'I don't know. Probably back in Belfast.'

'Look, it mightn't be Hughie. He's been with us a long time and he's been on operations that went smoothly. Don't assume it's him. Look at everybody who's close to you—'

'Close to *me*?'

'Yeah, you. You were in the vanguard on both operations.'

Tiny is discomfited at the direction this conversation is taking. 'Hold on there, Paul, are you calling *me* a tout?'

'If I thought for a second you were a tout, you'd be talking to the internal security unit, not to me. No, it's not you. Why do I know it's not you? Because touts are useful to their handlers only if they're at large in order to gather intelligence, whereas you, on the other hand, have spent the best part of your life in jail.'

Tiny cranks his neck away but a look of consternation is still fixed on his face. Any appetite he might have had to help find the informer has been severely trimmed. 'Paul, Hughie's my first cousin, and I'd prefer if you got someone else to carry out this inquiry.'

'I don't trust anyone else with it.'

'I appreciate the vote of confidence, but I'd still prefer it if you got someone else.'

'Are you not listening? I don't trust anyone else.'

'This is no small task you're giving me.'

'I know it's not.'

'The Army Council knew about those operations as did some members on the GHQ staff.'

'The Army Council knew about the operations, but they didn't know the logistics; they didn't know when and where the Proctor exchange would take place, for example. Our informer did. This tout threatens our entire movement. We have to weed him or her out.'

Tiny sighs. 'Okay, I'll get on it.'

O'Flaherty gets up and goes to the kitchen, followed by Tiny. The elder IRA man opens the fridge and looks in. He closes the door again. 'I'm ravenous. Fancy a Chinese takeaway?'

'I've already eaten, Paul.'

They walk back into the living room where O'Flaherty sits by the fire and lifts the phone from the coffee table. 'Hello? Can I order a takeaway, please?'

'I got a call from Dan Clarke earlier,' Tiny says casually.

O'Flaherty turns his head to Tiny and slowly hangs up the phone. He is surprised. 'And?'

'He says he's been rumbled.'

'What does he mean, "rumbled"?'

'His bosses know he's been talking to me ...'

'How do they know that?'

'He never said, but they've got a recording of one of my meetings with him.'

'Assume they've recorded all your meetings,' O'Flaherty says. He taps the arm of the chair. 'This isn't good.'

'It won't be good for me, if Clarke turns supergrass against me.'

'Will he?'

'He might, if he's no other option, especially if there's an offer of immunity from prosecution on the table.'

O'Flaherty lifts his face. 'I'm not sure about that. Giving dirty cops immunity would be seen as self-serving and would open a can of worms. People would ask – rightly – "Is this an attempt to hide the transgressions of other dirty cops?" It would be seen as the PPS conspiring to give one of their own a get-out-of-jail-card. It would set a bad precedent. They'd have to think long and hard over that one.'

O'Flaherty lifts the poker and jabs it into a turf log, sending yellow sparks up the chimney. On a roll, he suggests, 'Rather than give Clarke immunity from prosecution, the police and PPS might go for the lesser option and prosecute the two of you, with Clarke telling all and throwing himself on the mercy of the court.'

'Without evidence, it'd be his word against mine,' Tiny says.

'I wouldn't hang my hopes on that, if I were you,' O'Flaherty says. 'His word would carry a lot more weight than yours – especially if he admits his part in the conspiracy and you deny everything. And don't forget this: there'd be words whispered in chambers. A satellite file on your illustrious IRA career would be submitted to the judge – before the trial even begins. How many stiffs would be accredited to you in that file?'

'Too many.'

'So, what would any judge think when he reads about you stiffing ... what ... five?' Tiny holds up both hands, fingers extended, indicating the number ten. 'Y'see?' O'Flaherty says. 'Clarke would be offered a deal, five years, maybe.' The IRA supremo pokes the fire again. 'Now, the good news—'

'There's good news?'

'Oh, yeah. In your favour is the possibility that the police hierarchy might simply demand Clarke's resignation and hush the thing up: avoid the embarrassment of hanging out their dirty washing for all to see.'

'Nobody likes to see their dirty washing hanging out,' Tiny says.

O'Flaherty closes his hands on his chest, as if praying. 'Hold on a second,' he says, wagging his finger at Tiny, 'As I recollect from your recordings, Clarke always used "we" when he was referring to himself or those around him. Am I right there?'

'Oh, aye. Fucking sure. When me and Clarke were talking in Holywood, I suggested we might need the cops to look the other way when we were chastising dissidents ...'

'What was his reaction to that?' O'Flaherty says.

'He said he haven't the authorization to make a decision on that matter, but he'd pass on my comments.'

O'Flaherty is not taken aback. 'As I suspected. He was either acting under orders from his superiors, or he was part a rogue police cabal. Either way, he'd be asked in court to name his co-conspirators, and if he did, the question would arise: Why are they not in the dock? And if he *didn't* name them, he'd be held in contempt of court.'

'God only knows where this would finish,' Tiny says.

O'Flaherty warms his hands at the fire and looks at Tiny. 'You know, I could see a situation where the chief constable ends up being cross-examined in the witness box about whether or not his officers had his blessing to liaise with the IRA. He wouldn't like that. No, the more I think about it, the more I think the cops will want to bury it. You're on pretty good ground, Tiny.'

'I hope so,' Tiny says, ''cause I don't fancy doing any more time in jail.'

'You won't.'

'Oh, by the way, Clarke passed an interesting remark before he hung up. He called it a "parting gift from one old comrade to another."'

O'Flaherty laughs. 'One old comrade to another, was it? He has a good sense of humour – for a cop. So?'

'He said there's a gang of German neo-Nazis running around Dublin, and they're here for Goering's gold.'

'Now, that is interesting,' O'Flaherty says stroking his lower lip. 'How would they have known to come to Ireland? Is O'Hare thinking of doing a deal with them and cutting us up – *again?*'

'That blackguard's capable of shaking hands with the devil, Paul. Don't trust him.'

O'Flaherty shifts uncomfortably in his seat. *You're doing deals with Nazis now, Ructions?* he thinks. *And in Ireland too? You're making it difficult for me not to have you nutted.* 'Get stuck into this inquiry, Tiny. Spare no one. Any grief, get back to me.'

Ructions parks his car on the road at the bottom of Oughterard graveyard and looks to his left, across the expansive County Kildare countryside. As he walks up the gravelly road to the graveyard, he reads a tourist leaflet which states that Oughterard means High Place in Irish. There is a sign at the side of the gates saying 'Cosán Arthur,' or 'Arthur's Way.' Black, steel double gates and a coursed, eight-foot-high, stone wall mark the perimeters of the graveyard. Ructions walks up some stone steps and down the other side. He stops and looks around.

Trees surrounding the sides and back of the graveyard sway and hiss as if calling foul on the human invasion. To his right are remnants of a rough-stone, vaulted church with glassless arrow slits. Some relatively new gravestones stand upright, but most are old, weather-beaten, and lying at an angle, their fall from grace a result of vicious crosswinds and storms.

Ructions walks along the undulating, grassy ground towards the centre of the tiny cemetery and stops to observe what appears to him to be a prehistoric burial area, which is conspicuously marked by small upright stone tablets. He strolls into the centre of the stone circle, closes his eyes, puts out his arms, and slowly turns a complete circle. No voices are whispering in his ears, no one from the other side is giving his any clues about Goering's gold.

He steps into the church forecourt, his shoes crunching on the gravel. On the west end of the southern wall of the church is a sturdy monument, a doorway with concrete jambs, inlaid with an enormous stone, on which is written in weather-beaten lettering:

In the adjoining vault
Are deposited the mortal remains
of
ARTHUR GUINNESS
Late of
James's Gate in the city
and of
Beaumont in the county
of Dublin Esquire
Who departed this life on the 23d
of January AD 1803
Aged 78 years
and also those of
OLIVIA his wife
who died in the month of March 1814
aged 72 years
They lived universally loved and respected
and their memory will long be cherished

by a numerous circle
of friends, relations, and descendants.
In the same vault are also interred
the mortal remains of
RICHARD GUINNESS
Late of Leixlip Esq.
and those of
ANNE his wife
with those of some of their children
and grandchildren of the aforesaid
ARTHUR and OLIVIA

Ructions walks to a marble headstone that lies flat in the church-yard. 'To Richard Guinness,' he reads aloud. He looks at his tourist leaflet and discovers that Richard was Arthur's younger brother.

After returning to Arthur's grave, Ructions touches the gran-ite stone with his forehead. 'Hello, Arthur,' he says. 'It's a pleas-ure to finally meet you, sir.' Going over to a stone step at the side of grave, he takes off his shoulder bag, removes a notepad, and begins jotting down notes. A crack of thunder. His head auto-matically looks up. A frowning sky looks down. Ill-tempered grey clouds crash into one another. A large raindrop plops onto the open page of his notebook. *What's this?* he thinks, *Arthur's anger?* Ructions hopes not; he needs the good brewer's blessing. He closes the notebook and retreats to the shelter of church. The stormy weather will pass.

Standing in the sanctuary of the drafty old church, looking out on the enveloping squall, Ructions's imagination takes hold.

He shivers. Voices whisper behind him, voices that speak in Olde English, voices that cometh and goeth and passeth with the wind. He spins around. There's no one there. Looking all about, he can see shadows, or is it just a trick of light? Time to get out of there, pronto. He decides to brave the elements and runs to his car.

In his hotel room, Ructions is organising, getting things done. He hands Billy a page from the notebook, which Billy scrutinises. 'You want the lorries to carry the logo "Ingot Productions"?'

'Yes.'

'That's doable,' Billy says casually. 'Anything is doable if you've got the dough.'

'And the business cards?' Ructions asks.

'"Val P. Angley, Executive Producer, Ingot Productions,"' Billy says reflectively. 'Are we going into the movie business next?'

Ructions laughs. 'In a kinda way.'

'Five pairs of night-vision glasses, rubber mats ... how many?'

'Enough to soundproof the floor of the lorries.'

'Twenty sheets of three-quarter-inch plywood ... and so on and so on.' Billy smiles and thinks, *God only knows what you're up to, boy.* 'None of this should be a problem. Getting the cameras, the film equipment, and the lights ... that might be a toughie.'

There is a sense of purpose around the room, a sense that things are finally happening. 'Not for you,' Ructions says.

Billy reads on down the list. 'I'll have to get my skates on,' he mutters, looking at Ambrose. 'Mitzy Hagans?'

'Mitzy'll get you a tank, if the money's right,' Ambrose says.

Billy looks to Ructions. 'We're gonna have to run up to Dublin.'

'Fair enough. The bottom line is this,' Ructions says. 'Initially, at least, we need to look like a professional film crew to any Nosy Parkers. We must fit in. That means dressing appropriately.'

'How do film crews dress?' Ambrose asks.

'How do I know?' Ructions says. 'I'm the producer, so I'll be wearing a suit and a big hat.'

Dermot switches on his laptop. 'It says here' – he waves in the direction of the laptop – 'dress practically. I guess that means track bottoms?'

'Sounds like wise advice to me,' Billy says.

'And, guys, don't wear white clothes,' Ructions says. 'They reflect light. Probably, after say … half an hour, we turn off all lights and go to night vision.'

'What's this all about, Ructions?' Ambrose says.

'There's your first Nosy Parker,' Billy says.

'I was just—'

'Fellas,' Ructions says, 'we've twenty-four hours, at most, to put everything in place. We meet in the hotel tomorrow, at six o'clock. I'll let you know what's happening then.' Ructions puts his hand on the table and looks around the faces. 'Let's do this.'

Billy, Ambrose, and Dermot put their hands on top of Ructions's. 'Let's do this,' they repeat. As they break up, Ructions takes Dermot to the side. 'You stay with me.'

CHAPTER THIRTY-NINE

"ARE WE GRAVE ROBBERS?" DERMOT SAYS, STANDING in the middle of Oughterard graveyard, his hand stroking the top of a tombstone.

'That's a strange question to come out of the mouth of an archaeologist,' Ructions says. 'I thought you tinkered with dead people's bones and artefacts for a living?'

'I do, but that's for scientific reasons.'

'Would the stiffs know the difference? Just so you know,' Ructions says, 'We're not going to be touching anybody's bones.'

'That's very civil of you.' They walk on. 'Saint Briga's round tower,' Dermot remarks, looking off. 'Good Saint Briga founded a monastic settlement and that round tower there in 605, as I recollect. Or was it 615? Somewhere around that time, anyway.'

Ructions breathes in deeply, his chest expanding. 'This place is beautiful.'

'Enchanting. Like something out of a fairy tale,' Dermot says. 'No wonder Arthur wanted to be laid to rest here.'

Ructions stops and puts a finger to his lips.

'What is it?' Dermot says.

'Do you hear it?'

Dermot remains still. 'What am I supposed to hear?' he whispers.

'The silence of the dead,' Ructions whispers back. Dermot nods. He understands the importance of serenity.

They step into the churchyard. While Dermot looks at Richard Guinness's tombstone, Ructions runs his hands over the jambs and the granite stone at the entrance to Arthur's tomb. 'This vault was never to be opened.'

'What's that?' Dermot says, turning around.

'I said, Arthur and his family never wanted this vault to be disturbed. Look at this,' he says, pointing. 'The angel Gabriel wouldn't be able to move away this stone.'

The archaeologist approaches Ructions and says: 'Well, here we are. Now, do you want to tell me what's so important about this site? I take it has something to do with Goering's gold?'

'It's got everything to do with Goering's gold,' Ructions says. He holds up a finger. 'Question: Where was Leonardo standing when he started painting?'

'Leonardo?'

'The guy who painted this,' Ructions says, taking the painting out of his shoulder bag.

Dermot looks around. 'I don't know.'

Ructions walks out into the area in front of the church, Dermot following. He waves at the awe-inspiring vista below. 'Behold the Garden of the Lord.'

Dermot's mouth drops open. 'Oh, my ...'

'Over there,' Ructions says, pointing to the west, 'is the plain of Kildare and the province of Leinster. And down there are the Wicklow and Dublin Mountains.'

'You seem to know a lot about this site.'

'Not really. I looked it up on the computer.' Ructions takes the binoculars out of his shoulder bag and hands them to Dermot. 'And there,' he points in front of him, 'is Conolly's Folly. That small white building to its left is Castletown House.' Ructions holds up the painting.

Dermot looks through the binoculars and then at the painting. 'Yeah, this is it, but you only see half of Conolly's Folly. And it's much larger in the painting.'

'Spot-on,' Ructions says. 'I might be wrong, but I think the artist completed his painting from up there.' Ructions points to the vaulted roof of the chapel. 'That's where I'd go. More elevation. Better view. Come on. Let's see if we can get up there.'

Ructions leads Dermot back into the forecourt and into the church.

The historian in Dermot compels him to stop, to absorb the inner sanctum of the church. He looks up at the soggy, patchy ceiling and around the dilapidated, coursed walls. To the front of the church are three glassless, Gothic window frames. In his mind's eye, Dermot can see wigged men and bonneted women praying here, singing hymns, finding solace in their minister's sacred words. There has been happiness and sorrow in equal measure in this august place.

On the right side of the narthex is an opening to a spiral stairwell. 'Up here,' Ructions says. They navigate the twenty-two narrow, steep, slated stairs, gripping the steps in front of them and the jagged wall for balance. At the top of the church, they climb out onto the bevelled roof.

'Yes,' Dermot says, breathing deeply, 'I see what you mean.' Dermot again looks through the binoculars before turning to face Ructions. 'Okay. So, Lothair, old Hermann's artist, painted the scene on this roof.'

'And?'

'And he's not much of a painter. The Folly ... it's totally out of all proportion.'

Ructions wags a finger. 'Ahh, but the rest of the painting is perfectly proportioned.'

'Yeah, I can't argue with that.'

'So, what can we conclude from that?'

'That Lothair must have deliberately painted the outsized Folly.' Dermott studies Ructions's face, his mouth ajar. 'What are you saying, Ructions? What's this got to do with the gold?'

Ructions smiles. 'Look at the eagles in the painting.'

Dermot surveys the eagles and then looks at Ructions. His face is blank. 'What?'

Ructions nods to the painting. 'Look at the eagles on top of Conolly's Folly.'

Dermot again looks at the eagles. He takes out the magnifying glass, studies them at length but remains puzzled. 'What am I looking for?'

'Toucans.'

Dermot goes back to his magnifying glass and the painting. 'Ah! Well, okay, so, umm ...'

'And you a high-falutin' professor of archaeology at Queen's University too!' says Ructions.

'I just don't see what you see ...'

'What are toucans the symbol of?'

'Amm ... I don't know ... Guinness?'

'Correct!' Ructions points back down the spiral stairs. 'And who's buried down there?'

'Arthur Guinness? Wait, are you saying—'

'Yes! That's exactly what I'm saying! The old codger's been keeping an eye on the gold all these years.'

'But that's – that's preposterous!' Dermot stares at Ructions. 'Who'd hide gold in a man like Arthur Guinness's grave?'

'A man like Hermann Goering, that's who!' Ructions exclaims. 'Do you think for one second that Goering would've worried about a dead man's sensitivities? He signed the death warrant of six million Jews, for Christ's sake! Come on.'

Ructions leads Dermot back down the spiral staircase to the Guinness vault.

'Look at the fit of that tombstone,' Dermot says. 'It's a complete seal. In my professional opinion, this vault hasn't been opened since it was sealed after the Guinness children and grandchildren died in the nineteenth century.'

'But it *was* opened,' Ructions insists, 'because the Nazis opened it to hide the Reichsmarschall's gold in it.'

Dermot isn't convinced. 'I stand by what I said: this door hasn't been opened in over a hundred years.'

Ructions walks up and down, his hand caressing his chin. He stops and looks at the rounded, grassy top of the vault and cocks his head to the side, as if voices from beyond are burbling in his ear. He spins around and says, 'You're absolutely right. It hasn't been opened in over a century. They got into the vault another way.'

Now it's Dermot's turn to cock his head. 'How?'

'Through the brick roof.'

Dermot studies the roof. 'It's possible, I guess. But for it to work, and for no one to suspect the grave had been opened, they'd have to render the roof as it was before they accessed the grave.'

'That wouldn't be the hardest thing to do.'

Ructions climbs up a few stones until he is standing on the roof of the tomb. 'This vault is what?' Ructions says, studying the tapering grassy walls. 'Thirty foot by thirty? Don't know what depth it is, though. Still, it's big.'

'The structure of a rounded roof depends on the keystone,' Dermot calls up to him. 'That's the wedge-shaped stone at the top of the arch. It directs the weight of the structure downwards and outwards and holds all the other stones in place. You'd need to chip away the cement around the keystone and very carefully remove some wall stones, otherwise the roof will collapse.'

'Hmm, maybe too complicated,' Ructions admits. He walks to the back of the rounded roof and keeps walking. Dermot clambers up and joins him. 'What are you looking for now?'

'A hidden entrance.'

'Would the Nazis have built a solid door or tunnel and then concealed it?' Dermot asks.

'Now that's an interesting thought,' Ructions says. 'Why not? They're Germans. And what are Germans?'

'Very thorough.'

'Very, very thorough. And especially so because they were engaged by Goering himself.'

Suddenly, Dermot's head is spinning. He looks around him. 'You know what? You could be standing at the entrance to Arthur's tomb and not see me back here. I could work away in this spot all day, and no one would know I was here.'

Nodding, Ructions adds, 'And keep this in mind – back in

1944, this wouldn't have been the tourist attraction it is today.'

Both men continue to look for signs of a hidden doorway.

'What we need is a GPR transmitter,' says Dermot.

'What's that?'

'It's a ground-penetrating radar transmitter. It sends high-frequency radio waves into the ground and detects any anomalies in the subsurface.'

'I've no time for dillydallying. I need to be away from this site within two days – with or without the gold. Can you buy one of these GPR transmitters in the corner shop?'

'No, but I know where to get one.'

'Where?'

'At our dig in County Tyrone.'

'Can you get it here?'

'Ben can.'

'Who's Ben?'

'Ben Henry. He's our GPR operator. He's also my partner.'

Ructions hesitates. He is always wary of involving people he doesn't know personally in his business. 'I dunno ... Can he keep his mouth shut?'

'Yes.'

'You'd say that anyway.'

'Now, listen up, Ructions. You asked me to accompany you down here. I don't have to help you, and I certainly don't have to bring Ben along. And when we're on the subject, I don't have to take this tough-guy bullshit from you. You'll treat me with courtesy, or I'll pack up and go home.'

'Point taken,' Ructions says. 'My apologies. I can be an asshole sometimes.'

'We all can,' Dermot says diplomatically.

'Can you phone Ben?'

'He'll be looking to be paid.'

'He'll be well paid.'

'I'll phone him then, shall I?'

'Yeah, do that,' Ructions says, looking at his watch. 'I've meetings in Dublin. I need to scoot.'

'You go on. I'll wait in Celbridge for Ben.' As Ructions walks away, Dermot says: 'Hey ... amm ... what if there is no hidden entrance?'

Without turning, Ructions calls out, 'We go through the roof.'

CHAPTER FORTY

THERE ISN'T MUCH SERGE MERCIER'S NEPHEW, Antoine, doesn't know about boats. A fisherman all his life, it was he who had piloted the fishing boat that had picked up Ructions in Carlingford harbour, County Louth, along with approximately £20 million in unused notes that the Belfast man had stolen from the National Bank.

Now, years later, he drops anchor at the entrance to the Grand Canal at Ringsend in Dublin. Little does Antoine know that, sixty-four years earlier, not far from his anchorage, U-Boat Kapitänleutnant Ewald Rademacher's had transferred Hermann's Goering's gold onto a fishing boat, which had subsequently consigned it to a Guinness barge.

Serge comes up on deck, stretches his arms, and runs as fast as he can on the spot. 'I love Dublin!' he says, gulping air like a choking fish out of water. 'Don't you love Dublin?'

'I don't love customs and excise. They're on their way,' Antoine says.

'And rightly so. We can't have villains and vagabonds sailing the seven seas, can we?' Serge takes out his phone and dials Ructions's number.

'Hello?' Ructions says.

'Cad é mar atá tú, Monsieur?'

'*Go maith, a chara.* You sound very happy.'

'I'm always happy when I come to Ireland.'

'Any problems?'

'None at all. You may not believe this, but this little adventure has given me a new lease on life. I'm totally reinvigorated. *Cher ami*, I feel twenty years younger.'

Ructions laughs. 'Good for you. We meet tomorrow night at Lock 13. That's 13, now, not 12. Yes?'

'Yes. I've made the appropriate arrangements.'

'Good. I'll get back to you quite soon.'

'Do.' Serge hangs up.

At the Arbour Hill cottage where they had met previously, Ructions hands Keller his offshore bank details. 'Transfer the money into that account.'

'Before I can do that, my assistant will once more have to ensure the baton in the case is authentic.'

Ructions hands Gitte the case. She opens it and inspects the baton.

'Happy enough, Gitte?' Ructions says.

Gitte nods. Ructions smiles at her. She smiles back. Keller looks on with consternation. 'And you, Karl?'

'No, I'm not happy.'

'What's wrong now?'

'How do I know that you and your men' – Keller looks at Billy and Ambrose – 'won't steal the baton from me after I transfer the money?'

'We won't.'

'With all due respect, Herr Ructions, you're a thief, and we are in your domain.'

'And with all due respect, Herr Keller, you're a Nazi. Does that mean we can't do a trade?'

'No, it doesn't, but—'

'Okay. You need to do the transfer in a public place.'

'Yes.'

'Any suggestions?'

'Dublin Castle?'

'Too much security. Let's see … what about Trinity College in Dublin? Where the Book of Kells is on display?'

'Yes, I've heard of the Book of Kells.'

'I'll meet you at Brian Boru's harp in the Long Library in, say … two hours?'

'Brian Boru's harp?'

'You've never heard of Brian Boru?'

'No.'

'Brian Boru was the last High King of Ireland, and his harp is displayed in Trinity. A tourist guide will tell you where to find the Long Library. You can't miss the harp there.'

Keller looks baffled, then shakes his head. 'No. We go together.'

Ructions smiles. 'You're afraid I'll swap batons, aren't you?'

'I just think it's better we don't part until the deal is completed.'

'Okay, let's get this over with.'

At Oughterard graveyard, Ben, a tall man with long, fuzzy hair tied behind his head and a scraggly beard, is pushing a four-wheeled ground-penetrating radar machine at the rear of the Guinness vault. Dermot is walking beside him. Both are looking into a high-resolution touch screen between the handlebars of the machine, on which any anomalies or spaces underneath the surface of the ground will be evident.

'There,' Dermot says and points, 'what's that?'

'It's not as deep as the graves,' Ben says. 'And it seems to go this way.' He runs the GPR up to the raised ridge at the side of the vault.

Ben pushes the machine to the bank of the Guinness vault. 'It's definitely man-made,' Ben says. 'By the look of it, I'd say it's a small tunnel of some sort.'

'Go back again and see how far it runs away from the vault,' Dermot says.

Ben charts the length of the tunnel. 'It goes straight under that ledger stone,' Ben says, pointing to a flat marble stone at the back of the Guinness vault. He lifts the GPR machine on to the top of the ledger stone. 'It stops here,' he says.

Dermot looks at the ledger stone, '"Died 17 February 1809, aged sixty years, Anne Griffith, wife of Thomas Griffith, Temple Mill Celbridge and late of Manchester."'

'Clever,' Ben says. 'I can't see the main graveyard from here, which means no one in the main graveyard would be able to see me.'

'Well then,' says Dermot. 'I reckon there's a tunnel below this ledger stone that runs right up to the Guinness vault.'

IRA volunteer Hughie O'Boyle has been 'dark-roomed' many times, so he has no fear of what lies ahead of him when he walks into the house in Beechmount Grove in west Belfast.

Paddy Joe Delaney, a member of the IRA's Internal Security Unit, also known as the Nutting Squad, is sitting with his feet over the end of a chair, smoking and watching television. Lazily, he stirs. 'C'mon.' He brings Hughie upstairs onto a small landing. An open door throws a steam of light into a darkened room and onto a seat in a corner. 'You know the drill, Hughie. Sit on the seat, face the wall and don't look around.' Hughie complies with the command.

The door is closed, so the room is in complete darkness. Voices whisper. Someone behind Hughie clears his throat. 'Do you know why you're here, Volunteer O'Boyle?'

Hughie does not recognise the speaker's voice. 'Yes, I'm being debriefed.'

'What do you think you're being debriefed about?'

'The balls-up in Dun Laoghaire.' The interrogator does not comment, so Hughie feels compelled to elaborate. 'I was only the driver on that operation.'

'True, but you knew what was going down. You knew that an exchange was going to take place.'

'So did others.'

'Also true, and we'll be speaking to those people; have no worries about that.'

Hughie is slightly uplifted that he's not the only person who will be questioned.

The interrogator informs Hughie that they are also looking into the aborted Saint-Émilion operation. Hughie is nonplussed. In his defence, he offers that he was only following orders, that he had no level of involvement in the execution or planning of either the Dun Laoghaire or the Saint-Émilion operations.

'That's not what the issue is,' the interrogator says. 'You knew the logistics of both operations and—'

'I found out we were going to Saint-Émilion only at the last minute, like all the other volunteers.'

'Did anyone give you permission to interrupt me, Volunteer O'Boyle?'

'No.'

A thunderous silence pulses like a heart machine in the darkness. 'How is it that when you're involved in an operation, it invariably ends up in failure?'

'I've been involved in loads of operations that didn't end in failure. Ask Tiny.'

'Who's Tiny?'

Hughie wrings his hands. Any relief that he wasn't being specifically targeted by the Nutting Squad has dissipated. This isn't a usual debriefing; it looks like the finger of blame for those botched operations is being pointed at him. 'Where are you going with this? What are you trying to say?'

'I'm saying, Volunteer O'Boyle, that you're an informer.'

In the Irish police headquarters in Dublin's Phoenix Park, Thierry Vasseur, Pierre Robillard, and Manus O'Toole are watching a series of CCTV recordings of members of the Das Reich group arriving in Ireland. 'Do we know where these people are now?' Vasseur asks.

'Special Branch have them under twenty-four-hour surveillance,' Manus says.

Vasseur nods. 'And Keller?'

'He has vanished since he evaded surveillance on Monday.'

'Something big is happening, Manus. These terrorists wouldn't be in Ireland unless Keller sent for them, and he wouldn't have sent for them unless he envisaged a situation where he'd need armed backup.' Vasseur taps a pen on the desk. 'Would they have much trouble securing weapons?'

'I doubt it,' says Manus. 'Ireland is awash with arms at the minute and if you know the right people, they're easy enough to buy.'

'They didn't bring any firearms into the country with them, which means someone must have been sent ahead to buy the weapons for them,' Vasseur says.

'But to what purpose?' Manus asks.

'Gold,' Vasseur says. 'This is all connected to Goering's gold.'

'And Ructions,' injects Robillard.

'And Ructions,' Vasseur says. 'What's the latest on him, Manus?'

'He's vanished again. In Ireland, it's not unusual for IRA people and the like to drop off the radar for a while.'

'Hardly an endorsement of the Irish police,' Vasseur says caustically. 'I found Ms Proctor's kidnapping very disturbing, but what was even more disturbing is that the police didn't know she was being held by the IRA.'

'Hold on now, Thierry, you're talking about the Police Service of Northern Ireland, not An Garda Síochána.'

'Where is Ms Proctor now?' Robillard asks.

Manus looks to a text in front of him. 'She's in Christchurch, in Devon, England. It seems she's staying there with a cousin.'

'Have the British police been alerted?' Robillard asks.

'Yes. Special Branch are keeping an eye on her.'

Vasseur nods, leans back, and herds his thoughts together. 'They're all here: the neo-Nazis, the IRA, and the Irishman. He controls the game. We've got to stay close to him, Manus, or we'll miss the cut.'

As the crow flies, Ructions, still disguised, and Keller and Gitte, are all in Trinity College, a few hundred yards from Vasseur. They mingle with a large group of Scottish tourists in the Long Library. Also mingling with tourists, but unknown to Keller and his girlfriend, are Billy and Ambrose. Their eyes are clocking faces, making sure that none of Keller's Nazi friends will endanger their boss. Meanwhile, Ructions, seemingly perusing his tourist guidebook, is also scanning and logging the faces of everyone in the immediate vicinity.

The Scottish tour guide says: 'We are now entering the Long Hall of the Old Library. This magnificent library is sixty-five metres long. It was built between 1712 and 1732 and it houses over two hundred thousand books, many of which are early works—'

'How early?' someone asks.

'Let's see … *The Book of Armagh* dates back to the twenty-first of September 807, and *The Book of Leinster* to the twelfth century. Of course, these books, and other books from the Middle Ages, were written entirely in Irish.'

'This room has a Harry Potter feel to it,' a young woman with Doc Marten boots and spiked hair says out loud. The tourists laugh.

Ructions strolls towards Brian Boru's harp, followed by Keller and Gitte. He turns to face Keller. 'Transfer the money.'

'Now?'

'Yes, now. You wanted to do it in a public place. Well, it doesn't get much more public than this.'

'Okay.' Keller makes the call. 'The transfer has been made.'

Ructions walks aside and phones his offshore account in the Cayman Islands. He returns after a few moments. 'Good job.' He hands Keller the bill of sale, signed by Serge. Ructions comes alongside Gitte, takes off his shoulder bag and holds it out in front of him. 'Take it, Gitte.' Gitte takes the bag. Their fingers touch. Ructions broadly smiles, glances at Billy and Ambrose, and puts his arm around Keller's shoulder as if they were long-lost brothers. Billy and Ambrose stand directly in front of Keller, glaring at him. 'Have we a problem?' Ructions says smoothly.

'No ... no, Ructions.'

Ructions looks over Keller's shoulder and smiles at Gitte, who warmly gestures back. Then Ructions pushes past the neo-Nazi and strolls away.

Keller looks inside the bag and allows himself a wry smile.

Keller and Gitte head towards the exit and make their way to the Davenport Hotel, where he enters the toilets and closes the cubicle door behind him. He unscrews the end cap and holds the baton upside down. Nothing drops out. He looks inside the baton. Nothing. For a few seconds he shuts down, his mind frozen. Then he shakes his head. He starts muttering and foaming at the mouth.

I should've known. That Irish bastard! Four million euro! What will my backers say? They'll want their money back, and if I don't get it for them, they'll have me murdered.

Keller punches the toilet door.

Ructions is walking up Wicklow Street feeling his way along the pavement with a white stick, attached to which is a white rolling ball. Now, not only is he sporting the long beard, but he is wearing dark glasses, a flat cap, and a grey overcoat. He stops to cross the road at traffic lights. A Ford Expedition car pulls up alongside him. Sitting in the front passenger seat of the Ford is Thierry Vasseur. The beeping noise goes off, telling blind people it is safe to cross the road. Ructions rolls his stick in front of the Ford as he walks across the road. Involuntarily, he glances into the car and behind the dark glasses, his eyebrows involuntarily rise. Does he recognise me? he thinks. He shuffles on.

Vasseur stares at the blind man.

The lights change, and the car drives off.

Ructions makes his way to the entrance of a backstreet car park, where he folds up the blind man's stick and makes his way to his car. He is about to turn on the ignition when his phone rings. 'Hello?'

'You Irish cunt.'

Finding it difficult to suppress a belly laugh, Ructions replies: 'Now, what way is that to greet a business associate?'

'Business associate? You're no business associate of mine! You're a scoundrel, and a crook, and a—'

'Whoa! Back up, pal!'

'Don't you tell me to back up, you … you fucking rat.'

'This is very heavy, Karl. What's your problem?'

'You know what my problem is.'

'No, I don't. Now, calm down, unburden yourself. Talk to your uncle Ructions. C'mon.'

Keller again punches the toilet door. 'Calm down? Unburden myself? You are enjoying making a fool out of me, aren't you?'

'I've asked you before: What's your problem?'

Keller holds up a calming hand. 'Okay, okay … it's the baton.'

'What's wrong with it?'

'Part of it is missing.'

'Stop right there, Karl. You and I did a deal, did we not?'

'We did, but—'

'Did I not give you a bill of sale for the purchase of Hermann Goering's baton for four million euro?'

'You did, but—'

'And you were happy with the description of the item on the bill of sale?'

'Yes! Yes! Fucking yes!'

'No need to curse, Karl.'

'Fucking, fucking, fucking! Fuck you, cunt!'

Ructions had anticipated that this would be a funny exchange, but not this funny. 'Are you questioning the baton's authenticity?'

'No, I'm fucking not!'

'Then, what's your gripe, dude? You wanted to buy Hermann Goering's baton, and I sold it to you. End of story.'

'Part of it is missing. Someone opened the end cap and took something out.'

'Ah, I see. You mean the painting that points the way to Goering's gold.'

'It was a painting, was it? I thought it was written instructions. No matter. I want that painting. Do you hear me? *I want that painting.*'

'I daresay you do. But that'll be a separate deal.'

'It's the same fucking deal!'

'It seems to me you don't understand the barter system, Karl. The way it works is very simple. I have something to sell, and you want to purchase it; we agree on a price and complete the deal. That's what we did with the baton.'

'The interior of the baton was in the price. The painting was in the price.'

'That isn't on the bill of sale.'

'It's implicit.'

'Karl, I've never told you any lies. You should've made sure the painting was where you thought it was before you completed the transaction, shouldn't you? But you didn't want to be seen to open the end cap in front of me in case I pulled out of the deal. You were caught in your own headlights, buddy.'

'Ructions,' Keller pleads, 'My backers … they are business-people, but they are capable of exacting revenge, you know, especially if they think they've been … what is the English phrase … shit on. They expect a return for their investment and, if they don't get it, they could quite easily arrange for me to be murdered.'

'I'm sorry to hear that, but there's no twenty-eight-day money-back guarantee in a deal like this.'

'I need your help, Ructions. I'm begging you to give me the painting.'

'I'll tell you what I'll do, Karl, and I'm only doing this because I like you. Come along to the Duck Pub, Celbridge, and come alone, and I'll give you the painting. I'll even show you show you where the gold is. How's that?'

'That's very civilised of you, Ructions. Very civilised.'

'The price for my civility is two million euro.'

Keller gulps. *Good God*, he thinks, *this man's thirst for money is unquenchable. Play along with him – for now.* 'Another two million? By tomorrow? I don't think my investors will agree to that.'

'That's up to them. They might want to cut their losses and sell the baton, though I'm not sure they'll get anywhere near the four million they've already invested in it. On the other hand, for the price of another two million, they get tens of millions in return. Doesn't seem like much of a choice to me.'

Silence.

'Karl ... are you still there, Karl? Karl?'

'I hear you.'

'Well?'

'I don't know.'

'That's okay. If I don't hear from you by nine o'clock tomorrow morning, I'll assume you don't want to deal. Oh, and by the way, if you do go ahead, don't bring any heavies to the show because if I see any German-types lurking about, I'll not weigh in, and I'll not be contacting you again.'

'The Duck pub, Celbridge. Where is that again?'

'In County Kildare. Two million euro, Karl.'

Ructions hangs up.

CHAPTER FORTY-ONE

HUGHIE O'BOYLE IS FILTHY, NAKED, BRUISED, HAND- cuffed, and left dangling on a hook that hangs from the cross-beam of a dimly lit barn, with his toes alone touching the ground. His Tintin hair looks like it has been doused in motor oil, and his ribs ache every time he breathes. He tries not to breathe.

Nearby, two men wearing black overalls and woollen hats are sitting in old, brown leather chairs, their feet sharing a blue pouffe. They are watching a news show on an old television. It shows a blown-up photograph of a bank of gold bullion in a cave with armed U.S. World War Two soldiers standing guard. In the studio in front of the photograph is a reporter named Patrick Conlon, who says:

'By the end of 1944, with the Allies closing in on two fronts, it was Nazi policy to hide their gold in locations like the Kaise-roda mine in the tiny village of Merkers, in central Germany' – Conlon gesticulates with his hand towards the photograph – 'where, on the sixth of April 1945, members of the U.S. Third

Army discovered seven thousand sacks containing gold bullion, much of which is believed to have been extracted from the teeth of Jews in Nazi concentration camps.' The reporter crosses the studio to a large photograph of Hermann Goering. 'And this is Hermann Goering, Adolf Hitler's appointed successor in Nazi Germany, a man who stole art, jewellery, and gold from across Europe during the war. But did Goering have some of that treasure exported to Ireland before it fell into Allied hands?'

The reporter walks to a huge photograph of Ructions. 'Perhaps this man could tell us. He is James "Ructions" O'Hare, a former antiques dealer, who was acquitted in 2004 of the £36.5 million National Bank robbery in Belfast. Does O'Hare know the whereabouts of tonnes of Nazi gold in Ireland? Security sources in Ireland believe that he does, although it appears that he has gone to ground and has made himself unavailable for comment. Gail?'

Gail, the news anchor, asks, 'Who would own the gold, were it to be recovered by the Irish authorities?'

'That's a good question. Because it would be located in Ireland, the Irish state would lie claim to it. Any party wishing to claim thereafter would have to go through the Irish and possibly the European courts.'

Hughie lifts his head to look at the two men. 'Water,' he utters. No response. 'Water,' he says slightly louder.

One of the men looks over at him, then turns his attention once more to the television.

The barn door opens and Tiny, unmasked, walks in. The two men nod to him. Tiny looks at the television.

'Water,' Hughie groans. 'Water.'

'Hey, you,' Tiny says, shaking one of the men by the shoulder. 'Get up off your arse and give the man some water. What do you think we are? Fucking heathens?'

The man opens a bottle of water and gives Hughie a drink.

Something is bothering Thierry Vasseur, but he doesn't know what it is. 'That fish chowder was exceptional, Manus. Not as good as my own, but still very good.'

'I didn't know you cooked,' Manus says.

'I also play bass guitar very well.'

Manus laughs. 'Don't go hiding your light under a bushel now, big man.'

'Fortunately, I've never suffered the slings and arrows of outrageous humility, Manus.'

'Why would you? Dessert?'

'No, thanks.'

'You, Pierre?'

'Why not?'

Thierry looks away. *What is it?* He sips his mineral water and ponders … *What is it? Something happened. Where? When?*

The waiter approaches the table with dessert menus.

'Excuse me,' Vasseur says as he leaves the table and goes outside the hotel. Cars pull up to the traffic lights. The beeping noise that alerts blind people that it is safe to cross the road goes off. Vasseur tilts his head to the right. He frowns. His mouth opens. He can see the blind man crossing the road in Wicklow Street. He can see his cheeky glance into the car. Vasseur laughs aloud. He wasn't blind! He was looking at us in the car! He was Ructions!

Ructions pulls into the hotel in Celbridge where he has booked his party. He is dog-tired. His shirt is sticking to his back. He goes straight to his room, throws his shoulder bag on a chair, and kicks off his shoes. He looks out of his room window. Two lorries with 'Ingot Productions' written on their sides pull into the hotel's car park. Ructions allows himself a smile as he takes off his shirt. His phone rings. He lets the other caller speak first.

'Hello?' O'Flaherty says. 'Hello?'

Ructions would know O'Flaherty's croaky voice anywhere. 'Hello yourself.'

'Everything all right with you?'

'Sure.'

'No problems?'

'There are always problems. You know that.'

'Well, I'm just ringing to remind you that you've a meeting with me tomorrow.'

'As if I'd forget.'

'Don't be late. I don't like being kept waiting. And, more to the point, I don't like being disappointed.' Paul hangs up.

Ructions runs a shower.

Tiny has told the two men who had been watching television in the barn to get something to eat in the farmhouse.

Hughie is plopped down on one of the easy chairs, a blanket around his shoulders. His teeth chatter out an incomprehensible code. Tiny sits in the other chair. The smaller man has tears in his eyes as he looks intently at his boss. 'Tiny, I'm freezing.'

Tiny takes off his leather coat and puts it around Hughie's shoulders. 'How's that?'

'Better.'

'I'm sorry to see you like this.'

'Tiny … Tiny, can you help me?'

Tiny looks up and exhales, making smoke rings. 'You know the score, Hughie. Once this process starts, it has to run its course. I can't interfere.'

'But I'm not the tout.'

'I hope not.'

'I'm not.'

Tiny takes out a cigarette, lights it, and gives it to Hughie, who inhales. 'I can't raise my arms to take it out of my mouth.' Tiny takes the cigarette out of Hughie's mouth.

'If you were the tout—'

'I'm not.'

'But if you were, it wouldn't necessarily be the end of the world.'

'It's been the end of the world for dozens of other people.'

'Yeah, but that was during the war. There's a peace process now, Hughie. Politics have primacy. It's not as easy to kill informers as it used to be. Personally, I don't think you'll be nutted.'

'So what would happen if I were to admit it?'

'You'd still be punished, but it would probably be exile. You'd never be allowed to come back to Ireland to live.'

'And what's the alternative?'

'Those two Nutting Squad guys come back with a vengeance.'

'But I'm not a tout.'

'That's exactly what I'd expect a tout to say.'

Tiny makes a phone call. 'I'm sorry, Hughie.' The barn door opens, and the two men enter.

Hughie's head drops onto his chest and, without looking up, he says, 'Tiny, tell them, not the hook. Please don't hang me on the hook again.'

Tiny walks out of the barn.

'Pardon?' Thierry Vasseur says.

'The five Das Reich members have disappeared,' Manus O'Toole says. Embarrassed by the admission, he fiddles with a silver letter opener.

Vasseur makes no attempt to hide his disgust. 'That's unbelievable. That's … what sort of a police force have you? You had identified targets, very dangerous people, you arranged twenty-four-hour surveillance, and they've just' – Vasseur holds up the palms of his hands – 'vanished. Not one, but five of them. It's as if they were never in your country.'

'These people were obviously trained in countersurveillance.'

'And your people obviously weren't.'

'Thierry, they never left their hotels.'

Vasseur leans forward so that his words will not be missed. 'They never left their hotels by the front door – but they left them nonetheless.'

Manus stands up and glares at Vasseur. 'Superintendent, I've taken about as much disrespect from you as I'm going to take. You demand that vital resources be sucked into your absurd Hermann Goering conspiracy theory—'

'It's not absurd, and it's not a conspiracy theory.'

'It is until it's proven different. In the meantime, I've a raging drugs war, with people getting gunned down on the streets every other day, and a growing IRA dissident threat. Those are real. I'll wake up tomorrow morning, and they'll be there, in front of me. Against those realities, you insist that I pursue a man against whom I can't prefer a charge, even if I were to locate him. And these Germans … they've committed no crimes in Ireland, so I can't prefer charges against them either when we do find them – which we will. You and I have different priorities, and yours do not trump mine. You should remember that.'

Vasseur takes off his glasses and sets them on the desk. 'I appreciate that you have domestic problems, but I'm not going to hide my disappointment, Manus. Since I came to Ireland, I've seen nothing but gross ineptitude. Frankly, I expected better.'

'Perhaps your expectations were too high.'

'It seems so.'

'You have total confidence in France's security services, have you? You've never lost a suspect?'

'We know how to conduct surveillance operations.'

'You've never lost a suspect?'

Vasseur hesitates. 'Everybody loses suspects once or twice.'

'There y'are now. Maybe our terrorists are more unpredictable than your terrorists.'

Ructions walks into the hotel lounge, where Dermot and Ben are sitting in a booth. 'Ructions O'Hare,' Dermot says, 'this is Ben Henry.'

Ructions puts out his hand to Ben, who is dressed in jeans and a crewneck shirt. 'How's it goin', Ben?'

'Good, Mr O'Hare.'

'It's Ructions.'

'Ructions, right.'

'Good news,' Dermot says with a beaming smile. 'We've been over the ground at the back of Arthur's grave – it's a tiny plot, and it didn't take us long, and there's definitely a tunnel. Now, it's not big; you wouldn't be able to stand up in it, but it's there. It's only about twenty-two feet long by three feet wide, and it starts at the marble ledger on the grave behind Guinness's.'

'Good work, Ben,' Ructions says. Ben glows. 'And you, mister.'

'Thanks,' Dermot says. 'But here's the crux of it. This tunnel seems to have a small railway track. The actual rails are about a foot apart.'

Ructions smiles. 'You don't say? Germans … you can't beat their ingenuity. They run the gold along the railway lines into the vault. Fast, efficient, minimum exertion, and nobody looking at Arthur's grave would suspect it had been disturbed. Brilliant.' Ructions allows himself an indulgent smile. 'I wonder if there's some sort of carriage on the railings? It'd be very handy.'

'I'd say it's still down there,' Dermot says. 'Why would the Germans who stashed the gold have taken it away with them? The whole idea was to come back to retrieve the gold after the war ended. It's still there.'

Billy and Ambrose walk into the lounge. 'Did you get everything?' Ructions asks.

'I had to wait on the business cards,' Billy says, handing them to Ructions, 'but we got there in the end.'

Ructions examines the cards. '"Val P. Angley. Film and Television Producer. Ingot Productions." Sounds exotic.' Ructions looks around the table at everyone now sitting there. 'Leave any talking to me when we're on-site. Billy will be in charge of the extraction. Okay?' All nod. 'The crucial element to this is that once our opening gambit of being a film crew is played out, we go dead quiet—'

'Thence the rubber mats to kill the noise in the back of the van,' Billy says.

'Exactly. The tiniest sound travels for miles in the countryside, although' – Ructions looks out the window – 'it looks like we'll have a gale, and that's just what the doctor ordered. Also, once I give the signal, we go to night vision. No naked lights anywhere, except in the vault, once we go dark. And no smoking. We get in and out – fast. It'll be dark in half an hour. We head out in forty-five minutes.'

Fifty minutes later, the two lorries pull up on the road adjacent to Oughterard graveyard. Wearing a wide-brimmed hat, a yellow cravat, and a million-dollar smile, Ructions approaches the nearest house to the graveyard and knocks on the door. An elderly lady with grey hair and a wrinkled complexion answers the door. Ructions raises his hat as he introduces himself as Val P. Angley of Ingot Productions. He converses with the old lady before handing her his card. Reading the card, she nods, goes inside the house and returns with some keys, which she gives to Ructions.

Ructions walks over to the large gates and opens them with a key. He beckons the lorries, which move up the gravel laneway that runs to the entrance of the graveyard. After returning the keys, Ructions follows the trucks up the hill.

Once they stop at the top of the laneway, Dermot and Ben take out the paraphernalia that comes with setting up a film shoot: the generators, lights, and cameras. Meanwhile, Ructions quickly removes his cravat and hat and changes into a blue boiler suit. Ambrose and Billy, in boiler suits too and wearing night-vision goggles, join Ructions, and the three make their way to the back of Arthur Guinness's grave. Ructions whispers, 'Lads, we need to lift the ledger stone.'

Ambrose prises a large crowbar under the marble ledger stone and pushes it aside. A four-foot-by-four-foot concrete square slab, covered in dirt and insects, becomes visible. Ambrose digs down the side of the slab with the crowbar and creates a hole into which Billy can get his hands, but, despite the strongman's valiant efforts, he cannot move the slab. Ambrose loosens the soil on all four sides and wedges the crowbar into the bottom of the slab. He and Billy then manage to turn it over. They look into a dark hole with rustic, bricked sides.

Ructions looks down into the hole. 'Okay. Here goes.' Wearing woollen gloves and a safety helmet with an attached headlight, he climbs into the opening, turns on the helmet's lamp, and commences crawling on his elbows alongside the stony railway track. He notices a rope he suspects is attached – somewhere ahead of him – to the trolley he'd hoped for. In his right hand is a jammy bar. A solid wall confronts him.

'What do you see?' Ambrose whispers as he lies flat on his stomach, peering into the hole.

Ructions begins to dig into the soil-like wall with the jammy bar. The soil gradually gives way. Within a few minutes, he has punched a hole in the wall.

'What do you see?' Ambrose repeats.

Ructions widens the hole and looks into the tunnel. The beam on his headlight moves around the walls of the vault. 'Boxes. Dozens of boxes ... *and they've got swastikas on them.*'

Excited, Ructions pushes himself into the vault before realising that there is a five-foot drop. His fall is broken with the flat of his arms. 'Are you all right?' Ambrose asks.

'Yes,' Ructions hisses, then coughs in the stale, putrid air. Standing upright, he looks around the vault. Placed around the four white-tiled walls are dozens of boxes, stacked neatly from the floor to just below the roof, each one with a swastika and German words on them.

'Holy Christ!' Ructions exclaims. Then, trying to calm himself, he goes to the entrance of the tunnel. He cups his hand around his mouth and says in a muted voice, 'Send me down the small ladder, the Tilley lamp, and my shoulder bag.'

'Right,' Ambrose says.

Ambrose hands the items through, and Ructions takes the ladder and leans it against a stack of boxes. Climbing up, he reaches to grab one of the boxes on top of the pile, but as he pulls out the box, it slips from his hand and crashes to the tiled floor of the vault. He steps off the ladder. There, scattered on the tiles, are a dozen gold bars.

He lifts a bar and, holding it up to the Tilley lamp, reads the writing inscribed on the bar:

DEUTSCHE
REICHSBANK
I KILO
FEINGOLD
999.9
DRO766383.

He slowly looks around the walls of the vault. 'Fuck me!' he says softly. 'There must be seven hundred boxes here. No, make that eight hundred.'

He looks to his left, to the back of the vault and there, resting in niches in the wall, are coffins. He looks at the names on each coffin until he finds a black casket with a large, dusty cross on it. Ructions takes out a handkerchief from his pocket and wipes the clean the cross. Below the casket is written 'Arthur Guinness' and below that, 'Returned to God.' Ructions reverently cleans up the lettering.

Opening his shoulder bag, Ructions takes out a tin of Guinness, pulls the ring, and leaves the tin on top of the casket. He then takes out a small bottle of Jameson whiskey, screws off the cap, and leaves it on the casket, alongside the tin of stout. 'Drink them slowly, Arthur,' Ructions says. 'It's been a while since you've wet your whistle.'

With due respects paid to the great man, it was back to the business at hand. Ructions goes to the hole in the wall and says, 'Send up that trolley, boys! Send it up now! There's gold in this here graveyard.'

CHAPTER FORTY-TWO

RUCTIONS HAS CLIMBED OUT OF THE TUNNEL AND taken off the boiler suit. Dermot throws water over Ructions's hands and head to clean them and wipes dirt off Ructions's face with a soapy flannel. Ructions ties up his cravat and dons his hat.

Billy is now in the vault, industriously loading up the trolley. Ambrose sits at the bottom of the tunnel, legs apart, sweating like a Sumo wrestler in a sauna, awaiting the word from Billy to pull the rope attached to the trolley. Once the trolley reaches him, Ambrose loads the gold bars into a bucket, which is hauled to the surface by Ben, who loads them into a wheelbarrow. Dermot then pushes the wheelbarrow along a small plywood path the gold-diggers had laid along the outskirts of the graveyard to the lorry, whereupon Dermot puts the gold into the lorry.

Ructions, holding a phone to his ear, looks into the tunnel entrance and says, 'Now, you didn't mix up your locks?'

'I'm here. Lock 13,' Serge says.

'Excellent. We've broken into the vault, so we shouldn't be long now.'

'Do you need me to come to you?'

'No. I've people here. Have you brought the two briefcases along?'

'Yes.'

'Good.'

Dermot approaches. 'There's a car pulling up at the bottom of the road.'

'Someone's coming,' Ructions says into the phone. 'I've gotta go.' Ructions whispers to Ambrose to tell Billy to keep quiet before walking to the front of the Guinness vault.

A man steps into the forecourt. He has his hands in the pockets of a parka jacket with the hood up and he stares intently at Dermot, who is pretending to be working on a lighting system, and Ben, who is looking through a movie camera on a tripod.

Ructions has already removed his gloves as he approaches from the darkness at the entrance to the forecourt. He smiles, and walks towards the man, his hand outstretched. The individual pulls down his hood to reveal a pocked-faced man. He and Ructions shake. 'Hi. Val P. Angley,' Ructions says in a rich American accent. 'Ingot Productions.' He gives the man his fake card.

'Joe Fitzpatrick,' the man says. 'Celbridge Guided Tours Project. Can I ask you what you're doing here?'

'Sure, Joe,' Ructions says warmly. 'We're just shooting some footage and taking measurements, that's all. Not disturbing anything. Yeah, we're making a film about your national treasure, Arthur Guinness, trying to draw out the golden fabric that surrounded his life, even until death, y'know? And we're looking at night lighting and potential recording shots.'

'I'm surprised I wasn't told about this.'

'So am I, Joe. Didn't Kildare County Council inform you?'

'No, they didn't.'

'Well, pardon me ... I must apologise about that. Perhaps it's because we're just taking a few shots and not disrupting anything.'

'That might be it. There's no need for you to apologise for their mistake, Val.' Joe looks at Ben behind the camera. 'A film, you say?'

'Yeah.'

'There'd be work for the locals then?'

'Oh, once we get going, for sure. I'd imagine ... at least a hundred jobs, probably closer to two.'

Joe nods approvingly. 'Who's playing Arthur, then?'

'We're considering our options, but Colin Farrell ... he's looking good.'

'I like that lad.' Joe nods approvingly. 'Have you another card?' Ructions hands Joe a second card. 'Have you a pen?' Ructions gives Joe a pen. He writes on the card. 'That's my number, Val. If I can help you in any way, don't be afraid to lift the phone.'

'That's good to know, Joe. I'm gonna be about for maybe a week, getting a feel for the place. So, what do you say you and me get together during the week and raise a glass to Arthur?'

'No better man, Val. I'll look forward to that.' Joe starts to walk away.

Ructions waits until Joe has driven off before walking around to the back of Arthur's grave, where everyone, with the exception of Billy, has now assembled. 'Come on, boys, back to work; we haven't got all night.'

As Ructions moves away with some excess plywood, Ben asks Dermot why Ructions is using it to create a walkway to the graveyard's exit. 'I'd imagine so that there won't be any wheelbarrow tracks after we leave,' Dermot says.

'He thinks of everything, doesn't he?' Ben says.

Ructions is now in the back of one of the lorries, his cravat removed, his sleeves rolled up. He neatly places the boxes in the back of the lorry. Dermot returns to the tunnel area.

An hour later, and sweat rivulets are running down Billy's face. While the open entrance to the tunnel allows fresh air to penetrate the vault, the heat is nevertheless stifling.

'I'm burnin' up,' Billy says. 'I've gotta come out. Make way, Ambrose.' Billy scrambles up the tunnel and climbs out. He bends, his hands resting on his knees, straightens up, and breathes deeply, his chest expanding. Ructions comes along. 'What's the problem, Billy?'

'It's hotter than a pizza oven in there. I was on the verge of fainting.'

Ructions turns to Ambrose. 'You go in.'

'Me?'

'Yeah, you.'

'But my asthma ... I couldn't—'

'I'll do it,' Dermot volunteers. 'The inside of Arthur Guinness's vault ... who wouldn't want to see that?'

Ructions hesitates, throws a disparaging look at Ambrose, but says, 'Okay, get to it,' before going back to the lorry.

With the first lorry full up, Ructions is now in the back of the second lorry. He looks at his watch. They've been removing Goering's gold continuously for nearly three hours now. The first lorry is heavily weighed down, while the second is only a quarter full. Billy approaches with a wheelbarrow. 'That's it, Billy,' Ructions says. 'Wrap it up.'

'But there's lots more down there, Ructions, and it won't be daylight for another three hours!'

'We've got to have the gold transferred to the barge before daylight.'

'Do you want me to drive ahead with the full lorry?' Billy says.

'Nah. Better we stay together.'

'Got ya.' Billy lifts his boxes on to the lorry and Ructions stacks them. They hurry back to the rear of the crypt whereupon Ructions barks out instructions: 'Wrap it up, fellas. Bring everything,' Ructions says. 'The plywood: the wheelbarrows: everything. And put back the ledger stone. There can't be any trace of us ever having been here.'

Inside the vault, Dermot, stripped to his underpants, is surprisingly fresh, despite the heat and the hard work. One whole wall is cleared of gold boxes. Dermot reaches into his trouser pocket, retrieves his cell phone, takes photos of each coffin, and then talks into a visual phone recording. 'It's four a.m., on the twenty-first of November 2008, and I'm in the vault of Arthur Guinness and his family.' He turns the phone on himself and walks over to where the coffins sit in their niches. 'Look here,' he says, zooming in on the name on the nameplate. 'Olivia Guinness. Olivia was Arthur's wife.' His hand touches another nameplate. 'And here's the great man himself ... Arthur Guinness.

On behalf of millions of thirsty Irishmen down the ages, I salute you, King Arthur. This is Dermot McCracken, in Arthur Guinness's vault, Oughterard graveyard, County Kildare.'

'Dermy! Come on! Time to go!' Ructions says lowly.

As Dermot comes out of the tunnel, Ructions is waiting on him. 'Who were you talking to down there?'

'What?'

I heard you talking to someone.'

'I was just recording some shots of the interior for posterity.'

'On what?'

'My cell phone.'

Ructions put out his hand and wriggles his fingers. 'Give it here.'

'What? Why?'

'Are you insane? Have you any—' Ructions scratches his head with both hands in frustration. 'Your memento, your little fucking keepsake, is what is known as *evidence*. It puts you at the heart of our operation, and you can put us all at the heart of it. What do you think this is, man? A university dig?'

Embarrassed now, Dermot hands over his phone. 'Ructions, I didn't mean to—'

You're the reason why I hate working with amateurs, Ructions thinks. 'I'll buy you another one.'

It is only about a mile from Oughterard graveyard to Lock 13 along the Grand Canal. A large barge hired out by Antoine is anchored there. Once more, a human chain is formed. The transfer of Goering's gold from the lorries on to the barge is carried out seamlessly.

When the gold is safely on board, Ructions takes Dermot and Ben to the side and produces two thick, brown envelopes, which he holds out to the men. 'This is for you, lads. A thank-you from me.'

Dermot smiles. 'Much obliged, Ructions, but it was the whole experience for me. The money doesn't matter.'

'Everybody has to pay somebody rent, Dermy. Take the money.'

Ben interjects. 'Ructions is right. Take the money, Dermy.' Ben takes his envelope. Dermot smiles and takes his envelope.

While Ambrose settles himself in the ship's cabin with the gold, Ructions, Billy, Dermot, and Ben watch as the barge gets underway. They walk up the canal pathway where Ructions's car is parked.

CHAPTER FORTY-THREE

RUCTIONS MELTS INTO HIS HOTEL BED.

He is naked, lying in the foetal position, on a flat wooden bench, in a corner of a grey, spider-infested, round cell, which is only reachable by a ladder from above. A dark figure looks into the cell and floats down, through the air, towards him. He shivers. The figure is in front of him. It's an eighteenth-century wigged man with eyes that can see a man's soul. Arthur Guinness's pursed lips open wider, wider, as he sings in a hissing voice: 'And He shall reign for ever and ever ...' A ringing noise ... Ructions answers his phone.

'Are you up?' Billy asks.

'Yeah. Give me ten minutes.'

Hughie O'Boyle has the bewildered look of a prisoner who has been entombed in a twelve-by-twelve-foot hole on Devil's Island for ten years. His innocuous, twitching eyes stare down at the oak table. He is wearing overalls now and is in the kitchen of the farmhouse. The two interrogators stand on either side of him. Try as he may, he cannot grip the pen on the table because his fingers are broken.

'This isn't going to work,' one of the interrogators says. He takes a small recorder out of his pocket and lays it on the table beside Hughie, who stares at the device. Before turning it on, the same interrogator sits down beside Hughie. 'If I'd my way, tout, I'd blowtorch your balls, I would. No fucking sweat. But your good buddy, Tiny, he says my ways is the old ways, and you're only to be exiled. I ask you, what's the point? Where's the deterrent in that? Who's even gonna miss a piece of shit like you? Now say what you've gotta say into the fucking recorder and finish this. I've wasted enough time on you.'

He flips it on and Hughie coughs and leans over the recorder. 'My name is Hugh Michael O'Boyle, and I am a police informer ...'

'Speak louder.'

'My name is Hugh Michael O'Boyle and I am a police informer.'

Ructions walks into the open-air patio of The Duck pub in Celbridge, sits down on a tall chair, and lifts a menu. A very old man with grey hair, holding a walking stick, comes along and sits across from Ructions. Ructions concentrates on the menu.

'You must be Mr O'Hare,' the old man says.

Ructions is taken aback. He recognises the face from his computer screen and the heavy German accent. 'I am.'

The old man reaches over his hand, which Ructions takes.

'It's a pleasure to finally meet you. May I call you Ructions?'

'Sure, Kapitän Adelbert Keller.' Adelbert shows no surprise. 'Where's Karl?'

'He's about.'

'About where?'

'About where he needs to be. You're dealing with me now.'

'With you? What makes you so sure I want to deal with you?'

'Because you want to maximize your potential.'

Ructions grins. A waitress approaches. 'What would you like, Adelbert?' Ructions asks. 'It's on me.'

'I'll have a half-shot cappuccino, if you don't mind.'

'Not at all.' Ructions orders a black tea. The waitress leaves the table.

'I'm surprised you've shown up here, Adelbert. You must be …'

'Old.' Adelbert grins. 'Ructions, age is relative. If you live long enough, you'll understand that.'

'If I live long enough … that's a big *if*, wouldn't you say?'

'You never know. I never expected to live this long, and look at me now.' Adelbert stands up and touches his toes with his fingers.

'*Olé!*' Ructions exclaims.

The two men stare at each other.

'So, Adelbert, what's next?'

'I'm going to keep this simple. I don't want maps or diagrams or artist's paintings.' Adelbert places both hands on the table. 'I want you to take me to the gold. And, after it's confirmed that it is where you say it is and is in a quantity that makes it financially viable to conclude this deal, I am authorised by my friends to pay you the two million euro you are demanding.'

'You want me to take you to the gold *before* you hand over any money?'

'That's right.'

'And if I don't?'

'I finish my cappuccino and we never see each other again.'

Ructions stands up to leave, putting some money on the table. 'Enjoy your cappuccino, Mein Freund.'

'Good luck to you too, Herr Ructions.'

Before Ructions walks out to the car park, he takes out a one-kilo gold ingot from inside his coat and hands it to Adelbert. 'A memento of our meeting,' he says. 'Never let it be said that we Irish aren't gracious.'

Adelbert looks at the ingot and runs his thumb over the Nazi symbol. '*Danke schön,*' he says.

Ructions gets into his car. He is driving out of the car park when he sees that Adelbert is blocking his way. He stops. Adelbert gets into the passenger seat and melodramatically claps his hands. 'You played that exceptionally well, I must say.'

'You think so?'

'Oh, yes; yes, I do. You waited until there was an impasse and then you whetted my appetite to the point where I had no alternative but to give ground. You're a formidable opponent, Ructions.' The former SS soldier winds down the window and breathes deeply. 'I want to do a deal with you, Irishman, but the conditions have to be right. You appreciate that, don't you?'

'You've got my attention.'

'Ructions, you should know, I'm not Karl; he was too … shall we say … enthusiastic?'

'Enthusiasm has its place.'

'It has, but you're looking for two million euro before I even see the goods. Only a fool buys a product without seeing it.'

Ructions lights up a cigarette. 'But you have seen it.'

'I've seen an ingot.'

'I really do think we're finished here.'

Adelbert shows no signs of alarm. 'I can't believe you'd allow this deal to slip away.'

'Adelbert! I have the product and it's the most sellable product known to mankind. I don't need you.'

Adelbert's countenance changes. He now has a look of concern, a small furrowing on his forehead. 'But all I want,' Adelbert gesticulates with both hands, 'is to make a valuation of the gold in order to justify releasing such a large sum of money. Anything less would make me a hostage to stupidity. Don't you agree?'

'And if I bring you to the location of the gold without a down payment, what incentive would you have to pay me anything? Who's to say you wouldn't have me murdered?'

'I wouldn't do such a thing,' Adelbert says.

A prolonged silence follows as Ructions ponders Adelbert's words.

Then Ructions says, 'I presume you have people nearby?'

'Yes.'

'I have people also.' Ructions throws his cigarette out the window. 'Okay, okay, here's my final offer ... you will be detained while someone from your side goes with someone from my side to verify the location and the quantity of the gold. Once your guy is satisfied, he makes the phone call to you, you transfer the money, and you will be released.'

'How do I know you will release me?'

'Why wouldn't I release you? This is about money, Adelbert, and there's no money in holding on to you once we've been paid.'

Adelbert strains his neck. He purses his lips. Finally, he says: 'That is agreeable.'

'Let's do it,' Ructions says.

'Now?'

'Why wait?'

Billy and Karl Keller walk into the forecourt of the church in Oughterard graveyard. Keller looks quizzically at Billy, who points a finger at the Guinness vault. 'It's in there.'

Keller examines the large entrance stone. 'How do we get in?' he asks.

Billy takes the neo-Nazi to the back of the Guinness vault and points to Anne Griffith's grave. 'That's your way in.' Billy prises open the ledger stone with a crowbar and the opening to the tunnel appears. 'The gold is at the end of the tunnel.' Billy hands Keller a flashlamp. 'You'll need this.'

Ructions and Adelbert are sitting at the back of a country pub, each drinking a pint of Guinness. 'I must say,' Adelbert remarks as he crosses his legs, 'this is the most civilised hostage-taking I've ever been involved in.'

'Have you been involved in many hostage-takings then?'

'This is the first. That's why it's the most civilised.'

'You're a bit of a character, Adelbert. Much more colourful than your nephew.'

Adelbert sighs. 'Karl thinks he knows it all, and people like that are usually dull.'

'Can I say what I think?'

'By all means.'

'Didn't Hitler think he knew it all?'

'Someone like you would never understand the Führer. You never witnessed his power, his charisma; how he controlled a room; how he made every individual German feel like a god. He was the most extraordinary man I have ever met.'

'It's hard to imagine how someone as astute as yourself could be swept up in his madness.'

'It wasn't always madness. Take his ideas on eugenics, for example ... he wanted to improve the gene pool—'

'By murdering the weak and less fortunate?'

'By removing defectives. You may not know this, but the concept of eugenics wasn't invented by us Germans. Plato advocated it in ancient Greece in 400 BC. In fact, the United Kingdom, the United States, Canada, and most European countries had their own eugenics movements in the early twentieth century.'

'The difference with those countries and yourselves is that you Nazis took things to another level; you murdered tens of thousands of your own citizens who had mental or physical disabilities.'

'I didn't know about that then.'

'But you didn't disagree with it when you found out ...'

'Why would I? The principle was faultless. The greater should never allow itself to be the prisoner of the lesser.'

Ructions points a finger at Adelbert. 'You're still a Nazi at heart, Adelbert. Germany nowadays is probably the most progressive country in Europe, but you ... you haven't moved on.'

'Germany—' Adelbert's phone rings.

'Hallo?'

'Ja.'

'Bist Du Dir sicher?'

'*Ja.*'

'Danke.'

Adelbert ends the call and turns back to Ructions. 'Can I have your bank details, please?' Ructions hands Adelbert his bank details, and the latter transfers two million euro to Ructions's account.

Ructions phones up his bank to confirm the transfer. 'That's it, then,' Ructions says, closing his call.

Adelbert holds out his hand. Ructions looks down at it and walks out of the bar.

Sitting where he had met Adelbert at the back of The Duck pub, Ructions nods to the Arthur Guinness and toucan signs.

'Why Celbridge?' Tiny Murdoch asks.

Ructions says, 'In the first place, it has easy access to the Grand Canal—'

'And thus to Dublin port. Yes?' O'Flaherty adds.

'Exactly. And who would ever fiddle about with Guinness's grave?'

'You've fiddled about with it,' Tiny says.

'No, I didn't. I've been there to confirm that the gold is on-site, but that's all.'

'And is it?' O'Flaherty asks.

Ructions takes out a one-kilo gold bar and hands it to O'Flaherty. 'I anticipated you wouldn't believe me.'

O'Flaherty examines the gold bar and hands it to his comrade. 'Jaysus! Will ya look at this, Tiny?'

Tiny also studies the gold bar. 'How many of these are there?'

'Thousands,' Ructions replies.

'Holy Jesus and His Blessed Mother!' Tiny mumbles.

O'Flaherty coughs. 'Ructions, I'd like you to take Tiny to the site and show him—'

'Now, hold on, Paul, I'm out of this. I've done my bit. The deal was: I point you in the direction of the gold. I've done that. It's over to you now.'

'You're out of it when I say you're out of it.'

'This isn't right,' Ructions protests. 'This isn't—'

'I say what's right,' O'Flaherty insists. His manner softens. 'Look, all I'm asking is that you take Tiny up to the grave and show him how to get the gold out. Is that too much to ask?'

'And that's me gone?'

'That's you away.'

'And I can live free from IRA harassment or threat on the island of Ireland?'

'I don't have any gold, Ructions, but I have my word of honour, and it's worth all the gold in Fort Knox.'

'Fair enough.'

O'Flaherty puts a bottle of orange juice to his lips and takes it down again. All the while his eyes are fixed on Ructions. 'Are you trying to set us up, Ructions?'

'What?'

'It's simple enough; are you trying to set us up?'

'Set you up? Why would I do that? What's this all about, Paul?'

'Your German friends—'

'What German friends? I don't have any German friends.'

'What about the neo-Nazis who arrived in Dublin airport a couple of days ago?' O'Flaherty says.

Ructions holds out a questioning hand. 'What neo-Nazis? What's this all about?'

'He's good,' Tiny says.

'The neo-Nazis who are here for the gold,' O'Flaherty says.

'I haven't a clue what you're talking about, Paul.' Ructions's look of bewilderment is so convincing that O'Flaherty is almost certain he is genuine.

'Our intelligence has reported that a leading neo-Nazi called Karl Keller and five members of his party's paramilitary wing have arrived in Ireland,' O'Flaherty says, 'and they're looking for *our* gold.'

'They are?' Ructions says.

'So, you know nothing about them?' Tiny says.

'Never heard of them till you boys brought them up.'

'I don't believe him, Paul.' Tiny looks disdainfully at Ructions. 'You're burning the candle at both ends, bullet-dodger.'

'And you should've been shot dead instead of being kneecapped.'

Tiny pushes the table aside, jumps up, and throws a punch, which misses. Ructions pulls back his head, jumps up, moves towards Tiny, and pumps two left hooks into his ribs. The bigger man buckles over. O'Flaherty gets between the protagonists.

O'Flaherty points to Ructions. 'You! Get back!'

Deeply satisfied with the blows he'd landed, Ructions stands back.

'Deep breaths, Tiny,' O'Flaherty says, rubbing his comrade's back.

Even though he is still bent over, Tiny manages to wheeze out, 'We shouldn't … trust this boyo, Paul. He'd sell his granny for a quick buck.'

'Ghost a ghost a ghost! The shite I've to put up with for Ireland,' O'Flaherty exclaims. 'You're both assholes!' The IRA chief shakes his head. 'Nah,' he tells Tiny, 'he knows nothing about the Germans.'

'You're wrong, Paul!' Tiny gasps.

'I'm not wrong,' O'Flaherty says. 'I'm surprised at you for letting personal animosity get in the way of your professional judgement. This is IRA business. We never show emotion, y'hear?'

Chastened, Tiny nods.

'And you' – he turns to Ructions – 'show us the gold.'

Ructions, Paul, and Tiny step into the forecourt of the church in Oughterard graveyard. Ructions leads the IRA men to the Guinness vault and tells them that the gold is inside. He brings them to Anne Griffith's grave and prises opens the ledger stone with a crowbar, revealing the opening to the tunnel. 'That's the way into Arthur's grave.'

Tiny looks at O'Flaherty, who says: 'Go on. Get down there.'

Tiny takes the torchlight from Ructions and climbs down into the tunnel.

CHAPTER FORTY-FOUR

SERGE MERCIER STRETCHES OUT HIS ARMS, EXPANDS his chest, and gulps in the unpolluted Irish air. He is enjoying the barge trip down the Grand Canal from Lock 13, Celbridge, to Grand Canal Dock in Dublin. Sitting on a small, cushioned bench at the barge's stern and wearing a beige duffle coat with the hood up to offset the mizzling rain, he looks up at a brooding sky. Clouds are gathering. There will be thunder before long. A renegade thought drip-feeds into Serge's mind: this must be the slowest getaway ever. No souped-up Ferraris here; no helicopters waiting to evacuate the guilty; no one waiting to be beamed up to the mothership. No need to get too excited. He feels contented.

Just after passing Lock 9 and the townland of Ballymanaggin and Clonburris Great, an otter emerges at the side of the barge with a wriggling bream in its mouth. It looks up at Serge as if to say, 'What are you doing in my domain?' Serge raised his cup of hot chicken soup to the creature.

A police motorboat is coming in the opposite direction to that in which the barge is moving. 'We have company,' Antoine says.

'Who is it?'

'Police.'

Serge enters the first cabin of the boat and opens the door of the second cabin. Surrounded by tens of millions of euro in gold, Ambrose lies sleeping on a cushioned bench, his mouth open, his chest rising and filling between snores. Serge wakes him up. 'Police.'

The police boat pulls close and a garda on deck runs his finger across his throat, an indication that he wants Antoine to cut engines and pull into a nearby jetty. The lumbering barge pulls in. Two gardaí approach, one with a sniffer dog.

'Good day,' a garda says.

'Bonjour, monsieur,' Antoine says.

'May we come on board?'

'By all means.'

The two gardaí come on board. 'Is this your barge?' a fat garda with a grey moustache asks.

'No,' Antoine says, 'we hired it from Dublin barge hire.'

'Have you papers to that effect?'

'Sure. If you'll come this way, please.' Antoine goes into the first cabin, followed by the fat garda, while the second garda chats with Serge. The Frenchman lifts a briefcase from the top of a cupboard, takes out the barge hire contract and hands it to the garda, who reads it. The police officer looks around. 'How long are you planning to stay in Ireland, sir?'

'Actually, not long. My uncle' – Antoine nods towards the deck – 'he has terminal cancer, prostate—'

'I'm sorry to hear that. My father, God rest him, died of prostate cancer.'

'Yeah, well, then, unfortunately, you know what's involved.' Antoine winces and nods to a box of incontinence pads in the corner.

'Ah, yes. I've seen those before,' the garda says. 'How close is your uncle to ... you know?'

'This will be his last trip to Ireland, for sure. He loves this country. He's been coming here since his twenties. Went to the all-Ireland hurling final every year for almost sixty years with someone – I presume it was a lady friend – but he'd never confirm whether this person was a male or a female.'

'Those old-timers keep their cards close to their chests,' the garda remarks.

'He certainly does!'

The garda laughs.

'It seems he's intent on taking his secrets to the grave with him. Anyway, what was it you were saying? Yes, how long he has left ... Three months, maybe four.'

The garda grimaces. 'Then the hardest part is in front of you ...' The garda glances at the barge hire agreement. 'Philippe. I'm Patrick.' They shake hands.

In the second cabin, Ambrose has his ear to the door, a handgun by his side.

'Well, Philippe, we're looking for drug traffickers, not folks like yourselves. If I can have a quick look in there,' Patrick says, pointing to the innermost cabin, 'I'll be gone.'

'Feel free, Patrick.'

Patrick opens the door a few inches.

Ambrose, scarf around his face, has his gun pointing at the door.

Patrick's colleague comes to the entrance of the cabin and shouts in, 'Packy, we need to shift – pronto. The sarge and Big Dessie have intercepted Tempo and Skin Hughes on a barge at Sallins, and it's loaded up with coke and weed. The sarge reckons there's a hundred grands with the gear.'

'Righty-o.' Patrick quickly shakes Antoine's hand as he speeds out of the cabin. 'Good luck, Philippe.'

'Thanks.'

Ructions and Billy sit in a quayside coffee shop, waiting for the barge reaching the Grand Canal Dock. Ructions decides to ride his luck and walks outside to phone Eleanor – for the umpteenth time. The phone rings and rings, and just as he is about to hang up, the call is answered. 'Can you not take a hint?'

'El, it's me.'

'I know it's you, it's always you.'

There is a pause as Ructions tries to find the right words. 'Amm, sorry doesn't make it right, but I am sorry.'

'I bet you've a big mournful face on you right now.'

'I am sorry, El.'

'What are you sorry for?'

'For what I've put you through … for everything.'

'Can I tell you something, Ructions? I wish I'd never met you.'

'I can understand that completely, but I can't say the same, El. You've been the greatest thing that's happened to me.'

Eleanor's tongue is loosening up. 'You're a very understanding fella, Ructions, a big, kindhearted cotton ball. That's why you let me come back to Northern Ireland into the arms of the

IRA rather than pull the plug on your wee adventure. But then, you have a disease, don't you? A very nasty dose of greed. Potentially lethal, if not caught in time. Only one cure – gold – and plenty of it.'

'I deserved that, but I do love you, El, and you know it.'

'"I know it"? You ... you're so good at this bullshitting—'

'It's not bullshit; it's the truth.' Ructions hears whimpering on the other end of the phone. 'El, don't cry, I hate it when you cry.'

'Don't you bloody well tell me not to cry, Ructions O'Hare. I'll cry if I want to, you ... you—'

'Forgive me, love. Please, give me another chance.'

'How many chances do you want? You're a bastard for treating me like this.'

Eleanor hangs up.

Ructions considers whether or not to call Eleanor back. He decides against it. Then his phone rings in his hand. It's Serge, who tells him that they are close.

Ructions and Billy finish their coffees and make their way to the dock, where they watch Antoine navigate the barge alongside his docked fishing boat. They walk along the plankway towards the boats, passing rows of colourful barges. One barge looks as if it has a tree growing from its stern. Another looks like it is covered in ivy. Smoke comes out of the tin chimney of another. Most have curtains on their porthole windows and looked lived-in. Ructions's eyes travel directly across the canal from the barges to the large brown-bricked façade of the dilapidated Boland's Mill, where, during the 1916 Irish rebellion, Eamon de Valera, a future president of Ireland, and his Irish rebels had defied the might of the British army for six days. Now, the historical monument has foliage growing out of its dark stoned walls.

Ructions and Billy walk along the wooden pathways until they reach the location where the barge is berthed. They climb on board the barge as darkness is descending. The wind and rain have picked up, but the transfer couldn't be easier: the gold is placed in a net, hooked on to the barge's winch, and transferred in two lifts to Antoine's fishing boat, where it is then stowed in the hold.

Ructions brings Billy and Ambrose into the cabin of the fishing boat and hands them the black briefcases that Serge had brought on the voyage. Billy opens his briefcase, looks down at the rows of money, smiles, and nods affirmatively to Ructions. Ambrose does likewise. 'Thanks, mate,' Billy says. 'You didn't have to—'

'But I did, Bill. Thank you.' The two buddies hug warmly.

Ambrose shakes Ructions's hand before hugs are exchanged. Billy and Ambrose take their leave and walk away from the boat.

As the fishing boat, with Antoine, Serge, and Ructions aboard, sails out of Dublin harbour and into the open sea, it is tossed about by wrathful waves. Ructions, sitting in the cabin, looks at Serge, who is pouring two glasses of Guinness. He hands one to Ructions and says, 'What will we toast?'

'What about a toast to the man himself?'

They hold up their glasses. 'To Arthur!'

Tearing rain lashes the County Wicklow countryside. At the Oughterard graveyard, members of the Das Reich SS Division are extracting Hermann Goering's gold.

Karl Keller stands at the entrance to the tunnel. He exhorts his comrades to hurry up: *'Beeil dich!'* A subordinate comes along and tells him that the first lorry is full. Keller makes no reply. He looks at his watch. It is two o'clock in the morning. He climbs into the well of the tunnel. 'Franz?' he shouts.

'Ja?'

'Wie lange wird es dauern, um das ganze Gold herauszukriegen?'

'Wir sind noch nicht einmal halb damit fertig.'

There's more gold still in the vault than we've taken out? Karl is pleased. He makes a phone call and tells his pilot in the nearby Weston airport that he will be with him before long.

He is no sooner in the driver's seat of the heavily laden lorry, ready to head down the gravelly road when two cars with garda signs appear and are driven slowly towards him. Keller reaches for a handgun under his seat. He cocks it and puts it in his waistband before telling a member of his team to alert the others.

The garda cars pull up behind the lorry and the police officers get out of their vehicles. Keller notices that they are wearing heavy raincoats and are armed with Heckler & Koch MP5 submachine guns. Irish police don't usually carry firearms, he thinks. Why are the officers so heavily armed? A police officer comes around to the driver's seat.

Keller puts down the window and smiles.

'Terrible night for it, sir,' the garda says. Keller nods. 'Can I see your licence, please?' Keller passes over his licence. 'Karl Keller. You're German.' The garda turns his head and calls back to his colleagues. 'Karl Keller. German.' The gardaí cock their weapons and take up defensive positions around their cars. 'Can you tell me what you're doing here at two o'clock in the morning, please?'

'Can you tell me why my being German has led to your officers cocking their weapons?'

Still examining Keller's licence, the garda says, 'Mister Keller, we're responding to reports of a disturbance at this graveyard. Now, sir, I'll ask you again: What are you doing here at two o'clock in the morning?'

'Why don't you see for yourself?' Keller gets out of the lorry and leads the garda to its rear. He opens the doors. The garda shines a torch into the back of the lorry. 'What's in those boxes?'

'Gold. German gold. *Our* gold.'

'Pardon?'

Keller whips out the gun from his waistband and sticks it into the garda's face. 'Tell your colleagues to drop their weapons. Do it now!'

'Drop your weapons, boys.'

The members of the Das Reich Division appear silently, their weapons pointing at the gardaí. 'Tell your officers to come forward with their arms up and parade in front of your lead vehicle.'

'*Lassen Sie Ihre Waffen!*' IRA volunteer – and local German teacher – Dessie Lyons, barks. 'Drop your weapons!'

Shocked, Keller looks around.

A giant of a man, with an M60 machine-gun strapped across his shoulder, stands up in the field at the side of the road.

'*Lassen Sie Ihre Waffen!*' Dessie Lyons shouts again, as more men appear on both sides of the road, all armed with rifles.

'Karl Keller,' Tiny roars. 'Karl Keller, tell your people to lower their weapons. That gold is ours.'

'You're not the police,' Keller says in English.

'No, we're the IRA,' Tiny shouts.

'And what if we don't lower our weapons?'

'We'll kill you all.'

'Can't we talk about this, IRA? Surely there's enough gold for us both?'

'No.'

A sudden wind catches Tiny's word and whips it away. 'What was that?' Keller shouts.

'I said, *no*. We want it all for ourselves.'

'Are you prepared to die for it?'

'Try us.'

'Werden wir das Feuer eföffnen, Führer?'

'Nein.'

'Dessie, what did they say there?' Tiny screeches.

'He said, "Should we open fire, leader?"' Lyons says.

'Karl, listen to me,' Tiny bellows. 'There's no need for you people to die tonight, but if you don't do as I tell you, you'll all go down. Now, order your men to lower their weapons, and we'll let you walk away.'

'Aren't you're forgetting something?'

'What?'

'Him.' Keller nods to Stevie O'Shea, the 'garda' who had first confronted him. Keller has his gun pressed into O'Shea's cheek. 'If anything happens, he gets the first bullet.'

'Go ahead. Shoot him,' Tiny growls, 'but aren't *you* forgetting something? You get the second bullet.'

'What did you say?'

'I said, shoot the fucker.'

'I will. Don't push me, IRA.'

'Fucking shoot him, then. Sorry, Stevie.'

'But, Tiny—' O'Shea pleads.

'I will kill him!' Keller shouts.

'Hit the deck, Stevie!' Tiny roars. O'Shea elbows Keller in the ribs and throws himself forwards on to the ground.

Feeding his own belt of ammunition into the M60, Tiny rakes the front of the graveyard with machine-gun fire. Caught in the kill zone, the bodies of two Das Reich members contort and drop as IRA bullets rain down on the graveyard entrance. Das Reich member Gunther Klein steps out from behind the graveyard wall and, firing a submachine gun from the hip, lets off a volley of shots at Tiny. The IRA man beside Tiny, Peter 'Heffo' Heffernan, drops. Tiny is hit in the arm and grazed on the side of his head, but he keeps firing. Klein is almost cut in half by IRA bullets.

Amidst the cries and cordite, Keller rolls under the lorry. On his elbows, he crawls away along the graveyard wall hidden by the lorry.

As the two remaining members of Das Reich try to run through the graveyard, three IRA men cut them down in a hail of bullets.

'Cease firing!' Tiny yells. 'Cease firing!' The shooting stops. Tiny sets the M60 against a post. He takes a handgun from a holster, steps down onto the gravelly road, walks towards a wounded Das Reich member who is propped up against the wall, and shoots him in the face. 'Nazi bastard! No prisoners!' he shouts. 'Nut them all.'

Tiny turns around and bellows, 'Stevie! Stevie!'

Stevie O'Shea comes from around the lorry.

Tiny puts his hand on O'Shea's shoulder. 'Are you all right?'

O'Shea is stunned, his mouth agape. He breathes deeply, exhaling aloud. He finds his lilting County Kerry voice. 'You … you were going to let him kill me there.'

'He was never gonna kill ya.'

'How did you know that?'

'I saw it in his eyes.'

'In the pitch-black?'

'Get into the lorry—'

'You were gonna let that Nazi stiff me!'

'*I'll* fucking stiff ya!' Tiny retorts. 'You're an IRA volunteer, and you take your medicine like the rest of us! Casualties?'

'Just Heffo's bulletproof vest,' Rory Diamond says. 'It took three bullets. He's sore, but he's all right.'

'And I've been hit in the leg,' Dessie Lyons says.

'Rory, get Heffo and Dessie into the back of the lorry.' Tiny waves his gun in the direction of the cars and shouts, 'We're heading to MacIntyre's farmhouse and—'

'Hold on there, Tiny,' Rory says, inspecting his commander's head. 'You're bleeding.'

'Don't worry about it. It's only a graze. Now, get these fucking cars down the laneway. Everybody into the back of the lorry. Frank, you drive.' Tiny's phone rings. 'Right.' He hangs up and shouts, 'Stop! Cancel everything! The gardaí have set up roadblocks, and there's a large convoy coming our way. Into the fields, boys! Dessie, can you walk?'

'I can hobble.'

'Heffo?'

'Don't worry about me, Tiny. I'll make it.'

'Good man. C'mon, boys,' Tiny shouts, 'into the fields. Single file and we stick close to the hedges.'

The weeping clouds of County Kildare sob no more. Superintendent Thierry Vasseur, along with Inspector Pierre Robillard, walk along the gravelly road. Up ahead, garda forensic officers in white suits have set up a lighting system. Vasseur walks over to a lifeless body and looks into the dead Das Reich member's face. He walks around the dead, counting.

'There's five in all,' Manus O'Toole says from behind. Vasseur turns around.

'Das Reich?'

'Looks like it.'

'Head shots?'

Manus nods. 'They've all received multiple bullets wounds, including a *coup de grâce*.'

'Who did this?'

'The IRA.'

'Do you know that for certain?'

'It was them.'

'Won't this destroy the peace process?'

'No.'

'Why not? Aren't the IRA supposed to be on ceasefire under the terms of the Good Friday Agreement?'

'They are.'

'I don't understand.'

'Thierry, the magic of Irish politics is that it has the capacity to mutate when it needs to. The peace process has been a quarter of a century in the making and has involved every political party on the island, plus the British and American governments. Nobody's gonna blow a gasket over a few dead Nazis, who, incidentally, happened to have been running around Ireland in the middle of the night armed to the teeth. Besides, this will be put down to the Ructions O'Hare gang.'

'I didn't know he had a gang.'

'Neither does he.'

Vasseur turns to walk back down the gravelly road to the cars, followed by Robillard.

'Are you not staying, Thierry?'

Vasseur turns around. 'Look about you, Manus. The terrorists who murdered Clément Beauregard have been brought to the ultimate justice …' Vasseur spreads his hand. 'I have no further role here.'

'I don't think Keller is amongst those five.'

'He isn't. A pity.'

A garda sergeant approaches Manus. 'Sir, a Mr Joe Fitzpatrick of the Celbridge Guided Tour Project has arrived.'

'Right. What does he want?'

'Well, it's strange, because he says he was speaking to a Mr Val P. Angley in the cemetery last night. Angley, it seems, introduced himself as the executive producer of Ingot Productions.'

Thierry explodes into laughter.

'Here's an introduction card that he gave to Fitzpatrick.'

Manus looks at the card and gives it to Vasseur. 'Last night, you say?'

'Yes, sir. Apparently, Angley and several other men were filming night scenes in connection with a film about Arthur Guinness.' The sergeant smiles. 'Angley said he was endeavouring to "draw out the golden fabric that surrounded the man's life, even until death."'

Vasseur holds his stomach.

'That'll be all, sergeant.'

The sergeant goes back to the graveyard.

Manus looks aggrieved. 'It's not that funny, Thierry. By now, he could be anywhere on the continent.'

Vasseur tempers his mirth and says, 'By now, he's not in Ireland, that's for sure. That Ructions—'

'Ingot fucking Productions … he's making a right dick out of An Garda Síochána – and me – and you think it's funny. Well, it's not.'

'You shouldn't take it personally, Manus.'

'I don't like being made to look like a fool.'

'Nobody does.' Thierry puts his arm around Manus' shoulder. 'Look, a person can only look like a fool if they behave like one. The reality is, Ructions has made off with as much gold as took his fancy, and there's nothing you, me, or anybody else can do about it. But who's to say that he made off with anything? You, Manus? You're the SIO in this case. If you say you recovered all the gold, then you recovered all the gold.'

'Doesn't it annoy you that he's stolen the gold?'

'Why should it? Who owns it, anyway? Germany? The Allies? Who can legitimately show proof of ownership?'

'The gold was in Ireland,' Manus says, 'so it belongs to the Irish nation—'

'But only when it's in Ireland, Manus. If it were to be recovered on the European continent, the country in which it was recaptured would claim it, and moreover, there'd be no proof that it was ever here in the first place.'

'Thierry, it sounds to me like you admire Ructions.'

'Oh, but I do.'

'Why? He's a major criminal!'

'So what?' Vasseur laughs. 'Ructions didn't murder Clément Beauregard, and I doubt very much that he murdered any of those fascist bastards up there.' Vasseur nods up the gravelly path. 'But, I *do* think he set them up.' Vasseur lowers his head and puts out his extended hand. 'And if he did, he did me, you, and the world a favour.'

Vasseur walks on while Manus remains behind. 'Your friend Ructions,' he says to Vasseur, 'will face the full rigors of the law, like everyone else!'

Vasseur turns. 'For what? You recovered all the gold, didn't you?'

Manus stops in his tracks. 'Hmm ... maybe I did. I mean, I did, didn't I? I recovered all the Nazi gold.' Manus laughs.

'See? Why so glum? I wouldn't be surprised if you didn't end up the next garda commissioner,' Vasseur says.

'Garda Commissioner O'Toole,' Manus says, smiling broadly, 'the man who recovered Goering's gold. I like that.'

EPILOGUE

THE BLACK CAR DRIVES STRAIGHT ON ALONG THE R116 road towards Cruagh Wood in the Dublin Mountains. Hughie O'Boyle, his eyes taped and wearing dark, blacked-out glasses, is in the back of the car, wedged between two members of the nutting squad, both wearing balaclavas. The journey from the border farmhouse where he had been tortured into making a confession had been an emotional wrench for Hughie because, although his IRA inquisitors had indicated he had been sentenced to banishment from Ireland, he had been around IRA circles long enough to know that the Nutting Squad often spoke with forked tongues and that few escaped the ultimate punishment.

'I never been down this neck of the woods before,' the Nutting Squad member to Hughie's right says to his colleague.

'There's a lovely view of Dublin just up the road. Zack, there's a third-class road up ahead. Stop there for a few minutes, will ya?'

'I thought you said I was being taken to catch the Dun Laoghaire ferry?' Hughie says.

'You are. I've to meet a guy up ahead first.'

That answer gave Hughie no comfort at all. 'No, you're not. You're going to kill me, aren't you?'

The first Nutting Squad member looks across at his colleague. Hughie gulps. 'Tiny told me lies. I should have known. Oh, Jesus, oh sweet Jesus, have mercy on me.'

The van stops at the beauty spot, and Hughie is taken out of the car. 'Can I see Dublin?' he pleads. 'For the last time?'

'Don't try to make a run for it, Hughie.'

'I won't.'

One of the Nutting Squad removes the tape and the dark glasses from Hughie's eyes. He blinks repeatedly. 'You're right,' he says, 'it is beautiful. Can I have a cigarette?'

'No. Smoking is bad for your health. C'mon.'

Hughie is led into a pine forest and, after thirty yards, is told to kneel down. A gun is cocked. 'Any last words, Hughie?'

'Yeah. Tell Tiny he still has an informer problem because I'm not a tout. I'm a good republican. Tell my wife—'

'May God have mercy on your soul.'

Two shots ring out across the Dublin mountains.

Berlin, on a night of snow. Underneath a railway bridge, a bedraggled Karl Keller stands with some winos in front of an open fire in an old oil drum, warming his hands. He draws on the butt of a roll-up, almost burning his fingers in the process. A car pulls up across the road. Karl squints anxiously at the car. He smiles. It's Uncle Adelbert. He's come. It's going to be all right.

He walks over. Adelbert smiles. As Karl gets to within five feet of the car, his expression changes. 'No!' he shouts. 'Not that!'

Three soft puffs ring out from a handgun with a silencer on it. Karl falls to the ground. Adelbert gets out of the car, arm outstretched, and this time shoots Karl twice in the face. He looks at the winos. They look away. He drives off. None of the winos bother to come over to look at the body. He was not one of them.

At PSNI Headquarters at Knock, Belfast, Chief Superintendent Daniel Clarke is getting ready to leave his office after his shift. After an abrupt knock, two officers from the Discipline and Anti-Corruption Branch walk into his office. Clarke looks shocked. He is told that he is under investigation on suspicion of aiding and abetting terrorists and is cautioned that anything he says may be given in evidence against him. Then he is ordered to hand over his badge and gun. He is asked if he would like to say anything for the record and answers: 'No comment.'

At the exact moment that Karl Keller had been warming his hands at the fire beneath the railway bridge, Serge Mercier was warming his hands at the log fire in his study. He returns to his desk. Before him he has a first edition of Victor Hugo's Les Misérables. He gingerly closes the book and puts it back in the safe, then goes to the drinks cabinet and pours himself a large brandy. He goes to the window and looks at the falling snow. His phone rings.

'Allo? Qui est-a-l'appareil?'

'Hello, Serge,' a female voice says.

'I'm sorry, who's this?'

'My name doesn't matter, but you and I have a shared history.'

'I'm afraid I don't take calls from unidentified callers.'

'You'll want to take this one.'

'Why would I?'

'Because it was me who sent you the anonymous letters.'

Serge's interest in this conversation has been ignited. 'I'm sorry, what letters would those be?'

'Come, come, Serge; you know what letters I'm talking about.'

'No, I don't.'

'Do I have to spell it out?'

'I don't like intrigue, mademoiselle.'

Laughter. 'Then you shouldn't have pursued the Reichsmarschall's gold.'

'Ahh. Those letters. I see. Yes, I see now. I am indebted to you. May I have your name so that I can recompense you? I will be most generous.'

'*Cher monsieur*, you don't need to know my name. My interest in helping you was to make sure the Nazis didn't get their hands on the gold. It's not widely known, but six members of my family died in the Holocaust.'

'I'm very sorry to hear that.'

'Thank you. The point is, Serge, I couldn't let Keller and his gang of cutthroats get the gold, and once Ructions and you got involved, it was my duty to help you in any way I could.'

'I'm curious … how is Karl handling his disappointment?'

'Not very well. He's dead. Murdered by Das Reich.'

A silence. Serge says softly: 'That doesn't surprise me. Nazis aren't known for their compassion.'

'Adelbert certainly isn't.'

'Adelbert? The old Nazi?'

'That old Nazi has never changed, *cher monsieur*. The Führer? He may as well still be in residence in the Berghof, as far as Adelbert's concerned. Adelbert was and is the power behind the throne.'

'But I thought Karl—'

'Karl was only ever a straw man. It's been Adelbert all along.'

'That surprises me. It really does. Adelbert must be ancient.'

'He is, but he's never changed: *"Meine Ehre Heisst Treur—"*'

'I've read this on SS daggers ...' Serge says. '"My Honour is Loyalty."'

'Well done, *cher monsieur*. Adelbert has never forsaken his SS Loyalty Oath and, if given the chance, he'd still gas Jews.'

'Mon Dieu!'

'Serge, the Adelbert Kellers of Germany are vampires; they sucked the life's blood out of my country once before, and they'd do it again. But there are many others like me who are determined not to let them prevail again.'

Serge clears his throat. 'I'm so glad to hear that. And I'm very much obliged to you, mademoiselle. I know you want to keep your identity a secret, and I respect that, but if you ever need help, please feel free to come to me. I will not betray your trust in me.'

'I'll remember that. *Je vous dis au revoir*, Serge Mercier.'

Professor Gitte Meyer puts down the phone.

Tiny Murdoch is in a farmhouse in south Armagh, along with Paddy Joe Delaney of the Nutting Squad. He has his phone wired to a recorder as he phones Paul O'Flaherty, who is in a parked car outside the town of Ballymena, County Antrim.

O'Flaherty lowers the car window. He allows the phone to ring for more than a minute before finally answering it. 'Yes?'

'It's me.'

'I know.'

'Oh, right,' Tiny says. A silence. 'The bullet-dodger got away with the double cream. That shithead … how does he do it? He always comes out of these things smelling of roses, doesn't he?'

In a reference to the dead Das Reich members, O'Flaherty offers, 'He does, but I don't think he tipped off those other fellas, do you?'

'It's hard to say. He's a greedy fucker. One thing's for sure: he didn't tip off the gardaí. He had nothing to gain from doing that.'

'No.'

'I wonder who did?'

'I've been giving that some thought myself,' O'Flaherty says.

'I think we need an urgent meeting to discuss what happened, don't you? Where are you? I'll send one of the boys to pick you up.'

'You'll send one of the boys to pick me up?' O'Flaherty laughs generously. 'I don't think so.'

'Why not?'

'Tiny, this is me you're talking to, for Christ's sake. Are you forgetting? I invented the setup. I trained you.'

'Why would you think I'd be setting you up?'

'You're recording this conversation, aren't you?'

Tiny shakes his head at Delaney, puts his hand over the voice box, and whispers, 'He knows.' He takes his hand away to speak to O'Flaherty. 'So, you were the informer all along. You despicable bastard. You let wee Hughie O'Boyle take a bullet for you.'

'I was sorry about wee Hughie.'

'I blame myself.'

'And so you should.'

'I was too quick to focus on him because it never crossed my mind for a second that you, of all people, could have been the tout.'

'When did you realise it *was* me?'

'After Oughterard. Outside of myself, the only other person who knew the meat and spuds of Saint-Émilion, Dun Laoghaire, *and* Oughterard was you – and I *know* I'm not the tout.'

O'Flaherty smiles. 'I can't complain. I've had a good run. Thirty years. Do you know what my MI5 handler codename is? Enigma. After the enigma machine. Isn't that something? *Slán*, Tiny. It was—'

'Why?'

'What?'

'Why'd you do it?'

'Isn't it obvious? My brother, Iggy, was a priest. He saved souls. I saved lives.'

'But you ordered executions, an awful lot of them.'

'I think you need a history lesson, son.'

'And you're the boy to give it to me, huh?'

'No better man.'

'Go on then; let's have your best shot, you touting cunt.'

O'Flaherty ignores Tiny's insult. 'The Brits allowed some of their Atlantic convoys to be attacked by U-Boats during World War Two because to intervene every time the U-Boats were in a position to attack would have let the Germans know their codes had been broken. And although they could have prevented them, they didn't. It's all about the arithmetic, son. Tens of thousands of lives were sacrificed, but hundreds of thousands were saved. Bottom line? Greater good politics prevailed. There are dozens of people drawing breath this day because I prevented their deaths. So, once again, greater good politics prevailed. Put it like this, Tiny: you're proud of how many Brits' lives you took during the war. I get that. By the same token, I'm proud of how many peoples' lives I saved. You'll never get that.' O'Flaherty ends the phone call.

Sitting behind the steering wheel across from O'Flaherty is the thirty-five-year-old MI5 operative, Aaron Berkshire, who hands his asset an envelope. 'There's twenty grand in there.'

'Doesn't seem much for all that gold,' O'Flaherty says.

'What gold? The Irish copped all the gold. Besides, it's a lot more than you usually get.'

'I suppose.' O'Flaherty looks into the envelope and rifles through the fifty-euro notes. 'Fancy a drink, Aaron? My shout. One last hurrah?'

'Not possible. There's a plane waiting at RAF Aldergrove to take you out of the country.'

In a reflective mood, O'Flaherty says, 'I'll miss Ireland. I don't think I'll ever be back.'

'You never know.'

'But I do know. The 'RA will never forget or forgive this.'

'Are you all right?' Berkshire asks, glancing at the former IRA leader, who is shedding tears.

'Yeah.' O'Flaherty wipes his eyes, draws a deep breath, and exhales. 'Yeah, I'm okay. It's funny the way things turn out, isn't it?'

'What way is that?'

'Well, all Ructions ever wanted was to come back to live in

Ireland, free from the threat of being murdered by the IRA, right?'

'Ah-huh?'

'And, I, as chairman of the IRA Army Council, negotiated a deal with him whereby he could do just that, providing he either made the gold available to us or paid us four million euro.'

'I can't see the Army Council letting him return, can you?' Berkshire says.

'Why not? The deal is still on. Even more so, now that Ructions is gold rich.'

'But the Irish say they recovered all the gold.'

O'Flaherty sighs. 'The Irish also say that if you capture a leprechaun, it'll give you three wishes ... they say the Children of Lir were turned into swans ...' O'Flaherty leans towards Berkshire and waves an extended finger. 'We Irish are a lyrical people; we're master spoofs. Now, Ructions has got his pot of gold. Of that, I've no doubt. And believe me, the Army Council will be only too happy to accept the four million he and I agreed to — rather than walk away with nothing.'

'So, let me get this right ... he comes back to live in Ireland, free from the IRA threat on his life—'

'And I must flee Ireland and live the rest of my life abroad, with the threat of the IRA murdering me.'

'So, in real terms, the IRA threat on Ructions's life has been transferred unto you?'

'Precisely.'

Berkshire says, 'And because, officially, the Irish recovered all the gold, the gardaí won't be pursuing him for the gold that he stole?'

O'Flaherty smiles. 'The ironies of ironies, isn't it?'

Superintendent Thierry Vasseur sits at his desk in his office when a junior officer knocks on his door, comes in, and places a bulky envelope in front of him. 'Special delivery,' the officer says before leaving.

Vasseur looks at the envelope. He takes a letter opener, slices open the envelope, and squints inside. There is a smaller envelope. He takes it out and opens it, only to find that it contains an even smaller envelope. He runs his fingers around this envelope. There is something solid inside. He opens the envelope and turns it upside down. A one-kilo Nazi gold bar falls out. Vasseur's mouth opens. He holds the bar up to the light. He returns to the envelope and notices a note inside. He opens it. On it is written: 'We Irish are a generous race too. *Bonne chance*, Thierry. R.'

Vasseur bursts out laughing.

Eleanor is wearing a blue bikini as she lies on a sunbed on the beach in Nice. A waiter brings Daiquiri cocktails and sets them on a small table. Ructions emerges from the sea, a snorkel mask high on the crown of his head and flippers in his hand. He walks up to Eleanor, takes off the snorkel mask, flops down on the sunbed, and stretches over to kiss her.

'I wish I could swim,' she says. 'That looked like so much fun.'

'You won't let me teach you.'

'You'll drown me.' Eleanor laughs.

Ructions's phone rings. 'It's Paddy Gillen,' he says to Eleanor. She puts her ear alongside his. 'Hello, Paddy …'

'Hi, Ructions. Good news … They've accepted your offer. We're talking cash, aren't we?'

'Yes.'

'Look, I know you're on your holidays. I just thought you'd like to hear the glad tidings.'

'That's brilliant, Paddy. I'll talk to you when I get back.'

Eleanor has a troubled look on her face. 'We won't have a problem living in Dun Laoghaire, will we?'

'None at all.'

'All that IRA business is sorted out? They're gonna let us live in Ireland in peace?'

'Babe, that's all sweet.'

'You're not humouring me, are you? I couldn't go through any more of that trauma, Ructions. I couldn't take it.'

'It's boxed, El. That's it now. It's over.'

'I'm away to wet my feet.' Eleanor goes down to the water. Ructions's phone rings again. It's Serge.

'Salut, Le Français.'

'Salut, l'Irlandais.'

'What's up?'

'I thought you'd like to know we returned just over fifty-three.'

He feels giddy … We raked in fifty-three million euro! Well, thank you, Herr Reichsmarschall Goering. No, thank you, Herr Arthur Guinness.

'That's good.' There is a suspicious silence from Serge. 'What? What's up?'

'Nothing.'

'Something's up.'

'I've made a mistake. *Pardonnez-moi.*'

Ructions looks to Eleanor, who is paddling in the tiny waves. She looks up at him and smiles. 'Talk to me.'

'I might be able to put my hands on another painting.'

Ructions's eyebrows arch. 'Gimme that again.'

'I said I might be able to put my hands on another painting.'

'Like the last one?'

'I don't know yet for certain.'

'You don't have it?'

'Not yet.'

Ructions knows Serge is baiting him. 'But you might have it soon?'

'Possibly.'

'What are you saying exactly?'

'I don't think I have to explain myself, do I?'

'No, you don't.' Ructions hesitates. 'Might, possibly … that's two too many adverbs for me.'

'No pressure, *cher ami*. I'd hate to give you the impression I was putting a gun to your head.'

'You're not.'

'Good.' Ructions waves to Eleanor. 'Neither of us need this – especially you, with your illness.'

'You're probably right. I accept your decision. It's for the best.' Serge hangs up.

Ructions lifts a pen and draws an oblong image on the sand. On the image, he writes:

DEUTSCHE

REICHSBANK

I KILO

FEINGOLD

999·9

DRO766383

As Eleanor comes up the beach, Ructions rubs out the wr
on the sand.

'When we settle in Dun Laoghaire, I'm gonna learn to swi
she says. 'Maybe we can put in a pool; I think we should put
a pool. The property's big enough. It wouldn't have to be ar
more than eighteen metres in length. Do you think that's to
long?'

Ructions gives the odd 'Ah-huh' as Eleanor excitedly rattles
on about the new life that she envisages for them both ...

But in his mind, something porous and indeterminate is loitering with intent, clouding his happiness, causing flash flutters in
his belly. What could it be? On the face of it, he has everything:
Eleanor, the love of his life; riches beyond his wildest imagination; and at long last, a harmonious relationship with his former
nemesis, the IRA, after he had agreed to pay them off with four
million euro. Yet, his sixth sense is alerting him that his moon is
in danger of being eclipsed. By what? By whom?

His attention is drawn to the promenade, where, standing
looking directly at him, is a white-haired man with a walking
stick, in a short-sleeved Hawaiian shirt and khaki shorts. The
elderly man nods deeply to Ructions, clicks his heels, and brings
his arm up in a Nazi salute.

'Ructions ... Ructions ...' Eleanor says, 'are you listening to
me?' He turns around and watches her lips as words tumble out.
When he looks back at the promenade, Adelbert is gone.

iting

m,'

in

y

o